THE PEOPLE'S WILL

www.transworldbooks.co.uk

Also by Jasper Kent

TWELVE
THIRTEEN YEARS LATER
THE THIRD SECTION

For more information on Jasper Kent and his books,
see his website at www.jasperkent.com

THE PEOPLE'S WILL

Jasper Kent

BANTAM PRESS

LONDON · TORONTO · SYDNEY · AUCKLAND · JOHANNESBURG

TRANSWORLD PUBLISHERS
61–63 Uxbridge Road, London W5 5SA
A Random House Group Company
www.transworldbooks.co.uk

First published in Great Britain
in 2013 by Bantam Press
an imprint of Transworld Publishers

A CIP catalogue record for this book
is available from the British Library.

ISBN 9780593069547

Addresses for Random House Group Ltd companies outside the UK
can be found at: www.randomhouse.co.uk
The Random House Group Ltd Reg. No. 954009

The Random House Group Limited supports the Forest Stewardship
Council® (FSC®), the leading international forest-certification organisation.
Our books carrying the FSC label are printed on FSC®-certified paper. FSC is
the only forest-certification scheme supported by the leading environmental
organisations, including Greenpeace. Our paper procurement policy can be
found at www.randomhouse.co.uk/environment

Typeset in 11/14½pt Sabon by
Kestrel Data, Exeter, Devon.
Printed and bound by
CPI Group (UK) Ltd, Croydon, CR0 4YY.

2 4 6 8 10 9 7 5 3 1

For M.B.K. and E.B.K.

AUTHOR'S NOTES

Measurements
Much of the Russian Imperial measurement system was based by Tsar Peter the Great on the British system. Thus a *diuym* is exactly equal to an inch (the English word is used in the text) and a foot is both the same word and measurement in English and Russian. A *funt* is translated as a pound, though weighs only about nine-tenths of a British pound. A *verst* is a unit of distance slightly greater than a kilometre.

Dates
During the nineteenth century, Russians based their dates on the old Julian Calendar, which in the 1880s was twelve days behind the Gregorian Calendar used in West Europe.

In the text dates are given in the Russian form and so, for example, the death of Dostoyevsky is placed on 28 January 1881, where Western history books have it on 9 February.

With thanks to John Dunne for his knowledge of Saint George's Church in Esher, Stéphane Marsan for help with the French language and Seçkin Selvi for advice on Ottoman Istanbul.

Selected Romanov and Danilov Family Tree

Reigning tsars and tsaritsas shown in **bold**.
Fictional characters shown in *italic*
'#' indicates unmarried parentage.
Dates are *birth-[start of reign]-[end of reign]-death*

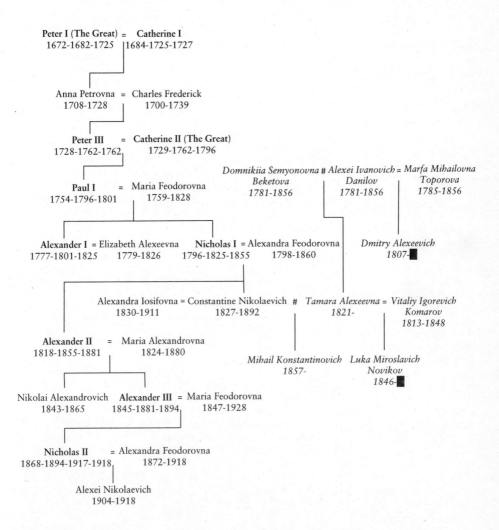

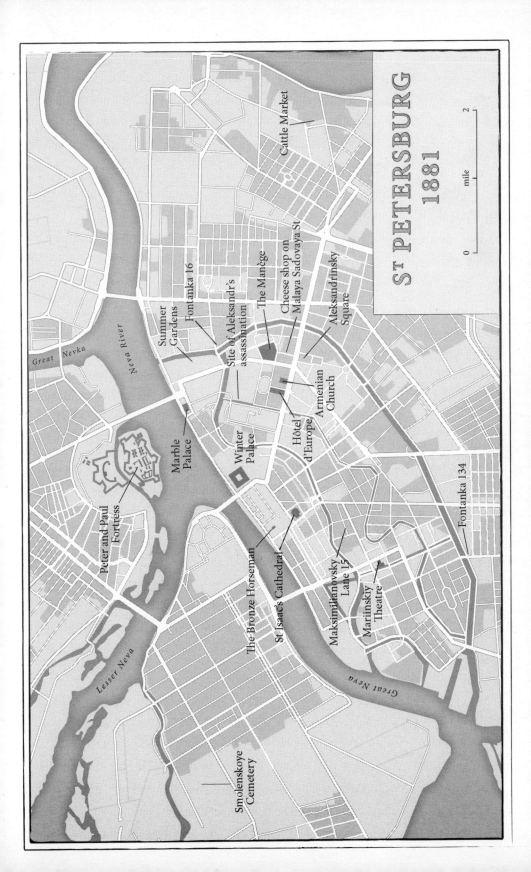

ST PETERSBURG
1881

0   mile   2

Cattle Market

Cheese shop on
Malaya Sadovaya St

The Manège

Fontanka 16

Site of Aleksandr's
assassination

Summer Gardens

Neva River

Great Nevka

Aleksandrinsky
Square

Armenian
Church

Hôtel
d'Europe

Winter
Palace

Marble
Palace

Peter and Paul
Fortress

Fontanka 134

Maksimilianovsky
Lane 15

Mariinskiy
Theatre

St Isaac's Cathedral

The Bronze Horseman

Great Neva

Lesser Neva

Smolenskoye
Cemetery

Only the scoundrels have forgotten that strength is with those whose blood flows, not with those who cause blood to be shed. There it is – the law of blood on earth.

Fyodor Dostoyevsky, writing shortly before his death in 1881

PROLOGUE

The verdict was unanimous. The sentence was death.

In the summer of 1879 the Executive Committee of *Zemlya ee Volya* – Land and Liberty – held a congress in the central Russian town of Lipetsk. There were eleven of them. It required twelve to constitute a jury, but they would be enough. The very idea of a jury was an innovation in Russia – one that had been instigated by the accused himself, a particularly august Russian. They came from all parts of the motherland – from Petersburg and Moscow, of course, but also from the south; from Gelendzhik and Odessa and Kiev. It was those from the south who argued most keenly for a death sentence. They knew poverty better, or had at least witnessed it more closely. None of the Executive Committee was truly poor, though some had parents who had been serfs – until emancipation, eighteen years before. Some might catch a hint of irony that the condemned man was also the emancipator, but sentimentality was a weakness. *He* would not be sentimental when it came to dealing with *them*.

Lipetsk was a spa town and the eleven of them – ten men and one woman – arrived in ones and twos, under the guise of patients. They drank the waters, bathed in the mud and rowed on the lake, gazing into its clear, fishless waters. Shiryaev suggested that the minerals which made the waters so healthy for men meant also that fish could not live in them. Shiryaev was a scientist. That would prove useful.

The lake was known to locals as the Antichrist Pond. It was Frolenko who asked how the name arose. The antichrist in question, so they were told, was none other than Tsar Pyotr I –

15

Peter the Great. The Executive Committee hid their smiles. Pyotr was the great-great-great-grandfather of the man they had come here to judge. When he had begun to reform Russian society at the beginning of the eighteenth century, many believed him to be the false prophet that the Bible foretold. Today the members of Land and Liberty held Aleksandr II in similar regard, though they cared little for Christian mythology.

On 15 June the Executive Committee made their way to a forest outside the town; though a popular spot for picnics, they managed to find a secluded glade. It was not their main purpose, but they too had brought food, wine and vodka. They were in a merry mood. On the way there Zhelyabov showed off his enormous strength, lifting a passing droshky by its rear axle and stopping the horse in its tracks. They did not mind drawing attention to themselves; no one would guess their true purpose.

After they had eaten, Aleksandr Dmitrievich Mihailov read out the charges against his namesake, Aleksandr Nikolayevich Romanov. The tsar, though not present to face his accusers, had but one defence. Mihailov dismissed it. 'The emperor has destroyed in the second half of his reign almost all the good he permitted to be done by the progressive figures of the sixties,' he explained to the others. Each of them was asked in turn whether the reforms of Aleksandr's earlier reign could win him a pardon for the evils of the present and for those he would yet inflict upon the country if allowed to live. From each came the same answer: 'No.'

The sentence was passed.

Then they went on to discuss how the execution was to take place and how, once the tsar was dead, the whole edifice of monarchy would be brought down. The second matter seemed simple, almost dull. Revolution would be brought about by the people. On Aleksandr's death the masses would sense their freedom. It would be more a question of how to guide the transformation of government than how to instigate it. Matters would be helped though if the tsar was not the only one to die. It would be easier if there was no obvious successor. The tsarevich, Aleksandr Aleksandrovich, should not become Aleksandr III. His son, though just eleven, should not become Nikolai II. There were those who would rally even to a child emperor if he bore the Romanov name.

But the tsar himself must be the prime target. As to how he would die, it was Shiryaev, the scientist, who made the suggestion – a new invention to bring about a new age: dynamite. It provided everything they needed. It would give the executioner the opportunity of escape; it stood the chance of dealing with those around the tsar as well as the tyrant himself; and it would be noticed. Land and Liberty had learned from their French predecessors that terror itself was a political statement.

And so the Congress of Lipetsk closed with much decided. The Executive Committee knew what had to be done. They knew how it was to be done. All that remained was to choose when.

But the decisions of the Executive Committee were not entirely popular among the wider membership of Land and Liberty. A further congress took place in Voronezh and within two months Land and Liberty was no more. Those who disagreed with the conclusions reached in Lipetsk formed their own party, Black Repartition, dedicated to a fairer distribution of land for the peasants, brought about by political means.

The Executive Committee, and many others, remained faithful to what they had decided; remained dedicated to carrying out the sentence which they had passed upon the tsar. They too chose a new name for their group, a name which described in simple terms that which they believed themselves . . . which they *knew* themselves to embody.

They called themselves *Narodnaya Volya* – the People's Will.

The verdict was unanimous. The sentence was death.

This trial had been a simpler affair, though it had preceded the events of Lipetsk by over a decade. It had taken place in Saratov in 1865. The accused was not a member of the imperial family, or the nobility, or even a citizen of Russia, though it was in Russia that his offences had been committed. With him there was no need to balance the good of his earlier years with the evils of his later life. There was no mitigation for his crimes.

Where the trial in Lipetsk would be forced to function with only eleven jurors, in Saratov there were just two. Even so, they followed the procedures of a trial, taking on all the necessary roles between them. For one of the two it was a game, for the other an obsession. It was the older of them, the woman, who spoke most. She was counsel for the prosecution and the chief witness. Other witnesses could not be present, so she represented them, retelling their experiences as best she knew them. She even acted as counsel for the defence. When the judge called on her to present her case she stood up, took a deep breath and then returned to her seat without a word. The judge giggled.

Then the jury – so recently acting as judge and counsel – retired. Unanimity between two was easier than between eleven, but there had never been any doubt as to the verdict. It fell to the judge to announce what they had decided. Some might see it as pointless that the only person he had to announce it to had moments before sat with him on the jury, but he understood the concept of play-acting.

Having discovered the verdict it was the judge's duty to pass sentence. The counsel for the prosecution made a strong case for death, against which the defence could find no arguments. The judge did not deliberate for long. He spoke the single word 'Death' in a whisper. It was an onerous decision for any judge to make, more so because it meant that one day he would have to take on another role – that of executioner.

More onerous still because the judge was a little boy – a little boy just eight years old.

CHAPTER I

OSOKIN GLANCED AT HIS WATCH. ONE MINUTE BEFORE NOON. 'Steady,' he said, his voice edged with suppressed excitement that he hoped wouldn't be read as fear.

Colonel Otrepyev didn't respond. He stood, or half stood, in the mouth of the side tunnel, too tall to fully straighten his back in the enclosed space. Ahead of him were the handful of troops that he'd brought with him on his mysterious late-night arrival, six days before, with orders from on high that his every whim was to be catered for. That side tunnel, the result of six days' labour, was more than a whim.

The main attack force was some way behind, at the mouth of the larger tunnel. Osokin had no plans to join them when they finally surged forward. His duty had been to undermine the city, not to invade it. Originally he'd intended to follow up with the rearguard, taking a little less glory for a little less risk, but since Otrepyev's arrival his ideas had changed. He wanted to see what lay at the end of that other tunnel.

'All set, Lieutenant?' he asked.

Lieutenant Lukin glanced up. He licked his dry lips and nodded curtly. He was the real genius behind all of this. He was scarcely more than twenty; only a few years out of the Imperial Technical School in Moscow. It was an odd route into the army, but an effective one. Science was the future of war; every officer knew that, all except a few geriatrics who'd have done better to die at Sevastopol in place of their men. But their time was past and a different breed of officer was eager to make its mark. Lukin knew his business – and his business was tunnelling and explosives. It was as though he'd been born for this job.

Osokin would never have guessed that they would get so far in so short a time. They'd started just two weeks ago, as 1880 had turned into 1881, and now they were ready. Above them, the massive citadel of Geok Tepe stood, ignorant of how it had been subverted, unprepared for the devastation to come. Each day it withstood a barrage of sixty Russian guns raining shell and shot down on the mud-brick walls. But today, at noon, the danger would come from a quite different direction.

It was quiet now. The beginning of the salvo was to be the signal. Ahead of them, down the tunnel – a safe, long distance ahead of them – lay five thousand pounds of nitroglycerin. Two thin copper wires led all the way back to where Lukin was crouched. In front of him sat a small wooden box with a little handle at the side and two metal pins sticking out of the top. Lukin had tried to explain, and though Osokin had no real idea how it worked, he understood enough. Lukin had simply to wind the handle, generating an electric current and then – boom – the walls of Geok Tepe would crumble. Joshua himself could not have done better, even with ten thousand ram's horns.

But Otrepyev's arrival had added further complications. Osokin had despised him on sight, and had to bite his lip to keep from muttering the word 'oprichnik' whenever the colonel walked past. The more correct term these days was 'ohranik', but whatever the name, Colonel Otrepyev reeked of the Third Section. Or he might have done if the Third Section had still existed. Its disbandment five months before had been a universal joy. But its work continued, and its stench lingered.

But the colonel's orders had to be obeyed. The extra tunnel had been dug and now another pair of wires emerged from it, at the far end of which lay more explosives; not as much as had been used for the main tunnel, but enough. Otrepyev and Lukin had discussed it all very carefully. Otrepyev knew where he wanted the tunnel to lead and Lukin knew how to get it dug. Lukin had been happy to assist. Perhaps he was too young to understand what Otrepyev was. Perhaps he was too smart to reveal his revulsion for a man who would spy on his own people. Perhaps he was just too fascinated by the work itself. Only minutes earlier he had twisted his detonation wires with Otrepyev's, and when the time came the larger explosion would mask the smaller.

When the time came.

Osokin looked at his watch again. It was a minute past. The sound of the guns would be muffled down here, but they'd be heard. Every day of digging they'd been audible, and that was above the crunch of shovels scraping unceasingly against the soil. Now all was silent. The loudest sound was Osokin's own breathing. In the dimly lit tunnel it was impossible to see the men waiting behind, or the bend in the passage ahead which would protect them from the blast. The tallow candles spaced out along the walls flickered, making the shadows jump back and forth. Lukin had suggested using electric light, but the resources were simply not available out here, closer to Afghanistan than to Russia.

When it came, it was more of a sensation than a noise, reaching Osokin not through his ears but his feet. He waited a few moments more, wanting to be certain. It was a different sound from that of the days before, when they had been digging. Now he could hear nothing of the guns themselves; the blasts of expanding gas forcing the shells from their muzzles. All that could be perceived was the shaking ground as the onslaught pummelled the city above. He glanced at Lukin, who had noticed it too.

'The men, sir,' said Lukin, jerking his head in the direction of the tunnel behind them. 'All those bodies – must be blocking the sound.'

Osokin nodded. He looked over at Otrepyev, who finally returned his gaze.

'Well?' demanded the colonel.

Much as Osokin would have liked to toy with Otrepyev's impatience, he knew his duty. The guns had begun firing; the rest must follow. He pressed his fingers against his ears.

'Do it!' he hissed at Lukin.

The lieutenant turned the handle rapidly, like a little boy playing with a *diable-en-boîte*. Just as with the toy, the exact moment at which his effort would bear fruit was unpredictable. Thus the blast, even though expected, was a surprise when it came.

It was testament to the glorious power of technology that so slight an action could have so devastating an effect. The sound from the side tunnel, the shorter of the two, came first, but only by a moment. Even with his ears covered it was possible to distinguish the scale and direction of the two blasts, until the one from the tunnel ahead became so loud as to drive out every other sound – every other thought. It was still growing in volume when Osokin felt its effects – first a wind rushing through the passageway towards him, and then a more solid impact, as though he had run into a wall, which threw him back on to the ground. For a moment his hands moved from the sides of his head in an attempt to break his fall and he experienced the full intensity of the sound hammering against his eardrums. He quickly covered his ears again, preferring to be bruised than deafened.

He lay still for a few moments. Clouds of dust and debris began to billow along the tunnel towards them. To his right he noticed that Lukin had removed his hands from his ears and was using them to cover his mouth and nose. Osokin did likewise, and squeezed his eyes shut too as the first flecks of pulverized rock began to pepper them. The noise was still loud, but now more of a slow rumble, as column by column the city's southern wall started to collapse into the pit that the explosion had created.

He waited a few seconds before opening his eyes again. The air was still thick with dust, making it impossible to see more than a short distance. Even so, Osokin could just detect the presence of daylight – something of which he had known little in the past two weeks. As they'd planned, the tunnel roof had caved in ahead. Here it was still intact, but at the end of the passageway the crater would be so large that no amount of rubble could fill it and block out the midday winter sun.

From behind him he heard a noise. It might have been a shout, but his ears still rang too much to make out what was said. A new sound assailed him, a rapid thump, thump, thump this time, again from behind. He turned, but the route back to the surface was veiled in dust, worse now in that direction than ahead. Shadows advanced, emerging from the thick smog. The shout he had heard was the command to attack. Whether the citadel would be taken by these men, streaming in through the tunnel, or by those on the surface charging across the detritus of the breached wall, no one could predict. So enormous a detonation could not be precisely calculated. It would come down to the relative sizes of the breach and the crater, and where the Turcomans chose to concentrate their defence.

Colonel Otrepyev had vanished. It was easy to guess where to. If Osokin stayed here, he would get caught up in the onslaught; either trampled underfoot or carried along by the crowd and into the sights of the defensive guns. He desired neither fate, and was still keen to discover what it was that Otrepyev had expended so much effort to get hold of before the marauding Russian army could fall upon it. He pulled himself to his feet and darted across to the side tunnel, into which Otrepyev had so recently disappeared.

Osokin had not ventured into this section of the mine before. Otrepyev said nothing explicit about its secrecy, but Osokin, like any Russian, understood without being told what was for him to know and what was not. Aside from the sappers doing the digging, only Otrepyev and Lukin had been down here – and Lukin pretty rarely. Even Otrepyev's select squad of men were walking into the unknown. Osokin knew he was taking a risk. Whatever lay ahead was Otrepyev's business. He might choose to have Osokin shot, but in the chaos that surrounded them it should be easy enough for Osokin to make an excuse for his presence.

The tunnel, as could be guessed from the time spent on it, was not long. It ended in an underground wall, constructed of large, heavy sandstone blocks – or at least it had done until the explosion. Now there was simply a jagged hole. Beyond was a corridor, constructed of the same stone. A greater amount of explosive might have brought the whole thing down instead of just one wall. The precise result was testament to Lukin's skill.

Osokin stepped over the rubble and into the corridor. It was brighter here – lit by oil lamps rather than candles. The breach had been made just as the passageway turned a sharp corner. One path led, as far as Osokin could tell, to the north-east, the other north-west, though both twisted and he could not see far along either. The sound of feet marching away came from the latter route, and Osokin took it.

He soon caught up with Otrepyev's men. They were moving swiftly, and it was clear that the colonel knew where he was heading, though it was hard to imagine he had ever been here before. In recent evenings, Osokin had seen him poring over maps that the other officers were not allowed to inspect. The route would not have been difficult to memorize.

From behind him, Osokin heard shouts. They were not Russian voices, but local Turcomans. Then footsteps – a single set – racing towards him. In a moment his pistol was drawn. He pressed himself into a corner of the wall and cocked the gun, raising it in front of him. He saw the shadow first, flickering against the stonework, and tried to guess where the figure would emerge. He squeezed the trigger.

His guess was wrong, fortunately for Lukin. The bullet ricocheted off the wall as the lieutenant raced along the corridor. His pace slowed momentarily in reaction to the shot, but as his eyes fell upon Osokin he seemed to comprehend the major's error. He flung himself against the hard stone wall just behind where his commanding officer was crouched and drew his own pistol.

'How many?' asked Osokin.

'Five,' replied Lukin. 'Maybe six.'

Even as he spoke, the first two appeared. Osokin had seen Turcomans from a distance, manning the city walls, but never this close. Their uniforms seemed almost medieval. They were dressed in some kind of mail, and carried small shields. They had rifles – supplied by the British, at a guess – but these were clumsy weapons to aim in an enclosed space. Osokin and Lukin's revolvers spoke moments apart, and the two men fell – their chainmail no protection against a modern bullet. But behind them, two of their comrades had managed to take aim.

Osokin felt a burning pain in his right arm. His hand fell to his side and he tried to reach over to take hold of the gun with his left. At the same time he felt Lukin grab his collar and drag him round the corner to temporary safety. But it would not take long for the Turcomans to advance, and Lukin alone would not be able to hold them off. Osokin tried to raise his pistol, but his arm would not obey. A body threw itself forward, lying stretched out on the ground in front of them, rifle aimed. Lukin fired, but the Turcoman's tactic had been clever – the shot went above his head. The man on the ground returned fire, but missed, and then two more figures appeared behind him, standing, the barrels of their guns raised.

Osokin heard a volley of gunshots – perhaps four detonations timed to the precise same moment. In the enclosed space, it was impossible to tell the direction that the sound came from, but the two standing Turcomans crumpled; the one already on the ground twitched and lay still, with nowhere further to fall.

Osokin turned to see four of Otrepyev's squad standing, rifles raised, wisps of smoke idling from the muzzles and twisting around the bayonets. Two of the men charged forward round the bend in the passageway. Osokin heard a scream, quickly strangled to nothing. He watched the soldiers' shadows as they thrust their bayonets forward. Then they reappeared, rushing past Osokin and Lukin as if they were not there.

'Can you walk?' Lukin asked.

Osokin glanced at his arm and put his hand across to feel the wound. It had numbed him, but the bullet had gone through and not broken the bone. He nodded and got to his feet. The two of them ran on in the direction the soldiers had gone.

Soon they reached the end of the corridor – or at least as close to it as they could. Otrepyev's elite squad blocked the way, and their way was in turn blocked by a heavy wooden door, with iron bands across it. One of the soldiers was bending down close to the lock, while Otrepyev leaned over him intently.

Lukin pushed forward through the men. 'Let me!' he shouted.

Otrepyev looked up, and then beckoned to Lukin. 'Move!' he snapped at the man beside him. The others parted to allow Lukin through, and Osokin took the opportunity to follow in his wake.

'This has to be quick,' growled Otrepyev.

Lukin nodded. 'Get them back,' he said.

Otrepyev ordered his men away and soon they were hidden behind a bend. Otrepyev stayed to watch Lukin, and Osokin did likewise. The lieutenant took the short stick of dynamite that his predecessor had been attempting to attach to the lock, and moved it to the other side of the door.

25

'The hinges will be weaker,' he explained. 'At least you've brought the right kit.'

He delved into the bag that the soldier had been using and brought out a handful of wet clay, with which he easily fixed the explosive where he wanted it. He struck a match and the fuse was alight.

'We've got about eight seconds,' he said, already on the move.

Soon they were with the others. Osokin held his breath. Otrepyev glanced at him and then at Lukin. The words 'Stay back and let *us* deal with this' emerged from his lips an instant before the blast. Even as sound came, Otrepyev's troops ran forward, and Osokin and Lukin had no choice, for the moment, but to obey.

It was Lukin who moved first, his curiosity evidently as great as Osokin's. Within seconds they were back at what remained of the door, the top hinge blasted by dynamite, the bottom smashed by a soldier's boot. The two officers gazed at what lay within.

It was like the inside of one of the cone-shaped chimneys used to manufacture glass; easily fifty paces across and twice as tall, with the curved walls converging almost to a point where one might expect to see a circle of daylight, though none was visible. By Osokin's estimation, they were still below ground level, but the peak of this strange cellar was surely above it.

The squad had scattered across the room, brutally dealing with the Turcoman warriors they discovered inside. The defenders outnumbered the Russians by at least two to one but seemed no match for Otrepyev's men, who happily slaughtered them with sword, bayonet and pistol. If the place had merely been some kind of barracks, then the effort of blasting their way in here would have been superfluous. But Osokin could see that the Turcomans were not here for their own comfort. They were here to guard something.

And what they were guarding stood at the very centre of the room.

It was a chair; a wooden chair – sturdy but surely not comfortable. The word 'throne' might have been more apposite, given its slightly raised, central position and the evident fact that this room – this throne room – existed solely to house it. But the man sitting

26

in it was no king, those surrounding him no loyal courtiers. He did not move. At first Osokin suspected he might be dead, but looking closer he saw the man's eyes constantly flickering, taking in what was happening around him.

Osokin walked forward, oblivious of the melee that was taking place. With his injured arm, there was little he would have been able to do to defend himself, but he found he was strangely removed from what was going on all around. The Turcomans' objective did not seem to be the repulsion of the invading soldiers, but was more like a retreat; a retreat which the Russians were intent on hindering. But how they might escape was unclear. There was only one door to the chamber – the one which Lukin had so effectively blown from its hinges – but the Turcomans did not head for it. Instead they were making for two muster points, towards the back of the room on either side of the chair, marked by pieces of machinery whose detail Osokin could not make out. None tried to defend the chair itself, though no one save Osokin was attempting to approach.

As he got closer, he could see more clearly why the occupant did not move: he was bound where he sat. On his forearms and shins, thick leather straps fastened him to its arms and legs and, as if this might not be enough to fetter him, chains added a further layer of constraint. A strap stretched across his shoulders, and his head was kept still by yet another across his forehead, pressing his unkempt blond hair tight against his skull and binding him to some extension of the chairback that Osokin could not see. The prisoner – there could be no doubt as to what he was – strained every sinew against his bonds, but could do nothing to free himself, or even to move.

It had become lighter. Osokin looked around, realizing that it had been no gradual process but a sudden increase in illumination beyond what was provided by the oil lamps. He looked up and saw that the dark circle at the apex of the chamber's coned ceiling was now partially lit, almost like a waxing moon. Sunlight was spilling through and illuminating the wall, the line between dark and shadow gradually moving, soon to reach the floor as the gap above opened further.

A shot rang out. Osokin looked and saw Otrepyev holding his

pistol, his arm outstretched. Following its line, he saw a Turcoman slump to the ground. Beside him was one of the machines that Osokin had observed. It was fastened to the wall; a large wheel with a crank handle, which two of the dead man's comrades continued to operate.

Otrepyev did not expend any more bullets, but strode over towards them, sabre in hand – the height that had so restricted him in the tunnels now giving him impressive speed without his having to break into a run. One of the men let go of the wheel and drew his sword in an attempt to defend his post, but Otrepyev quickly dispatched him with a backhand blow to the neck. The remaining guard desperately tried to turn the handle more quickly. Osokin could see now that from the wheel a long rope ran up the wall to a pulley, after which its path could not be seen, but it was clear enough that it was this which was gradually drawing aside the shutter that had been blocking out the sun, and allowing its light to spill into the room.

Why this action should be of such vital importance to the Turcoman was unclear, but it most certainly cost him his life. Otrepyev brought his sword down on the man's hands. The Turcoman snatched them away from the wheel and held them up in front of him, as if hiding his face in fear. But one hand, lolling from his wrist by the fragment of skin and sinew that had been left by Otrepyev's blow, provided no cover. Otrepyev quickly put him out of his misery, his pistol firing at close range into the middle of the face the Turcoman had seemed so eager to protect.

Next Otrepyev grabbed the rope that stretched out above him with one hand and hacked at it with his sword. It was soon cut through and the colonel let it swing freely across the chamber. Almost instantly another Turcoman broke free of the swordfight that had been engaging him and leapt high into the air, grabbing the dangling rope and pulling it down so that the panel above opened a little further and the line of sunlight progressed another step across the room. The Turcoman tugged and jiggled on the end of the rope, swinging back and forth as he did so, but his weight was insufficient to encourage any additional movement. As this human pendulum came past him, Otrepyev took a short run and flung himself into the air – an impressive feat for a man of his years. At the apex of his flight he hacked at the rope again with his sword, cutting it in a single stroke. The Turcoman fell to the ground, still clutching his end of the rope like a valued treasure. Otrepyev landed comfortably on his feet and turned, but he had no need to deal with his adversary. A swarm of Russian soldiers rallied to the prone figure and finished him with their bayonets.

That so many of them were free to do so showed that the fight had turned in the Russians' favour. There now remained only a small group huddled against the wall, furiously working on the other device that Osokin still could not see. Otrepyev shouted an order and pointed towards the Turcomans. A number of his men moved towards them. At the same moment one of the Turcomans gave a cry which Osokin guessed to be an exhortation to his god. There was a sudden movement among the group, two of them falling to the ground, and Osokin could at last see what they were working on: a great iron lever set into the wall which they had finally managed to pull down from the vertical to the horizontal.

Osokin heard a sound above him, as did Otrepyev, who looked to its source and then broke into a run towards the chair at the centre of the chamber. He quite deliberately barged one of his own troops out of the way, pushing him across the room so that he blocked Osokin's view of the chair and the prisoner. As the soldier's head turned towards Osokin, a look of horror appeared on the man's face and he attempted to throw himself backwards. But he was already off balance and could do nothing. Behind him Otrepyev could be seen, still dashing towards the chair.

Osokin felt a whoosh of air above his head and a dark shape appeared in front of his eyes, as though some great black raven had swooped down from its nesting place high in the wall. But as it moved away Osokin saw that it was no bird. Two long, straight poles stretched up from it to a pivot in the ceiling by which it swung, released by the lever he had watched the Turcomans operate. At the end of the poles was a thin horizontal sheet of metal, which was travelling at huge speed now that it approached the bottom of its arc.

The Russian soldier in front of him had had no time to move. The horizontal blade hit him with gruesome precision just a little way above the middle of his Adam's apple. The man's body fell to the ground like a marionette whose strings had been cut; as though the head had been holding up the body instead of the other way round. The head itself remained momentarily *in situ*, given a slight upward momentum by the impact and spinning frantically in the air, repeatedly showing and hiding the gaping red cross-section of its hewn neck. Osokin felt a splatter of blood across his face, and then another.

But the impact had done little to slow the blade's progress. As the soldier's head continued to turn in the air, behind it Otrepyev had launched himself off the ground, his feet out in front of him, as if aiming a drop kick at the prisoner. But instead the impact was just to one side of the captive's head, to the wood of the chair itself.

The blade was level with Otrepyev's own head as his feet made contact with the wood. It was a race between the two of them. If the blade were to be the victor it would fulfil its design – there could be no doubt that all of this was planned – and sever the prisoner's head. The chair back received the full force of Otrepyev's lunge. The room was filled with a screeching, tearing sound as the chair's legs ripped away from the nails and bolts that fixed it to the platform beneath.

The prisoner gazed at the blade, now only inches from him, and then seemed to look upwards as the chair finally began to tip back under the force of Otrepyev's assault. For a few moments, the blade continued to make ground, closing faster on the prisoner's neck than the falling chair could move him away. But then he began to fall quicker, down as well as back, and the blade finally skimmed over him, just missing, or perhaps just catching, the ball of his chin.

The chair and the prisoner and Otrepyev and the spinning, severed head all continued to fall, each matching the others' speed in response to the same gravitational force. There was a loud crash – nothing compared with the blasts that Osokin had heard earlier in the day – as the two men and the chair hit the ground. At the same instant the head landed and, still revolving, began to roll eagerly towards Osokin's feet, coming finally to rest just in front of them, its dead eyes gazing upwards. It had been only seconds since the blade's release.

Over by the lever, Otrepyev's men had dealt with the last remaining Turcomans and were already wiping their bayonets clean. Otrepyev himself was pressed against the floor, aware that the swinging blade was still loose. Osokin could see it returning already, level with his eyes and hurtling towards him. He stood his ground. It had missed him before, and would follow the same path back. He felt his hair ripple as the blade flew over his head and relished his bravery, or at least the power of his intellect to overcome his native fear. It swung past again, on its way down.

'Deal with it!' shouted Otrepyev from his position on the floor.

Two soldiers approached warily, knowing full well what the blade had done to their comrade. They kept to the side of its path, jabbing at it with their rifles and each time taking a little of its momentum. When it had slowed enough, one of them felt sufficiently brave to grab at it, but he couldn't keep hold. The other man was knocked to the floor, but the blade had lost its power to kill. Soon they had it under control and let it come to rest at its natural position, just above where the chair had been, at the height of the prisoner's neck.

Otrepyev pulled himself to his feet and dusted down his greatcoat.

'Get him up,' he snapped.

Two more of his men ran forward and grabbed the chair, dragging it across the chamber, away from the dangling blade. Then they began to tip it back upright, the prisoner still bound to it as tightly as ever.

Osokin stepped closer, keen to see the man who had been the focus of so much effort, both on the part of Otrepyev to get at him and, it seemed evident, on the part of the Turcomans to ensure that he was not taken alive. The others gathered around too. Osokin noticed that Lukin was among them. Whether he had taken part in the battle or, like himself, had been merely a bystander, Osokin could not tell.

With grunts and gasps the chair was finally lifted back to an upright position. Otrepyev leaned forward and stared into the prisoner's eyes. Osokin had a clear view of both men. They were of about the same age – late forties, perhaps fifty – but apart from that, in appearance they were almost opposites. The prisoner was

not short by any means, but compared with the towering Otrepyev he seemed puny. His blond, straggling, unkempt hair contrasted with the neat dark brown of Otrepyev's. But his cold, grey
eyes spoke of a fierce intelligence which, Osokin guessed, was not
nearly matched by that of the colonel.

One thing, however, was beyond doubt: that these two men
knew each other. The entire chamber became hushed. One of
them would have to speak; the prisoner or his . . . rescuer, if that
was what Otrepyev truly was.

In the end, it was the captive's lips that moved first.

'It's been a long time, Dmitry Alekseevich,' he said.

CHAPTER II

IT HAD BEEN ALMOST TWENTY-FIVE YEARS SINCE IUDA LAST SAW
that face, in circumstances remarkably similar to those in
which the two vampires now found themselves. Then Dmitry
had cast Iuda into a dungeon. Today he acted as liberator. No,
that went too far. Iuda may have been free of the Turcomans, but
that did not mean he was free. That would depend on the reason
Dmitry was here. And there would be a reason. Iuda's freedom
– his life itself – would depend on his ability to fathom Dmitry's
motivation.

He'd got it wrong before, terribly wrong, the last time they had
met. He'd pondered it over the years – particularly during that
first year, when he'd had little else to do – but still he could make
no sense of it.

Dmitry had been a vampire for only a matter of weeks back
then in 1856 – Iuda for thirty years. They'd been down there in
the tunnels beneath the Kremlin: Iuda, Dmitry, Dmitry's half-
sister Tamara and their father Lyosha.

Lyosha – a man who had seemed able to defeat Iuda even as
he died, pathetic and old. It was a common enough diminutive
for the name Aleksei; Aleksei Ivanovich Danilov. He'd returned
from exile. He'd been half drowned and shot, and still, somehow,
he'd goaded Iuda into a mistake. No. It wasn't Lyosha. Iuda had
made the mistake all on his own. He'd wanted to twist the knife,
to destroy not only Lyosha but what Lyosha loved. And that
meant his son. And Iuda *had* destroyed Dmitry; transformed him
willingly into a vampire. And yet it was nothing if Lyosha did not
know it.

But in all that consideration of Lyosha, Iuda had failed to take account of Dmitry. Rather than let his father hear the truth, he'd chosen to protect him. He'd kicked out with both feet and knocked Iuda into one of his own dungeons, then drawn the heavy bolts across and turned the lock.

Iuda was trapped.

He'd designed and built the dungeon himself, with one end in mind – to make a prison that could hold a vampire. The chamber he was in now, beneath the citadel of Geok Tepe, was constructed with much the same intent, but on a grander scale. But in Moscow in 1856 he had known that he could not escape a prison of his own design. He would have to wait. Someone would come.

Sustenance was not an immediate concern. Although he had built this cell to be the cage for a *voordalak*, he'd been using it as a larder. There were four humans in there with him. They'd even attacked him, wrapping their chains around his neck and dragging him down as Dmitry bolted the door. But they were weakened, and chains were no weapon against a *voordalak*. He soon subdued them, and returned the shackles to their correct use – restraining the humans themselves; making them available when his hunger surfaced.

But they would not live for ever. There was a little food for them, left from their last meal, but even with the most careful rationing it would eventually rot. The humans lasted three weeks. He knew which one would be the last he left to die: Marfa Mihailovna. In saving his father from the truth, Dmitry had been quite happy to sacrifice his mother, whom he'd known full well was in there. Once again, it made little sense.

Of the four prisoners, Marfa Mihailovna's blood had been the least appetizing, but that was not why he had kept her alive. The hope had been that she would offer some amusement. By goading her over the fate of her son and her husband, described in exquisite and revolting detail, he expected to raise in her some reaction that might make his imprisonment less tiresome. But it was too late. She was already a broken woman, and Iuda had only himself to thank for that. Occasionally though, in moments of lucidity, she would ask where Dmitry was. At first he believed she had genuinely forgotten her son's fate, but later he realized she was merely reminding him – reminding him, with a hint of pride, that it was her son who had locked him in there.

At least before she died – as she died – she could facilitate Iuda's eventual escape. He had taken the last of her blood, but had not drunk it. He lay in the dungeon, dormant thanks to the lack of nourishment, for fourteen months. Eventually someone had bothered to break down the door and investigate the cellars below and had found the various rotting bodies that lay there, along with Iuda's strangely undecayed corpse. They had carried it back up. Somewhere on the short journey they'd twisted or jolted their load, and the small vial of human blood – the blood Iuda had taken from Marfa and lodged in his own throat before losing consciousness – was spilled. It was so little, but it meant so much. He was recalled to life.

When he awoke, he was lying on the floor of his own office. He barely recognized it. Dust sheets were thrown over the furniture and repainting had begun. The stairs led up to the Kremlin above, but Iuda did not need to see the glimmer of light shining down them to know that it was mid-afternoon – he felt it in his gut.

He could hear voices down in the cellars below, and footsteps ascending. There were two of them. Normally, he would have no concerns about defeating them, but he'd consumed such a tiny amount of blood that he was still weak. He would hardly be able to stand without support.

'Let's get on with it then.'

The timbre of the voices had changed; the men had climbed the steps and were now in the office. He sensed them moving towards him and then leaning over. He let out a groan. He felt them grip him and begin to lift. They hadn't noticed. He coughed a little and felt the hands release him.

'Jesus Christ! This one's alive.'

'Bollocks. It's just air escaping.'

Iuda coughed again, letting his body convulse a little.

There was silence – a stunned silence, he presumed. Then the second man spoke. 'What do we do?'

They clearly needed guidance. Iuda opened his lips, flexing them after months of disuse. He tried to make his speech appear weak, but discovered he had little need to pretend. He allowed

35

his eyes to flicker open and saw the two men peering over him. One of them knelt down and bent his head forward to listen more closely. His ear hovered above Iuda's lips, meaning that his neck was not far away. Iuda sensed the blood pulsing in the man's jugular vein – so close that only a slight movement would allow Iuda to bury his teeth deep into the sweet pink flesh. But it was not worth the risk. He raised his head just a little.

'Water,' he muttered, and then fell back, closing his eyes as if the effort had exhausted him.

'What?' asked the man standing.

'Water. He wants water. Go find some.'

Iuda heard feet pattering up the stairs to the Kremlin. He opened his eyes. The first part of the plan – to separate them – had worked. The other man was still there, his hands clasped to his chest, his eyes raised upwards, his lips moving in a rapid whisper. Iuda suppressed the urge to laugh at the realization that the man was praying for him. He'd have need to pray for himself soon enough.

Iuda began to speak again, mumbling without any thought as to what he was pretending to say. The man squeezed his arm reassuringly.

'It's all right. You're safe now.'

Evidently this was going to require a little more bait.

'No, please, listen,' Iuda croaked. 'There's not much time.'

The man looked down, puzzled. 'What do you mean?'

'It's about . . .' Iuda allowed his voice to die away. The man bent forward, but not close enough. Iuda raised his arm and beckoned, letting it fall again with an exhaustion he had little need to feign. He could not be sure he even had the strength to do this – but it would be his only chance. The man leaned over him again, just as he had done before, his ear close to Iuda's cracked lips.

Iuda pounced.

His hands clamped on to the man – one to his head, the other to his back. Iuda's nails dug through his hair and into his scalp, twisting his head to one side. The man pulled away. Iuda felt his emaciated muscles scream at him in pain, but he held on. The man was strong and was soon halfway to his feet, but he brought Iuda with him. Iuda bit. The instant rush of blood was bliss, but his first need was not to drink. The blood would take time to invigorate him, time which his prey could easily use to fight him off. The man must die and die quickly. Iuda bit again, and pulled his mouth away, bringing with it a mess of artery and sinew. Blood cascaded over Iuda's face – an appalling waste, but the job was done.

The man fell limp, collapsing on top of Iuda and forcing his weakened body back to the ground. It had been a quick death – a sudden, catastrophic loss of blood pressure to the brain. But Iuda had a better purpose for the blood. He rolled the man's lifeless corpse off him. The two of them lay side by side, like exhausted lovers who did not care to embrace one another after the act.

The urge to remain there in silence, resting, was powerful, but Iuda knew he had work to do. They would not be alone for long. He crawled over and placed his lips to the ragged wound in the man's throat, almost mimicking the posture of the man when he had been listening to Iuda. Drinking blood this way was neither pleasant nor easy. The blood of the dead was stale. Nutritionally it had only a little less value than living blood – Iuda had established that by experiment years before. But it tasted like a cold, thin, flavourless soup.

Worse than that, it had to be drawn from the body. To drink from a living victim one had only to pierce the artery and let the beating heart force gush after gush of blood into the mouth, weakening in strength as it gradually deprived itself of that which it most needed in order to live. With this lifeless slab of flesh, Iuda had to suck the blood for himself – harder still in his starved condition. If he'd had the time and the strength he would have imitated a butcher and hauled the cadaver up on a rope to let it hang upside down, allowing gravity to do the work that the heart was no longer capable of. But he had no strength. In the end he resorted to lapping at what had spilled on the floor, like a cat. It was degrading, but no one would see, and it would give him the strength for better things soon.

It was only a few minutes before the dead man's workmate returned, racing down the steps two at a time and clutching a bottle in his hand. Iuda was seated in his chair – the same chair that had been there when the room had been his office – in a dark corner where he would not be seen by someone coming in from the daylight. Even after so little time and so little blood, he felt renewed. He was not quite his old self, but he was strong enough to take his next meal in a more dignified manner.

He'd placed the corpse in the position where he himself had been lying. The differences between his cold, dormant body and the bloody remains that now took its place would be quickly noticed, but not quickly enough. From the bottom of the stairs, the returning man took only a glance at it, not realizing who it was.

'Sergei?' he shouted, looking around. 'Sergei?'

There was, unsurprisingly, no reply. He didn't seem too concerned. He went over to the body, uncorking the bottle as he went. He began to kneel.

'Here you are, old fella. We'll soon have you feeling—'

He leapt upright and took a step back, staring down at what remained of his workmate, saying nothing, his face showing bewilderment rather than fear. That would change.

'I have to say I'm already feeling much better, thank you.' As Iuda spoke he felt stiffness in the skin of his face, where the splattered blood had begun to congeal.

The man turned in the direction of Iuda's voice, peering into the darkness to make out its source.

'Your friend, however,' Iuda continued, 'is beyond all hope.'

He stood and began to walk, not straight towards the man, but on a path that would put himself between him and the stairs. The man's head followed him as he moved, realization dawning on his face.

'You. But . . .'

Iuda would not have been easy to recognize. In a few short minutes the effect of new blood must have taken twenty, perhaps thirty years off him. With only a little more, he would be fully restored.

'I sent for a doctor. He'll be here soon.'

It was difficult to determine what he meant by it. Was he still concerned for Iuda's health? Or was he simply giving a warning that they would not be alone for long? Iuda would not need long.

He stepped forward and put his hand over the man's mouth,

pushing him back towards the wall. He felt the man try to resist, and lifted him upwards, revelling in his returned strength. The man's feet scraped and tapped on the floor, but could find no purchase. He hit the wall with a thud and began to scream, but the sound was muffled by Iuda's hand. His arms flailed, beating against Iuda's sides and back, but with no effect.

Iuda bit. His primary purpose was still sustenance, but he now felt confident in his abilities. A hungry man might rush the appetizer of his first meal, but he would allow time to relish the main course. He sealed his lips over the wound he had just inflicted and allowed the blood to pump into him, as though his mouth, oesophagus and stomach had become an extension of the man's circulation, a one-directional extension that took blood and did not return it. Iuda knew that at this moment his victim would share something of his mind. He tried to make it clear that there was no hope of survival.

Soon the blows from the man's fists became more feeble, his screams turned into gasps for breath. Within a minute he was unconscious; within two, dead. Iuda was replete. Now a different weakness took him – not the powerlessness of the starved, but the lethargy of the glutted.

'It must be down here.'

The voice came from outside, at the top of the stairs. There were at least two of them. Iuda could probably have dealt with them, but was in no mood. He let the drained body drop to the floor and headed for the other flight of stairs, the one that went down to the dungeons. He stepped through the archway and examined the door. The lock had been smashed, probably not long before, when the cellars had finally been broken into. Fortunately the door itself was intact.

He slid the bolts across as quietly as he could. They would find the two bodies in moments, and he did not want to leave any clue that the killer was near at hand. For the moment he was trapped in the cellars, almost as he had been trapped in that one dungeon for fourteen long months. This time it would only be until sunset. Once the sun was down he would make his way through the tunnels that led down to the Moskva, and then he would be able once again to walk the city's streets.

He had lain down and slept, and when evening had come, he had been free, and had continued to be free for twenty years.

And now, as he sat strapped to the wooden chair in Geok Tepe from which he had been unable to move for three years, he wondered if he might soon be free again. He maintained his gaze into Dmitry's eyes, searching for some hint of what was to come.

Dmitry spoke.

CHAPTER III

'SHALL WE CONDUCT THIS INTERVIEW IN ENGLISH?' DMITRY asked. There was little chance that anyone in the chamber beneath Geok Tepe would understand the subject matter of their conversation, whatever language they spoke, but it wouldn't hurt to keep it from them.

'I didn't know you spoke English,' replied Iuda.

'I've travelled since we last met. One picks these things up.'

Dmitry wondered just how well he really spoke the language; how thick his accent was. Iuda would be the man to know. He was, when it came down to it, an Englishman – although that had been a long time ago.

'I can imagine,' said Iuda.

Dmitry did not want to waste time.

'As you'll have realized,' he continued, 'I need you alive. So tell me – what other traps are there?'

'You've seen it,' said Iuda. 'There's the sunlight,' he attempted to jerk his head upwards, but the strap across his forehead still restrained him, 'and the guillotine. The guards all used to carry wooden stakes, but one of them got the jitters – tried to kill me out of pure fear. He got close, but I managed to deal with him.' He grinned and ran his tongue across his teeth to clarify the point.

'So they gave that up?'

Iuda tried to nod. Dmitry suspected it was a pretence – after so long he should have been used to his immobility. What he thought to gain by it, Dmitry could not guess; anything to unnerve his opponent.

'Yes,' said Iuda as an alternative to the gesture. 'They took all the stakes away. They want me alive. The only circumstances in which I should die are . . .' he smiled, 'those in which we now find ourselves. The shutter and the guillotine take more than one man to operate, you see, which makes them safe, but slow.'

'Luckily for you.'

'That, I think, remains to be seen.' Iuda eyed Dmitry, trying to determine why he was here. Dmitry ensured that his face remained inscrutable. 'They could have been a little quicker off the mark,' Iuda continued, 'but I suppose they saw this as a genuine Russian assault, not a feint to disguise your more personal business. You did well to arrange it.'

Dmitry gave a brief snort. Iuda was probing. Even so, it wouldn't hurt to let him know a little of what was going on around him.

'Oh, the attack was real enough. "Is", I should say – it's still going on, up there. All part of what you English call the Great Game. We call it the *Turniry Tyenyey* – the Tournament of Shadows.' He added the English translation simply to annoy Iuda, whose Russian was perfect.

'Next stop Afghanistan then?'

'For them, perhaps,' Dmitry nodded towards Osokin, Lukin and the others, 'but I, and you, have a different path to take.'

'You chose your path a long time ago.'

Dmitry narrowed his eyes. Was that a hint of reproach in Iuda's voice? Had he really expected Dmitry to remain by his side once he'd become a vampire? Iuda had groomed him since he was a child, with a foresight that would startle even the most ancient *voordalak*. As Dmitry had grown into manhood, they had become friends – closer even than that. Dmitry had loved Iuda almost like a father, in some ways more than he loved his true father, Aleksei. Dmitry had found it hard to forgive his father's infidelity to his mother. Iuda, on the other hand, had always carried an air of sainthood in Dmitry's eyes. It was laughable, and Dmitry deserved to be laughed at for being taken in. He was different now, and thankful for it; in becoming a vampire he had become a cynic. He'd rarely been fooled since – except by himself.

But as far as Iuda's interests had been concerned Dmitry was merely a stepping stone. The real enemy was Aleksei – always Aleksei. Dmitry could not be sure that Iuda had planned exactly the dénouement that had taken place beneath the Kremlin twenty-five years before, but it had been something along those lines. Iuda had wanted to take Dmitry and show him to Aleksei, to dangle the son before his father's eyes and say, 'I have taken him. For all you loved him he is mine now.' It would have broken Aleksei's heart.

And for his father's heart, Dmitry did not care a jot. Since the moment he became a vampire, Dmitry had cared for no other creature but himself – and perhaps a little still for Raisa, his vampire 'mother'. Down in that low, dank corridor, when Iuda had begun to reveal Dmitry's fate to Aleksei, Dmitry had felt no pity for his father. Iuda's words might break Aleksei's heart, but it would mean nothing to Dmitry – a heart that has died cannot be broken.

Instead Dmitry had thought of himself. He had been Iuda's pawn, and he did not like it. He could look back on himself and be amused by his own credulity, but it stung his pride to have been a bit player in the story of his own life. And he was still a mere supernumerary. Iuda, Tamara, Aleksei – they all had their roles to play, but for Dmitry there had been nothing to do but stand there, and let Iuda complete the plan that he had formed as long ago as 1812 when he first set eyes on that five-year-old boy. Dmitry did not care whether the plan succeeded or failed, but this time success or failure would be down to him.

The thoughts had crossed his mind in an instant, and he'd known that he must act. He would not let Iuda make the final move; would not let him reveal the truth to Aleksei. Dmitry kicked out and, for the first time ever, acted on his own volition. The expression on Iuda's face as he fell back among his prisoners would have been satisfaction enough, but the knowledge that Dmitry had taken control was what mattered. As he walked away, with the key to Iuda's dungeon in his pocket, he had been in charge. Later, he might return to release his former mentor, or he might leave him there to rot. In the end he left him, but the decision had been his.

It was only hours afterwards, when it was too late, that he realized what he should have done. He pictured it in his mind. He would still have kicked Iuda into the cell, still locked the door and taken the key, but he would not have left, not right away. He would have bent down to his dying father, so that Aleksei could see him with his failing eyes, and would have whispered the words, 'Papa, it's me, Dmitry. And I have become a vampire.'

It would have been the best of all: to take control and then to instigate the climax of Iuda's plan for himself – and it was a wonderful plan, there was no doubt about it. He would even have told Aleksei how he'd left Marfa, his own mother, locked in there with Iuda, just to extinguish any hope for his humanity that might linger in his father's mind. But he would not cry over a missed opportunity. He had had many opportunities to live his own life since then, and had rarely declined to take them.

'What matters is to *have* a choice,' he said, staring down at Iuda, flicking his eyes across the bonds that held his arms and legs and head.

'And you chose to come here?' replied Iuda. 'To rescue me?' Dmitry remained silent, but Iuda did not need to be told that this was no rescue. 'To *fetch* me?'

Dmitry was tempted to turn away, but he knew Iuda was just guessing. Any reaction might tell more than was necessary. He'd find out soon enough, anyway.

Iuda continued to goad, his voice heavy with sarcasm. 'Now who on earth would send his minion to fetch *me*?'

The answer was obvious, but Iuda was still guessing.

'Where is it?' Dmitry asked, tired of wasting time.

'Where is what?'

'Ascalon.' Dmitry whispered the word, afraid to say it in front of so many, even though they would little understand its meaning.

'And what would you want with that?'

'That's no concern of yours.'

'Nor, I would suspect, of yours. Something else you've been sent to fetch?'

'I know you've been searching for it. All that time you spent at Chufut Kalye, and you never spoke to the Karaites about it?'

'And you think that since I've been searching for it, I must have found it? That's a very flattering estimation of my abilities.'

'You must know something,' said Dmitry.

'I might.'

'And you'll tell me.'

'Why should I?'

'Because you want your freedom.' Dmitry was not sure that it was an offer he was empowered to make, but that did not matter; Iuda was unimpressed.

'Such an exchange would require trust between the participants. You lost my trust years ago, Mitka.'

'So who would you trust?'

Iuda spoke slowly. 'I've lived a very long time. That's not achieved by trusting.'

Dmitry paused. He was getting nowhere, just as he'd expected. 'Perhaps not for much longer,' he said. It was meant to be a parting shot, but Iuda continued.

'Your father understood trust, of course,' he said. 'Faith, if you like. That's why I could never quite handle him. But it was his faith that allowed him to choose Dominique over your mother. Perhaps it was only one side of his family that inherited it.'

Such insults meant nothing to Dmitry any more – though they would have cut him deeply when he had been human. But the mention of that side of the family gave Dmitry an opportunity to play one of his few trump cards.

'You'd trust Luka Miroslavich then?'

'Who?' Iuda's voice was casual, but he kept his face a little too still in repressing his surprise. Or perhaps that was deliberate. It was Iuda who'd brought the conversation to that point. Had he finessed Luka's name out of Dmitry? It was too late now to go back.

'My nephew, if you like to call him that,' Dmitry explained, 'on the more faithful side of the family. Tamara Valentinovna's child. She gave him away.'

Iuda stared at him blankly.

'We know you've befriended him . . . much as you befriended me,' Dmitry continued.

But Iuda's focus was not on his relationship with Luka. A gentle smile played across his lips, smug and victorious. He allowed Dmitry a moment to observe it before offering by way of explanation a single, simple word.

'"We"?' he asked.

Dmitry felt his jaw tighten. An anger grew within him that was not entirely his own. He turned away, suspecting that Iuda had learned far more from the conversation than he had. He rubbed his chin angrily. Suspected it? He knew it for a fact.

It was early in the afternoon, only a day since Geok Tepe had fallen and since they had come into this underground chamber with its strange, solitary prisoner. Colonel Otrepyev had departed soon after his initial discussion with his captive and not returned. He left orders with Major Osokin, but Osokin knew that it was merely out of form, a sop to his status as senior officer. The men that Otrepyev had brought with him seemed well capable of carrying out their duties alone.

'And see if you can find a way to get that roof closed' had been the colonel's final instruction. It was an odd preoccupation, but Osokin had noticed the colonel eyeing the clear patch of sky above them for a while. He seemed older now than when he had first arrived.

'I'll see what can be done, sir,' he'd replied. 'Should we allow the prisoner to stretch his legs?'

Otrepyev laughed heartily, but briefly. He was eager to get away. 'No. No, I wouldn't recommend that. I'll be taking him away before long.'

'I assume we should feed him?'

'Don't even go near him.' And with that Otrepyev departed.

Attempts to converse with the prisoner, even to discover his name, proved unsuccessful. Osokin tried Russian and French, but with no response. He was pretty sure that Otrepyev and the prisoner had been using English when they spoke, but he knew nothing of the language.

'*Sprechen Sie Deutsch?*' had been his last attempt, as he bent forward, peering closely at the man, trying to judge whether he was even aware of his surroundings. No reply was forthcoming. Osokin stood upright and took a step back, still in close examination of the figure in front of him. There was no point in asking the men; perhaps the lieutenant.

'Lukin!' he called.

'Sir?'

'Don't suppose you speak English, do you?'

'Afraid not, sir.'

And that was the end of it, but in that brief exchange Osokin had at last noticed some slight reaction from the prisoner, though to which precise words he could not tell. Perhaps he was just reacting to the word 'English', presuming it was similar in both languages.

'Any idea how to get through to him?' Osokin asked the lieutenant.

'Best leave him be, I'd have thought. The colonel seems to know what he's doing.'

It was sound if unimaginative advice. Osokin left the chamber. The bullet wound to his arm had been crudely bandaged by one of the men, but it still throbbed uncomfortably. It would be worth getting a field surgeon to have a look at it. And he was eager to see how the battle in the rest of the city had played out.

It had not been his nation's finest hour. Granted, they had achieved victory, but many of the men – the commander-in-chief, General Skobyelev, for one – had desired more than that. They had been seeking revenge – revenge for the humiliation of a little over a year before when Russia had first attempted to take the city of Geok Tepe, under the command of General Lomakin. Then there had been no undermining, and the assault had come after too short a period of bombardment. The attackers had been thrown back, and then Turcoman defenders – Teke tribesmen, most of them – had poured out of the city to counterattack. Seven hundred Russians were killed; as many captured. Back home some people had compared it with Khiva in 1717. In Europe the papers called it the Lomakin Massacre.

But today, for seven hundred, revenge had been taken on seven thousand – perhaps more. Hundreds had died in the initial explosion, for which Osokin felt no guilt. It had achieved its goal and allowed the Russian cavalry and infantry to swarm in. As they had arrived, the Turcomans had fled out into the desert to the north. Some Russians had pursued. Those they caught they killed, but they didn't catch many. Perhaps that was why they dealt so brutally with those who hadn't escaped.

On the other hand, drunkenness was as likely a cause. Osokin had seen enough of it in Bulgaria against the Turks. It was the men, not the officers, but the officers did little to discourage it. Some thought it inspired a foot soldier to be braver, but in truth it just served to quieten their consciences. There was nothing brave about many of the killings that had taken place during the battle. It was not just enemy soldiers; the old, the young, women too – there was no sector of the population that did not have its losses. Some of the women had been raped first – even some of the children.

And there had been looting, of course. Osokin couldn't object to that, up to a point. It wasn't like the old days, when an army had to finance itself as it marched, but any little extra picked up along the way could help. But you couldn't leave the enemy destitute, otherwise they'd turn to crime and half your troops would be busy just keeping the peace, instead of marching on to greater victories.

General Skobyelev – the White Pasha, as the Turks called him, thanks to the colour of his charger and matching uniform – decided to take things a step further. On the day after the battle he commanded the women of the city – the surviving women – to hand over all their gold and silver jewellery by way of a war contribution. There was a tradition among the locals that at a woman's wedding she should be decked with so much jewellery that she could not stand unaided under its weight, so there was plenty to be taken, even from the poor. At first the women resisted, but then they looked at the bodies of their mothers, sisters and daughters.

Osokin saw the loot for himself. Two large carpets had been laid out to receive the offerings, but had disappeared from sight, obscured by piles of jewellery that stood taller than a man's height – and still the women came to pay their tributes.

Some brave staff officer, lower in rank but higher in nobility than Skobyelev, asked what it was all supposed to achieve. Wasn't victory enough? But for Skobyelev, this was not about war; it was about the permanence of the ensuing peace.

'The harder you hit them,' he explained, 'the longer they stay quiet.'

Osokin had the dressing on his arm changed and then returned to the tunnels and to the strange conical chamber with its solitary captive. At least now the bodies of the dead had been cleared away – particularly the awful headless torso that had lain in the middle of the place. But bloodstains still marked the point at which each man had fallen, and one didn't need to venture too far along the corridor outside to discover them all, stacked up, awaiting a mass burial.

'Take an hour or so,' he said to Lieutenant Lukin. 'You might as well see what we've conquered.'

'I'll be all right, sir,' Lukin replied.

'Just do as you're told!' The boy – that's all he really was – didn't deserve to escape the consequences of what they had done. However brilliant he might be at digging tunnels and laying explosives, he needed to learn that it was about more than just making precise mathematical calculations. He needed to see the result.

Lukin reluctantly obeyed.

Otrepyev's men had achieved little success in drawing the shutter back into place above them. They'd managed to reach the dangling rope, but in pulling it they had only opened the gap a little further. There was no obvious mechanism to reverse the process. The whole contraption had been devised to be used just once – to open the roof, which would never then need closing.

One of the soldiers had managed to shin his way up the support for the swinging blade that had so efficiently beheaded his comrade the previous day. But its pivot was not close enough to the skylight. He reached out as if expecting his arm to suddenly grow in length and bridge the gap, but it was hopeless. His fingers lost their grip and he fell with a cry, landing at the feet of the prisoner, still in his chair, who glanced down with an expression of contempt. Even if he'd escaped breaking any bones, the fallen man must have been horribly bruised, but he looked up into the eyes that stared down upon him from the chair and in an instant was scrambling away like a startled crab. He huddled against the wall, nursing his aching limbs.

It was all very peculiar: the prisoner himself, the two strange contrivances – one to open up the roof, the other to behead the prisoner. It was clear that the man was not meant to be captured alive. What reason could there be for that? And if he needed to be killed, why not a simple bullet or a blade? There was one answer that crept into Osokin's mind, but it came from the past – from childishness and superstition. The Turcomans though were a backward people; a hundred or more years behind Russia. At the time of Empress Yekaterina, might not many of even her most rational subjects have taken such myths for truth? There were tales from as recently as the Patriotic War, of monsters preying on Russians and French alike. It would be the same for the Turcomans today. But if it was just these primitives who believed it, why had Colonel Otrepyev been so keen to cut that rope?

His contemplations were interrupted by a sudden sound; a heavy crash of wood against stone. He turned to see that the prisoner, and his chair, had fallen backwards. Both lay there, in much the same position as when Otrepyev had kicked them over. None of the soldiers was nearby. Osokin could only guess that it was the prisoner himself who had managed to rock the chair over as part of some failed attempt at escape. But there was no way he would be able to free himself of those bonds – whatever he might be.

'Get him up!' instructed Osokin.

Two of the men rushed forward and pulled the chair back upright for a second time. Osokin supervised. He ran his eyes over the prisoner to check his condition.

'You injured?' he asked, forgetting for a moment his earlier failure to communicate.

'No,' replied the prisoner, and then, after a pause, 'Thank you.'

Osokin said nothing, merely nodding an acknowledgement. It was no real surprise to discover that the prisoner was well able to understand.

'I wonder,' the prisoner continued, his Russian still flawless, 'if I might ask one favour.'

'What?'

'Could you turn the chair a little? The light hurts my eyes.'

In falling and being righted again, the chair had moved a little way across the chamber. It was now closer to the area of sunlight that shone in through the roof. It was bright, but not so bright as to be uncomfortable, not for Osokin at least. But it fitted into the picture that he was, against his better judgement, building of the situation. Or perhaps the prisoner was just toying with his suspicions. Osokin considered for a moment, and then nodded his assent at the soldiers. They began to rotate the chair.

'That's perfect. Thank you,' said the prisoner meekly, after he had been turned through a right angle. He was now roughly side on to the line marking the boundary between sunlight and shadow and facing directly towards the mangled doorway. Was he planning something? Osokin could not imagine what. Anyway, Otrepyev would return soon, and then it would be his problem.

At least Osokin hoped it would be soon.

It was a tricky choice, after so little acquaintance: to appeal to the bad in him, or to the good? To say 'Please don't throw me into that briar patch,' or just the reverse? For most Russian officers, and even more of the men, Iuda would have asked for what he didn't want, and got what he did. But in this major – Osokin was what Dmitry had called him – he'd detected a little more sentimentality. He'd seen the look of disquiet on Osokin's face as he'd returned to the prison chamber, having presumably surveyed the aftermath of the battle above. It would make him more sympathetic to the well-being of a prisoner of war. At least, so Iuda had hoped.

Luck was on his side, and not just in Osokin's agreeing to turn his chair. The first stroke of luck had been that Dmitry had departed. It was to be expected; his hunger was obvious, certainly to another vampire such as Iuda. His ageing skin would be noticeable even to a human. Dmitry must have been so dedicated to his pursuit of Iuda that he had neglected to sustain himself. Now his hunger would have become overwhelming. He'd been forced to leave and seek blood among the defeated Turcomans, even if it meant leaving his captive alone. It was understandable, but a mistake nonetheless.

The very fact that the chair had fallen was not part of Iuda's plan. He'd been moving himself oh so gradually, inch by inch, his only means of locomotion being his toes and heels. Until yesterday it would have been impossible, with the chair bolted to the floor, but now it could be done. It took every ounce of his inhuman strength, but it could be done. But then he had become stuck –

the chair leg caught in a ridge in the flagstones, he guessed. He'd pushed hard, beginning to rock the chair to what extent he could, trying to free the leg, but had gone too far. He felt himself falling, then came to a halt with a crash.

And then came more luck. In resurrecting him, the soldiers had moved him to almost precisely the spot where he desired to be. Once Osokin had had him turned it took only a few fine adjustments with his toes for him to be within inches of where he wanted.

Now he waited, and allowed the Earth to continue its inexorable rotation. He remembered a room in an abandoned house in Moscow in 1812 and the sun's slow progress across the floor, creating a tightening trap for any vampire. That was when he had first wondered whether Lyosha might prove a worthy opponent. Lyosha had proved more than worthy. Dmitry was a disappointment, as much to Iuda as an adversary as he would have been to Lyosha as a son, if only Lyosha had known the truth.

He also remembered an escape, by a *voordalak* named Ruslan, who'd later gone by the name of Kyesha – the very creature that had eventually turned Iuda into a vampire. He had been Iuda's prisoner, the subject of his experiments. He had been manacled in a cave in Chufut Kalye and exposed daily to sunlight so that Iuda could measure his reactions. And then, one day, he had vanished. It had taken Iuda hours to imagine how he might have done it, but once understood it had been obvious. Today Ruslan's method needed only a little modification.

The line between light and shade moved closer. Iuda could not perceive its movement directly, but every time he glanced down it had taken a step towards him. He felt a cold, visceral fear of it and became filled with the urge to flee, but even had he yielded to it his bonds would have held him in place.

For nearly three years he had not moved from that chair. How would it feel to be free? He knew that the muscles of a vampire did not atrophy to the same degree as those of a man, but he would still be below his peak. He was well fed, at least. The Turcomans had been told to keep him alive, and they were too afraid to disobey. It was always the same procedure. They would loosen the restraint to his head, allowing him some little movement, and then the victim would be held close and he would feed. It was, and was intended to be, a humiliation – being hand-fed like a baby rather than using his own arms to hold his prey close. But it kept him strong. He would need his strength for what was to come – regrowth demanded the greatest strength of all. Usually it had been some criminal that they gave him, who would have died anyway. The thought made it even less enjoyable. More recently they had brought him captured Russians. That had been enough for him to know that an attack was imminent. His last feed had been only the day before the assault.

He felt a stinging pain in his ankle and tried to pull it away. The sunlight had reached him. If his foot were to burn, so be it, but it was not intended as his primary sacrifice to Apollo. The sunlight worked its way up the wooden chair leg, like a slow incoming tide, ready to engulf him as he sat, commanding the waves to go back. But he knew it would not engulf him, and he would not command it to stop. It would reach him, do its work and then recede. He had calculated its path, and seated himself accordingly.

He felt a prickling in his leg as the sunlight squeezed through the weave of his trousers. He wondered how much damage would be caused. Would it be like sunburn? He wished he could look. Later he would experiment. Now the light had turned a corner. It crept stealthily along the top of the chair's arms. Soon it would reach his hand.

He braced himself and then watched, fascinated, as his fingers and then his hand and then his arm began to dissolve.

Osokin sniffed and looked around. Whether it was the stench of the thousands of rotting corpses above or the few out in the corridor mattered little. He had smelt the aftermath of battle many times before, though this was a little different; not the usual miasma of putrefaction, but something more like mildew, mixed with burning – burning hair. He glanced around the room, but saw nothing. The soldiers were sitting or standing idly, awaiting the return of their commander. The prisoner remained in his chair. The light of the setting sun was close to him now. If Osokin's preposterous imaginings had been true, then the prisoner would not have happily sat there. Unless it was that he sought death. If so, thought Osokin, let him die.

'Everything in order, sir?'

Lukin had returned. He too sniffed the air, and paled.

'Don't worry, Lieutenant, you'll get used to it.'

Lukin looked at him, puzzled. 'Has something happened with the prisoner?'

'He managed to knock his chair over, that's all.' Osokin glanced over, but the figure sat immobile.

'Best give him a quick inspection, don't you think, sir?'

Without even showing his superior the respect of waiting for a confirmation, the lieutenant flicked his fingers to attract the attention of one of the men. There was no response and so he repeated the gesture, at last gaining some reaction. He pointed to the prisoner and the soldier strode towards him, Lukin a few paces behind. Osokin felt the urge to reprimand him, but he was curious to see how the lieutenant would deal with the taciturn captive. He sauntered after them.

'Shit!'

The one, explosive word came from the lips of the soldier an instant before he was hurled across the room, slamming into the sloping wall opposite. Lukin took a step back and Osokin broke into a run. Even as he approached, he could see what had happened. Somehow the prisoner had freed his right arm. Osokin drew his revolver and stood at a safe distance, holding it out in front of him in both hands. Even so he could see it shaking, his right arm still too weak and painful to keep it steady. The prisoner's arm threshed from side to side, almost wildly, but the look of calm concentration on his face told Osokin that the action was quite deliberate.

'Keep back,' he instructed Lukin. He would have told the others too, but having seen the fate of their comrade, none of the remaining soldiers dared approach. It was as if they knew what was happening.

Osokin assessed the scene. He could see nothing amiss with the bindings that should have been holding the prisoner's right arm. The leather and chains appeared intact – and yet they were too tight for the prisoner to have slipped his hand out. But, looking at the hand, maybe that wasn't so certain. It was more of a stump. There was the hint of a thumb, but the whole thing was smeared with blood and pus. The prisoner reached over with it, as if trying to undo the bonds that held his other wrist, but without fingers there was nothing he could do.

And yet now there were fingers – not complete fingers but three short sticks of bone that protruded from the prisoner's bloody, shapeless fist. He began to flex them, just like he might have done if they had been cold, or if he had slept on his arm. As he did so, they grew and were joined by a fourth.

Osokin stood in frozen inaction, unable to determine what he could or should do. If he went close, then that arm might deliver a heavy blow, but apart from that was there any danger? The prisoner still had no chance of escape. A shout broke into his thoughts.

'Get over here! If we can hold him now we may have a chance!' It was Lukin, shouting to the other men, but without effect. For all his technical abilities, the lieutenant had no great air of authority about him – not enough to overcome the men's fear. But to Osokin, his and their concern seemed misplaced. There was no serious threat.

The prisoner reached over again, his nailless fingers out-stretched, scrabbling for where his bonds were fastened. His hand was almost complete. The skin had returned – smooth and shiny, as though scalded, but even as Osokin watched it became firmer and more textured, matching the complexion of the rest of the prisoner's body. The prisoner grunted and strained with his left hand, and with a splintering of wood it was free. He stood, his lower legs still fastened tight to the chair legs, and looked around him, breathing heavily. Then he bent forward.

'Sit back down!' Osokin's words sounded calm, at least to him-self. They had no effect on the prisoner, other than causing him momentarily to look up from his work on the straps that held his legs. 'Sit, or I fire.'

Still there was no response. Osokin let loose three shots. In his bent position, the only target the prisoner offered was his head and shoulders. Osokin was sure that at least one bullet entered the brain. The prisoner stood and Osokin fired again, noting the slight recoil as the bullet hit his chest.

Now there was no doubt in Osokin's mind. He was facing a creature of his nightmares – a *voordalak* or something very like it; names did not matter at this moment. His gun was useless. He looked around him, trying to think what he might use as a weapon, but time was short. The prisoner had bent down again and had already begun to free one leg. Perhaps a sword or a bayonet would help, although legend said that the blade used against a vampire must be wooden. The room itself had two weapons – sunlight and the guillotine – though how either could be put to use, he could not guess. There was only a small patch of daylight left now, but at least it might provide protection. Osokin backed towards it.

At the same moment, he witnessed an act of preposterous bravery. With the prisoner still bending down, Lukin ran forward and leapt towards him. It was no direct attack. Lukin's booted foot landed square in the middle of the prisoner's bent back and then the other launched him from the back of the chair, sending him flying through the air to where he managed to grab the end of the dangling rope.

The canopy above shifted, and the line of daylight moved a little closer to the prisoner, but now it was no longer so much of a threat; the prisoner was free. With a shake of his leg the last strands of leather dropped to the floor. The last chain fell and coiled itself on the ground like a snake, clinking instead of hissing. The prisoner looked around.

Now the troops that Otrepyev had left on guard were stung into action. Some rushed to surround the prisoner, sabres drawn or rifles raised, bayonets pointing upwards. Most, though, went over to Lukin. After his initial success, his efforts on the rope had made no further progress. One of the soldiers jumped up, reaching up for his ankle, but missed. A second attempt found its grip and the soldier dangled from Lukin's leg. The lieutenant managed to keep hold of the rope and the shutter moved again. The soldier began climbing up Lukin's trouser leg, and calling on his comrades to add their own weight.

The prisoner was well aware of events. He had seen the shade recede and turned to take in the cause. He reached forward and grabbed at the rifle of one of those surrounding him. The soldier fired, but it mattered little whether the bullet found its target or not. The prisoner wrenched the gun from his hands and then rammed it forward. The butt hit the soldier in the face, splitting his cheek and lip and dropping him to the floor. Another man struck with his sword. If the blow had kept true it would have split the prisoner's skull, but at the last moment he jerked his head to one side and the blade caught his right ear. It was impossible to see what damage had been done for the flow of blood, but the prisoner was unperturbed. He swung the rifle again, knocking the swordsman to the ground, then he plucked the bayonet from the muzzle and cast the gun aside. He turned and flung the blade at the dangling figure of Lieutenant Lukin, from whose legs three other bodies now hung, with at last some significant effect on the speed at which the roof was opening.

Osokin did not see where the bayonet hit, but Lukin's grip slackened immediately and all four men tumbled to the floor. The three *ryadovye* quickly pulled themselves to their feet, but the officer remained motionless on the ground.

The prisoner – though it was now far from appropriate to consider him a captive – strode towards the doorway. Although it was still daylight outside, there was a maze of tunnels out there – both those that were a part of the city and those that the Russians had dug for themselves – and he would easily find a safe place to hide until it was night. One of the soldiers threw himself on to the creature. It was brave, but it was no real attack. The prisoner caught him with one hand and drew him closer, so that they were almost face to face. There was a scream and Osokin saw a spurt of blood spray across the ground, quickly ebbing to nothing. The prisoner did not pause to drink, but hurled the corpse away. It landed against the wooden wheel that had once operated the canopy, shattering it. The prisoner turned and looked back at the room, stains of the soldier's blood on his chin and neck. No one else moved to intercept him.

But Osokin did move, neither towards nor away from the prisoner, but laterally, in the direction of the wheel he had just destroyed. Osokin looked down, kicking the shards of broken wood with his toe until he saw what he wanted. It was one of the spokes of the wheel, still in one piece and sharpened at one end where it had been driven into the hub when the thing was constructed. He raised it in his right hand, and turned towards the prisoner.

The expression on the creature's face was a fitting reflection of the futility of Osokin's action. He did not know why he couldn't simply let the vampire leave. He did not know whether such an implement really would be effective, or whether it would be as useless as the bullets that had already been tried. He did not even know if he would have the skill and the strength to drive it home. And yet some force deep in his gut told him that he must fight this thing – must destroy it.

The prisoner grinned and took a step away from the doorway, as if to prove that he was able to leave and that he chose not to. He and Osokin began to circle one another. He did not cut an impressive figure. He was of about the same height as Osokin, but carried no great bulk. And yet Osokin knew how futile it was to assess his appearance as if he were a human. Everyone in the room – everyone still alive – had seen what the prisoner could do.

Osokin now had his back to the door. He took a step forward, but the prisoner made no move. Osokin jerked the stake out in front of him and the prisoner raised his hands a little in mock surrender, taking a step back. Osokin moved forward again and the prisoner echoed his movements, keeping a constant distance between them. Osokin prayed that his adversary had not noticed what he could plainly see. While most of the men watched in numbed silence, one of them had begun to move, crawling on all fours and positioning himself behind the prisoner. It was the sort of trick that belonged to the schoolyard, but it might just work.

Osokin gave a roar and began to run, hoping to see the prisoner react and tumble over the obstruction behind him. The creature did move, but far more swiftly than Osokin could have imagined. He turned and picked up the soldier from the floor behind him, holding him by his belt and collar, then he straightened and hurled the helpless man into Osokin's oncoming charge. There was nothing Osokin could do. He heard an obscene noise and felt the stake press against his hands as it entered the man's body.

His nostrils caught the scent of human ordure. He fell backwards under the impact, letting go of the stake. The soldier rolled aside, groaning in agony.

Osokin tried to sit up, but he had no time. The next moment, the prisoner was upon him, his eyes blazing, his mouth open to reveal his fangs. Osokin fell back once again and felt the prisoner's hand on his chin, pushing his head upwards to reveal the pale white flesh of his throat. He began to pray, not that he would live but that he would truly die. He braced himself against the pain.

But no pain came. Instead, he heard a strangled, gurgling cry and felt the prisoner's weight lifted from him. He opened his eyes and raised his head to see what had happened.

Colonel Otrepyev had returned, and had come prepared.

Around the prisoner's neck was a loop of wire rope, which was tightened like a dog's leash. Otrepyev held the other end and now that he had pulled his captive away from Osokin, he had his foot in the small of his back, so that he could further tighten the noose. The prisoner's hands were at his throat, scratching in search of some way to relieve the tension, but they could find nothing.

'Bind him.' Otrepyev's command was to the two men who had returned with him. They had brought a wooden trunk which they emptied on to the floor. A pile of metalwork lay before them, chains, manacles and other devices. Otrepyev maintained his grip on the wire rope, while the soldiers moved in. First they placed a helmet over the prisoner's head. It was not solid but made of strips of metal so that his eyes, ears and nose were not covered. His mouth received no such favour. A steel tongue forced its way between his lips as the device was fastened. Osokin had seen such a thing before, in a museum in Leipzig. It was called a *Schandmaske* – a scold's bridle.

Next they manacled him – both his hands and his feet. The wire rope was looped through the bindings at his wrists and tied off on those at his ankles. Now Otrepyev released his grip, confident that there was no chance of escape. Finally the prisoner was bound with chains, across his arms and torso, at about the level of his elbows, and around his knees.

Under Otrepyev's direction, the two men lifted the prisoner and began to carry him across the room. Osokin was on his feet now and could see more clearly the box they had brought in. It was no simple crate. The sides, top and bottom were constructed of thick, solid oak, and additionally there were bands of iron, hinged so that the lid could open, and fitted with hasps so that they could be locked. From its shape anyone would guess that the box was intended for use as a coffin – only those who had witnessed the inhuman powers that had just been displayed would understand the need for it to be so strong.

The prisoner offered no struggle as he was lowered inside. Otrepyev lifted the lid and took one last, long look at the creature within before allowing it to drop with a slam that echoed around the inside of the conical chamber. Padlocks were quickly applied as a final security measure.

The two men picked up the coffin – whose weight must have been doubled by all the additional metalwork – and carried it from the room. Colonel Otrepyev took a final glance around the chamber, as if checking he had not forgotten anything.

He pointed to a couple of his men. 'You two, come with me. I'll need you to load the crates. The rest of you can return to your regiment.' Then he turned to Osokin, offering a salute. 'Thank you very much, Major,' he said. With that, he was gone.

Osokin felt the urge to laugh. He'd always despised men like Otrepyev – men who worked for the Third Section, or now the Ohrana. Was this really what they spent their days doing? If so, it was now clear that Colonel Otrepyev was a brave man. A hero. And yet still the question niggled at the back of Osokin's mind; why couldn't they have just left that creature to perish in the sunlight?

He looked around him, at the bodies of the injured, dying and dead. He knew he must act. They needed a doctor. He was about to leave when he saw something on the floor – bloody and gnarled, but still recognizable. It was a human ear. At least it appeared human, but Osokin knew where it had come from. He had seen it being cut from the prisoner's head during the struggle.

And that was enough to expel any doubt there might have been in Osokin's mind. The creature – the prisoner – was irrefutably a *voordalak*. Osokin had observed him closely as they had clamped the *Schandmaske* over his head and seen for himself with absolute clarity. The ear, whose twin now lay in the dirt of the cell floor, was perfectly intact on the prisoner's head. There was only one explanation: it had grown back.

CHAPTER IV

LIEUTENANT MIHAIL KONSTANTINOVICH LUKIN LEANED ON THE railing of the boat and gazed north across the Caspian Sea. The breeze was cold, but even now, in the middle of January, it was nothing to what he had known in Moscow or even in Saratov. To the north, the sea often froze in the winter, and Mihail could see a few solitary chunks of ice drifting gently by. Here though, and further south, the sea was deeper and warmer, and ice, so he was told, rarely formed.

He looked down at the two letters in his hands, one to him, the other from him, the arrival of the former making the completion of the latter superfluous. He'd known what the letter to him had been about without the need to open it. He'd felt the small, hard lump inside and understood immediately what it was, and what it meant.

The bayonet that Iuda hurled at him had not done any serious damage. It caught him in the back of the left hand, almost dead centre, and had gone right through. Mihail had been forced to let go of the rope and so he and the others had fallen. He landed badly, and was knocked out, waking the following day inside a mosque that had been commandeered for use as a field hospital. Major Osokin had told him of the prisoner's strange departure.

He'd spent two further nights in the hospital. His concussion was not serious, but the doctor was concerned about his hand. The bloody mark on his palm might have been taken for a single stigma. The doctor told him he was lucky not to have lost a finger or two, and Mihail had smiled quietly to himself. But the wound was bad enough to justify his taking some leave; that and his commendation for the mine works. He was more than happy to get away from the place, after what he'd seen of the Russian army's treatment of the vanquished citizens of Geok Tepe – they'd given him no warning of the barbarity of his own army during his training at the Imperial Technical School. The only hold-up had been in waiting for the slow machine of military bureaucracy to fill out the paperwork. But ultimately it was a lucky delay. The letter arrived on the morning of his departure – three weeks after it had been sent.

He'd taken the road north-west from Geok Tepe towards Krasnovodsk. There was plenty of traffic in both directions; supplies travelling one way and empty carriages holding a few dispatches being sent back. It was slow, but he doubted his quarry would be travelling much faster, and it gave him time to think. After Kyzyl-Arvat, the railway began; General Skobyelev's great scheme for keeping the army supplied as it marched ever closer to the British Empire. But even by train, the pace was infuriatingly slow. The track had been started with a narrow gauge, and then the decision had been made to switch to the standard used throughout the Russian Empire. In places the carriages were pulled by steam engines, which broke down, in others by horses, who struggled to find a grip in the winter mud.

Once at Krasnovodsk, it was a simple task to book a passage across the Caspian. The sense in every soldier on that boat that once ashore they would be on home soil was palpable – though Baku was very different from any truly Russian town.

He might have chosen a different route across that vast inland sea, heading north and then following the path of the Volga – by boat if it still flowed or on land if it had frozen – up to Saratov, the town of his birth. But the place held little for him now, and the only clue he had to guide his quest pointed towards a quite different city – to Saint Petersburg, far in the north.

Mihail had listened intently to that conversation between Dmitry and Iuda, though his eyes had been closed and his head had lolled idly against the stone wall of the chamber. His mother had insisted that he learn English from an early age, even though she spoke not a word herself. The reason she held it so important, she had told him, was that English was the language of Cain's journal. Whether he was truly an Englishman, no one had been able to determine for sure, but that he used it in writings intended only for himself to read suggested that the language was close to his heart. Mihail had been a little surprised to learn that Dmitry could speak English too, but as he'd suggested, he'd had plenty of time to learn.

Only a fool – and neither Dmitry nor Iuda fitted into that category – would expect that speaking in a foreign tongue was a sure protection against eavesdroppers, but little of what they discussed would be comprehensible to the uninitiated. Most of it Mihail already knew. He'd followed the clues that led inescapably to the fact that somewhere deep beneath Geok Tepe there was a secret prison which held a captive so terrible that he was never allowed even to rise from his chair. In Kyzyl-Arvat he'd witnessed the interrogation of a captured Teke who described the appearance of the man – his straggling blond hair and cold grey eyes.

Mihail had never met Iuda, but he'd heard the monster's description even as he suckled at his mother's breast. She'd tried to draw him, but without much skill, although when he'd finally seen Iuda face to face, bound to that chair, Mihail had begun to review his assessment of his mother's abilities. Of course, when she had known him his hair had been dyed black, but they'd both guessed – and guessed right – that he was happier with it in its natural blond state.

Mihail did not stare too long into Iuda's eyes, no longer, he hoped, than any officer might upon encountering so strangely fettered a prisoner. He saw no hint of recognition in those eyes, but why should there be? Mihail's mother had always claimed to see a family resemblance in her son, but he suspected she was just trying to flatter – for her there could be no greater compliment.

It was only when Major Osokin had mentioned Mihail's surname, Lukin, that there had been a flicker of recognition in Iuda's eyes, and perhaps a flicker of fear too. It would be almost seventy years since that name had meant anything to Iuda, but he might still be wary of revenge. If he was, he was wise. He might suspect revenge if he heard other surnames too, the names Savin and Petrenko. But he would experience the greatest terror if he knew Mihail's true surname. He would learn it soon enough. He would have discovered it there and then, on the day that Geok Tepe fell, if things had gone according to Mihail's original plan, and would have died with that name on his lips, but it turned out that Mihail was not the only one who had been able to piece together the clues.

Dmitry's arrival – under the pseudonym of Colonel Otrepyev – had been a complete surprise. At first, Mihail had not even been certain it was Dmitry; his mother's description of him had been less precise – she held for him none of the hatred that she felt for Iuda. She wondered even if he might be counted on as a friend, but warned Mihail not to trust him. It was his height that was the most recognizable feature, though it was not unique. But Otrepyev's evident interest in and knowledge of the prisoner put into Mihail's mind the list of people who might come so far to find him. And 'people' was not the right word. Mihail knew that Dmitry was a *voordalak*, just as he knew Iuda was. He watched Otrepyev and saw that he never went out of the tunnels during the day. He watched Otrepyev's men too, but they led more normal lives. Mihail felt sure that they were not vampires; most of them, at least. He knew the error of presuming that most meant all.

With Dmitry and his squad present, Mihail knew he would have little chance to kill Iuda. He could have helped as the Turcoman guards tried to spring their traps, but that might well have resulted in his death too. And it was more than that; it was not enough for Iuda to die. He had to know why he was dying and who was killing him – Mihail's mother had been insistent upon that. This was to be an execution, a punishment for a crime – for many crimes. It meant nothing for the criminal to be shot quietly in the back of the head when he least expected it.

When Iuda had escaped, Mihail's attempt to grab at the rope and bring sunlight into the room had been an act of self-preservation, not revenge. He was almost glad he had failed. Perhaps whatever Dmitry had in store for Iuda would be worse than anything that Mihail could have conceived. And Dmitry, of course, was not working alone – his 'we' had given that away to Mihail as much as to Iuda. Both could take a good guess as to who the other half of the 'we' was. Even so, it would not be enough. No punishment, no death would be enough if Iuda did not at that moment look into Mihail's eyes and see in them the eyes of his mother, and of his grandfather.

And so it had become clear that, thanks to Dmitry's intervention, Mihail would not take his revenge – not that day. He had been happy to listen to the two of them, and to learn. In all they had said, there were two things of particular interest.

One was Ascalon. It was not a word that Mihail had ever heard before, but it seemed to be of importance to both vampires. Mihail had asked around, mentioning the word to Osokin and others he encountered during his brief stay in hospital. The only meaning anyone could put upon it was the town of Ascalon, or sometimes Ashkelon, a place on the coast of Asia Minor, not far from Jerusalem. The padre had even recalled a mention of it in the Bible, in the second book of Samuel:

Tell it not in Gath, publish it not in the streets of Ascalon; lest the daughters of the Philistines rejoice, lest the daughters of the uncircumcised triumph.

It didn't seem likely to be helpful. Mihail considered going there, but Petersburg was the better bet. He didn't think that the Ascalon in question was a place. Admittedly Dmitry had asked where it was, but if he was talking about the city, that question would be simple to answer. And then Iuda had talked about fetching it, which made no sense if it was a town. Dmitry had mentioned the Karaites. Mihail had heard about them from his mother too – a Jewish sect, a group of whom had lived at Chufut Kalye in the Crimea. But Mihail had already been there – it was one of the first places he'd looked in his search for Iuda. The Karaites were long gone and rubble still blocked the mouths to Iuda's caves below. Mihail had not dug down – fearful of what he might uncover.

No, Petersburg was the place to go. That would be where Dmitry was taking Iuda, secured in that coffin-prison. Dmitry himself would presumably travel in a similar manner, though without the constraints. Mihail knew because of a second name he had heard them speak of.

Luka Miroslavich.

Mihail had never met his brother – his half-brother – Luka Miroslavich Novikov. Luka had been adopted years before Mihail was born and taken the name of his new family. They had different fathers, but the same mother: Tamara Alekseevna Danilova. And Tamara's brother – again, her half-brother – was Dmitry. That was why Dmitry could rightly call Luka his nephew.

Just like her son, Tamara had been adopted, years earlier, but she'd always known in her heart that the man and woman who had raised her were not her true parents. Once she was old enough she had gone in search of them – and been reunited only to see them both die within hours of each other. It was obvious to Mihail that she hoped Luka would one day come looking for her, just as she had gone in search of her parents, Aleksei and Domnikiia. But Luka never came. It made her bitter towards him, even though she had loved Luka's father, her husband Vitaliy, more than she could ever love Mihail's, a passing encounter. She'd had two other children with Vitaliy. Both had died. Mihail often tried to imagine Milenochka and Stasik – his sister and brother – but Tamara was loath to talk of them.

Neither did she speak much of Mihail's father, but of all the things she had told him – drummed into him since before he could remember – this was the aspect over which he most doubted her.

It would be untrue to say he had not doubted other things. For a boy brought up in the second half of the nineteenth century to be told every day, by the woman whom he is by nature itself compelled to trust, that the *voordalak* – the vampire – was as real a creature as the wolf or the bear was, to say the least, unusual. She had told him of Baba Yaga and Zmey Gorynych, but never pretended that they were real (though she had debated whether Zmey Gorynych might have had a child and called him Zmyeevich).

When he had gone to school, the other children had laughed at him for his beliefs. Mihail had felt humiliated and realized in an instant that everything his mother told him had been make-believe. She was mad, and whatever the cause, she had moulded her son to believe in her madness. He had ranted and screamed at her, but she had held her ground, though for years after she scarcely spoke of vampires, or of Iuda, or even of Aleksei. Then she had shown him something that had convinced him, the evidence of his own eyes proving that at least part of what she had told him was true and, by inference, that the whole of it was true. She had scolded him for that last leap of misplaced logic.

But even then, there was nothing she could do to prove to him the identity of his father. She had told him how she, when young, had suspected that *her* real father was a prince, and not just any prince – specifically Prince Pyetr Mihailovich Volkonsky – but Mihail's supposed father was of a higher rank even than that. He was, Tamara insisted, a grand duke – Grand Duke Konstantin Nikolayevich Romanov, the tsar's eldest brother. It was preposterous, and yet no one denied there were Romanov bastards scattered across the country. There was no certainty that Mihail was not one of them, but it seemed unlikely. Tamara had told him to go and see his father, and how to prove their kinship, but Mihail had always been afraid, afraid of his own humiliation, but afraid most of seeing his mother's dreams exposed as rambling self-delusion.

But now he had to go, for the first time in his life, to Petersburg. Petersburg was where, as far as he knew, Luka still lived. And both Dmitry and Iuda knew of Luka and so to find him might be to find them. Perhaps it would be a good time too to attempt to make himself known to Konstantin and discover whether his mother's claims could be anything close to the truth. Now of all times, there was least to lose if they proved a lie. Now of all times, Mihail needed a father.

He read again the words of the letter he had begun writing in hospital:

My dearest Mama,
    I have seen him, face to face. He was just as you described him. I will not waste your time by recounting my feelings, but must tell you immediately: I failed. I failed in the sole task that you have raised me to accomplish. He escaped me, but he is not free, and I shall soon hunt him down again.
    Let me tell you from the beginning . . .

At that point Mihail had put down his pen to think, and soon after the letter to him had arrived, and there was no need to write any more.

The letter was from Saratov, from Nadia Karlovna Lukina, the matriarch of the family whose surname Mihail had adopted. Tamara had gone to Saratov with Mihail still in her womb and sought out the family, knowing – praying – that they would help her, out of their respect for Aleksei. In the Patriotic War, Aleksei had fought alongside Maksim Sergeivich Lukin. It had not ended well for Maks, but the two men had been firm friends, and that friendship extended to his family. On her arrival at their house, four and a half decades later in 1857, the pregnant Tamara had only needed to mention Aleksei's name to be taken in and cared for.

Nadia's letter brought the news that Mihail had expected and feared. The item inside, which he had felt through the paper of the envelope and immediately recognized, was an icon – a small oval icon showing the face of Christ – hanging from a silver chain. It was old now; at some point the chain had snapped and been hurriedly tied in a fine knot. Tamara had not known when – it had happened before the icon was given to her. She had always worn it around her neck, ever since Mihail could remember, and always promised that Mihail would have it when she died.

And now Mihail did have it. It hung around his neck and nestled against his chest, beneath his shirt. Tamara had been only four when her father had given it to her – it was one of her few memories of him from back then. He in turn had been given it by his wife, Marfa – Dmitry's mother, but not Tamara's – as he set out to do battle against Napoleon in 1812. That Mihail now wore it meant that his mother was dead.

He read through Nadia's letter again, but there was little it could tell him. It corralled many words into expressing a simple concept – a death. It explained how Tamara had found it harder and harder to breathe, and how every day she coughed up blood more regularly. It explained how Tamara did not blame her son for being absent at the moment of her death, in such a way that suggested that though Tamara might not, Nadia perhaps did.

Mihail did not blame himself and knew that his mother did

not blame him either. She had raised him to have but one destiny, to fulfil one goal that she knew she was too old and too weak to achieve. Although he had failed on this occasion, nothing would have given her more pleasure than to know that at the time of her passing, or close to it, he was face to face with the creature that had caused the death of her father, of her mother, and destroyed her life. If she had lived to see that destiny fulfilled, all the better, but Mihail knew she had died in the knowledge that her son would one day achieve what she had sent him out to do. She would have died happy.

Mihail folded the letter from Nadia and slipped it into his pocket. Then he crumpled his own letter to a ball and let it drop from his hand, watching the wind catch it and take it away from the hull of the ship before flinging it into the sea. His eyes followed as it floated away and became entangled with the foam of the ship's wake, never to be seen again.

He reached inside his shirt and stroked his thumb across the face of the icon, remembering his mother, remembering what she had told him of her life, and how most of that had been the story of her father's life, recounted to her in short, painful breaths in the few hours before his death. Beside the icon hung another item that Tamara had given to Mihail and that Aleksei had given to her. This one was a locket, square and made of silver. Aleksei had handed it to Tamara moments before his death. She had given it to Mihail the day he left to go to university in Moscow.

He had only looked inside once, but Tamara had already explained what was in there: twelve strands of blond hair, coiled into a circle. It was the same blond – the same hair – that Mihail had seen on the head of the prisoner in Geok Tepe just a few days ago. Aleksei had ripped it from Iuda's head as he'd tried to drown him in the frozen Berezina, seventy years before. One day, Mihail would reunite those hairs with their owner, and complete the job his grandfather had begun.

And those few hairs were not the only memento he had to remind him of Iuda. The other was buried deep in his luggage. Major Osokin had shown it to him as he lay in the field hospital – Iuda's severed ear. Osokin had scarcely dared to voice the implication of what he had witnessed, and had almost wept with relief when

Mihail had unquestioningly agreed with his interpretation of what had taken place. He had gladly handed the lump of flesh over to his subordinate, hoping to forget all that had happened.

Mihail did not know what use he would make of it. However distant, it remained a part of Iuda's living body. If he exposed it to the sun and let it burn, then Iuda would feel it burn – but that was not a pleasure to be squandered. When Iuda finally died, then the ear would crumble to dust with the rest of him. If that were to happen at the hands of another then at least Mihail would know. But his hope was to be there, to destroy Iuda for himself and in the monster's dying moments to reveal his heritage and his true name.

Until then, he would stick with Lukin. It was the name by which he was known in the army, and so it would make life, and travel, much easier if he kept it. And his revenge was not just in Aleksei's name. Iuda had killed Maks too, and Vadim, and it was for them that Aleksei hated him so. Mihail was happy to carry Aleksei's hatred along with his own – his mother had taught him that.

But once he had Iuda in his power, once there was no chance of interruption from inconvenient uncles, once it was time for the sentence passed against Iuda to be carried out, then Iuda and the world would know Mihail's true name:

Mihail Konstantinovich Danilov.

CHAPTER V

NOW HE WAS MAKING PROGRESS. THE BOAT ACROSS THE Caspian had been speedy enough, but from Baku Mihail once again had travelled over dirt roads, either in creaking carriages or on the back of post horses so old that he suspected it was only his riding them that kept them from becoming a part of that evening's stew. He'd headed north-west at first, sticking to the Caspian coast and observing how quickly it got colder as he progressed. At Petrovsk-Port the road turned inland and the journey continued by the same slow, unreliable means.

But at Vladikavkaz modernity returned – in the form of the railway. Now he travelled at thirty, sometimes even forty versts an hour. The track had turned almost due north and the change in the climate became more obvious with each passing hour. The train was slowing now, coming into Rostov-on-Don. The journey from Baku to Vladikavkaz had taken five long days. From Vladikavkaz it had taken scarcely twenty-two hours. Even so, it was now nine days since he had left Geok Tepe; twelve since Dmitry and Iuda's departure. From here the journey would speed up, and that meant that those two might almost be in Petersburg by now. Mihail had no wish to tarry, but there wasn't a train until the afternoon. There was little he could do but wait.

The town sat on the river Don, still a good forty versts from the Sea of Azov into which it emptied. A little way across that sea was the town of Taganrog, where Aleksandr I had died. That was the official story; Mihail knew better. Aleksei had told Tamara everything, and she had told Mihail – even down to the name that

Aleksandr had chosen for his new life: Fyodor Kuzmich. It was dangerous knowledge, though less so now. Kuzmich must surely be dead – otherwise he would be over a hundred. But Tamara and Mihail both knew a way that that might be possible. Iuda, by their reckoning, was around that age.

In Rostov Mihail found a bathhouse and some lunch and returned to the station in good time for the Moscow train. On the platform he felt uneasy. He looked around him, but in the clear light of day he had no fear of vampires. He felt the same discomfort that every Russian experienced, especially when travelling. He was being watched; they all were, by the Ohrana – the secret police that had so recently taken over from the Third Section. Dmitry had been posing as one of their agents, or perhaps more than posing – he could well be a genuine operative – but his aims within that organization would be quite different from those of its more regular employees, which were to ensure that the people remained in their place.

Mihail could not despise the Third Section the way that others did. His mother had been one of their agents and had taught him much of what she had learned – anything that might help him in his quest. She believed that much of what she had done had been good work for the benefit of the nation. She loved the tsar, as a matter of principle, but in all her concern about bringing Mihail up to hate her enemies, she had neglected to make him an unquestioning royalist. He was no socialist either. Government by and large was an irrelevance; how would a change of government help him in his one goal, to destroy Iuda? Perhaps he was a nihilist, to use Turgenev's definition – 'a man who declines to bow to authority, or to accept any principle on trust, however sanctified it may be'. *Nullius in verba* – take nobody's word for it – was another way of putting it. For a moment Mihail paused, wondering how he knew the phrase, then he gave a wry smile. They were the words that Aleksei had seen on the cover of Iuda's notebook, years before – the motto of the Royal Society in London.

In current times, he could hardly blame the tsar for being fearful of his own people, or for sending out spies to keep an eye on them. His people had done enough over the last few years in attempting to kill him. It was less than twelve months ago that they had exploded a bomb in the Winter Palace itself, and not long before that they had blown up what they thought was the imperial train, only to discover that they had done nothing more than exterminate His Majesty's luggage.

That was why the railway stations drew so much attention. Mihail could see two men on the platform who were obvious *ohraniki*, but there would be at least the same number that he hadn't spotted. He suspected that they posted the ineffectual ones – the ones who peeped over the tops of newspapers that they never read – just to lull the terrorists into a false sense of security. It was the ones you didn't notice that you had to worry about.

'I beg your pardon, sir, but have you seen a porter?'

Mihail looked around and then down. She was a short woman, but pretty; the same age as Mihail, or a little older. Her blonde hair was pinned up on the back of her head. She did not look well. Her skin was pale and moist, like clay, and her green eyes, which might have been her best feature, bulged a little in their sockets. Beside her were two cases – one almost half her height, the other smaller. Perhaps it was the effort of carrying them that had caused her so much strain; perhaps not.

'I just dismissed one,' said Mihail. He looked around in the direction that the porter had gone, but could not see the man. He smiled. It would be a long journey, and there was no one on the platform with whom he would rather spend it. 'I'm sure I can manage if you'll allow me.'

Before she could agree he had picked up the larger bag and begun to lift it into the carriage, ignoring the pain in his wounded hand. It was heavy, but he tried to make it seem like a matter of no effort. He placed it at the end of the compartment, just next to where the porter had put his own trunk, and then returned to help the young lady with her other bag. She had already lifted it and was halfway up the iron steps to the second-class carriage. He reached out, but she ignored him, continuing to manhandle the bag herself and forcing him to step back.

At last she sat down. He took the seat opposite.

'You wouldn't prefer to sit by the window?' he asked.

She shook her head curtly, and then raised her hand to her temple as if the action had hurt her. 'I prefer the shade,' she said.

His mother had always taught Mihail to be prepared, to notice the signs and be ready to act upon them. And here there were signs enough: an aversion to sunlight; the pallor of the skin. But it was only a few hours after noon and she had been standing out on the platform. Admittedly it was winter, but the sun was clear, reflecting off the piles of shovelled snow as brightly as it shone in the sky. Mihail leaned forward, pretending to flick a speck of dirt from his trousers, and breathed in through his nose. Sometimes there was an odour to them, particularly if they'd recently eaten. What Mihail smelt was quite different, and yet very familiar to him. It confirmed a quite different diagnosis of what she was.

'Might I introduce myself?' he asked, smiling. 'I'm Lieutenant Mihail Konstantinovich Lukin.'

She returned his smile. 'My name is Nikonova,' she said. 'Yevdokia Yegorovna. My friends call me Dusya.'

Mihail didn't really have friends. His mother had called him Mishan and he doubted he would ever want to hear that name from anyone else. He said nothing and felt uncomfortable at the silence.

A man entered from the far end of the carriage. Mihail did not recognize him as one of the *ohraniki* he had seen on the platform, but in tow he had a uniformed gendarme, which somewhat gave the game away. They began questioning the passengers. Mihail glanced meaningfully at Dusya and then back in the direction of the two men. She twisted to look before turning back to face Mihail. She was even paler than before, if that were possible.

Mihail winked at her. She gave him a puzzled look but said nothing.

Soon the *ohranik* and the gendarme came to them.

'Papers!'

They both handed over their passports. The *ohranik* examined Mihail's first, while the gendarme swung his gaze up and down the carriage, trying to appear necessary to the whole business.

'Name?'

'Mihail Konstantinovich Lukin. Lieutenant – Grenadier Sappers, Pyetr Nikolayevich Battalion.' The rank and battalion were evident from his uniform.

'Not with your regiment?'

'On leave.' Mihail held up his bandaged left hand. Blood had started to seep through from the effort of moving Dusya's bag.

'Turkmenistan?'

'Geok Tepe.'

The *ohranik* nodded approvingly. 'That was good work Skobyelev did out there.' He turned to Dusya, examining her papers. 'And you?' he asked, without looking up.

'Yevdokia Yegorovna Nikonova.'

'Mrs?'

'Miss.'

He glanced between her and Mihail. 'You two travelling together?' he asked.

Dusya opened her lips to answer, but no sound came. Her eyes fell to the floor.

'Yevdokia Yegorovna is a friend of my brother,' said Mihail. He could have left her to her fate, but she was pretty and he enjoyed the thrill of taking an unnecessary risk.

Dusya looked up, her eyes fixed on him. She might have blushed, but with her sickly skin it was impossible to tell.

'We're engaged to be married,' she said, a little too quickly. She was not used to this, and seemed inadequately trained.

'She and my brother, I should say,' explained Mihail casually. 'Not she and myself.' He gave a slight chuckle and Dusya joined in, more naturally this time. 'It's pure chance I bumped into her,' he added, distancing himself in case his ruse proved insufficient.

'I see. How far are you going?'

'To Petersburg,' said Mihail.

'Only as far as Moscow' was Dusya's response. Was that a hint of apology in her eyes?

'I'll be returning to Moscow in time for the wedding,' Mihail added. He said no more. It wouldn't do to be *too* helpful.

The *ohranik* nodded and he and his henchman moved on. Mihail raised his hand to his face and as he did so slipped his thumb between his first two fingers, making the sign of the *sheesh* at their backs. They could not see, but the gesture was not for their benefit. Dusya saw and her face suppressed a smirk. The *ohranik* turned, but already Mihail's palm was open and innocent. He watched them as they questioned the remainder of

76

the carriage's occupants, but they didn't look back again. At last they were finished, and climbed down to the platform. A moment later Mihail heard a slow creak followed by a clang as the brakes were released and the train began slowly to ease its way out of the station.

Somewhere behind Mihail a man stood up and walked down the carriage in their direction. He was tall – as tall as Dmitry – and heavily built, with a thick beard. He took another seat a little way ahead of them, but Mihail noticed the glance that was exchanged between him and Dusya as he passed. Mihail, it seemed, might have done well as an extemporized guardian for the young lady, but she had never been alone.

The train was fully up to speed before she dared to look him in the face again. She seemed keen to say something, but uttered not a word. She rubbed her temple again and her eyebrows became pinched.

'Don't worry,' said Mihail. 'You don't need to explain.'

She gave a meek, embarrassed smile and turned away again, but she had misunderstood. She didn't need to explain because he understood perfectly well. Beyond that familiar odour – a scent that made Mihail feel almost at home – there were the symptoms: the bulging eyes, the pallid complexion, the headaches. He'd been warned about them on almost his first day at the Imperial Technical School, and he'd seen it more than once in the field, in men who were less than familiar with the tools of their trade.

They were the symptoms of prolonged exposure to nitroglycerin.

The train slowed and finally came to a halt. It was impossible for Iuda to determine where he was, but it had been twelve days since they left Geok Tepe. They'd travelled by land, then by water, and then by land again, until finally his coffin had been loaded on to a train. They had changed trains once more since then. One thing he felt sure of, although he could see nothing of the outside world, was that the nights were getting longer, which meant they were heading north.

It wasn't the most pleasant of journeys. He'd travelled by similar means before; nailed into a crate and then shipped as freight, but usually of his own volition and to a destination of his own choice. Today, he didn't know where he was going to end up – though he could take a good guess – and in addition to being in the crate, the other constraints that Dmitry had placed on him rendered him quite immobile. It wasn't painful, but he despised the sensation of being unable to move his hands, and the halter at his neck really did interfere with his breathing, and the metal tongue of the scold's bridle poking into his mouth tasted of someone else's saliva.

He felt himself being lifted, and then carried, and then dropped on to a hard stone floor. He was picked up again and placed on a wagon, which began to trundle slowly across the snowy ground. He felt sure he was close to the end of his journey, and would soon discover his fate.

Anything would be better than the three years he had spent imprisoned in Geok Tepe. It had been his own fault. He'd overplayed his hand, and underestimated his opponent; Ibrahim Edhem Pasha was a subtle man.

After the escape from his own dungeons in 1858, Iuda had been forced to remake his life. He could no longer wander down the corridors of the Third Section, rubbing shoulders with the powerful and pretending that his every action was bent towards the protection of the tsar. For a start, he'd been doing that for too long. Soon enough, someone would notice how he never seemed to age, and then someone else would look into his history and it would all be over. He returned to his earlier way of life – the life he had led before becoming a vampire. He became a traveller, a mercenary of sorts, but always with an emphasis on persuasion rather than brute force. It wasn't that he lacked the ability to overpower his enemies, but it always seemed like less fun – cheating almost, especially now that he was so much stronger than any mortal. He preferred to use the faculties of brain which he had been born with to those of brawn which he had acquired. That wasn't to say he didn't enjoy the pleasures of the flesh as much as any other *voordalak*, but such occasions were made far sweeter if the victim had first been manoeuvred into a situation from which death was the only escape.

But he had to be circumspect. He had his enemies, and they

would recognize the signs if he left too many mysterious deaths strewn across Russia and Eastern Europe. The Romanovs were an enemy, though he felt sure they would leave him alone if he did the same for them. There was Lyosha's daughter, Tamara, but she had vanished without trace. Perhaps she was dead; perhaps she had chosen to live out her life in quiet contemplation. But of all people, she was the one who must hate Iuda most, out of love for her father. But then shouldn't Dmitry feel the same? Iuda had never been quite sure where Dmitry stood – he still wasn't. But it was none of these who truly made Iuda feel afraid.

Zmyeevich was the real enemy. Once they had been allies, but they had never trusted each other. They had gone their separate ways, and Iuda had twice managed to defeat Zmyeevich, or at least thwart him in some minor way, and Zmyeevich was the sort of creature who would repay even a small inconvenience a thousandfold.

He had almost caught Iuda, in 1877. Once again Russia and Turkey had been at war, and this time Russia was winning. Iuda had allied himself with the tsar's troops at Plevna, just south of the Danube. It was familiar territory. The city was besieged for over four months. Each night Iuda would climb its walls – walls unassailable by man, but simple for him – and feast inside the city. It helped Russia's cause, but it was mostly Iuda's own pleasure that brought him there.

But then the Romanians entered the fray – under Prince Carol – and among them the Romanian that Iuda feared most.

One night in September, after returning from another successful sortie, he had been summoned, along with several other Russian officers, to meet a newly arrived Romanian commander – a Colonel Flaviu Stanga. They assembled in a clearing by the light of flickering camp torches. Colonel Stanga emerged from his tent.

It was fifty-two years since Iuda had last met Zmyeevich face to face, but the great vampire had not changed. The high, domed forehead was hidden under a military cap, but was still unmistakable, as were his bushy eyebrows and arched nostrils. The iron-grey moustache was neatly trimmed. His skin was young and unwrinkled; he had eaten recently. He wandered down the line of officers, talking amiably about his plans for the siege, pausing at each man, looking him squarely in the eye and shaking him by the hand.

Until he drew level with Iuda.

He came to a halt and stopped speaking, staring intently down into Iuda's eyes. He took Iuda's hand, his grip firm. Iuda remained impassive, hoping that time enough had passed for Zmyeevich not to recognize him. Zmyeevich began speaking again, keeping to the subject of military tactics, and Iuda thought he had succeeded, but still he gripped Iuda's hand. And as he moved away, Zmyeevich twisted his wrist, forcing Iuda's hand down and revealing the back of his own and the ring that he wore – and had always worn, whenever Iuda had seen him. It was the figure of a dragon, with a body of gold, emerald eyes and red, forked tongue. He was making sure that Iuda recognized him, and knew that he in turn was recognized.

If Zmyeevich had chosen to kill him there and then, he had the strength to do it, and to slay every soldier who tried to stop him. But Zmyeevich remained calm. He continued his speech, moving on to the next man and the next. When he was finished he asked if there were any questions, but none came. Colonel Stanga dismissed the men.

Iuda fled; fled the camp, fled the army and fled the country. He lived as best he could, like vampires had done for years in these parts, sleeping in churchyards and feeding off peasants. And as he fled south so the Russians advanced south, and with them came Zmyeevich.

Finally, like most of the sultan's army, Iuda was trapped in the south-eastern extremity of Europe. There was only one city in which he could hide: Constantinople. He went by his real name of Cain and spoke English like an Englishman. A year before, at the Constantinople Conference – the Shipyard Conference as they called it locally – Britain had been keener to do a deal favourable to Russia than to the Ottomans, and so the English were not universally popular. But at least Britain had not joined in the war on Russia's side. And Iuda did not come empty-handed – he brought with him the gift of information.

It took only the mention of Zmyeevich's name – not in its Russian translation, but in a form known better to the Turks

– to allow Iuda access through the layers of administration of Ottoman government and into the Sublime Porte. He was granted an audience with His Imperial Majesty, the Sultan Abdülhamid II, Emperor of the Ottomans and Caliph of the Faithful, in the throne room of the Dolmabahçe Palace. The Grand Vizier – the Greek, Ibrahim Edhem Pasha – stood at his sultan's side. He was by far the wiliest of all those in the room; apart, of course, from Iuda – or so Iuda had thought.

Ibrahim Edhem did the talking.

'So you're aware of our empire's history with Ţepeş?' Even then, they dared not use Zmyeevich's full Romanian name, and stuck to that short epithet.

'I know much of him – especially of his dealings with your enemy, Russia.'

'Then you understand he is no friend of the Romanovs?'

'He would like to be more than a friend.'

Now the sultan himself spoke. 'You understand the blood curse he holds over them?'

Of that, Iuda knew more than anyone but Zmyeevich himself. He knew of the bargain between Zmyeevich and Pyotr the Great, and of how Pyotr had broken it. He knew that Zmyeevich had drunk Pyotr's blood, but that the tsar had not reciprocated. And he knew how every other Romanov was thus vulnerable to the possibility that he might one day drink Zmyeevich's blood, and die with it in his body, and become a vampire, subject to Zmyeevich's will. And if that Romanov were to be or to become tsar, then Zmyeevich would rule Russia. And then where would these Ottomans be?

'I know that if he takes Russia,' said Iuda, 'your throne will be next. He will make their armies victorious.'

Ibrahim Edhem glanced at his sultan, and then spoke again.

'How do you know all this?' he asked.

'I myself took Ţepeş's offer to Tsar Aleksandr.'

'You have spoken to His Majesty?' The Grand Vizier hid his surprise well.

'To Aleksandr Pavlovich,' Iuda explained. 'Aleksandr I.'

There was muttering around the court, and then the sultan spoke again.

'So you are . . . like him? A vampire?'

'And so I know whereof I speak,' confirmed Iuda.

'And what are you offering us?' asked the pasha.

'I know where Țepeș is. I know what name he is travelling under. If you move swiftly, you could take him.'

'A trick! Intended to divert us from the tsar's real intent.'

'He marches with the Russians. Dealing with one is not a distraction from the other.'

'And even if we could reach Țepeș,' added the sultan, 'what would we do then? He is invincible.'

'He can die, like any other vampire,' said Iuda.

'Like yourself?' asked Edhem.

Iuda acknowledged the comment with a smile, but he felt safe. Although the guards standing on either side of the sultan were armed with sabres that could easily sever his head, there were tall windows close by that he could reach in moments, and it was dark outside. Besides, they would be fools to kill him before learning all he knew – and Iuda prided himself that he knew a lot.

'Only by destroying Ascalon can Țepeș be overcome,' said the sultan.

'And if I could deliver Ascalon to you?' asked Iuda.

'It's been missing for centuries,' said the Grand Vizier. 'What would you know of it?'

'I was once Țepeș's closest ally.'

'So why would you betray him now?'

'I've already betrayed him,' explained Iuda. 'That is why I fear him. That is why I would have you deal with him.'

'He's pursuing you?'

'He would, if he knew where I was.'

'You're certain that he doesn't?'

'Quite certain,' replied Iuda, hoping he spoke the truth.

Ibrahim Edhem Pasha leaned forward and whispered into the sultan's ear. The sultan looked at him for a moment and then nodded.

'Go now,' said the Grand Vizier. 'You will be summoned.'

Iuda had turned to leave, but the meeting was not quite finished. It was the sultan who had the last word.

'And mind you don't feed during your stay in the city. These are my people. My duty is to protect them.'

Iuda departed, fully aware of the sultan's meaning.

Two days later he received a message from Ibrahim Edhem Pasha requesting a private meeting, 'in the Sunken Palace, away from the sultan's ears'.

The Sunken Palace was an ancient Roman cistern, built beneath the city by the Emperor Justinian to store drinking water. The entrance was not far from Hagia Sophia, and a safe distance from the Dolmabahçe Palace, on the other side of the Golden Horn. It was half an hour before midnight, the time for which Edhem had requested the meeting. Iuda descended the stone steps.

The space below was cool. There wasn't much water in there now, scarcely enough to reach his knees, but beneath that were centuries of accumulated mud and silt that could suck a man down and drown him as effectively as the water above. Huge columns rose up out of the water to support the arched vaults of the roof, upon which in turn the city stood. Some had collapsed, leaving stepping stones across which the great, dark space could be traversed. A few of the pillars had oil lamps hanging from them which gave illumination in some places, but left deep shadows in others. Even with Iuda's heightened ability to see in the dark, he could not penetrate the gloom to see the far end of the cistern. But the fact that the lamps had been lit at all showed that he was expected.

He skipped from stone to stone into the darkness. Soon he was near the centre of the vast chamber. None of the walls was visible. All was silent.

'Edhem!' he shouted. 'Ibrahim Edhem Pasha!'

His voice echoed, reflecting from the water, from the walls, from the columns and from the vaults, throwing itself back at him. It seemed like a minute before all was silent again, and from the evanescent sound emerged the quiet ripple of a boat breaking through the still water. Soon a figure began to materialize out of the darkness. It was the Grand Vizier, a long pole in his hand as he pushed the low, flat boat towards Iuda. The intended impression would seem to be that of Charon taking the dead across the

Styx, but Iuda was reminded more of his days at Oxford, punting on the Cherwell.

'Have you followed His Imperial Majesty's prohibition?' asked the pasha.

'Of course,' replied Iuda. He had not consumed any blood since arriving in the city. It would have been foolish to so directly contradict the wishes of his host.

'Then you will be hungry.' Edhem nodded downwards and Iuda saw that in the bow of the vessel was huddled a young man, bound and gagged. He wore the uniform of a Russian *ryadovoy*. 'Eat!' the Turk commanded.

Iuda was not starving, but he did not know when he would next get the chance to feed. He wondered if the offering of a Russian soldier was a test, to see whose side he was really on, but they must know that even if Iuda were working for the tsar, he would have no qualms over the death of one of his subjects. The Grand Vizier noticed his hesitation.

'Go ahead,' he insisted. 'The sultan's protection does not extend to kafirs.'

Iuda stepped into the boat and lifted the *ryadovoy* up by his collars. Aside from his own hunger, he knew that it would be a breach of etiquette to refuse such hospitality. He had grown to understand how important these matters could be to some. And Edhem had done everything right. The Russian was not dead – he was not even unconscious. His eyes scoured Iuda's face, searching for some sign of pity, some hint that Iuda might be his rescuer. Iuda bared his fangs and saw the young soldier's hope turn to terror. It was too much to resist. He leaned forward and bit, drinking slowly, pleased that Edhem understood his needs so well. The soldier was in no position to resist.

The Grand Vizier continued to speak as Iuda indulged himself.

'We have considered your offer,' he explained. 'As you are well aware, Ţepeş – Zmyeevich, as you call him – has been an enemy of our people for many years; for centuries. But we have not been constantly at war. At times we have occupied his lands, and he has tried to repel us. Currently, his nation is not part of our empire. It is Russia who threatens us, not him.'

Iuda lifted his head. The *ryadovoy* was scarcely conscious now, but his blood was still vibrant. Iuda began to speak, but felt dryness in his throat. He coughed. 'Țepeş is an opportunist,' he said. 'He will let Russia lead, but he will follow.' He returned to his repast, feeling more compelled now to drink than when he began.

'He is, but he is also a pragmatist.' Ibrahim Edhem's voice was louder now. 'He knows when to fight and when to cooperate. When he sailed through the Bosphorus to join you in Taganrog, do you think we were unaware? And do you think we were unaware of your experiments in Chufut Kalye?'

'You weren't even born.' Iuda noticed that his own voice was slurred.

'I was – just – but I am only the latest of those who have protected our empire over the generations. We have known for centuries things that you have only learned recently – for all your science.'

'And what do you know?' Iuda spoke quickly and returned his mouth to his victim's throat. The man was dead now, but still he felt compelled to drink.

'We know, for example, that Țepeş and Flaviu Stanga are one and the same. We know of the hatred between you. We know of your experiments and how your own kind despise you for them. We have even reproduced much of what you have discovered: how to kill the vampire, how to control him. We've learned of toxins that will render a creature such as you incapable – and we know how to administer them.'

Iuda understood in an instant, but it was too late. He spat out an unswallowed mouthful of blood, yet still yearned to drink more. His intellect prevailed, but he had already consumed enough. He felt no pain, no knotted agony in his gut. That just went to show how well Ibrahim Edhem had chosen the poison. He looked up and saw the silhouette of the pasha's head and shoulders as a blur. He was still talking, but Iuda could make no sense of it. The image in his eyes began to collapse, as though it were a freshly painted canvas left out in the rain. He slumped forward into the boat, hearing a splash as his victim's body fell from his grasp and into the water. Then there was nothing.

When he awoke, he had not moved far. He was still in the cistern, lying face upwards, the stone columns soaring above him. He sensed wooden walls at his sides, which made him feel secure, reminding him of a coffin. He tried to move, but found that he could not. He wondered if he might still be paralysed by the drug that he had drunk from the soldier's body. He racked his memory for what the poison might be, but as his senses returned he realized that his immobility was due only to the fact that he was bound by heavy chains; not simply hand and foot – his whole body was wrapped in them, leaving only his head free, as though captured by some giant spider that spun a web of iron and steel instead of silk.

Ibrahim Edhem Pasha's face leaned over him.

'You'd have done better to have killed me,' whispered Iuda, his voice weak.

'I think it would be better to preserve that pleasure for someone who will really enjoy it.'

'You're going to ransom me? To Ţepeş?'

'We're going to try.'

'You're a fool. He will come here and take me, and you will get nothing.'

'Here?' There was a twinkle in the Pasha's eye. 'We're not going to keep you here.'

'Anywhere in the empire. Your people will not be safe.'

'Then perhaps we should find you a prison outside the Ottoman Empire. We have friends. Ţepeş will not find you, unless we choose to hand you over to him.' A pause. 'Or you could simply tell us the whereabouts of Ascalon.'

Iuda said nothing. The Grand Vizier gave a signal to one of his men and a heavy wooden lid was placed over the crate in which Iuda lay. He'd listened to the sound of nails being hammered home, and then felt the rough shaking of being moved up the steps, on to a cart, on to a boat, and so on for many days. It was the same sensation he now felt as he was carried on the last leg of his journey away from Geok Tepe. Back then he had not known his destination, but he had been told on his arrival, as they strapped him into the chair that was to be his resting place for the next three years.

He often wondered if there was meant to be some joke in it, a connection between the name Ţepeş and Geok Tepe. But the words came from different languages. Tepe was the Turkic for hill – Geok Tepe meant 'the Blue Hill'. Țepeș was Romanian and meant something quite different – it meant 'the Impaler'.

Iuda's coffin was set down on the ground with a thump. He could hear no voices outside. Minutes passed. He tried to push away the memories of his betrayal and his three years in Geok Tepe, but he could not do so entirely.

It had been too long, and in all that time, one fact had remained. Țepeș, or Zmyeevich, or whatever he might call himself, had not paid the ransom. He had chosen not to deal with the Ottomans and their Turcoman allies.

Iuda noticed the minutest change in air pressure within his coffin as the iron bands across its lid were unclamped. He saw a crack of light appear between the lid and the side, and feared for a moment that it would soon be the end of him, but then realized it was merely lamplight.

A hand reached inside and pushed up the lid, and as he saw it Iuda was sure of what he had previously suspected; Zmyeevich had not paid any ransom because he did not need to.

On the middle finger of the hand there was a ring; a ring in the form of a dragon, with a body of gold, emerald eyes and red, forked tongue.

CHAPTER VI

DMITRY TOOK LITTLE PART IN THE TORTURE. HE WOULD NOT have objected, but neither would he have drawn particular enjoyment from it. If the victim had been human, it would have been a different matter, but Iuda was a vampire, and Dmitry could experience little pleasure in his pain.

Zmyeevich, on the other hand, relished the concept. And so Dmitry was happy to sit and watch – and learn; learn both the techniques of a master and whatever information Iuda might reveal.

It would be familiar territory for Iuda. The wire rope that still dug tightly into the flesh of his neck – now the only thing restraining him – was fastened at its other end to an eyelet in the ceiling of an underground cell that lay deep beneath an office that had once been the Moscow centre of the Third Section. It was the lair in which Iuda – under the name of Vasiliy Innokyentievich Yudin – had based himself for almost a decade and it was in these dungeons that he had tortured so many who had information which might protect the life of Tsar Nikolai I, along with those he tortured for reasons more personal to him.

In the subsequent years Dmitry too had made his mark in the Third Section, and so now, although the organization no longer existed, it had been easy enough to requisition these rooms beneath the Kremlin and make them a base for himself and Zmyeevich while they stayed in Moscow; and for their prisoner. Iuda had chosen the place for himself as the ideal haunt for a vampire. They would trust his judgement.

Light would have been the most effective tool in the armoury of a vampire torturer, and yet down here it was the one thing of which they were deprived. They might have taken him up and held him close to the door above, opening out on to the Kremlin, but even if they hadn't been seen, Iuda's cries would have been heard. Down here it was much safer. It did not matter; Zmyeevich knew other ways to inflict suffering upon a fellow vampire – ways that Dmitry would never have dreamed of.

To cut him, to make him bleed, to sever a finger or an entire limb; these were all things that would inflict pain upon the victim, but a *voordalak* could withstand most pain – certainly one of the age and the experience of Iuda. He could easily reassure himself that he would heal – that however great the agony there would be no lasting effect, not even a scar. The worst that could happen was that the vampire would die – and that could never be to the benefit of the torturer.

Zmyeevich had tried these basics, cutting and severing. In total Iuda now had thirteen fingers and three thumbs, the excess scattered on the floor, his hands replenished by regrowth. Zmyeevich – with a little help from Dmitry – had drained Iuda of blood until he was almost dry. Normally that would bring on a light-headedness in a vampire, a mood of compliance in which the creature might reveal its darkest secrets. Iuda was made of stronger stuff. They had needed to feed him in order to be able to begin again. It had been easy to get hold of a victim – a young boy who had been impressed by Dmitry's uniform and thrilled at the offer of a visit to the Kremlin Armoury. It was better that it was a child – less blood. They didn't want Iuda to become too strong.

But it had all taken time. Now it was almost a day since they had arrived in Moscow, Dmitry travelling, like Iuda, in a crate. For him there was always the liberty, at least during the night, to open up the lid and step outside, but he rarely indulged himself. For most of the journey, Dmitry had been as much a prisoner as Iuda. But now things had changed.

After Iuda had fed, Zmyeevich switched to a different set of techniques in his attempts to extract the information he wanted. He made small cuts in Iuda's body using a sharp steel knife. They would have healed rapidly and hurt little, but Zmyeevich had quickly inserted small shards of wood – he'd brought along a whole sack of them for the purpose.

'A wooden stake through the heart kills a vampire because the flesh cannot heal rapidly enough,' he explained. 'Wood in any wound will have a similar, if less terminal effect. Hawthorn is best, though it is not essential.'

Soon Iuda's belly, back and thighs were a latticework of short, deep cuts, from every one of which protruded a twig or a stick. Iuda screamed as each one was inserted, and screamed again whenever Zmyeevich took hold of one and chose to twist it, pressing it into the wound.

'And then there's always this,' he said after a little while.

He cut Iuda once again, just as he had before, and this time slipped a clove of garlic, skinned and cut in half, into the wound. He repeated the process half a dozen times, and each time Iuda screamed as the white flesh of the vegetable penetrated his own.

'This is where the myths about our fear of garlic come from,' Zmyeevich explained. 'The smell, the taste, the sensation on the skin – these are nothing. But buried in the flesh, it becomes something quite different.'

Dmitry nodded. He'd known even as a human of the belief that vampires feared garlic, but had never experienced it himself. Now, perhaps, he would be a little more wary. Zmyeevich continued the process until there was scarcely an inch of Iuda's body that had not been implanted with either wood or garlic. Iuda screamed and shuddered with each new penetration, but did not grow weak. By the end of it, Dmitry saw Iuda more as a leg of mutton, prepared in a Petersburg hotel by some expert French chef who knew how to get the flavour of garlic to infuse every last fibre of the meat.

'Come and look,' suggested Zmyeevich when he was finished.

Dmitry approached, and peered closely at Iuda's wounds, first examining one where a thick splinter of oak held open a flap of skin and fat just below Iuda's bottom rib. Around it the flesh attempted to grow and reform, just as might the flesh of any wounded *voordalak*, but whenever it touched the wood, it was repelled, and so the laceration was in a constant state of flux, always trying to heal – never succeeding.

90

Next he looked at where Zmyeevich had placed a sliver of garlic. Here things were far worse. The flesh made no attempt to regrow. It lay dead and black, leaving a gaping hole in Iuda's side. Yellow pus oozed from somewhere in the dark crevice that Dmitry couldn't see. Even to a human the smell would have been repellent. To a vampire – smelling rotting vampire flesh – it was unendurable. Dmitry stepped away and breathed deeply.

'Just an address.' Zmyeevich was talking to Iuda now. 'You must have had another home here in Moscow. Simply tell us where it is.'

It was only the second time Zmyeevich had bothered to ask, the first being right at the beginning, before he'd even laid a finger on Iuda. But Iuda would not have forgotten. It was a subtle approach; none of the great questions, along the lines of 'How much of my blood have you hoarded?' or 'Where is Ascalon?' It was just a simple question that could do little harm. And once Iuda was broken and told them the answer, everything else would follow.

But Iuda did not answer.

Zmyeevich turned away and let his eyes wander across the panoply of equipment that he had brought with him. His eyes fell upon an item and he walked over to it – a simple wooden bowl. He placed it on the floor and knelt down in front of it, rolling up his sleeve as he did so. He reached to the pile of knives – of every shape, size and purpose – and selected from them a lancet. He held the blade against the flesh of his forearm, touching it at one place and then another as though attempting to select the perfect spot. Then, without hesitation, he cut. Blood flowed quickly, running across his skin and dripping from his bare elbow into the bowl below.

While he had shown not a glimmer of fear or pain as he made the cut, now Zmyeevich's face became contorted with strain and concentration. Dmitry understood the reason. If nature were left to run its course then the tiny cut to Zmyeevich's arm would already have healed, with scarcely a few drops of blood shed. Only by the force of his will could he keep the wound open and deliver from it sufficient blood for his purpose – whatever that might be.

Soon he had enough, and he relaxed, breathing deeply, sweat

glistening on his forehead. The flow of blood waned and died, and the gash began to close. Within seconds there was only smooth skin.

'Hold his head,' instructed Zmyeevich, standing and bringing the bowl over to Iuda. Dmitry did as he was told, though unsure of Zmyeevich's intent.

'Open his mouth,' Zmyeevich barked.

Dmitry complied, forcing his fingers between Iuda's lips and then his teeth, still failing to comprehend what was to come. Zmyeevich held the bowl of his own blood close to Iuda's mouth and began to tip it forward. Iuda had not seen Zmyeevich bleed himself – his eyes had been closed and his head hung as he tried to cope with the pain of his myriad wounds. At the hint of blood on his lips he opened his mouth a little wider and drank greedily. Dmitry took the opportunity to push his fingers in deeper, so that Iuda would not be able to change his mind.

After a moment, the flavour of it hit Iuda. Dmitry could well imagine it – the blood of one *voordalak* tasted foul to another, at least at first. Even for those who wanted to imbibe, it had to be forced down, like medicine. With practice the instinct could be overcome, but Iuda was far from that point. He tried to spit, but had no strength, and the blood flowed out over his bottom lip and chin.

'Tastes like piss,' he muttered, forcing out more blood as he spoke.

'No.' Zmyeevich's voice was almost soothing, like a mother trying to persuade her infant to eat. 'You must drink it all down. You must savour the blood of your master.'

At these last words Iuda raised his head and looked into Zmyeevich's face. Suddenly he seemed to understand whose blood it was. At the same moment Zmyeevich raised the bowl again, and began to tip the thick, warm liquor into Iuda's mouth. Dmitry held his head firmly, but as the fluid dripped on to his tongue a second time Iuda began to writhe, thrashing his head from side to side and kicking out with his legs, his actions a desperate attempt to force the drink from his mouth and to break free of Dmitry's grip.

Zmyeevich smiled triumphantly, but Dmitry was bewildered.

Vampire's blood might taste foul to the uninitiated, but it was nothing worse than that. Why should the thought of drinking it produce such terror in anyone, particularly in one usually so calm, as Iuda was? And that it was the blood of a *voordalak* of the eminence of Zmyeevich should make the consumption more an honour than a humiliation.

At last Iuda ripped his head free of Dmitry's grasp. He jerked it forward and brought the bridge of his nose into contact with the bowl, knocking it to the ground and spilling its contents across the grey flagstones. Dmitry felt a pang of regret at the loss of so precious a fluid.

'Don't worry,' said Zmyeevich, addressing Iuda rather than Dmitry. 'There's plenty more.'

He righted the bowl and picked up the lancet once again, preparing to yield another portion of his own vital fluid.

'No,' muttered Iuda. 'Not that. I'll tell you.'

Still Dmitry could not comprehend why the taste of Zmyeevich's blood should be regarded by Iuda with such horror, to the point that it had broken him where all Zmyeevich's twigs and garlic cloves – still protruding from his lacerated body – had failed. .

'You'll tell me what?' asked Zmyeevich.

'Zamoskvorechye,' he whispered. 'Klimentovskiy Lane – number 14.'

His knees buckled and he slumped forward, hanging with the wire rope around his neck as his only support, finding even that more comfortable than standing.

Zmyeevich looked at Dmitry and said one word.

'Go!'

Dmitry was on his way.

Number 14 stood opposite the Church of Saint Clement, after which the road was named. The building was rendered in red stucco, like the church itself. It was not a long walk from the cellars beneath the Kremlin: out through the Nikolai Gate, across Red Square, down the hill past Saint Vasiliy's to the Moskva Bridge. It was all very familiar, the same pathways that Dmitry had taken in his youth, when he'd first come to Moscow to train as a cavalry officer. Much had changed, but most remained the same. Once over the bridge it was only a short walk, crossing the Vodootvodny Canal, and he was standing outside the building.

It seemed empty, but not abandoned. It must have been three years, probably a little longer, since Iuda had had the chance to visit. They had not asked about keys; there would have been little point – Iuda certainly did not have them in his possession. Presumably somebody kept them for him, perhaps kept an eye on the building too. They could be watching now. It could all be a trap – but Iuda's fear had been genuine. Dmitry tried the door and was not surprised to find it locked. He glanced up and down the lane, but saw no one. It was well past midnight now. He threw his shoulder against the wooden panel and the lock broke away easily from the doorframe.

Dmitry stepped cautiously inside. He remembered the swinging blade that could so readily have decapitated Iuda in Geok Tepe. It was by no means beyond Iuda to have rigged up something similar – probably something far better – to deal with the unwary intruder. Dmitry fetched a paraffin lamp from his bag and lit it.

His inspection of the ground floor and first floor was cursory. Every window was curtained and shuttered, and the rooms themselves were empty of all but a few scraps of furniture. The layers of dust were suggestive of far longer than three years' disuse, but Dmitry knew Iuda would not have spent much of his time here; the instinct for any vampire was to be underground.

The steps down to the cellar lay directly beneath the main staircase. Dmitry opened the door at the top and descended, still circumspect in case of any snare that Iuda had left. What might it be? Would Iuda have merely been defending his lair against human trespassers? Or would he have been afraid of his own kind coming in here and discovering his darkest secrets? It would be like him to cover all eventualities – but there could be no doubt as to which of the two species harboured his truest enemies.

Dmitry reached the bottom of the stairs safely. He was faced with another door. He reached for the handle and opened it. Beyond, the cellar was vast, taking up half the ground plan of the entire building. At its centre was a stone plinth, and on that lay a simple wooden coffin. Its place of honour in the middle of the room reminded Dmitry of the solitary chair that had held Iuda fast in Geok Tepe.

Dmitry approached. The coffin lid was in place. Still there seemed nothing to protect the slumbering figure of Iuda on those occasions when he lay here. But today he was *not* here. It made sense that he would not have set a snare to catch himself on his own return. Dmitry drew his sword and held it out, slipping its blade into the crack beneath the coffin lid, then twisting and pushing it to one side. If there were any trap installed, he hoped he was standing far enough away.

The lid fell to the floor with a low clatter, but there were no other consequences of Dmitry's action. He glanced around; nothing in the cellar had changed. He approached the plinth and looked inside. The coffin, as he had expected, was empty, its silk lining still showing the slight imprint of where a body had once lain. This was not what they had been expecting at all. Zmyeevich had been sure that there would be documents, journals – with luck even some of Iuda's experimental samples. They hadn't expected Ascalon itself, but at least some clue. But Dmitry had examined the entire house, and this coffin was the only thing that suggested Iuda had ever been here.

Dmitry raised his sword and used the sharp tip to make a long, straight incision in the coffin's lining, down the whole of its length. He ripped away the smooth material and hurled the bundle into the corner of the cellar. But beneath, there was nothing – just the hard wooden sides and bottom of the casket, and . . .

Something caught Dmitry's eye, just where the side and bottom panels joined, about halfway down: a small metal ring attached to a wire, which disappeared into a gap in the wood, no bigger than a wormhole. On the other side was a similar arrangement, except that a longer stretch of wire was visible. The mechanism for some secret door? Dmitry doubted it. More likely it was the switch to activate whatever traps Iuda had to protect him while he slept; one wire to switch them on, when he lay down, the other to disable them before he rose. Dmitry would leave things be, for now.

He returned upstairs and considered. Why would Iuda have bothered telling them, if there was nothing here to be found?

For a momentary respite from his suffering? To allow him the chance to overpower Zmyeevich and escape? It was possible, but it would not get him very far – Zmyeevich could deal with him perfectly well. Merely for the amusement of wasting their time? That seemed feasible, but Dmitry was still doubtful.

In his mind he retraced his steps around the house – upstairs, downstairs and in the cellar. And then he saw it: a gap in the lay-out of the rooms, on the ground floor, between the stairwell, the kitchen and the large room that looked out on to the street. He walked around it, trailing his fingers across the wall, feeling for any secret latch. The space was definitely there, large enough for a sizeable room, and with no windows – no outside walls – ideal for a vampire.

And that meant the entrance would not be through any of the main rooms of the house. Iuda would want to be able to rise from his coffin in the cellar and go straight to whatever was hidden in there, without passing by any windows and the inconvenience of daylight. Dmitry returned to the cellar steps. He did not go down, but closed the door at the top and examined the wall that had been hidden when it was open.

The switch was easy enough to find. With a click Dmitry felt the panel in the wall loosen. He pushed and it swung back. He stepped through.

It was a study. The walls were lined with shelves and in the centre stood a desk and chair, facing the door. A great mirror with a gilt frame hung quite unnecessarily on one wall, to the side of the desk. Dmitry stood and gazed into it, but saw no reflection of himself, just as Iuda would not have seen himself when he stood there. The small room behind was visible in every detail, but of Dmitry – of any vampire – there could never be any sign. Why would Iuda have put it there? It could be that it dated back to a time when Iuda was human, but it seemed improbable. More likely it was there only to serve Iuda as a reminder of what he was – a *memento mori*, but of what had passed, not what was to come.

It was a reminder for Dmitry too, but as ever when he looked unseeing into a mirror it was not his own death that came to his mind, but that of Raisa Styepanovna, the creature who had taken him from humanity – his vampire mother. He did not know quite how she had died – and thus could not decide how she was to be avenged – but whenever he saw a mirror he felt a sense of horror and revulsion that he knew came from her in the hours leading up to her death. She had gone mad, but the last lucid thought he had shared with her was her anticipation that soon she would once again be able to see her face.

He turned back to the room and began to search. The shelves were empty. He inspected them all and saw faint markings in the dust that suggested they had once been filled with papers, but either Iuda had taken them away himself, or someone else had got here before Dmitry. He turned his attention to the desk. There were a few items on its top – a dried-up inkwell, a paperweight, a candle – nothing of any interest. There were nine drawers, four on either side and one in the middle.

Dmitry pulled at the central one. It wasn't locked, but stuck after he had opened it only an inch. He tugged, and it gave with a click. At the same moment, Dmitry heard a scraping sound behind him, and realized what a fool he had been.

He flung himself to one side, half rolling, half sliding across the desktop before landing heavily on the dusty carpeted floor. He stared back at where he had been standing. In the shelves behind the desk, right behind his back, a panel had dropped open, revealing behind it some contraption whose nature he could easily guess at. There was a grinding, squealing sound and something began to move in the darkness. Then the movement stopped with a clunk and a long, thin cylinder rolled sideways and fell to the ground. All was still.

Dmitry got to his feet. He bent forward and picked up the cylinder. It was essentially an arrow, though slightly thicker, made of wood except for the feather fletches at the rear end. The front had been sharpened to a point. The mechanism from which it had fallen was a crossbow, aiming the wooden bolt at the heart of whoever had so incautiously stood and opened that drawer. But such a complicated mechanism needed care and maintenance, and this had received none for many years. Some of the metalwork was rusted, and Dmitry could see the marks where rats' teeth had gnawed into the wood. A few pieces of string hung loose where once they would have been taut, presumably thanks to the same cause.

Dmitry laughed, both at his luck and his stupidity. He could easily have been the victim of Iuda's little trap, and it was down not to him but to fate that he had survived. Why was that a matter for laughter? He closed his mouth and the room was silent again, but still in his head he could hear someone laughing – laughing at him. There was no voice to it, no timbre or pitch that he could recognize, but the sentiment behind it was clear. It had the same mocking tone he had heard from Raisa, even as she took his mortal life. But it could not be her – she had shared a part of his mind, but no longer. Who then could it be?

He pushed the thoughts away and examined further the trap that had failed to catch him. When Iuda had last been here, he would have ensured that everything was in order. The metalwork would have been well oiled; the rats would have been poisoned. But when Iuda last departed, he would not have been expecting such a long period of absence. What was he thinking now, Dmitry wondered, as he sat beneath the Kremlin with Zmyeevich, awaiting Dmitry's arrival? Had he realized how decayed his machine had become? Dmitry would be pleased to see the look on his face when he returned.

In the meantime, he had work to do. The open drawer was brimming with documents. Dmitry began leafing through them.

Iuda followed Dmitry's progress in his mind. It was pure guesswork; there was no mental connection between them as there would have been if one of them had inducted the other into the *voordalak* race. Iuda simply employed the power of reason. He knew how Dmitry behaved; he knew what Dmitry would find. There would be details over which he was mistaken, of course, but for the most part everything would go according to Iuda's plan.

Once Dmitry departed, Zmyeevich had begun to remove the twigs and splinters of wood and cloves of garlic that perforated Iuda's body, and he had begun to heal. Even so, it was a slower process than normal. In some wounds, depending on the type of wood, sap had oozed into his flesh and inhibited regrowth.

The same was true with the juice from the garlic. Iuda had to acknowledge some admiration for Zmyeevich. In all of his experiments on the functioning of a *voordalak*'s body he had never thought of trying anything like this. Zmyeevich, with his great age and experience, knew much that Iuda was yet to discover.

They did not speak. Zmyeevich walked out of the cell and Iuda heard him heading up the stairs. Iuda was glad of the solitude and of the chance to consolidate his plan for escape. It began with Dmitry's trip to Zamoskvorechye. Iuda had acquired the property not so very long after becoming a vampire; he'd had plenty of time to prepare.

Dmitry would go down to the cellar first, Iuda imagined. He'd be wary of traps – he knew Iuda well enough for that. Would he touch either of those two cables hidden on each side of the coffin? One side might not make him taller, but the other would most certainly make him shorter. Iuda had come up with the idea long before his gaolers at Geok Tepe.

Would Dmitry perceive the missing space in the middle of the house? Would he find his way in there? If not, he would return empty-handed and Iuda would have to let slip another clue. It wouldn't come too easily, not without a little more persuasion, but Iuda could cope with the pain of the wooden shards and the garlic. He could even cope with a little more of Zmyeevich's blood; that was a slow, cumulative poison.

But Dmitry was no fool – not in that way. He'd find that secret room, Iuda would give odds on it. Would he avoid the crossbow? Would it even work after all this time? It would be a shame if that got him, or the guillotine in the cellar. Iuda remembered explaining once to Dmitry's father how disappointing it could be in a game of chess when an opponent fell into one of the inconsequential traps that were set not to catch him, but to guide him towards the true finale. The dénouement would not take place in Moscow at all, but in Petersburg. But first they had to get there.

He heard footsteps approaching and the sound of voices speaking softly. Zmyeevich entered, followed by Dmitry. Iuda tried to let his face show a little disappointment, as if he'd not been expecting Dmitry to return, but instead thought he'd be reduced to a cloud of dust by the wooden bolt that pierced his heart. It was by such little things that Iuda had managed so often to deceive, ever since he was a boy.

Dmitry was carrying a bundle of papers. That was good. He laid them out on the wooden table, next to the tools of Zmyeevich's trade, and began to pore over them. Dmitry explained what he made of them. Iuda could not see exactly what they were looking at, but he could listen.

'These all relate back to his time in the Third Section. They're mostly just authorizations for interrogation.'

He was right, that's all they were.

'Any names you recognize?' asked Zmyeevich.

Dmitry shook his head, but with none of the dismissiveness the papers deserved. There was nothing important in any of them, they were just dross, padding so that the real item of substance would not be too obvious.

'These are letters from his bank, but they're ancient.'

'And all sent to the house in Zamoskvorechye, so even the bank would be able to tell us nothing new.'

Shame. Keep trying.

'What about this?' asked Zmyeevich. 'It looks like a rental agreement. Is there an address?'

Dmitry spoke after a pause, with a slight laugh. 'It's just Papa's old apartment on Konyushennaya Street. We've already looked there.'

Was that a hint of nostalgia in Dmitry's voice? It was where he had grown up.

'This one I can't make out at all though,' said Dmitry.

Aha!

'It looks like a builder's plan . . .'

Indeed it was.

'But I can't tell what for.'

Iuda sighed inwardly. He hoped he wouldn't have to help them further. He began to think of how he could let the information slip without making it too obvious, hoping it wouldn't come to that. They should both have been familiar with what they were looking at.

'It looks big,' Dmitry concluded, unhelpfully.

Zmyeevich considered, his fingers stroking his moustache. He began to nod, slowly at first, but speeding up. He turned to look at Iuda, smiling broadly, then back to Dmitry.

'Oh, I know where this is,' he announced.

'Where?' asked Dmitry.

'Get him back in the crate,' said Zmyeevich, nodding in Iuda's direction. 'We'll have to take the railway.'

'But where are we going?'

'We're going,' said Zmyeevich, 'to Saint Petersburg.'

CHAPTER VII

PETERSBURG WAS IN UPROAR. MIHAIL'S TRAIN HAD ARRIVED the previous day and even then the news was beginning to circulate. That was Wednesday 28 January 1881, a day that would go down as one of the saddest in Russia's history. Now on Thursday everybody knew. Everyone in Petersburg would have awoken, like Mihail, some of them happy, some of them sad, some indifferent, but after a few moments they would have remembered the news, and wished it had been a dream.

Dostoyevsky was dead.

Mihail had read everything that Fyodor Mihailovich had ever published – as should every Russian of his generation, even those who despised him for his conservatism. Mihail had seen him in the flesh and heard him speak only the previous year, in Moscow at the unveiling of the statue of Pushkin. Mihail had elbowed his way into the rear of the auditorium to listen.

Looking back, he found he couldn't agree entirely with the great man's message. It had been a call for national unity – a fine sentiment, but one which in Russia would require such compromise by the different factions that it would never be achieved. But the way Dostoyevsky had spoken and the words he had used had been mesmerizing. The small figure had taken to the stage quite unassumingly, so distant that Mihail could not make out his features and had to strain to hear his voice. But by the end, his presence filled the entire hall.

When he had finished there had been a brief moment of silence, and then the audience erupted. There was clapping, cheering, the banging of chairs on the floor; handkerchiefs were waved, hats thrown into the air. Ivan Sergeivich Aksakov was supposed to speak next but refused, knowing he could say nothing that would compare to what had just been heard. If anything could achieve national unity, then it was this speech and the almost Christ-like reputation of Dostoyevsky himself. Here was a man who had been a radical, who had faced a firing squad and been pardoned just seconds from death. And yet still he could see the good in Russia – the good in humanity.

The mood had faded quickly, but not completely. After Dostoyevsky's speech there had been no further assassination attempts on His Majesty. After Dostoyevsky's speech the Third Section had been abolished. After Dostoyevsky's speech, so rumours had it, Aleksandr and Loris-Melikov, his Minister of the Interior, had begun plans for a constitution. No one could swear that these events were the result of his speech, but to some degree he seemed to have captured the nation's zeitgeist.

Mihail was surprised how deeply the death of a writer – a stranger he had never met – affected him. When he read the morning paper he found something that made it all the more personal. He saw Dostoyevsky's date of birth: 30 October 1821. He had been born just six months after Mihail's mother, Tamara. He had outlived her by less than six weeks. They had each packed more than a single lifetime into their fifty-nine years.

But there was no time to dwell upon it. It was Mihail's first visit to Saint Petersburg, though his mother had described it to him in such detail that it seemed strangely familiar. There were two reasons to be here; two relatives: a father and a half-brother. In each case he had to presume his mother was to be believed. He had more confidence with regard to the latter than the former. It was illogical to doubt her. Every other thing she had told him had proved true, yet all of it was immeasurably more preposterous than the idea that a grand duke should take a lover, and that the lover should conceive a child.

Tamara had even told him where it had happened. As he'd taken the final leg of his journey – the train from Moscow to Petersburg – he'd looked out for the stations; somewhere between Bologoye and Okulovka. It gave a certain verisimilitude to the story, that degree of detail. With the help of an old railway timetable, he might have been able to determine the exact time of his conception too, but he didn't bother.

By then he had been travelling alone. Dusya had not been true to her word. She'd claimed to be going all the way to Moscow, the end of the line, but had in fact alighted at Ryazan, the previous station. The tall man with the beard had got off there too, though still there was no direct communication between them. Dusya and Mihail had spoken a little more on the long journey, but he had never mentioned his suspicions over her. They had talked mostly about his part in the campaign against the Turcomans, and so he had been forced to lie to her. But he spoke in great detail about his work with explosives, and tried to gauge her reaction. At every opportunity he exaggerated his own radicalism. Like all Russians he had heard of these terrorists, but until now he had never met one. She was not as he had imagined and he was intrigued to find out more.

At Moscow he'd had only a few hours to change trains and once in Petersburg, having taken in the news of Dostoyevsky, he had checked into a hotel and taken his first real bath since Rostov and then spent his first night in a real bed for many months. By morning he had decided which of his relatives he was going to visit. He would need proof, of course, with a story like his, and Tamara had provided it for him in two ways. One was a simple letter. It conveyed the information, but was unlikely to convince; it could have been written by anyone. The second was far more substantial.

He sat on his bed and looked at it, cupping it in his hands; a large pink gemstone, with a hint of blue, the last of five that made up a necklace that Konstantin had given to Tamara as a birthday present. Again it could all be part of a fantasy world in which she lived, but the gems were real. Pink sapphires, so she told him, and jewellers confirmed it – how else could they have lived so long on the money made from selling them, along with the smaller diamonds, and the silver setting?

But she had insisted they never sell this last one, not until Mihail had presented it to Konstantin and said to him the words 'I am your son.'

He slipped it into his pocket and set off. It was wonderfully cold. Saratov, his home town, had cold winters. In Moscow, where he'd studied, it was colder still. But in the south, around the Caspian, where his quest for Iuda had taken him, there was no real winter. Here in Petersburg, it felt Russian. Mihail set out north from his hotel and crossed the Moika, heading towards the English Quay. The surface of the Great Neva was frozen solid, though he knew that the cold waters still ran beneath. It was a beautiful city, and he was sorry that it had taken almost twenty-four years of his life for him to visit it. His mother, having lived in both, preferred Moscow, but then she had the most horrific memories of Petersburg and of the cholera epidemic that had claimed her family. Now people understood cholera. It persisted, but only thanks to the government's inaction.

Tamara's mother, Domnikiia, had never visited Petersburg, and Aleksei had always preferred Moscow – not least because Domnikiia lived there – and so Mihail sensed quite a familial pressure, channelled through his mother, to favour the old capital over the new. But he had only experienced Petersburg for a few hours and decided to give the city a chance.

He marched onwards, the snow creaking beneath his boots, passing the foot of the Nikolaievsky Bridge. There was nothing like that in Moscow, but then the Moskva was nothing like the Neva. It was not at its best frozen over. He would make sure to see it in the summer, when all its glory would be on display, a swathe of glittering azure cutting through the city. Soon he turned inland, walking across Senate Square until he was at the base of the statue. The Bronze Horseman – Pyotr the Great – gazed into the sky from the back of his horse, oblivious to Mihail's presence. And yet Mihail, supposedly, was his great-great-great-great-grandson. Today the truth of it would be known. Mihail felt the urge to linger, to leave the truth for tomorrow, or the day after that.

So much had happened here, to both sides of his family. It was here that Zmyeevich and Pyotr had met in 1712; here that Zmyeevich had drunk Pyotr's blood and shared with him his knowledge; here that Pyotr had refused to drink Zmyeevich's blood and thereby condemned the Romanov family through the generations; here that Zmyeevich had thrown himself into the billowing Neva and left Russia, but not left it alone.

It was here too that Aleksei had confronted Iuda, in 1825; here where he had discovered the influence that Iuda had had on his son's life; here they had fought, out on the frozen river; here that Aleksei had killed Iuda, shot him in cold blood; and here that Iuda had cheated death, drunk the blood of a vampire, and become a vampire himself.

Perhaps it would be near here too – and soon – that Mihail would finally deal to Iuda the fate he had so long deserved. And Mihail would learn from his grandfather's mistakes; he would not be tricked.

He turned back to the embankment to continue his journey, taking one last look at the statue. Behind it Saint Isaac's loomed, its dome glittering in the morning sunlight. Back then, when the Decembrists had risen against Nikolai I, the construction of the huge cathedral had scarcely begun. To a newcomer like Mihail, it seemed so permanent. He had only his guidebook to tell him of its history.

He carried on alongside the river, heading roughly eastwards, past the Admiralty and then the Winter Palace. But neither of these was his destination, although the man he sought often frequented them. Across the Neva, to his left, he could see the Peter and Paul Fortress, the spire of the cathedral within reaching high into the air, but his destination was on this side of the river. At last he was there: the Marble Palace. The Petersburg residence of His Imperial Highness the Grand Duke Konstantin Nikolayevich Romanov – 'Papa'.

He looked up at the building. The marble reliefs on the walls were impressive enough, but they were dull compared with the Winter Palace. It was a fitting residence for a grand duke – elegant, but not so extravagant as to make the tsar feel even a twinge of jealousy. By which door, Mihail wondered, had his mother made her clandestine entrances and exits on her visits to Konstantin? He struggled to picture it. His images of Tamara were recent; of her sallow skin and hollow cheeks – one horribly scarred – and of the continual pathetic coughing. It was hard to imagine that in her youth she had been a beauty, or that she had ever loved. Life had hardened her.

He already knew Konstantin's habits. He and his mother had

studied them in the newspapers, even from distant Saratov. If he was at home and if his brother, the tsar, was at home – and the Romanov standards flying above both palaces showed that they were – then he would most likely make the short journey from the Marble to the Winter Palace at some point in the mid-morning. Mihail turned away from the river and towards Millionaire's Street. The doors of the palace opened on to a courtyard from which gates led out on either side. The far side opened on to the embankment, but to reach his brother, Konstantin would use the gates through which Mihail now peered. It was scarcely nine o'clock, but already quite a crowd was gathering, waiting to get a glimpse of royalty as it hurried past. It would not make things easier.

He took the small, square piece of notepaper from his pocket and looked at it again. The message was brief, almost curt.

> *My Dear Kostya*
> *This is your son.*
> *With many affectionate memories,*
> *Tamara Valentinovna Komarova*

Mihail had asked his mother if she didn't have more to say, but she was not sentimental; this would be enough. She had used the name by which Konstantin had known her. Mihail could explain the rest, if it was appropriate. On the back of the note Mihail had scribbled his own name, and the address of his hotel. Now all he had to do was wait.

He glanced at the faces in the crowd. Most looked like foreigners – French, German and English come to see what they imagined to be a spectacle. Some were merchants or professionals, part of a new class that had money but no family connections. Among the aristocracy, only a few had easy access to the royal family, but those who did not would not accentuate the fact by standing out in the cold, waiting for a glimpse of one of them. The scattering of peasants or workers who watched were merely passing by. They waited for a few moments, hoping to be lucky enough to spot the mighty grand duke, but did not have time to linger; they had work to do.

And then there were two others that did not fit into any group. A man and a woman – apparently unconnected to one another, but giving the impression of having some common purpose. Mihail was reminded of hidden glances exchanged between Dusya and the bearded man on the train. His heightened awareness was no accident; being brought up to fear creatures that lurked in the shadows made him perceptive of the world around him.

The man was barely twenty, with a square head of untidy swept-back hair and no beard. He had flat eyebrows and a broad, squashed nose. The woman was somewhat older, though it was difficult to judge. Her blonde hair and bright blue eyes gave the impression of youth, but other features indicated a greater maturity. She was plainly dressed and would have been pretty if it were not for her large forehead, which seemed to dominate her face.

In the palace courtyard there was a commotion. Mihail looked and saw horses being made ready. He pushed his way to the front of the crowd. He was the only figure in uniform there, and the people let him past as if to do so was in their very nature. When the entourage emerged, it came quickly. First two mounted Cossacks, then the royal carriage itself, then two more Cossacks. It was not just the tsar who needed a bodyguard in these turbulent times. The gates opened and the carriage slowed to turn on to Millionaire's Street. Mihail grabbed his chance.

It took him only two strides to reach the coach and then launch himself from the ground. His hand caught the frame of the open window and his feet scrabbled momentarily before finding a secure place to settle on the running board. Konstantin turned, his expression not so much startled as offended. The two men locked eyes for only a fraction of a second, and then Mihail reached forward with his free hand, offering the grand duke his mother's note. The coach continued to move, carrying them away from the crowd. Mihail waved the slip of paper.

'Take it, please!' he said, loud enough only for the grand duke to hear.

Then hands grabbed him and he fell back, landing in the snow. Booted feet began to kick his sides. One hit his cheek and he covered his face with his hands, still clutching the note.

'Stop that!' came a shout.

The barrage of blows ceased. Mihail lowered his hands. There were two Cossacks standing over him, rifles aimed, their muzzles almost touching him. A little way away, a third was doing his best to hold back an angry crowd, although the two misfits that Mihail had noted earlier were no longer a part of it.

In the other direction the Cossack captain was looking up into the open coach door, in conversation with Konstantin, whose face could not be seen but whose hands poked into view as he gestured with them. Mihail heard the crump, crump, crump of quick-marching boots on the snow, and saw more guards arriving from the palace, some to take their places in the group guarding Mihail, others to help fend off the crowd. The captain strode over and spoke to one of his subordinates.

Mihail was hauled to his feet. His sword was removed from its scabbard and a mercifully superficial search revealed no other weapons. They didn't even discover the note, which he had managed to slip into his glove. They held him by the arms and marched him away to the east. Behind him, the Cossacks remounted and the procession set off once again.

Mihail's journey was not a long one. On the right they passed a vast parade ground, which he guessed to be the Field of Mars. Then they turned left, walking alongside a small canal until, right on the Neva embankment, they came to a stone bridge, arched like a cat's back, by which they could cross. They carried on along the embankment, past a beautiful park with a tall wrought-iron fence and over a larger canal via a three-span bridge. Then they turned away from the river again, along the side of this second canal.

At last they came to a squat, anonymous, three-storey building into which Mihail was led. They took him up the stairs to the top floor. An iron gate blocked their way, which a sentry opened. The corridor beyond had a blank wall on one side and doors on the other. Mihail was taken through the second door into a room that contained just a chair, a mattress and a table.

They left him there. The door slammed shut and the key turned in the lock. Things were not going according to plan.

*

Naturally they had been forced to wait until it was dark. Fortunately, at this time of year, darkness came early to Petersburg. It wasn't even five o'clock. That was one of the things that had brought Zmyeevich to the place to begin with, him and his friend Pyotr Alekseevich Romanov, all those years ago. Pyotr's reasons had been different. He wanted a northern port for his empire, and a fortress to hold back the Swedes. But they had managed to work together, for a while.

Zmyeevich looked up at the Bronze Horseman. It was a close enough likeness, as far as he remembered. The statue hadn't been cast until fifty years after Pyotr's death, but there were plenty of portraits to base it on. And Zmyeevich too was immortalized in the statue – as if one already immortal needed such an honour – but for him the likeness was more symbolic than naturalistic. Under the hooves of Pyotr's steed a serpent writhed, vanquished by the great tsar. The Empress Yekaterina had known the story when she commissioned the monument. Every Romanov did – they'd be fools not to pass the warning down to their children. She had put Pyotr in the role of Saint George and cast Zmyeevich as the dragon. How much had she really known, Zmyeevich wondered, to have come so close to the deeper truth?

It was almost on this very spot, just a little closer to the river, that Pyotr had betrayed his comrade. It was all very different now from 1712, the year that Petersburg had become the capital. So much building had gone on since. Zmyeevich had been lucky to escape with his life, throwing himself into the river and swimming to freedom. Not so easy at this time of year, with the Neva sealed under an inches-thick layer of ice.

It had been rare for him to return to Russia since then. Once he had done so, in 1762, to offer the new tsar, Pyotr III, the chance of immortality. Again he had come in 1812, but on that occasion had only made it as far as Moscow and had not seen the tsar. He'd been in Taganrog, or as close as he'd dared, in 1825, when prospects had seemed at their best, but every time he had failed.

He had not failed; his emissary had failed – his unprofitable servant. On those two occasions it had been the same man, now no longer a man, now Zmyeevich's captive: Cain, or Iuda, or whatever name he chose to go by. Zmyeevich had been a fool to trust him, both to trust his abilities and to trust his fealty. Zmyeevich had, for a while, regarded himself as minor European royalty; his rank of count did not come so far down the scale. But royalty was decadent, and he had tried to emulate it, sending subordinates to do work he would have done better himself – work that he would relish. That would change.

True, he still had servants. Dmitry Alekseevich was one. Might he not, like Iuda, prove to be unworthy of the tasks assigned to him? It was possible, but unlikely. There were stronger bonds that tied him to Zmyeevich than there had been with Iuda. The two had sought each other out after Dmitry had become a vampire. Dmitry knew of Zmyeevich by reputation; Zmyeevich knew Dmitry through his father, a worthy adversary. His son might make a worthy ally. And so it had proved.

Zmyeevich turned his head and saw the two figures standing in the shadows, Saint Isaac's dwarfing them in the background, so much more imposing than the tiny church on the site when Zmyeevich had last been here, no more than a consecrated barn. Iuda was manacled and the wire rope meant he could not run far from Dmitry. It was not the safest arrangement for such a creature, but they had to bring him, otherwise they would never find their way in. And Dmitry was a stronger vampire by far. If anyone cared to question the strange arrangement, Dmitry's rank and uniform were enough to see them off.

Zmyeevich took one last look at the statue of Pyotr. Truly, they had been friends, as far as Zmyeevich could have one – as far as Pyotr could. It was back then that he had first taken on the Russian form of his name. Pyotr had told him that if he were to become a great boyar, then his name would have to be Russian. Zmyeevich was a simple translation of the original. They had debated whether 'Son of the Dragon' fitted better, but had gone with Zmyeevich – 'Son of the Serpent'. And besides, there already was a Zmyeevich in Russian folklore – Tugarin Zmyeevich – though there was no connection between them. Zmyeevich used the Russian form in Russia, but everywhere else he preferred the original Romanian.

He strode across the square to where Dmitry and Iuda waited, circling round to look the prisoner in the face.

'So now we are here,' he said. 'Will you show us the way?'

Iuda nodded sullenly, and they began to ascend the steps to the cathedral doors.

It had made no sense to Dmitry, but he wasn't surprised that Zmyeevich had quickly recognized the floor plans to be those of Saint Isaac's, and noticed the scribbled modification in the north-eastern corner. It was hard to conceive that Iuda might have been able to influence the construction of the building to such a degree, but at the time he'd had a powerful position in the Third Section. He could have made any excuse about its purpose: a hiding place for spies; a secret dungeon. The church elders did not see the world so very differently from the tsar – not back then – and would have happily acceded. Even today they showed respect. When the three men entered, the only occupant was a priest, going about whatever his duties may have been. He frowned at the intrusion, but then saw Dmitry's uniform. Dmitry jerked his head and the priest scampered away, leaving them in peace.

Iuda led them towards the Nevsky Chapel, to the left of the Beautiful Gate at the centre of the main iconostasis. Beside the side chapel entrance, in the north-eastern corner of the nave, was a tall mosaic of a saint, framed by columns of green malachite. It was unmistakably Saint Paul, with his long sword and open Bible, to which he pointed. Iuda turned his head to look at his captors, his grin showing a little pride in his creation – perhaps justified.

'I'll need my hands,' he said, raising his bound wrists and with an expression of humble entreaty upon his face.

'Tell Dmitry what to do,' Zmyeevich replied.

'Very well, but . . . there are traps.'

Iuda could easily have been bluffing, but it wasn't worth the risk. Zmyeevich paused for a moment in consideration, then nodded. Dmitry handed him the end of the wire rope to hold while he unlocked the manacles that kept Iuda's wrists behind his back. The rope still shackled him at the neck. He flexed his fingers, putting on a show. When they had first known each other, and for years afterwards, Dmitry would have been taken in by it all, but not any more.

Iuda reached up and pressed his thumbs against the mosaic tiles, somewhere close to the saint's big toes. The lock released without a sound. Iuda stepped back and the entire icon swung outwards, revealing a dark, narrow brick passageway, far smaller than the icon that had hidden it, its floor at the level of their chests.

'Let him go first,' said Zmyeevich.

Iuda required no second bidding. He pulled himself up the high step into the passageway and disappeared into the darkness. Dmitry felt the rope tighten in his hand and yanked it back, telling Iuda not to go too far ahead, as though he were a disobedient mongrel. The corridor was tight for Dmitry, but he was used to such things. Any fear of enclosed spaces that he had felt in life had vanished the moment he had awoken in his own coffin, deep under the soil. He felt Zmyeevich at his back.

The corridor ran only a few feet before arriving at a descending spiral staircase. They went down, Iuda still leading the way, until the steps ended in another corridor, long and straight. Dmitry felt that they must be below the level of the crypt, but he had lost his sense of direction on the twisting stair; he could not say whether this new passageway led out under Senate Square, or back beneath the cathedral, or in any other direction. All he could do was follow.

At last the tunnel opened out into a chamber. It was a large space, about half as tall again as he was. The arched ceiling was supported by eight brick columns. The place smelt of damp; Dmitry guessed that they must be close to the level of the river.

'Welcome to my humble abode,' said Iuda.

Dmitry tugged at his leash again, and he fell silent. Zmyeevich traversed the room, lighting the various lamps and torches that hung from the walls with the candle he had brought from the cathedral. The columns cast a criss-cross of shadows over the brickwork of the floor.

'You had all this built?' asked Zmyeevich, with genuine wonder in his voice.

'No, no,' admitted Iuda. 'This has been here since Yekaterina's time, perhaps longer, but lost for decades. I merely ensured that there was an entrance to it.'

That would make sense. The whole construction had a much rougher, more functional feel to it than had the cathedral.

'And an exit?' Zmyeevich asked.

Iuda glanced in the direction from which they had come. The door back to the passageway had been open when they arrived. Zmyeevich strode over and slammed it shut. The key was in place. He turned it and slipped it into his pocket. Dmitry began to look around, still keeping a tight hold on the rope, but moving some way from Iuda. In the middle of the chamber, where a ninth column might have been expected, stood a pool of water, almost like an ornamental fountain, except for the lack of the fountain itself. Its raised stone sides came to waist height, and water filled it almost to the brim. Dmitry had not realized how cold it was in the room, but the water was frozen over. Even here underground, embraced by the warm earth, it was impossible to entirely escape the chill of a Russian winter. But the ice didn't look particularly thick. Dmitry rapped it firmly with the back of his fist, and a crack spread across the diameter.

'I suspect this place was once a chapel,' explained Iuda. He nodded towards the pool. 'A font?'

'Where are we?' asked Zmyeevich.

'Somewhere beneath Senate Square,' answered Iuda. 'I could show you precisely on a map.' He pointed, upwards and ahead of them. 'The statue of Pyotr is just there.'

From the walls, on both sides, hung a number of cupboards. They were closed, but had no visible locks.

'What's in these?' asked Zmyeevich.

Iuda raised an open palm in the direction that Zmyeevich was looking. 'Be my guest.'

Zmyeevich gave a short laugh, but wasn't fooled. 'I think not. You may have the honour.'

Iuda shrugged and walked forward, reaching up to one of the cupboards, but not the one which Zmyeevich had indicated. Dmitry tightened the rope to stop him.

'This one, I think,' said Zmyeevich, indicating his original choice.

Iuda went over to it and raised his hands, placing them on the two handles. He glanced from side to side, taking in the positions of his two captors. Then with a sudden motion he flung open the double doors of the cupboard, at the same time stepping back, away from it.

Dmitry tensed, but Zmyeevich remained calm. Iuda was teasing them. They stepped forward and examined the open cupboard. Inside they found shelf upon shelf of bottles, flasks and vials. Some contained powders, others potions, many of which had evaporated almost to nothing. Dmitry cast an eye over them, but the names scribbled on faded labels meant nothing to him. Zmyeevich lingered a moment longer, but he was no more a man of science than Dmitry.

He pointed to the next cupboard and Iuda opened that. Much of its contents was similar, but in addition there were a number of notebooks and papers. Zmyeevich picked one up and flicked through it.

'English,' he said with a sneer, before adding in that language, 'but that shouldn't prove to be a problem.' Even to Dmitry's ear his accent had a strange intonation. He put the papers back down. 'We'll examine them in detail later.'

He opened the next cupboard himself, satisfied that there were no booby traps. It contained much the same.

'Do you have the samples of my blood that you took?' asked Zmyeevich.

'I'm not sure,' said Iuda. 'If I did, they'd be in there.' He pointed to a cupboard and then strode quickly over to it, but Dmitry was faster. He opened the doors before Iuda could reach it. Inside were further vials, each containing a small amount of red liquid that Dmitry knew instinctively to be blood, and guessed to be vampire blood. They were all neatly labelled in Latin text and ordered alphabetically. Dmitry looked to the bottom right, where Zmyeevich would have been.

'Nothing,' he announced. 'Perhaps he's used it all up.'

'Perhaps,' said Iuda.

'And what of Ascalon?' asked Zmyeevich. 'Do you have that here?'

'Why would I have it?'

'Perhaps you found it here. We're beneath the very place where Pyotr took it from me.'

'And you think he might have built this, to hide it?' said Iuda. He thought about it for a moment, but then shrugged, seeming unconvinced. 'It's possible, I suppose.'

'When did you first come across this place?' Dmitry asked.

'When they were building the cathedral,' Iuda explained. Behind him, Zmyeevich began opening other cupboards, examining their contents. 'They found the tunnel when they were digging the foundations; you have to go deep to build anything stable with the mud round here. It was years later that I got to investigate. I told them it was unimportant, but I made sure the stairs were built.'

From the corner of his eye, Dmitry could see that Zmyeevich had opened the last cupboard on that wall. He stood gazing into it.

'To be honest, I've not made much use of it,' Iuda continued chattily – uncharacteristically, 'but when I'm in the city . . .'

Zmyeevich hadn't moved. His hand still rested on the door handle. The door itself was half open, hiding whatever Zmyeevich had uncovered from Dmitry's view. It all looked quite innocent, but somehow Dmitry knew that Zmyeevich was in terrible pain. He dashed over.

The cupboard was empty. It had no bottles, no papers, not even shelves. Like the others, it was only around four inches deep, but its back wall, rather than being the dull brick of the rest of the cellar, was a mirror – and not a particularly refined one at that. It was cloudy, and seemed to be made of many small sections rather than a single sheet of glass.

But the oddest thing about it was that Dmitry could see Zmyeevich's reflection. A moment later he realized that he could see his own.

Or at least he could see a figure at the place where his reflection should be. He had never seen himself – not since the moment he had become a vampire, but he had assumed he remained unchanged from what he was in life. Now he knew different. What others saw in him, what he could see in himself when he looked down at his own hands, it was all an illusion. What he saw in that mirror was not sharp and distinct – and that was a blessing – but he knew without doubt it was a truer representation of himself

116

than he had ever laid eyes on before. He peered closer, trying to see through the hazy glass. Various shapes and textures caught his eye, but they did not form a clear image. He did not want them to. He wanted to tear his eyes away before they could fully take in what he saw, but he was unable. He could not step away, nor raise his hands to cover his face, nor close his eyelids, nor even move his eyeballs to look in a different direction. With each passing moment that he gazed into the mirror, the clearer what he saw became, and the greater was his desire to see it.

And through all this came a memory – a memory that he had witnessed such a thing before, and yet a memory that was not his own. It was something he had never understood in the past, but which was now quite clear to him. He knew that the sight of this reflection had led to death. It had done so before and it would do so now.

And then he was no longer staring immobile at the thing reflected in the mirror. He was lying on the ground, on his back. Above him he could see the arched ceiling and, looming closer, Zmyeevich. The ancient vampire's hands gripped his shoulders, unable to let go after holding him so tightly to drag him away from the mirror, his eyes squeezed shut. His tongue protruded from his lips and his teeth bit down on to it. His precious blood seeped from the corners of his lips. His fingers dug still harder into Dmitry's flesh.

Dmitry dashed Zmyeevich's hands aside. He scrambled across the floor, on his back, keeping his eyes averted so that there was no chance of seeing the mirror. When he was far enough away he stood, and edged back along the wall until he was able to slam first one door then the other back over the obscene looking glass. Then he knelt down beside Zmyeevich. His eyes were open now, but he appeared shaken, old, as though he hadn't fed for weeks.

Dmitry helped him to his feet. He looked over to the mirror, and sighed deeply when he saw that the doors were shut. He turned back to Dmitry, holding on to him for support, his eyes full of fear.

'What was that?' asked Dmitry, his voice shaking.

'I saw . . .' Zmyeevich spoke softly, but then paused to think. He seemed to become instantly stronger, and stood upright, stepping away from Dmitry. 'I saw what I have always known,' he concluded.

Dmitry wondered if he himself had always known of what he had seen, but pushed the thought from his mind. He had caught only a glimpse of his own image; he did not want to learn more. Zmyeevich was now almost completely himself again. His head twisted from side to side as he scanned the room.

'Iuda!' he hissed.

Dmitry looked around too. He looked at the door by which they had entered, but it remained closed. He strode over and tried it but it was still locked. It had been only a matter of seconds that they had stared into the awful glass, but in that time Iuda had vanished.

CHAPTER VIII

THE ICY WATER EMBRACED HIM, INFILTRATING EVERY CREVICE of his body. For a vampire such as Dmitry, it was not a discomfort but it was still a piercing sensation. The cold could not kill him, but it could slow him and weaken him. If it became cold enough for his body's fluids to freeze, then he would become dormant, but at some point before that ice crystals would begin to form in his blood, and his limbs – and his mind – would stiffen.

It had taken only moments for them to deduce where Iuda had gone. The wire rope that had bound him by the neck was discarded on the floor. In the middle of the cellar the ice on the frozen pool, which before had displayed merely the single crack that Dmitry had caused, was now smashed to a thousand floating, bobbing lumps. The glassy mosaic reminded Dmitry of the mirror into which they had just gazed, but he knew it would require something more than mere ice to make him see his own reflection.

Dmitry dived in in pursuit, while Zmyeevich headed back to the surface via the cathedral. The pool was an illusion; appearing simply to be standing on the cellar floor, it in fact went beneath it. From there the pipe turned to the horizontal and narrowed. It was too tight for Dmitry to make much use of his arms, but he kicked hard and propelled himself through. He could hold his breath for a long time, but if the pipe didn't come to an end eventually, then the lack of air would subdue him in just the same way that the cold might. But Iuda would face exactly the same problems – and Iuda had come this way in full knowledge of what lay ahead.

Dmitry's pursuit of Iuda had a new passion to it – a hatred that he had not been able to feel towards anyone since becoming a vampire. But in that time, there had always been one regret – that Raisa, the woman who had turned Dmitry into a vampire, was dead. His feelings for her were not the romantic love or corporeal lust that had attracted him to her in life. It was more of a pack instinct; the sense of loyalty that a dog has to its own kind. There was a practical side to it too – the fact that he could learn so much about his new state from her – but her loss had affected him more viscerally than could be dismissed with so rational an explanation. It still did.

Because she had made him, part of her mind had been in him, guiding and teaching him. With her death, that had gone, all except one tiny splinter which stuck in him like a bee's sting after the insect itself has fallen away: a desire for vengeance. For Raisa's death to be avenged would do her no good, but still that bit of her which remained inside Dmitry sought it on her behalf. It would act as a warning to others; even from beyond the grave, they would be punished.

But until today, until he had gazed into that mirror, he'd had no idea what had befallen Raisa. In the hours before her death her mind had become confused, unhinged, incapable of his understanding. And today, for a few moments, he had felt the same. The jumbled images of her last hours had suddenly coalesced. He still did not know just how she had died, but he knew that she, like him, had gazed into a mirror that had the power to let her see her own true appearance. Whatever effect that might have had on Dmitry or Zmyeevich, the impact on Raisa – a woman who loved her own beauty – had been devastating. Perhaps it hadn't caused her death directly, but it had prevented her from defending herself when she most needed to.

It had all come from looking in a mirror. The mirror that Dmitry had seen today had been created by Iuda and Iuda had tricked them into looking at it. The mirror that had destroyed Raisa's mind had been created by Iuda, and he had tricked her, or enticed her, or cajoled her into looking at it. Iuda had brought about her death, and now Dmitry would kill Iuda – whatever Zmyeevich might say about needing to keep him alive.

Dmitry kicked his legs more vigorously. Ahead he could see the dimmest circle of light, like the moon forcing its way through thick cloud. A second later he became suddenly colder still. He no longer found his arms constrained by the sides of the pipe, nor his kicking to have any effect whatsoever on his motion. He was swept sideways, far faster than he could propel himself by swimming.

He was out in the Neva. It was as he had suspected – the only way that Iuda's escape route could make any sense was if it led to that vast waterway. Dmitry had no idea how many millions of barrels of water flowed each day from Lake Ladoga out into the Gulf of Finland, but he was now a part of it, and it was indifferent to him.

He exercised what little control he had over his body, and swam upwards. Within seconds he hit the ceiling of the underwater world, and fully understood just how quickly he was travelling, as his fingertips scraped across the underside of the ice sheet. As a *voordalak* he had discovered the ability to find texture in even the smoothest wall in order to climb it, but here he could find no purchase. Even if he'd managed to hold on, he doubted it would have helped him much. This was no thin covering like that over the pool into which he'd dived. However he might kick and beat his fists against it, he would achieve nothing. All he could do was let the current take him until, somewhere out in the gulf beyond, the ice began to part. Iuda would be long gone, but with luck Dmitry would still be conscious, though he would have no chance to breathe before then. He must make the best use of the air he had. He tried to relax.

He came to a halt with a painful thud which propelled the air from his lungs and into his mouth. He tried to keep hold of it, but saw bubbles rising up in front of his eyes. He had hit the pier of a bridge – it could only be the Nikolaievsky. Now he had some slight hope. He scrambled up the stonework, still feeling the Neva pressing against his back and trying to carry him away. Soon he reached the ice again, but here it was nothing like the solid barrier he had encountered before. Where the river met the pier, the ice was broken and fragmented. He thrust himself upwards through it and felt the night air against his face. The river still grabbed at his legs, and blocks of ice barged into him, threatening to crack his skull.

He swam forward through the barrage of miniature icebergs and found the lip of the ice shelf. He pulled himself up out of the water and prepared to fall forward, to allow himself a few moments to catch his breath and to dispel the coldness that was beginning to affect even his vampire body. He felt light-headed – a combination of the cold and the breathlessness, and perhaps the lingering influence of Iuda's mirror. It had been enough to drive Raisa to insanity – it was possible that there might be some effect on him.

But before he could compose himself he saw in front of him a figure running across the ice. It could only be Iuda. He must have followed the exact same path through the water that Dmitry had, just seconds ahead of him.

Dmitry hauled himself to his feet and resumed his pursuit. Iuda was heading back upriver, in the direction they had come, but veering towards the northern bank. He reached it at the Menshikov Palace, almost directly across from Senate Square. Dmitry didn't bother to see whether Zmyeevich had yet emerged to join the chase. He ran with long strides, wary of the slippery surface, but knowing that the real problem would be to stop or make a sharp turn. Iuda chose not to attempt to climb the stone embankment, but instead ran alongside it, looking for the next point at which steps came down to the water's edge. Dmitry was able to see the location and head straight for it, gaining ground on his quarry.

But as Iuda reached the steps he hesitated. Dmitry heard shouts and saw that on the embankment a small band of soldiers had spotted Iuda, who did not seem inclined to deal with them. He changed his plan of getting up on to land and continued along the frozen river. His feet slipped as he tried to accelerate and it took him seconds to get up to speed. Again, it was all a chance for Dmitry to get closer. The soldiers – six of them in total – split into two groups. Some came down on to the ice and the others ran along the bank, paralleling Iuda's movements below them. Dmitry could only guess that they had seen his uniform and realized that he must have good reason to be chasing a fugitive at this time of night. He had discarded his greatcoat back in the cellar, but his tunic was enough for them to recognize his seniority.

Iuda swung away from the bank, out towards the centre of the river, making good speed again. Ahead of him stood the pontoon bridge, spanning the river from the Winter Palace to the Stock Exchange. In the summer it offered a convenient but somewhat undulating route out to Vasilievskiy Island, but now it was held firm by the ice. Dmitry remembered it stretching out from Senate Square on the day of the Decembrist Uprising, but it had long since been moved upstream. Iuda disappeared beneath it, under one of the central spans.

Dmitry was close to him now, and the three soldiers who had come down on to the river were not far behind, but the men who had remained on land had made far quicker progress, running over snow rather than ice. Soon though they would have run out of land as they came to the fork at which the Great and Lesser Nevas split. Instead, they turned on to the pontoon bridge itself, running across it at almost the moment Iuda darted beneath.

Seconds later, Dmitry was under it too, and he saw Iuda ahead of him, heading out to the middle of the widest part of the river, trying to leave as late as possible the choice of which branch to take. But out there, the ice was at its weakest and he might easily fall through. Perhaps that was his plan, to return once again to the water, where his capture would be impossible.

From the bridge above him Dmitry heard shouting. Shots rang out and Iuda fell. Dmitry looked and saw the three soldiers on the bridge, their rifles still aimed. The bullets would do little permanent damage to Iuda, but they had knocked him down and left him scrabbling on the slippery surface, trying to regain his footing. Within seconds Dmitry was upon him.

The two *voordalaki* slid further out across the ice, carried by Dmitry's momentum. He looked into Iuda's face – a face which he had in his time regarded with both love and indifference. Now he felt only hatred. It was almost a separate part of his mind, that fragment of Raisa that remained in him. It was she who wanted revenge, and Dmitry was happy to comply.

It was a rare thing for one *voordalak* to kill another. Dmitry had never seen it done, but he had heard talk of it. He and Zmyeevich had discussed it, aware of the fate that eventually must befall Iuda. There were many ways, but in present circumstances one seemed obvious.

Iuda was lying on his back, his head towards Dmitry. Dmitry pressed his knees against Iuda's shoulders and then took his head firmly in his hands, one under his chin, one at the back of his skull. Decapitation would kill a vampire, but it did not have to be the neat, clinical severance of a sharpened blade. Iuda writhed and struggled, but Dmitry knew he had the strength; together he and Raisa had the strength.

But then he stopped. He could not say why. It was as though some third presence in his mind had said 'No' – and that third voice held sway. Dmitry tried to ignore it, but already it was too late. A semicircle of three soldiers had formed beside them. The other three had climbed down off the pontoon bridge, and were already approaching.

'What the hell's going on here?' barked one of them, a captain, before adding 'sir' as an afterthought.

Dmitry rose to his feet, gazing down at Iuda with loathing but trying to appear calm and dignified. His heart beat fast from the chase and the cold and the lack of air, and his head still reeled, pulled in different directions.

'This man is in my custody,' he said, aware of how heavily he had to breathe. 'My commendation for your help in his recapture, but I'll take it from here.'

It was a sign of the times that a captain would dare question a colonel, even in these strange circumstances. It would not have happened in Dmitry's day.

'Sir, are you really sure?' he said. 'You're wet through and frozen. God knows you could be wounded and you wouldn't feel it.'

'I'm perfectly fine, thank you, Captain.' Dmitry emphasized the man's rank.

'Sir, look,' the captain persisted, pointing across the ice. 'The fortress is just there. What better place for him, if only overnight?'

Dmitry looked. The captain was quite right. There stood the Peter and Paul Fortress, the stronghold at the heart of Pyotr's city, and also its prison. There was no need for him to comply. He could easily deal with these six and do with Iuda as he chose. But that would mean six corpses, and he knew that his and Zmyeevich's presence in the city would be better kept secret. And still his mind was in turmoil.

'Very well,' he growled.

One of the soldiers hauled Iuda to his feet. Iuda's eyes darted around, looking for a chance to escape. Once he was away from Dmitry, he might not find it so difficult. Dmitry reached into his pocket and drew out the manacles that he had taken from Iuda back in the cathedral, scarcely half an hour before.

'Use these,' he said.

The captain complied.

'And be careful with him. You don't know how dangerous he can be. Put him in the deepest cell they've got. Don't take the cuffs off him. Don't let him even see a window.' Dmitry hoped he sounded casual.

'Absolutely, sir.' The captain knew his place better now that he had got his way.

'Don't let him out for exercise and don't let anyone question him without my authority, you understand? Colonel Otrepyev.'

'Sir. Do you require an escort, sir?'

'No. I'll be fine. Carry on.'

The captain saluted and turned. He and his five men led Iuda away to the Neva Gate, the gate from which Dmitry's father had departed on his journey into exile, half a century before. It would take them only a couple of minutes to cross the ice to the fortress. When they thought they were out of earshot, one of the men said something that raised a laugh. The captain snapped at them and order was re-established. With discipline like that they might just survive the short journey. If they did, then perhaps it would all prove to be for the good. Keeping Iuda captive was a burden to Zmyeevich and Dmitry – if His Majesty was happy to take on the responsibility, then who were they to complain? If they could get him as far as the cell, then even Iuda would not be able to escape.

All the same, Dmitry did not relish having to relate what had happened to Zmyeevich. He turned and headed back. On the quay, just beside the Winter Palace, the dark figure stood silhouetted, waiting for him.

It hadn't taken Mihail long to work out where he was. His mother had told him of the place – she used to work here. This was Fontanka 16; the building beside the chain bridge; the head-quarters of the secret police. In her day it had been the Third Section; now it was the Ohrana, but it all meant much the same.

He'd tried to rest, lying on the thin mattress and letting the hours pass. The food they'd brought him had been unrecognizable as such, but he'd forced it down, not knowing when he might get more. The army had been good training for that. He wondered what would become of him. He tried to think of the best outcome – tried to believe in it, not because believing would make it true, but because expecting the worst would drive him to despair. Tamara had told him how they worked here – the first task was to break a man's will.

He'd not had a weapon; that was in his favour. He'd had a sword at his side, but so did any officer in uniform. And he was a hero of Geok Tepe – he still had the wound to show it. His hand was almost healed now, but it was still bandaged, and beneath the linen the scar looked worse than it felt. He'd still need a story to tell them. He could say that he'd been so overcome with joy at being close to the grand duke that he'd felt the urge to rush to him and thank him for his family's support of the army. Perhaps that was taking it too far; he would be more convincing if he was petitioning for better rations for the men. Neither made absolute sense – Konstantin's power lay in the navy, not the army – but it was the best he had. He spent the day inventing further details for his story, but no one came to question him.

He still had the note, and the sapphire. He could do nothing with the gemstone, but he wondered whether he should try to get rid of the letter from his mother. It undermined his story, but if they found it, they might take it to the grand duke and Mihail's ends would be achieved after all. But more than that, he couldn't bring himself to destroy the last communication from his mother to his father, however brief it might be.

He heard the rattle of keys in the door, and then it opened. A sentry looked in, then withdrew. He heard a voice outside.

'I'll be perfectly safe. It's imperative that I speak to him alone.'

Mihail turned his chair away and stared at the wall, not wanting to appear too eager to begin his interrogation. The door slammed and there was a moment's silence, followed by a slight cough. Mihail turned.

It was Grand Duke Konstantin Nikolayevich – his father. Mihail leapt to his feet, turning as he did, knocking the chair to the floor. He tried to speak, but was tongue-tied. He could not tell whether it was down to coming face to face with his father for the first time, or to being in the presence of so high-ranking a Romanov. He reached into his pocket for the note.

'You . . . you must read this,' he stammered.

Konstantin shook his head. 'No, I have no need to read anything. Do you think I cannot see your mother in your eyes? Do you think I cannot see myself in . . . in everything about you? I know you are my son.'

He opened his arms in preparation to embrace Mihail, but the gesture was not a comfortable one. Mihail hung back. However unconventional his upbringing might have been, he was still a Russian, and a Russian did not embrace a grand duke, even if he was his bastard son. In an instant Mihail understood how little he really cared for his absent father; he was interested in him, he might grow to like him, but there was no aching gap in his heart that would now be filled. He suspected Konstantin felt the same.

His father chuckled and offered Mihail his hand. Mihail grasped it firmly and shook.

'It seems we're very much alike already,' said Konstantin. 'But tell me. Tell me everything. I don't even know your name.'

Mihail picked up the chair and offered it to Konstantin, who sat down. Mihail himself sat on the mattress, leaning against the wall. Too late he realized that he should not sit without permission, but his father didn't complain. He looked up at the man, now in his early fifties, and managed to see a little of himself, but still he felt a greater sense of excitement than affection. He took a deep breath – there was much to tell.

'My name,' he began, 'is Mihail Konstantinovich Lukin.'

'Mihail.' Konstantin thought about it for a moment. 'After the archangel.'

'Actually, no.' Tamara had always been quite clear about it. 'After Mihail Maleinos.'

Konstantin chuckled again. 'The protector of the Romanovs? That was good of her. And Lukin, where does that come from? Has she married again?'

The name Lukin meant so much: the name of the family that had cared for Tamara and Mihail when they had arrived in Saratov; the name of Aleksei's closest friend. But there was no need for Konstantin to hear of it.

'Lukin's not my real name. And no, she never remarried.'

Konstantin guessed the implication of those last words. 'You mean . . . ?'

Mihail spoke quickly, avoiding his father's eyes. 'She died. The end of last year.'

Konstantin stood and paced the room. 'I see. I wish you'd come to me sooner.'

'It's not easy.'

'I know. I know. And why have you come now? You want something? Money?'

Mihail shook his head. 'Nothing like that. I still have this, look.' He slipped off his boot and from inside took the pink sapphire. He handed it to Konstantin, who lifted his spectacles from his nose to peer deeply at the stone.

'I remember,' he said softly. 'Did she have to break the necklace up?'

'When would she have worn it?'

Konstantin nodded wistfully. 'That's just what she said.' He handed the sapphire back and returned to the present. 'You can have money. She could have had. Anna Vasilyevna and the children have a dacha to themselves in Pavlovsk.'

Mihail had heard rumours enough to know who Anna Vasilyevna was. He knew that Tamara had not been his father's only lover.

'Really, no,' he insisted. 'I still have money – and a career, in the army.'

Konstantin nodded. 'A lieutenant, I see,' he said, gesturing at Mihail's uniform, 'in the grenadiers.'

'Grand Duke Pyetr Nikolayevich Battalion. I was at Geok Tepe.'

'A great victory. General Skobyelev has made a name for himself.' Konstantin's voice hinted that this was not a good thing for the general to have done. There was a pause. It was surprising how quickly father and son had run out of things to say. Mihail broke the silence.

'What I wanted from you – other than to meet you, of course – was some information.'

'You only have to ask.'

'I was wondering if you knew the whereabouts of my half-brother.'

'I'm afraid you'll have to be a little more specific than that, you know. You have more than one half-brother. Two of them are grand dukes.'

Mihail knew that he was being teased, but he noted the small number of grand dukes. It was common knowledge that Konstantin had sired four legitimate sons – along with God knew how many other bastards – but the youngest of them had died a few years before, aged just sixteen. The eldest, Nikolai Konstantinovich, was still alive, but had been banished to some distant corner of the empire after a scandal. Technically he was still a grand duke, but in his father's mind he had evidently been stripped of the title, if not of existence itself.

'I meant on my mother's side,' replied Mihail. 'He's called Luka; Luka Miroslavich Novikov.'

'I know. I know,' said Konstantin soothingly, sensing his attempt to play the fool had been misplaced. 'Your mother told me of him. I hoped to keep a watchful eye over him, but I'm afraid I failed.'

'He's dead?' It would be a surprise, given what Iuda and Dmitry had said.

'No. No.' Konstantin reached into his pocket and brought out a folded piece of paper. 'As soon as I saw you yesterday, I thought you'd ask. Here's his address.'

Mihail looked at the paper. He did not know Petersburg well enough for it to mean anything to him, but he would easily find it.

'I don't suppose you even know what he looks like,' said Konstantin.

Mihail shook his head. Konstantin reached into his pocket

again and handed over a photograph. Mihail could not see much of himself in Luka, but recognized a little of Tamara. The man was in his thirties, his hair longer than was popular at the time, but well kempt. He had a moustache, but no beard. He was handsome. The real oddity was that Konstantin should have a photograph of him – but the style and pose of the picture gave away its origin. It was taken from the files of the Ohrana.

'He's a criminal?' asked Mihail.

'A suspect – nothing has ever been proved.'

'Suspected of what?'

'Have you heard of the People's Will?'

Mihail nodded.

'It was they who tried to blow up my brother's train; they who exploded a bomb at the Winter Palace.' Konstantin's voice rose with suppressed anger. 'A dozen guardsmen died; ordinary men – the very people they're supposed to be fighting for.'

'I'm sorry,' said Mihail quietly.

'They want us to react, but we won't. We'll give them liberty – we have done already – but we won't let them take it.'

'And Luka's one of them?'

'He knows people who are – the police aren't sure about *him*.'

'I'm guessing you don't want me to see him.'

'He's your brother,' said Konstantin. 'I wouldn't stop you. But be circumspect. They have as many spies as we do – even in here.' He glanced around with an air that hinted of paranoia.

'Here?'

Konstantin nodded gravely. 'Just yesterday they arrested one – a clerk named Kletochnikov. No wonder we'd made so few arrests; he'd been warning them, just in time.'

'There are others?'

'Who knows? Perhaps your brother can tell you.' He paused for a moment, then changed the subject. 'Why did she go so suddenly?'

It was obvious he meant Tamara. 'It was nothing to do with you,' Mihail explained. 'Family stuff.'

'Did she ever find her parents?' Konstantin asked. 'She told me she was looking.'

'She did.' Mihail felt warm just to speak of it, to be reminded of his mother's happiness, however short-lived it had been, however tragic the circumstances. 'Though she didn't know them for long.'

'And that's why she went away?'

Mihail nodded. It was time to test the water regarding another matter on which Konstantin might have information. 'I mentioned earlier my name isn't really Lukin,' he said. 'I get my true name from my grandfather. It's Danilov. He was Aleksei Ivanovich Danilov.' Konstantin looked blank. 'He was a colonel under Aleksandr Pavlovich.'

'Against Bonaparte?'

'And later. But then he was exiled – after 14 December.'

'Ah! And then he came back after my brother's pardon. That would explain it.'

'You've not heard of him?'

Konstantin shook his head. 'I'm sorry.'

Mihail felt anger welling inside him. After everything his grandfather had done to protect the Romanovs, with all the secrets he could have revealed to save himself from exile, still he'd remained loyal. At the time it had been necessary, but now, so many years on, he was forgotten, regarded as no different from any of the others who had genuinely stood against Nikolai. It was a disgrace, but Mihail was in no position to say anything.

Konstantin stood. 'I must go. But we'll talk again later.'

'You're leaving me here?'

Konstantin looked shocked. 'Goodness, no. You'll be released in a few hours. You understand . . . ? There has to be a gap.'

Mihail nodded.

'Where are you staying?' asked Konstantin.

Mihail gave the address of his hotel.

'I'll be in touch,' said his father. He walked over to the door and was about to rouse the guard, but then he turned. 'What was it you wanted me to read – when I came in?'

Mihail reached into his pocket for the note. 'It's what I was trying to give you on the coach,' he explained, offering it to his father.

Konstantin read it – presumably several times, given how long he took. Then he looked up at Mihail. 'You think that's a fair summary – of her feelings? "Many affectionate memories"?'

Mihail nodded. 'Did you really feel any different?' he asked.

Konstantin cocked his head to one side, thinking. 'And did she love you, as a son?' he asked.

Mihail believed she did, but all the time he had known her, her capacity to love had never been as great as her capacity to hate. But that was not down to Konstantin, and he did not need to be concerned with it.

'I know she did.'

Konstantin gave half a smile. 'That's all an absent father can really ask.'

He turned and left.

It was a step in the right direction; a step away from Zmyeevich. Three weeks before Iuda had been in a gaol built to hold a *voordalak*. Now his cell was constructed merely to hold a man. Getting out should not prove too much of a problem.

His escape from Dmitry and Zmyeevich had progressed just as he had envisaged. There was nothing much of real value in that cellar beneath Senate Square – he'd moved everything to a far more fitting residence, still within the capital. He'd put the mirror there to do precisely what it had done. It didn't really matter whether he opened the cupboard, or some other vampire did. If it had been him he could simply have closed his eyes and waited until Zmyeevich and Dmitry came over to look. He doubted it would produce in either of them the devastating breakdown it had in Raisa, but it had caused a moment's disorientation – and that was enough.

It had taken him a long time to understand why a vampire showed no reflection in a mirror – to realize that in fact a mirror reflected the monster's true, monstrous image and that the mind of human and vampire alike was forced to block it out, preferring to see nothing. It had taken him longer still to work out how a mirror might be constructed to trick such a mind into perceiving the reality that it so feared. And even then it had been time-consuming and expensive to import and assemble so much of the necessary crystal: Iceland Spar. None of the final stages of the work could be done by him, for fear that he might catch even the briefest glimpse of his own reflection. But after he had watched

Raisa's reaction to seeing her own true face, he had known it would be worth the effort. And so it had proved.

He still had no idea what Zmyeevich and Dmitry had seen in the looking glass. He had never dared look upon his own reflection. Perhaps one day.

It was in the fast waters of the Neva that things had gone awry. Iuda had known that his quickest route out of the water was to run into the bridge, and had tried to steer himself to that end. Dmitry should have been dragged on between the piers. That the current should carry him along exactly the route that Iuda had taken was pure bad luck. It was bad luck too for that patrol to be at just that place at just that time. In the end though, perhaps they had saved his life. He hadn't expected Dmitry's attack; why had Dmitry tried to kill him, then, after so much effort to keep him alive?

His last chance for freedom might have been under that escort to the fortress, but the guards were wary, and the cold had weakened him. Just as Dmitry had commanded, they had given him a deep, dark cell. High up on the wall, near the ceiling, was a tiny window, the size of just one brick, but it was no danger. The sun was low and the light that shone through stayed high above Iuda as it worked its way across the cell, its journey lasting just a few hours each day.

The cell was old – part of the oldest building in the whole of Petersburg – but it was solidly built. The door was newer, and Iuda doubted he would be able to break it down. It did not concern him; he had only to wait for an incautious guard to enter and he would be free. A pair of water pipes ran along one wall of the cell, just inches from the ground, emerging from the stonework at one end and disappearing into it at the other. Periodically these erupted with the sound of tapping, but currently all was silent; there was a pattern to it – the prisoners were clearly communicating in some form of code. Most of them in here would be political – they'd probably been taught the code as part of their indoctrination, in preparation for their inevitable arrest. The Peter and Paul Fortress had always been a place for that kind of prisoner, since the beginning. The walls of the cell were testament to it – a thousand messages scratched into the stonework, some long, others just names or initials. They dated back all the way to the time of Pyotr. The authorities could have sanded them away, or painted over them, but they didn't. Perhaps they felt a sense of history; perhaps they knew it would demoralize the prisoners more to see how many had come before them, and to know that they had failed; the Romanovs still reigned.

Iuda examined the various graffiti; it passed the time and provided some amusement – particularly when he saw the same name or initials repeated with different dates, months or sometimes years apart. He paused at one and smiled broadly.

А.И.Д. – 16.xii.1825

It was beyond coincidence: A.I.D. – two days after the Decembrist Revolt. It could only be Aleksei Ivanovich Danilov – Lyosha. There was no question he would have been sent here, to the Peter and Paul Fortress. Why shouldn't it be the same cell that Iuda now occupied, fifty-six years on? Their paths had crossed so often, but no more. Lyosha was long dead now.

The tapping on the pipes began again, interrupting Iuda's thoughts. He sat down on the lumpy straw mattress that was the cell's only furnishing and listened, trying to identify patterns, trying to make sense of them. It should be easy, as long as he applied the proper scientific method. It was just as his father had always told him, had sometimes beaten into him, but it had served Iuda well – it would serve him now.

Iuda's father, the Reverend Thomas Owen Cain, was the parish priest of Esher, in the county of Surrey, in England. Iuda himself – Richard Llywelyn Cain – had been born in the rectory of Saint George's Church on 28 June 1778, killing his mother, quite accidentally, in the process. By the time Richard was old enough to discern such things, he noted that his father seemed none too perturbed by the loss of his mother, and Richard chose to adopt a similar attitude. Thomas Cain's chief interest, aside from his flock, was in science – particularly its application to maritime navigation, a matter of increasing importance with the rapid expansion of His Majesty's vast empire.

Thomas seemed almost to regret that the problem of longitude had been solved, not because he did not admire the solution, but because he had spent so many of his earlier years trying to deal with it by a quite different approach. But he was not disheartened. Even now that the issue of accurately knowing the time was resolved, there were still vast and complex measurements and calculations that needed to be made in order to combine that time with the observed positions of the sun or the stars and thus calculate a ship's location, allowing it to sail safely across the oceans. The loss of the thirteen colonies, when Richard was just five, was a shock to the whole nation, but Thomas became convinced that they could be won back if only a fleet could be sent that had sufficient navigational agility to outmanoeuvre the rebel forces.

The solution was his 'Navigational Engine', a device, in its ultimate form, the size of a small table, with concentric wheels on its surface which allowed the positions of stars to be marked off, the time set and – so Thomas insisted – a course to be plotted. Richard had little interest in it, but that was not a concept that his father could even consider. Each year – sometimes with greater frequency – Thomas would come up with a new generation of his device, with additional features and refinements that would guarantee its effectiveness, and then he and it and young Richard would board a carriage and head out for the Royal Observatory at Greenwich.

On some occasions the trip would take the whole day – a third of it for the journey there, another third for the journey back and the remaining third sitting, waiting for the committee to find a moment to allow Thomas admittance to their presence. On others they would set out the day before the appointed meeting and spend the night with Thomas's brother, Edmund, across the Thames in Purfleet. There, as his father snored beside the fire, Uncle Edmund taught Richard to play chess. After the age of ten, Richard never lost a game to him.

Whether their travels took one day or two, the actual examination and discussion of the Navigational Engine took only minutes, and the result was always the same. Travelling out there, Thomas would be full of optimism. He and Richard would look out of the carriage window and he would answer Richard's questions about the flora and fauna they could see. But the return journeys were more sombre. Thomas would emerge from his discussions with ostensible cheer, speaking of the points which the committee had liked and the recommendations they had made for further improvement, but as the journey home progressed he would fall into a morose silence, his face flushed and scowling. On occasions he would grab the white powdered wig from his head and hurl it on to the floor of the carriage, revealing the sparse ginger hair that naturally topped his scalp; hair which Richard was thankful not to have inherited. On those dark days Richard knew not to ask about or even to look at the world that sped past.

Richard's fascination had always taken him more in the direction of living things than of astronomy and mathematics. At first his father had discouraged him, telling him that nothing would ever come from the study of plants and animals, but later he had relented, reasoning, Richard supposed, that it was better for his son to show an interest in something, however unimportant it might be to the fate of the empire, than to be interested in nothing.

Even so, Thomas Cain was not prepared to allow his little boy merely to take pleasure in the beauty of the world that God had created; he must experiment and he must discover. Richard's approach, like his father's, should be scientific and methodical. It was not enough to marvel at the beauty of a butterfly; the creature must be caught and pinned in a case to be studied and documented. It was not enough to ponder the mathematical symmetry of a spider's web; the web must be broken, and the steps taken by the spider to mend it recorded; a fly must be placed on the web, and the speed at which the spider scampered over to devour it measured. It was not enough to watch a rat devise and execute a plan to steal grain from a sack that the farmer had thought beyond reach; the creature must be trapped and dissected in order to gain a better understanding of how its organs operated, and compare it with the same organs in other animals and then – perhaps one day at university – with those of a human being.

Richard had not enjoyed it at first – it was tiresome, mundane work, with little reward, but it was incentive enough to keep his father happy and to keep the cane (Thomas never tired of the pun: 'Master Cain, the cane awaits!') in its place on the mantelpiece. Later, though, he began to get a sense of satisfaction when his pages of notes and measurements revealed some general principle of which he had not previously been aware: that the spacing between threads on a spider's web was proportional to the size of its body; that a rat could not vomit.

By the age of eleven, Richard had already filled a dozen volumes with his observations. Such subjects were not studied at school, but even there he did well, with Latin a particular favourite. But he had no interest in divinity – his father had bored him with the subject before he began school, and the more he learned of the detailed mechanisms of nature, the more he doubted that the Lord could have created them in the space of just a few days. More than that, even if the Bible were true, he despised it for the cursory disregard with which it so fleetingly skipped over the magnificence of what God was supposed to have achieved. Six verses to deal with every animal of the sea, the air or the land. Where was the respect? Where was the wonder? Richard could have spent six chapters simply describing the wing of a butterfly.

Richard's disregard for religion inescapably led to a disregard for his father, for whom, as God's representative on earth, religion played an important role. But it was more than that; it was Thomas Cain's failure as a scientist that inspired the most loathing in his son. As the expectant journeys out to Greenwich – and the disappointed trudges back – came and went, Richard began to understand more and more the gap between his father's ambition and his ability. Others around them saw it too – parishioners, the bishop – but in them it inspired sympathy, an admiration for the heroic failure. But he was not *their* father and they didn't have to grow up worrying that one day they might end up like him. There was little Richard could think of that might solve the problem of his father, but at least he could make sure that he did not become him.

But it was when Richard was just eleven, in 1789, that the revolution in France changed everything. This was far more terrifying than the loss of the colonies; this was on England's very doorstep. Richard's world changed in a hundred ways as his country came to terms with what had happened to a fellow monarchy of equal age, pedigree and grandeur. But for Richard there was one great practical benefit.

Within a few years of the Revolution, thousands of French émigrés had left their homeland and come to England, many to live in Surrey. And it was among these émigrés that Richard was first to make the acquaintance of a vampire.

CHAPTER IX

KONSTANTIN WAS TRUE TO HIS WORD, AND LATE THAT EVENING Mihail stepped from the gates of Fontanka 16 a free man. He went straight back to his hotel, but slept badly. He lay, gazing up through the darkness towards the ceiling, trying to work out what he felt. But the answer he began with was the one he ended with. It was quite, quite simple.

He felt nothing.

Konstantin seemed an amiable enough individual. Mihail had enjoyed his company, but in his short career in the army he'd met several men he could have said that about, many he'd liked less, a few he'd liked more. Throughout his life he'd downplayed the prospect of this event. His mother had told him of his lineage as a fact, not as something in which she took joy or pride. And on top of that Mihail had always doubted that what she had said was even true.

He wished he could have the chance to apologize to her for that. He still felt a greater love for his grandfather, Aleksei, who had died before he was born, but that too came from Tamara. And Aleksei had loved his tsar – had saved him from the plans of Zmyeevich and Iuda. It would be the act of a hero to emulate him, and yet if he did so it would be for the sake of his grandfather's memory – not out of any love for his father.

And today his task was to unearth another relative for whom he could find in himself no familial love – his brother, Luka. So why seek him out? Why add further worries to the life of this young man whose fate would seem to be to die in a failed attempt to assassinate the tsar? Even towards that, Mihail felt indifferent.

In principle he loved and obeyed his tsar, but he could not stir in himself any hatred towards Luka for holding a different position. Mihail had only one hatred, for Iuda. And that was why he knew he must seek out his brother: Iuda and Dmitry had spoken of Luka. Either directly or indirectly, Luka might lead to Iuda.

Mihail walked alongside the Moika, frozen over by the January cold. The river meandered a little, always taking him in a direction that led roughly to the centre of town, but before he reached Saint Isaac's Square he turned off and soon found himself at the address Konstantin had given him: Maksimilianovsky Lane 15, apartment 7.

He asked the *dvornik* whether Luka Miroslavich was in, but the man just shrugged. It was rumoured that half the *dvorniki* in Petersburg were in the pay of the Ohrana – they saw who came and went and knew the names of all the tenants of their buildings. It would explain how Konstantin had unearthed the information about Luka so easily.

Mihail climbed the twisting stairs up to the third floor and knocked on the door of apartment 7. The man who answered looked nothing like the picture of Luka. This one was in his late twenties, with a trimmed beard that did not cover his cheeks. He was thin and pale, with a sharp nose on which sat a pair of pince-nez.

'Oh!' He seemed disappointed at what he saw. Mihail had changed out of his military uniform, thinking it unwise for his sojourn in the Petersburg underworld. He hoped his profession didn't shine through even without it.

'You were expecting somebody else?' Mihail asked.

'Yes, I was rather.'

'I'm here to see Luka Miroslavich Novikov. Is he in?'

'He's not here.' The man kept glancing over his shoulder, back into the apartment. He kept the door almost closed, with his weight against it so that Mihail could not push his way through, not that he had attempted it. None of it served to convey an impression of innocence.

'Will he be long? Might I wait?'

'He moved out weeks ago. I don't know where he went.'

With that the door was closed. Mihail went back down the

stairs and out into the street. Not far away, on the corner, was a tavern. He ordered tea and found himself a seat by the window where he could look back towards number 15. He was the only man in the place who didn't have a cigarette between his lips. He breathed deeply of the smoky atmosphere, the smell bringing his mother to mind. He could rarely remember her without one. In a provincial town like Saratov, it had been a minor scandal for a woman to smoke in public.

The passing minutes turned into hours as the citizens of Petersburg wandered up and down the snow-covered street. Mihail drank more tea and ate some lunch. It was already afternoon when at last two figures emerged from the building. They walked in Mihail's direction and he easily recognized one of them as the man with the pince-nez whom he had spoken to, now sporting a shabby coat and a battered, black top hat. He did not recognize the other one, who was somewhat younger than the first, with neatly parted straight hair and a pencil moustache. There was a hint of Tartar blood to his features. It certainly wasn't Luka. An hour later he saw a woman stop and speak to the *dvornik*. She clearly got a better response from him than Mihail had, because she didn't bother to go in. She just carried on down the road in the direction of the tavern.

It was when she was about halfway towards him that he recognized her. It was Dusya, the girl he had met on the train from Rostov; the girl who had been handling explosives. Given what Mihail had learned, it wasn't so very surprising to see her paying a visit to that particular apartment.

He turned his face away from the window, but he didn't think she had seen him. He threw a few coins on the counter to cover his bill and then made for the door. Dusya had turned south and walked along Fonarniy Lane until she hit the Yekaterininsky Canal, where she headed east. The path of the canal twisted even more than that of the Moika. Mihail did his best to follow without being seen, but he was a stranger in the city and Dusya, he presumed, was on the lookout for any *ohranik* who might be on her trail. But she made no effort to lose him.

He recognized Nevsky Prospekt when they crossed it. Dusya's path continued to follow the canal, but before long it merged with another waterway that Mihail's understanding of the city's geography told him was the Moika once more. They had not taken the most direct route. They followed the river a little further and Mihail found himself once again on familiar ground. They turned into a park which Mihail recognized as being the first thing he had seen on exiting the Ohrana building at Fontanka 16. This was the Summer Gardens – though it achieved an exquisite degree of beauty even in winter.

Now that they were in a more open space Mihail could – and needed to – keep a greater distance between himself and Dusya. The park was laid out in a regular grid of crossing pathways, separated by trees and hedges. Under other circumstances Mihail could have followed these at random, and not worried if he had walked past Dusya more than once, as any two people walking in a park might pass each other. But even if she saw him once, she would recognize him, and though their re-encountering one another was genuinely a coincidence, he would prefer her not to know he was there.

She did not walk through the park for long, but made directly for a bench, upon which a man was already sitting. As she approached he stood. He took her hands in his and they kissed. It was not prolonged, but tender enough for Mihail to construe the depth of their relationship. From a distance he could not clearly see the man's face, but already he could hazard a guess as to who it was.

The couple sat down – the man making an exaggerated show of wiping the snow from the bench, even though he had evidently already done the same on his own arrival. They began to talk and Mihail realized he had been standing watching for too long. He walked away along one of the paths, but soon returned along another. Still, he was not close enough to properly see the man's face. He took a chance. Dusya's back was to him, and she was busily gazing into the eyes of her beloved as he spoke to her, so it was unlikely that she would turn. Mihail risked walking past them.

He kept his eyes fixed on the path in front of him, his head down as if to avoid the cold. Dusk had fallen, but there was still sufficient light to see by. Only for a moment did he look up. At the same moment the man looked at him and Mihail knew instantly that he was staring into the eyes of his brother. Whether he saw anything of Tamara in them was hard to say, but the waved hair and the moustache were just as Mihail had seen in the police photograph. In reality he was perhaps a little more handsome. It must have come from his father.

Mihail walked on as though his inspection had been merely a passing glance. He almost laughed. It seemed that the subterfuge which he and Dusya had extemporized on the train was proving to be true. Whether or not she was actually his fiancée, Dusya was most certainly a friend of his brother – and an intimate one at that.

And why should Mihail not share the joke with them? His intention when he set out that day had been to speak to Luka openly, but having followed Dusya here, he had fallen into the habit of subterfuge. It was preposterous. Dusya would be pleased to see him, and Luka more so to be united at last with his long-lost brother. Mihail almost turned to face them there and then, but still he felt the urge to be, as his father had put it, circum-spect.

He turned right, right and right again, knowing that at the next junction he would be revisiting his path of moments before. Still he could not decide whether this time he would walk by or would stop and sit, and that his brother would at last become his friend.

He turned the final corner and looked, and saw that the bench was empty.

It had been many weeks since the Executive Committee had formally assembled. The chairman had not been in Petersburg, but in the meantime work had continued. Mihailov was supposed to have been in charge, but had got himself arrested. He was a pawn anyway. Now that they were all gathered there was much to be discussed. It was Sofia Lvovna who spoke first. Of all of them, she had the noblest blood in her veins. Her father was Count Perovsky, once the military governor of Petersburg, who had been forced out of office as the early liberalism of Aleksandr's reign had begun to wither. Sofia had inherited his blue eyes and prominent forehead.

'Towards the end of 1880 we rented a basement property on Malaya Sadovaya Street.' Sofia's speech was clipped and formal. 'The owner is Countess Megdena, but she has no direct involvement with the property. It consists of three rooms: the shop, a storeroom and a living room.'

None of this was news to the chairman, but it had so far been kept secret from many of the others present. The choice of the shop had been his alone, and made carefully, but using criteria that would mean nothing to the rest of the committee. He'd already been down in the tunnels below, and made sure they led where he wanted.

'Comrades Bogdanovich and Yakimova will run the property as a cheese shop,' Sofia continued, 'posing as husband and wife.'

The chairman glanced over at them. It was a sensible choice; they would not take the roles of a loving couple too far and become distracted from their work. The same could not be said of many of the People's Will – Sofia included. The women saw it as a liberation to choose when and to whom to offer their bodies; the men took it as an opportunity.

'We've taken the name of Kobozev,' explained Bogdanovich.

'And how's the cheese business?' asked the chairman.

There was general laughter.

'Does it matter?' asked Bogdanovich.

'It matters if an *ohranik* notices a cheese shop that never sells any cheese!' The chairman's voice was raised.

Bogdanovich nodded. 'We'll keep it in mind.'

'And what of activities beneath the shop?'

Sofia turned towards Kibalchich, who stood. He removed his pince-nez and wiped them on his shirt before returning them to his nose. Even so, he never seemed to look directly at the chairman as he spoke, or at Sofia, or anyone in the room.

'After the failure of the explosion at the Winter Palace, I think we all realize the need for getting the correct amount of nitroglycerin in place.' Kibalchich was making a point. For that operation he had insisted they would need more explosive to blast through two storeys of the palace and get at the tsar, but he'd been overruled. Whether it would have actually made a difference was open to debate. 'Thankfully,' he continued, 'our efforts in that direction have gone well. Yevdokia Yegorovna returned to Petersburg only yesterday with the final sticks of dynamite.'

'Where is she then? Why isn't she here?'

All eyes turned to Zhelyabov. The big, bearded man spoke calmly. 'My duty was to act as escort on the train and ensure the safe arrival of the dynamite in Petersburg. I've no idea where Dusya is now; nor Luka.'

He was right; Luka was not here either and, given their relationship, there was an obvious inference to be drawn as to the reason for their joint absence. Zhelyabov drew attention to it in contrast to his own relationship with Sofia, which neither of them ever allowed to interfere with their calling.

The chairman grunted. 'Perhaps it's for the best; the fewer who know exactly what's going on at the shop the better. And what of the tunnel itself?' he asked.

'Since you were last down there, it's not been so good,' replied Kibalchich. 'The layout is just as you said it would be, at least down below. But on the main tunnel we hit a sewage pipe which flooded back almost to the shop and we had to virtually start again. Even so, it's not going well. Since Shiryaev was arrested I've had no one to consult with. To be honest, none of us really has the expertise in this sort of work, particularly not when you have to keep everything so quiet.'

'Do we know of anyone who's got the right experience?'

There were general shrugs, indicating an answer in the negative, and so the chairman moved on. 'We're sure of when the tsar will travel along Malaya Sadovaya?' he asked.

'We've been out in the city for several months watching his movements,' explained Sofia. 'There's little regularity to them, except on Sundays when his return from the Manège usually takes him that way.'

'Usually?'

'If we don't get him one week we'll get him the next. More recently we've been watching other members of the royal family, though I think it's better to focus on the main target.'

'We?'

'Rysakov's been helping me.'

'Is he reliable?'

Sofia was about to reply, but the chairman raised his hand to silence her. There were footsteps on the stairs outside. A second later the others heard them. All held their breath. There was a knock at the door: three raps, then one, then two. It was the correct signal. Zhelyabov was closest to the door. He unbolted it and Dusya entered, followed by Luka.

'You're late!' snapped Sofia.

'We were followed,' Luka explained. 'You wouldn't want us to bring an *ohranik* here.'

'You're certain?' asked the chairman.

'It was me he was following, I think,' said Dusya. 'I don't know where he picked me up, but he was there at the Summer Gardens. Luka saw him.'

'Did you recognize him?'

'*I* didn't,' said Luka. 'But I described him to Dusya and—'

Dusya interrupted. 'I think he's the same man that I spoke to on the train from Rostov.'

'Well, that's marvellous!' exclaimed Sofia. 'They must know everything.'

'I don't think so,' said Dusya. 'On the train he helped me – lied for me.'

'And why would he do that?' Sofia's voice oozed scepticism.

'Who knows? He's got no love for the Ohrana, that's for sure. Perhaps he just, you know, liked me. He was a soldier; on leave. You know what they're like.'

'For what it's worth,' added Zhelyabov, 'that's what it looked like to me.'

'And it was pure coincidence that he was in the Summer Gardens today?' asked Sofia.

'Perhaps he wanted to take things further and decided to look me up. I told him my name.'

'Your real name? Why would you do that?'

'I was about to show my passport to an *ohranik*! You want me to get caught lying?'

'This chap,' interrupted Kibalchich. 'About my height? Clean-shaven, side whiskers, curly auburn hair, brown eyes – piercing?'

Dusya nodded. 'That's him.'

'He was at the apartment on Maksimilianovsky Lane. He must have watched us leave and then seen you arrive.'

'You're sure?' asked the chairman.

'I'll check with Titov, the *dvornik* – he'll have seen,' replied Kibalchich.

'Who else was there?'

'Just Mihailov.'

'Mihailov?' The chairman tried to hide his concern. Mihailov was supposed to be rotting in a gaol cell. If he were free it would be a threat to the chairman's position.

'A new recruit,' explained Sofia. 'Just a kid. No relation to Aleksandr Dmitrievich. He might prove useful.'

The chairman grunted, then turned back to Dusya. 'It would be easy enough for a soldier to trace you, *ohranik* or not.'

'So what we have,' said Zhelyabov, 'is either a very subtle police spy or a soldier with some slight sympathy for our cause, and holding a candle for young Dusya here.'

'I think, Dusya, that you'd better tell us everything you know about this man,' said the chairman.

She sat down and began. 'Well, he's a lieutenant in the grenadier sappers – an engineer. Knows everything about undermining and explosives and all that sort of thing. Went on about it for ever. He'd been supervising the tunnelling in that place . . . you know . . . General Skobyelev.'

'Geok Tepe?' suggested the chairman.

'That's it,' Dusya confirmed.

The chairman leaned back with a smile. 'Comrades,' he announced, 'I think we may just have found our expert.'

Not so very far from Saint George's Church in Esher, about eight miles away, just on the other side of Leatherhead, stood Juniper Hall. In 1792, when Richard Cain was fourteen, the hall was leased to a group of French émigrés who had fled to England to escape the terror that they correctly guessed would soon come to their homeland. For many in the area – particularly for the children – there were immediate benefits. Richard's study of French, while moderately successful, had been limited by his hearing it spoken only by his father and other staid Englishmen at his school who regarded the French people's pronunciation of their own language as degeneration that needed to be corrected. Once he was able to converse with those for whom French was a necessity rather than an affectation, his love for it – and for all languages – blossomed. Ever the methodical child – as his father had raised him to be – he systematically discovered and then memorized the French names of every creature he had studied and previously known only in Latin and English.

But the French occupation of Juniper Hall brought more than mere language to that corner of Surrey. It also brought death. The first body was found in the ditch beside the road from Oxshott to Chessington. The European obsession with vampires had not at the time reached England's shores and so, while the wounds to the man's neck were mysterious, their cause was not as immediately obvious as it might have been to a Slavic observer. The victim was never identified. In the end it was concluded that he was one of a gang of footpads who'd fallen foul of his comrades.

But Richard Cain jumped to no such precipitate conclusions. He simply noted in his journal the time, location and manner of the death and wondered – perhaps hoped – whether such a thing would happen again. He had no reason to suppose that it was anything but a solitary happenstance, but instinct told him there would soon be more of the same. His instinct proved correct. Within two months four other murders had come to light. More followed.

The locations of the deaths formed a rough circle, with reports from as far afield as Crawley and Guildford marking its extremities. He never identified Juniper Hall as the precise hub of the wheel, but was unsurprised when he learned the truth. As far as he could tell the events all occurred at weekends, on either a Friday or a Saturday night. Richard recorded them in a calendar and plotted them on a map, and slowly saw the pattern emerging.

And all this might have been spotted by others attempting to investigate the crime had it not been for a series of additional deaths, again with the same wounds to the throat. The difference, and the cause of the confusion, was that in these cases the victims were not men but animals.

Richard was not confused. He knew perfectly well there was

no single killer out there, but that the killer of the animals – a dog, several rabbits, a cat and a deer – was a different creature from the killer of the men. He knew it because he had killed the animals. He had taken no pleasure in it – not in the slaughter itself – but it had been a challenge to reproduce with so great a degree of accuracy the neck wounds that were the distinctive trait of the killer.

The first step had been to get a good look at the bodies. There had been no real trouble there. Two of them had been buried in the cemetery of Richard's father's own church, and so it was no problem for him to borrow a set of keys and creep into the deadhouse – if the rickety shed beside the church merited such a name – to look closely at the bodies before they were interred. On many occasions, he wasn't alone. By the age of fourteen he had acquired a number of friends, although his later understanding of human nature led him to question the term. They were the boys who in general chose not to punch him on the way to or from school. Richard soon learned that one way to maintain this peaceful state was to distract them with the sight of something gruesome. A dissected frog or a spider devouring a fly would normally be enough, but a visit to look at a corpse – particularly the victim of a murder – might keep Richard free of their unwanted attentions for a week or more. For his own part, Richard studied the wounds, took notes, made measurements – in short he behaved exactly as his father had taught him. And yet at no level did he feel that in doing so he was being a 'good boy'. There was no self-delusion that his actions could, through misinterpretation, be justified. He knew that he was twisting his father's wishes to an end which the rector would not have desired, and the knowledge pleased him.

It was not only the boys from school to whom Richard provided tours of his world of the macabre – there was also a girl. Susanna Fowler was the daughter of Edward and Lucy Fowler, who kept house for Richard's father. She was a year older than him, and while in their younger days they had lived very much apart, Susanna had for several years been old enough to share much of the housework with her mother, and so she and Richard came increasingly into contact.

They often talked as friends. He would learn from her about the world outside his somewhat cloistered upbringing at the rectory, and he would tell her of his world, reading from his journals and showing her the remarkable diversity of animal life that could be found without venturing outside the churchyard. He even described to her the mechanisms of reproduction, not as handed down to him by his father – that conversation had never taken place – but from his observation of animals. He had seen what dogs and cats did, and what the oxen in the fields did, and learned from the farmers that it led to calves. He was not surprised to learn from Susanna that people procreated in much the same way. He had assumed it based on extrapolation, but was pleased to have it confirmed, and noted the discovery in his journal. He noticed, as they discussed the matter, that her manner changed slightly and that her face became a little flushed. He himself felt unusual – a little more excited than at most of his scientific discoveries. He noted down these observations too.

And so it was quite natural that Richard should show Susanna each of the two mutilated bodies that rested overnight in the deadhouse. With the boys he brought them in as a crowd, but with her it was just the two of them. On the first occasion, she remained quite calm. Richard suspected she was hiding her fear and made an effort to describe to her in detail everything he had observed about the wounds to the neck. Still she showed no outward signs of apprehension, and so he had pulled back the victim's head, holding it by the chin, thus allowing, as he described it, a full and clear view of the damage done to the internal structures of the neck. She fled. Richard savoured the moment, enjoying the knowledge that he had managed to in some way control her, without any need for coercion or force.

She had come to ask him to show her the second body that had been laid there. Richard gladly obliged and on this occasion she seemed to have prepared herself, to have stiffened the sinews and summoned up the blood, and no amount of detail on Richard's part had made her show any desire to flee. Even so, after they had left the deadhouse together and stood facing each other, shaded by the pale stone wall of the church, Richard had noticed a stiffness in her movements and a shortness in her speech that hinted she was still hiding her emotions. It was most enjoyable to observe.

And then, quite unaccountably, he kissed her. From where inside him the urge arose he could not say, but it could only be related to her terror. For a moment she remained very still, her fear now augmented by surprise, but then he felt her hands on his head. Her mouth opened and he felt the moisture of her tongue on his own lips. It was a kiss that he had begun, but which she had taken over. It lasted only a few seconds and then she pulled away. She looked at him, smiling, her hands still cupping his head; then she giggled and ran off. Even a century on, it remained a pleasant memory.

Richard had now gathered enough information to be able to recreate the wounds on the murder victims. Their most notable feature was that, in all the mess and devastation of the attacks, there were always two points of incision. Richard quickly came up with a mechanism to mimic the injuries. He took two knives and placed them side by side, so that their handles touched and their blades sat parallel, pointing in the same direction. He bound them together with twine. The first animal he practised on was a rabbit. The reproduction of the wounds was remarkably accurate.

Richard chose a much simpler pattern in which to lay out the corpses of the animals with which he baited his trap, one that would be easy for the genuine killer to understand. In terms of 'when', Richard followed the same calendar – always killing at weekends. The 'where' was in a circle, a much smaller circle than the killer used. This one had a radius of just a furlong, and its centre was his father's church.

Each weekend Richard would kill an animal and place its body somewhere on that circle. Then he would return to the church and place a lighted candle in one of the arched vaults of the crypt that just managed to peep above the level of the ground. He would hide in the branches of the great yew tree that hung over the churchyard and wait.

If the killer had been only what Richard was expecting – some deranged lunatic with a lust for blood – then it was madness for a fourteen-year-old boy to try to capture him on his own. If Richard had understood what he was truly dealing with, a supernatural creature with strength ten times that of any man, he would have fled, knowing his task was hopeless. But his ignorance robbed him of fear. Perhaps on a thousand other occasions it would have been hopeless; in a thousand other worlds Richard would have lain dead, the blood sucked from his body, and he would not have grown to be the creature he was today; perhaps some malign spirit was watching over him. Whatever the cause, Richard was lucky.

It was on the seventh weekend, on the Friday night, that Richard observed the figure of a man skulking through the undergrowth, heading, by a twisting path, towards the candle that had been set to trap him. When a few yards from the opening to the crypt, the figure paused. It shouted in French: 'Are you there?'

With no response forthcoming, the figure moved a little closer to the crypt, crouching almost on its hands and knees, and called again. It crawled further, so that it was now peering into the space beneath the church, its hand perched on the ledge. Richard moved. He covered the ground between him and the church in seconds and charged the figure with the full force of his shoulder. It was taken quite by surprise and tumbled forward into the crypt. The fall was only six feet or so, and was unlikely to harm even a man – but by the same token, even a man might quickly escape. But Richard was prepared. He slammed down the old iron grate that he had propped open when placing the candle and slipped the lock back into place. His prisoner was secure.

He peered down into the dark crypt. The candle had been knocked over and extinguished in the tussle. Outside the light of the half-moon was bright enough, but it did not penetrate far into darkness. It didn't need to. Seconds later hands gripped the iron bars and a face appeared, twisted with rage, its lips bared in a ferocious snarl which revealed to Richard its long, sharp pointed teeth.

And at that moment, although he might not yet fully appreciate the import of the word, Richard knew that he was looking into the face of a vampire.

*

That had been eighty-nine years before, and now Richard preferred to call himself Iuda, and now *he* was a vampire, and a prisoner in a cell with only one small window high up in the wall. But he would not climb up there and snarl at those who passed by – it would do no good. Iuda had better plans for escape, perhaps even for rescue. But to get help he must be able to call for help, and there the continual tapping of the prisoners on the pipes would be his salvation.

He had analysed the signals and observed that the smallest unit of communication was a pair of numbers – tapped against the pipe with some metal object and separated by a pause. The first number was never greater than five and the second never greater than six. This gave a combination of thirty possibilities – close enough to the thirty-seven of the Russian alphabet, within which there were a number of letters that were rarely if ever used, being virtual duplicates of other letters. The whole system was ripe for revision. Thus 'I' could be replaced by 'И', 'Ѳ' by 'Ф', 'Ѣ' by 'Е' and 'V' by 'В'. At a push, even 'Щ' and 'Ш' could be treated as a single letter. The hard and soft sounds – 'Ъ' and 'Ь' – could be ignored, and that reduced the number of letters to thirty. Iuda arranged them alphabetically on a grid.

	1	2	3	4	5	6
1	А	Б	В	Г	Д	Е
2	Ё	Ж	З	И	Й	К
3	Л	М	Н	О	П	Р
4	С	Т	У	Ф	Х	Ц
5	Ч	Ш	Ы	Э	Ю	Я

Originally he drew it in the dust of the floor, but it was easy enough to memorize and he soon wiped it away so that no guard would see. Any letter could be transmitted by a pair of taps. 3 and 5 would signify 'П'; 4 and 6 gave 'Ц'. Iuda's own name was

153

2,4 – 4,3 – 1,5 – 1,1. He listened to the messages coming through the pipes and analysed them. They all made sense.

Iuda picked up the tin mug that the guards had given him and threw the water from it on to the cell floor. Then he squatted down beside the pipes and began to tap out a message of his own.

CHAPTER X

SATURDAY BEGAN MUCH AS FRIDAY HAD DONE, WITH A SHORT walk to Maksimilianovsky Lane, a nod to the *dvornik* at number 15 and a march up the stairs to apartment 7. This time the door was opened by a familiar face – familiar from a photograph and from one passing glance in the Summer Gardens the previous day.

'Mihail Konstantinovich Lukin, I presume,' said Luka, opening the door wider to allow Mihail in.

There was no one else in the apartment. Mihail had half expected to see Dusya there, or one of the two men he had observed leaving the previous day, but he was alone with his half-brother.

'How do you know my name?' asked Mihail. The answer was obvious enough. He had told Dusya his name; somehow she had seen him.

'How do you know my address?' countered Luka.

'We have a mutual friend.'

This much appeared to pique Luka's interest. He gestured towards a chair, which Mihail took.

'Tea?' Luka asked.

'Thank you.'

Luka went over to the samovar, which was already hot, and drew two glasses. Mihail glanced around the apartment. The sitting room, on to which the front door opened, was quite large, with two further doors opening off. Three or four cheap watercolours provided the only real decoration. The room was well furnished with seating for over a dozen people, either on the divan or on a number of padded chairs or even more hard ones, none of them matching. Mihail knew that one thing these revolutionaries did like to do was meet and talk, and this place seemed quite suited.

What the room lacked was any hint of written materials. The shelves on the walls were empty. There was a desk but apart from the samovar its surface was bare. He could not see in the drawers, but guessed that they would be the same. There would be no clues if the place was raided by the Ohrana.

'And who is that?' asked Luka, sitting on the divan and leaning back. He seemed calm – almost amused.

There Mihail was at something of a loss. The identity of the mutual friend – mutual acquaintance – was simple enough: Iuda. But Iuda was a creature of so many aliases that it would be a challenge to hit upon the right one. 'Iuda' itself seemed unlikely and though Tamara had told Mihail of others – Richard Cain, Vasiliy Denisovich Makarov, Vasiliy Innokyentievich Yudin – there could be many more besides, by any one of which he might be known to Luka.

There was, of course, another connection between Mihail and Luka – another who was closer than any friend: they shared a mother. But Mihail had decided not to reveal that – not until he knew just where his brother stood with regard to Iuda. He thought back to what he had heard Dmitry and Iuda say, back in Geok Tepe. There was very little, just Dmitry's words: 'We know you've befriended him . . . much as you befriended me.' Iuda had befriended Dmitry when he was just five years old, and had been his hidden guardian as the boy had grown into a man. How close was the similarity with Luka?

'I take it you know you're adopted,' said Mihail, approaching the issue obliquely.

'Of course.' If Luka was surprised at Mihail's knowledge he hid it well. 'My parents never lied to me about that.'

'What happened to your real parents?'

'My father died in the cholera epidemic in '48. My mother went mad. They had to take me away from her.'

It was brutally close to the truth; perhaps it would have been kinder for them to invent a lie.

'Any brothers or sisters?' asked Mihail.

156

Luka shook his head. 'My parents couldn't have children of their own.'

'It must have been lonely.'

Luka allowed a little of his irritation to seep through. 'Look, what's all this about? You said we had a mutual friend.'

Mihail continued with his line of attack, a plan forming in his mind.

'I'm an only child too – and brought up just by my mother. But I was lucky enough to have a benefactor.'

'And who was that?' Was that a little flicker of acknowledgement in Luka's eyes? Had Iuda played that same role for him?

'He was shy about using his full name – he liked his good deeds to remain anonymous.' It was wild guesswork – a parallel of the way Iuda had worked on Dmitry. 'I usually just call him "Uncle Vasya".' Of the pseudonyms that Mihail knew, Vasiliy was the only repeating factor.

Now Luka showed an even greater reaction. He leaned forward in his seat. 'Vasya? Vasiliy?'

'That's right. I can tell the name means something to you.'

'Perhaps. Tell me more about him.'

'Well, he was a friend of my mother's,' explained Mihail. It was all extemporization now, but it did not matter – Luka was hooked. This was mere reeling in. 'I don't mean there was anything like that going on; Vasya's not like that. But he saw immediately that I missed my father, and tried to take on the role – when he was in town.'

Luka nodded, sharing the experience.

'He used to buy me toys, and books when I was older, and tell me of history and of the world.'

'What does he look like?' Luka asked eagerly.

'Striking. You wouldn't fail to recognize him. He's quite tall – a little taller than me. And he's got blond hair; it's very distinctive. He wears it long – at least for a man of his age.'

'Anything else?'

'His eyes; grey. Some people think they're cold, but not when you get to know him.'

Luka nodded, his hands at his mouth, hiding his joy. 'It's him,' he said. 'The same man. Vasiliy Grigoryevich Chernetskiy.'

Another alias to add to the list. 'How do you meet him?' Mihail asked, trying to reflect his brother's joy.

'My story's much the same as yours – except that Vasya knew my father rather than my mother. But whenever Papa had to go away on business, Vasya always kept an eye on us. And I know that Papa once got into debt, and Vasya made him a loan which saved him. He's got money – from land, I presume – and he knows how to do good with it. The country would be a better place with more like him.'

Mihail nodded. 'You're not wrong.' In some ways it would be sad to finally prick the bubble of the man's affection for Iuda; in others a joy. It would have to be done sooner or later.

'And so . . . what?' asked Luka. 'Vasya told you about me? Said you should look me up?'

'Not quite. I've known about you for some time. But as fate would have it, Vasya and I found we would both be travelling to Petersburg at the beginning of the year. We planned to meet up and then call on you together.'

'You mean . . .' – Luka was excited now – 'he'll be here soon?'

Mihail allowed his face to fall. 'That's just the problem. I'm quite unable to find him. He should have arrived in the city before me, but I've been to the hotel where he said he'd be staying and his club, and there's no sign. I wondered if he'd contacted you.'

And there it was: the reason for Mihail's coming to Petersburg; the hope that there might be some thread of a connection whereby he could find Iuda.

Luka threw himself back on the divan and raised his hands in despair. 'I've heard nothing. He hasn't even written to announce his visit, which would be usual. You think he might be in trouble?'

'That's my fear.' It was more than a fear. Iuda was Dmitry's captive. There was no reason to suppose he had escaped, but there was plenty to suggest they had come to Petersburg – not least that Luka himself lived there.

'What can we do?'

'Keep our ears to the ground. You know Petersburg better than me. Does he have an apartment here, or anywhere else he might be able to stay?'

Luka thought, perhaps for a little too long, then shook his head. 'Nowhere that I know of – nowhere fixed.'

'He mentioned a place on Great Konyushennaya Street.' It had been Aleksei's home once, but Iuda had managed to acquire it, along with Aleksei's wife and son.

Luka shook his head. 'No, he sold that years ago – and even then he never lived there.'

'Then all we can do is wait. If he is here and something has happened to him, you'll hear of it I'm sure.'

'How shall I get in touch?'

'Here's where I'm staying.' Mihail handed him a card with the address of his hotel. 'And I'll find you here if I learn anything.' He stood, preparing to leave.

'One more thing, Mihail Konstantinovich,' said Luka, standing also. An edge had crept into his voice.

'Anything.'

'You said we had a mutual friend – in Vasya – but it seems we have another.'

'Another?'

'Dusya.'

'Dusya?'

Luka tutted. 'Don't play the idiot. We know you followed her yesterday. I saw you in the Summer Gardens.'

'Ah!' Mihail tried to blush, but did not know if he succeeded. 'You saw me. That's a pity.'

'Why?'

'Well, I don't know how much Dusya may have told you, but we met on the train from Rostov a few days ago. I couldn't help but find her a very attractive young lady – she did nothing to encourage it, I assure you. You'll imagine my surprise when I saw her paying a call on the very house where I knew you to live. But all the same, I felt the desire to become reacquainted with her.'

'And so you followed her. Why not just speak to her?'

'That would have been wiser. But Vasya's disappearance has got me worried. When I saw her with you – not that I knew then who you were – I realized she already had a beau, and I gave up all inclinations in that direction.' Mihail paused. He should have reacted to the apparent coincidence earlier. 'I hope she's not going to come between us. Vasya would be so disappointed.' Mihail resisted the urge to chuckle – that last comment was below the belt.

Luka held out his hand with a smile that didn't quite convince. 'I don't see it being a problem.'

They shook hands and with that Mihail departed. There was no immediate lead to Iuda, but he had not expected one. Luka, however, was not a man without associates. If Iuda was anywhere in Petersburg, perhaps the People's Will would hear of it. If not, there was always that other connection, through Dmitry. It was unlikely that Luka even guessed at the existence of his uncle, and Mihail was not going to overplay his hand by mentioning it just yet.

He turned on to the street and headed back to his hotel. It was getting on for lunchtime. He passed the tavern where he had eaten the previous day, but chose not to partake of its cuisine again. There must be a hundred better places to eat in the city. As he walked past the door, a man stepped out dressed in a heavy brown overcoat and with his *ushanka* tied tightly under his chin. He looked down the street away from Mihail, but then set off in the opposite direction, bumping into Mihail heavily, almost knocking him over in the slippery snow. Both men apologized and continued on their way.

It was only a dozen or so paces later, as Mihail replayed the minor incident in his mind, that he recalled the slight unnecessary pressure to his chest. He turned, but the man had vanished. He ripped off his glove, slipping his hand into the inside pocket of his jacket, where he had felt the pressure. With relief he found that his notecase was still there. He pulled it out and opened it. None of his paper roubles were gone. It was inconceivable that a pickpocket could have taken them and replaced his empty wallet, but still he'd felt the urge to check. He returned it to his pocket, and it was then he noticed the extra slip of paper that had been planted there. The man had possessed the skills of a cutpurse, but he had used them not to take but to give.

Mihail opened up the note and discovered that it was a summons; a summons from his father.

*

Once he had begun to send his own messages, and listen to those that came back, Iuda managed to gather a clearer understanding of what was going on – not just in the Peter and Paul Fortress, but in the whole of Petersburg.

There were at least twenty inmates who were in some way connected with the People's Will, plus others arrested for more normal crimes and a few from organizations with similar goals to the People's Will, but quite independent. None of these were allowed to know the code – least of all the other revolutionary groups – though Iuda had no doubt that a few would have been smart enough to crack it. He had managed it in only a day, and there were plenty who'd been incarcerated here for longer than that.

Nor was it outside the realms of the imagination that the authorities understood something of the code – indeed it was almost essential that they did. While prisoners within the fortress could communicate with relative ease, it would be of little benefit to anyone if messages couldn't be got out and in. At some point in the chain there had to be a corrupt guard to act as courier to the wider world. But that meant that the inmates had to be circumspect; beneath the surface of the simple code of tapping there were other layers of subterfuge. Pseudonyms were used rather than real identities – both for revolutionaries and their intended targets. Iuda had been familiar with most of it at one time but his long incarceration by the Turcomans had left him out of touch. Even so he could tell that something momentous was afoot, and that before long there would be another attempt on Aleksandr's life.

But that was not Iuda's most pressing concern; he was becoming thirsty. He had not fed since Dmitry and Zmyeevich had provided him with the meagre feast of the boy in Moscow. Before that there had been nothing since Geok Tepe. The sentries at the fortress delivered food twice a day, but it was of no use to him. He wasn't yet on the point of becoming weak or lethargic, but the time would come. He needed to get out.

He had faced a similar problem with the vampire he kept prisoner beneath his father's church in Esher. His first instinct, on discovering that what he'd captured was not human, had been to kill it. He was still young enough to have an instinctive sense of what was good and what was evil, and to have a revulsion for the latter, but his first problem had been to devise a mechanism. He knew little of vampire lore. He'd heard tales that daylight could harm them, but while some stories said it would bring death, others were quite clear that it would merely weaken the monster. During the day the creature lurked in a dark corner of the crypt and so Richard never had the opportunity to experiment on the effect light might have on it, except to make the observation that it was afraid of the sun. But even as he realized the difficulties he might have in killing the creature, he also began to question the need for it. His father's attitude continued to hold sway; the rat and the butterfly were not killed for killing's sake, but in order to study them. If more could be learned from a live specimen than from a dead one, then life should remain.

He boarded up the small window by which he'd trapped the monster and instead gained access to it through the church. His father never went down into the crypt, and Richard now stole the appropriate keys so that he would not be able to, even if the whim took him. The entrance was hidden behind the triple-decker pulpit that stood almost midway down the nave, overlooking the Chamber Pew where the local nobility – the Pelham family – could worship in isolation from the masses. Richard's father could preach directly at them, either from the top tier when he delivered his sermon, the middle when he read the lesson or the bottom when he had more secular announcements to make regarding the parish. It was from behind this bottom level that steps led down to a wooden door, and beyond that there was an iron gate leading to the crypt. Richard could sit between the two and converse with his specimen in complete safety.

It was two days before he got any reply to his questions.

'Yes, I am a vampire.'

His English bore a heavy French accent, though Richard had already suspected his nationality from the manner of his dress.

'Your name?' Richard asked.

'*Je suis Honoré Philippe Louis d'Évreux, Vicomte de Nemours.*'

'You're staying at Juniper Hall?' Richard stuck with English.

'Not any more, it seems.'

Richard smiled. 'But you were?'

The *vicomte* nodded.

'How long have you been a vampire?'

'Twelve years.'

Richard noted it down in his journal. 'And before that, you were a normal man?'

'*Oui.*'

'And how did the transformation take place?'

Richard copied down every detail of Honoré's story, occasionally interrupting to ask questions but generally allowing him to tell it in his own way. That battered exercise book was to become the first volume of Iuda's vast collection on the study of the vampire. He spent every moment he could down there, learning of Honoré's strange life. His father scarcely noticed his absence. Only Susanna made any comment on his recent unusual behaviour, but he told her nothing. There had been a time when he might have been tempted to take her into his confidence, but since their kiss he had felt wary of her – afraid of the power she might have over him.

It was after two weeks that the issue of Honoré's sustenance had arisen. It came in the middle of their normal interrogation. Honoré had never asked anything of Richard and when the words came from him, it was more of a plea than a demand.

'Feed me.'

Richard had already been considering the issue. There was a series of possible solutions, each with increasing risk, and the increasing prospect of excitement.

'Will animal blood do?' Richard asked.

Honoré shook his head. 'I've tried it. I can force it down, but it does nothing to relieve my hunger. Perhaps others can stomach it, but not I.'

'How much do you need?'

The vampire shrugged. 'Whatever I can get. A little regularly – a lot occasionally.'

'Would my blood do?'

'Certainly. Come over here and press your neck against the bars.'

Richard chuckled. 'I mean if I were to draw a little and give it to you.'

'Where would be the pleasure?'

Richard drew out his double-bladed knife. He no longer needed it to mimic the vampire's teeth, but he had grown fond of it – proud of the fact that its wounds were his unique signature. He drew one blade across the palm of his left hand, then smeared the oozing blood on to the flat of the metal. He held the bloodied knife with an outstretched arm, approaching Honoré with utmost caution.

The vampire snorted. 'When I said a little . . . You'd do better to save your strength, Cain, and use it to catch me bigger prey.'

Richard doubted whether his strength was up to the task, but he had his cunning. He stole a bottle of his father's wine. Brandy would have done the job better, but it would be missed, whereas the cellar beneath the rectory was plentifully stocked with wine.

It took another two days before he found a suitable victim. Honoré asked him constantly how he was progressing but Richard told him to be patient. Eventually he saw the man, a vagrant wandering down the Portsmouth Road. Richard watched as he plodded along and then eventually settled down for a night's sleep. Richard sat down beside him and began to chat, eventually offering him the wine. The tramp drank eagerly, but Richard had underestimated his capacity for alcohol. He had hoped that an entire bottle would render him insensible, but it merely made him talk more, and with less coherence.

In the end, that made things easier. Richard would have had trouble carrying the unconscious body back to the church, but all he now had to do was tell the vagrant that he knew where more wine could be found, and the drunken fool happily walked to his own death. Richard led him down under the church and then pointed through the locked gate while pretending to look for the key.

'It's all in there,' he said encouragingly. 'Have a look.'

The tramp peered forward, his beard pressing against the iron bars.

Honoré struck.

Richard sat a little way away and took notes. There was nothing that the tramp could do once the vampire had got hold of him. Honoré's hands clasped him by the back of the head, pulling him close so that his neck lay bare against the bars, allowing Honoré to drink. The man's hands scrabbled against the stone walls and his legs kicked wildly, but with ever-decreasing vigour as his blood drained away. Soon he was unconscious. The vampire let go and the vagrant slumped backwards on to the floor, his head hitting the stonework with a crack.

'I need the body,' Honoré hissed.

Richard considered. The only way he could hand over the tramp's body would be to open the gate, but that would be an idiotic risk. And yet he yearned to discover what the vampire would do. He wished he'd been able to further restrain his captive. He had a heavy chain and a padlock ready, but he could think of no safe way to get close enough. He decided to do the best he could with the hand he'd been dealt.

'Step away from the gate then,' he said. 'Get right back, but where I can see you.'

The *vicomte* complied. Richard kept his eyes fixed on him as he unlocked the gate, prepared for any attempt to rush forward, but none came. He managed to drag and kick the tramp's body forward, noticing a slight groan, indicating that some life remained. Once he had got the body through he slammed the gate closed and locked it. Honoré scurried forward and dragged the tramp away into the shadows. Richard never discovered what it was that he did with it, or with the bodies of the other victims Richard went on to provide. Later he learned, through both observation and personal experience, that for many vampires the taste of human flesh was sweeter even than that of their blood.

Richard left Honoré to spend the night alone with his repast, but he did not go to sleep. He spent the whole night reading, comparing his recent notes of how he had seen a vampire feed with some of his earliest on how a spider devours a fly, noting down the similarities and the differences. It was all quite fascinating.

He kept his specimen locked down there beneath the church for two years, feeding it regularly, but not extravagantly. It was not always easy to find passing itinerants who would not be missed, but Richard was not without imagination. His friends from school already knew that an invite to the church to see something gruesome was worth responding to. Richard made them promise to tell no one, not even where they were going. That way, when they failed to return no suspicion would fall upon him. Honoré always kept back from the gate when Richard opened it, allowing his schoolfriend to walk inside and disappear into the blackness. Often he saw nothing of their fate, happy merely to sit on the steps down from the pulpit and listen to their screams.

But through it all, Richard could only hide his terror. The more he learned of Honoré the more he understood how dangerous a creature he was holding captive – how lucky he had been to capture it at all. Honoré gave no hint that he was planning to escape, but Richard knew that it must be so – it was what *he* would have done.

As time went by, Richard became more ambitious, providing victims not simply to sate Honoré's thirst but also to settle his own personal scores. Of all the boys at his school, the one he hated most was Charles Armitage. They had been friends once, but at some point in his life Charles had made the decision that social success was best achieved by joining the crowd and de-riding Richard's quiet interest in the natural world, rather than sharing it. The worst of it was his hypocrisy – while he would goad Richard in public, he was fascinated to talk of nature's glory when they were alone. It was to be his undoing – though it was almost Richard's too.

Richard tempted him down to the crypt as he had the others. He walked to the gate and checked to see where Honoré was. After a moment he saw his eyes, a safe distance away in the shadows, glinting in the light of Richard's lamp. Richard opened the gate and beckoned Charles forward, promising him a thrill far greater than anything he had seen previously in the deadhouse. As he spoke he caught a movement from the corner of his eye. It was only then that he realized his mistake. Whoever's eyes he had seen, they were not Honoré's, nor was there any life behind them; he had given the vampire enough material to produce a convincing replication.

Honoré moved quickly and slammed the gate against Richard, trapping him between it and the stone wall and knocking the wind out of him. The pressure was released and Richard slumped to the floor. The vampire stood above him, fangs bared. Richard tried to crawl away, but he made little progress. Even so, Honoré allowed him to move, confident that he could not escape. Richard knew that if he could just make it to the church above, where daylight streamed through the clear windows, then he would survive. But Honoré knew that too. Before Richard even made it to the bottom step, the vampire leapt, pinning him to the ground and gazing into his eyes, his foetid breath infiltrating Richard's nostrils. Even at such a moment, Richard wondered how that stench might be related to the creature's diet, and how he might devise an experiment to understand the connection better.

'You should have killed me, Cain,' he snarled.

He opened his jaws wide, revealing his fangs, and raised his head in preparation to bring them down on Richard's neck. Richard turned away and tried to close his eyes, but still his curiosity forced him to look – to try to learn even in the moment of his own death. But Honoré did not strike. His head fell back. A whimper escaped his lips and he froze for a moment, his eyes closed, as though in thoughtful contemplation. An instant later he collapsed into Richard's chest. Behind him stood Charles, a huge piece of masonry in his hands which he had brought down on the vampire's head. It would have caved in a man's skull and killed him in a moment, but Richard already knew enough to doubt the effect would be the same here. In seconds he was up on his feet, pushing Honoré's body off him, and confirming as he did so that the creature was not dead.

'Quick!' he snapped at Charles. 'Drag him back in there.'

Whatever presence of mind had allowed Charles to find the chunk of stone and bring it down on Honoré's head had now deserted him. He stood shaking, his arms dangling loosely by his sides, tears welling in his eyes.

'Now!' shouted Richard, moving to grab Honoré's feet and haul him back into the crypt. His action spurred Charles into movement and soon they had dragged the vampire's inert body through the open gate. Richard bent down close to examine the wound at the back of his head, and saw that it was already healing. As he peered, Honoré emitted a groan.

'Jesus Christ!' whispered Charles.

Richard looked up at him. 'Thank you,' he said. It seemed the natural thing to do, but there was no sincerity to it.

'How could he . . . ?' mumbled Charles. Then, with greater conviction, 'We should get out of here.'

'No!' snapped Richard. He saw in the moment an opportunity, but not one that would be available to him for long. He dashed through the gate again and back towards the stairs, Charles in tow, but he did not ascend. In an alcove he found what he had left there, the chains he had wanted to use on Honoré. Back in the crypt the creature was beginning to stir, but Richard acted swiftly. Soon the chain dug tightly into the vampire's throat, fastened with a padlock, its other end secured to the bars at the window through which he had first been thrust into his prison.

Charles had been of no further help, and was eager to leave. 'He's waking up. Let's go.'

Richard was calmer. 'It's safe now – now that he's bound. Let's watch.'

Richard stood by the gate and did as he'd suggested, Charles beside him. He knew perfectly well that it wasn't a safe place to be. He'd made sure that the chain was long enough for Honoré to reach every corner of the crypt. He also made sure that Charles was a little further into the crypt than he was. The two boys stood, watching with different mixtures of terror and fascination as the vampire came to. His eyes fell upon Richard and he leapt to his feet, then stopped and raised his hand to the chain at his neck, sensing it for the first time.

'You're wise to chain me, Cain,' he said. 'But you'd have been wiser to kill me.'

'Perhaps one day I shall,' replied Richard. 'Or perhaps one day I'll free you. For now I want you alive. And for that you must feed. *Bon appétit.*'

Charles didn't even notice that Richard had stepped to the other side of the gate. It was only when he heard the lock turn that he understood what was happening. He had proved a useful ally – an indispensable one – when Honoré had attacked Richard, but there was no chance that he would keep what he had seen to himself.

Richard at least did his friend the courtesy of not staying to watch his end. Even after he'd locked the wooden door and begun ascending the steps he could hear Charles's muffled voice shouting after him.

'Richard! Richard! Richard!'

It didn't last long.

Honoré never attempted to escape again, and their previous routine resumed. Richard fed the vampire and questioned him, and received the answers he sought. It was during their conversations that Richard first came to know of Zmyeevich, though that was not the name by which Honoré referred to him. It was thrilling enough to know that vampires were not rare, certainly not in Europe, but more fascinating still to learn of one so old and so powerful that he struck terror and obedience into every one of his kind. Honoré spoke of Zmyeevich's hatred for the Romanov family, but knew nothing of its origins.

When Richard was sixteen his father summoned him to his study. Richard guessed what the conversation was to be about and was excited by the prospect. At last he would be free.

'Sit down, young man,' his father began. 'As I'm sure you're aware, you've reached the age in life when a gentleman of a certain status and intellect should be looking forward to going to varsity. We haven't spoken of it recently, but we both know that it's always been my intention for you to go up to Oxford, just as I did.'

Richard remained silent; his father preferred a speech to a conversation.

'Now, I won't beat about the bush, Richard,' the reverend continued. 'I'm sorry to have to tell you that this is not to be. You won't be familiar with these things, but a rector's stipend isn't very much. I'd hoped that my Navigational Engine would make me a rich man, but with all the changes the Admiralty wants me to make . . . well, it's turned out to have cost me more than the return is ever likely to be. So I'm afraid I can't afford Oxford. We'll have to sort out something else; an apprenticeship maybe – something decent – in London perhaps.'

He paused, but Richard said nothing.

'You do understand, don't you?' For a moment there was the hint of an apology in his tone, but it was too late for that.

'Yes, sir,' whispered Richard. And with that their meeting was at an end.

Richard fumed. His instinct was for revenge. He was tempted to take his father down to the crypt there and then and thrust him in with Honoré. Better still, he would do the dirty work himself, with his double-bladed knife. But even then he knew that vengeance was a tepid dish. He was too young ever to have seen hangings at Tyburn, but it was not the only gallows in London. He had looked into the eyes of the convicted and known that their deaths would not change the world one jot. The people who jeered in the square might find their spirits momentarily lifted by the swinging rope, but they would not sleep any safer in their beds. Richard had no objection to men's deaths – be they guilty or innocent – but it was wasteful for a death not to have a practical purpose. Thus to kill his father would be a mere gesture – an admission of defeat. It would not get him to Oxford.

It took four months for Richard to devise a way to give his father a useful ending. He'd turned his mind to methods by which he might raise the money he needed. An early thought had been that his father was simply exaggerating his penury, but a quick examination revealed he had been telling the truth. Moreover, if he were to die, Richard would get very little. Even the house they lived in belonged not to Thomas Cain but to the Church of England.

But then he found the answer. In nearby Ewell there lived a dowager by the name of Lady Agnes Truslove. She and her brother had been the children of a parish vicar and had been orphaned at a young age, thus preventing the brother from going up to Cambridge. He'd been forced to enter the army and had been killed at the Battle of Plassey. She, however, had married well, and was now a rich widow and had used her husband's vast fortune to establish a fund to assist the education of those who could not afford it themselves. The one criterion was that beneficiaries of the fund must themselves be orphaned sons of the clergy.

Richard was no orphan, but things could change – could change very rapidly if he put his mind to it. He would have liked to effect the transformation from son to orphan himself, but there might be those who were suspicious. There had been sufficient deaths and disappearances in the village that tongues were already wagging. It would be better if he were a long way away and in company when it happened.

He put the bargain to Honoré.

'Why don't you just send him down here, like the others?'

'Because there must be a body,' Richard explained. 'If he merely disappears then I may not get the money – certainly not quickly.'

'So you propose to let me go, and as a last favour to you I kill your father, leaving you in the clear?'

'That's about the size of it.'

'Why should I do you any service?'

'Because I'm letting you go.'

'Excuse me, no.' Honoré shook his head. 'You will already have let me go. I will be free to do as I please.'

'You'll be hungry and he'll be there, quite unprotected.'

'So will many people in the town. Why should I do something for you, my gaoler of two years?'

'I could have treated you worse. I fed you, didn't I? And not just anybody.' Richard felt his throat tighten as he spoke.

'This is true.'

'So will you do it?'

'Release me and you will find out.'

It was the best Richard could hope for. A direct yes he would have taken for a lie anyway. If Honoré didn't keep up his end of the deal then Richard could always commit the deed himself and forget about the alibi. But Honoré was a member of the French aristocracy. Surely he'd have some sense of honour, as the name suggested.

Two weeks later the opportunity arose. It was after evensong one Sunday. As Thomas's flock departed, one of their number, Mrs Tregaskis, suggested that Richard should join her and her family for dinner. Her intent was, and had been for some time, to pair off Richard with her daughter Beatrice. Richard had no interest in the girl, at first because of Susanna and now because of his hoped for departure to Oxford. But the circumstances were perfect. He explained to his father, who was quite happy to let him go. Everyone in the church saw father and son part, with the father in perfect health.

Then Richard slipped down to the crypt. He stood close to the iron gate and peered inside, holding his lantern high to penetrate the shadows, but saw no one. He turned the key in the heavy lock and swung it open. Still there was no sound and no movement from within. He took the key to the padlock that fastened Honoré's chains and flung it into the darkness, listening to it clatter across the stone floor.

'It's tonight, Honoré,' he said. 'Thank you and adieu.'

'*Au revoir,*' came a voice from the shadows.

Richard turned away and as he did so the light of his lantern fell briefly upon what looked like a face, white like the full moon against the darkness. But it could not be – not that face. He looked again and it was gone.

He hurried back up to the church and departed in the Tregaskises' carriage to enjoy a pleasant dinner at their house in Leatherhead. Soon after the meal he complained of an upset stomach and a feeling of light-headedness, with only a partial need to affect the symptoms after what he had seen. Mrs Tregaskis insisted that he should stay the night, while the glint in Beatrice's eye suggested she thought this was some sort of ruse on his part. It was, but not to the end she had in mind.

He accepted their hospitality with the proviso that a boy be sent to Esher to inform the Reverend Cain of his son's predicament. The lad was dispatched and Richard retired to bed. The sun had not risen when he was shaken from his sleep to be told the tragic, horrible news of his father's murder. Not an ounce of suspicion fell on him.

After that the rest of the plan fell into place just as he had known it would. Lady Truslove happily gave him the funds he required – and a little more besides in consideration of the awful circumstances of his father's death. Richard never knew precisely how awful those circumstances had been. He heard descriptions of the wounds; it was obvious that Honoré had done his duty and then, presumably, gone his merry way. But Richard never went down to the crypt again to check, out of fear for what he might find there.

And so, just after Michaelmas 1795, Richard Llywelyn Cain arrived at the College of the Holy and Undivided Trinity in the

University of Oxford to begin the next stage of his education.

Honoré's imprisonment, under Richard's watchful eye, had lasted for two years, but in the end he had been able simply to walk free. In the Peter and Paul Fortress, Iuda planned to do the same, and was not prepared to wait nearly so long. But he would need help. There was only one man in Petersburg he could trust – and even then he had begun to fear that his trust might be misplaced.

He began to tap a message on the pipes, knowing it would be relayed across the fortress, transferred to some sentry or visitor who was able to walk freely out through the gates, and that soon it would be with its intended recipient. And soon after, Iuda would have a visitor.

CHAPTER XI

KONSTANTIN'S NOTE HAD BEEN BRIEF. 'TAKE THE 1.15 TRAIN. You will be met at Pavlovsk.'

The officer who met him there, a colonel of the Semyonovskiy Regiment, did not give his name, but escorted Mihail to a sled which took them from the station through the town to the gates of a large estate. This, it was easy to guess, was the Pavlovsk Palace, Konstantin's country retreat. The sled took them through the estate and past the great palace itself, but stopped ultimately at a much smaller building in the grounds.

The colonel remained seated, but indicated to Mihail a door in the side of the modest house. It opened on to a long corridor, at the end of which Mihail saw his father in earnest conversation with a slightly built woman in her thirties. In the army Mihail had heard all the rumours and guessed that this was Konstantin's mistress, Anna Vasilyevna Kuznetsova. Perhaps this was even the house he had set aside for her, so close to the home of his official family. It was an appropriate place for a man to make a rendez-vous with his bastard son.

Konstantin noticed Mihail's arrival and held up his hand, signalling that Mihail should not come any further. Mihail obeyed and Konstantin finished the conversation with his lover. She disappeared and the grand duke beckoned Mihail forward, then went through a door. Mihail followed.

Konstantin was not alone. Another man stood in the room – some sort of study – facing the hearth, his hands clasped behind his back. He was tall; immense in comparison with the diminutive Konstantin.

Konstantin strode across the floor, grasping Mihail's hand in both of his and shaking it vigorously. He seemed warmer than he had done two days before.

'It's good to see you, my boy,' he said.

'You too, sir.' Mihail did not know where the 'sir' came from, but 'Papa' still did not seem appropriate.

Konstantin turned to his companion. 'Here he is then, Sasha.'

The tall figure turned to face them. Mihail recognized him immediately, though he had never before seen him in the flesh. He bowed deeply, driven by the same instinct that had made him call his father 'sir', but magnified a thousand times.

'Your Majesty!' he whispered.

Mihail straightened up to see Konstantin turning once again to his brother, Tsar Aleksandr II. 'Sasha, may I introduce my son, Mihail Konstantinovich.'

The tsar looked Mihail up and down, but did not offer any form of greeting. He turned to his brother.

'He's a fine boy, I'm sure, Kostya, and I know you must be proud of him, but I really don't see the need to be introduced to every one of your offspring.'

Mihail felt much the same. It was all a little excessive. He had revealed himself to Konstantin only for the sake of his mother's memory, not to inveigle his way into royal circles.

'There's a little more to it than that,' Konstantin explained, walking behind Mihail as he spoke. 'This young man, you see, has a very illustrious grandfather.'

'Well of course he does!' snapped the tsar. 'His grandfather is your father – and mine. He was a tsar of Russia as appointed by God. You don't get much more illustrious than that.'

'I was meaning on his mother's side.'

The bemusement on Aleksandr's face reflected Mihail's own feelings.

'I haven't mentioned,' Konstantin continued, 'this young man's surname. It's Danilov. His grandfather was Colonel Aleksei Ivanovich Danilov.'

Aleksandr turned his head a little to one side, as though attempting to hear more clearly. He stood frozen in the pose for perhaps a second, then lunged forward, seemingly on the point of dropping to his knees, but then regained his composure. He grasped Mihail's hand and pulled it to his lips, kissing the knuckle of his middle finger. He stepped back.

'I never got to meet the man – to thank him on behalf of our family. I thank you in his place.'

Mihail had no doubt as to what the tsar meant. He'd heard it all from Tamara, who'd heard it from Aleksei in his dying hours.

Konstantin turned to Mihail. 'I'm sorry to have deceived you the other day, but when you mentioned his name I was too shocked even to think. I could never have dreamed that Tamarushka was Danilov's daughter.'

Mihail thrilled a little at Konstantin's affectionate name for his mother. Suddenly, for the first time he could imagine his mother and father together as a single entity, and himself as *their* son, not just hers. And yet at the same time he couldn't ignore how easily Konstantin had deceived him. Mihail prided himself on his ability to catch people in their dishonesty, and yet his father had been utterly convincing. It was a trait that had helped the Romanovs to survive the centuries.

'I presume you've verified his claim.' Aleksandr had become stiff again after his lapse. Mihail felt a glimmer of pity for him; in how many members of the Romanov dynasty did the blood of the father not run in the veins of the son? Mihail could at least be confident of his mother's side of the family.

'As soon as I heard I went back and looked at Volkonsky's papers,' Konstantin explained. 'Danilov had a daughter, Tamara, who was put into the care of a man called Lavrov and her upkeep paid for by Volkonsky himself. This was when Danilov went into exile after the Fourteenth. The woman I knew was most certainly Danilov's child, and I have no doubt that this is her son – and mine.'

The tsar looked at Mihail gravely. 'Sit down, Mihail Konstantinovich,' he said.

Mihail sat, as did the other two men. The tsar continued.

'You know, I take it, of the great service that your grandfather did for our uncle, Aleksandr I.'

Mihail nodded. 'He and Prince Volkonsky helped Aleksandr to

counterfeit his own death. Aleksandr went on to live the life of a normal man. He called himself Fyodor Kuzmich.'

The tsar sat upright in his chair. 'You even know the name he took?'

Mihail nodded. 'Aleksei told Mama and she told me.'

'But no one else?'

'Iuda tortured my grandfather to get the name, but he failed.' Mihail felt his face redden as he spoke. The image of Iuda ducking his aged grandfather beneath the water and screaming at him for a name was something that Mihail had never witnessed, but his mother's description of it had been vivid. It was adopted memories such as this that kept his hatred for Iuda alive.

'Iuda?' interjected Konstantin.

'Cain,' clarified Mihail.

Aleksandr nodded. 'You know why Cain was so interested in my uncle?'

'Because of Zmyeevich. He believes Pyotr the Great betrayed him. He believes that if he can persuade one of Pyotr's descendants to drink his blood and die with that blood in their veins then they will become, like him, a *voordalak*, and be sway to his will.' Mihail felt momentarily foolish, just as when he had first spoken the word '*voordalak*' in front of his schoolfriends, and they had laughed at his beliefs.

No laughter came from either of those present.

'You can imagine what that would mean if the Romanov in question were tsar,' said Aleksandr grimly.

Mihail nodded. 'That was the genius of what my grandfather and your uncle planned. Once Zmyeevich had tried to wield his influence on Aleksandr – tried and failed – he had no power over any other Romanov of that generation. While Aleksandr lived, Zmyeevich was powerless against any other Romanov, and yet Aleksandr himself – Fyodor Kuzmich – was a nobody.'

'Fyodor Kuzmich died almost twenty years ago,' announced the tsar.

Mihail had guessed as much. 'He outlived my grandfather, then.'

'From what my father told me, Aleksandr regarded Aleksei as a friend.'

'Tsar Nikolai knew, then?'

'Volkonsky told him, but every tsar has known of Zmyeevich. Since the days of Pyotr the knowledge has been passed down. Every tsarevich must be told by his father.' He paused and his face grew sallow. 'It is a duty I have had to perform twice.'

Mihail understood. The current tsarevich, Aleksandr Aleksandrovich, was not the tsar's eldest son. The first tsarevich, Nikolai Aleksandrovich, had died aged just twenty-one. 'And your other brothers? They know too?'

'Just Kostya.'

Mihail swallowed. How was he meant to put the next question? 'And have you . . . heard from Zmyeevich?'

The tsar stood and walked across the room, his hands clasped behind his back once again. He stood in front of a tall mirror and gazed at Mihail in its reflection, as if to prove that Zmyeevich had not taken him already.

'I have seen with his eyes,' he said.

'What?' It was evidently news to Konstantin.

'For the past few months I have seen things that I should not see. I have looked down at my hands and they have not been mine. They are old, and there is a ring shaped like a dragon.'

'You should have told me,' said Konstantin.

'It was just as Papa said it would be, though he never experienced it himself. Aleksandr spared him that.'

'But Zmyeevich has attempted nothing more?' asked Mihail.

'He has not approached me directly, nor sent his emissary.'

'Cain, you mean?'

'Cain must be dead by now, but Zmyeevich will have found another.'

'No,' explained Mihail. 'Cain is not dead. He has become like Zmyeevich, though they're no longer allies.' He paused, unsure how they would take the news. 'I believe that they are both here, in Petersburg.'

'Here?'

'Cain is Zmyeevich's captive.'

'Why hold him captive? Why not kill him?'

'I think Cain has knowledge that Zmyeevich wants. It's unlikely he'd kill him – he had the chance and didn't take it.' Mihail chose not to mention Dmitry. After the awe with which they had spoken of Aleksei, Mihail could not bring himself to reveal the fate of his son.

'How can we help?' asked Aleksandr, returning to his chair.

'I really don't know, not until I have more information. Perhaps you're in a better position to find out than I am.'

'This is not your battle,' said Konstantin.

'You're right,' Mihail answered without hesitation, 'it's not. But to the degree our interests coincide we can help one another.'

'Your interests are not in saving your emperor?' It was hard to tell whether Aleksandr was more astonished or amused.

'I'm interested in only one thing: Iuda – Cain. All I ask is that you leave him for me to deal with. Do what you will with Zmyeevich.'

Aleksandr glanced at his brother, who replied with a shrug. The tsar considered for a moment.

'We'll see how things develop.'

'How shall I contact you?' asked Mihail.

Aleksandr thought for a moment. 'If you need either of us, go to Fontanka 16. You know where that is?'

Mihail eyed his father ruefully and received an apologetic smile in response.

'Ask for Colonel Mrovinskiy,' Aleksandr continued. 'He's the man who escorted you here. He'll convey your messages – or arrange a meeting.'

Aleksandr stood, as did Konstantin a moment later. Mihail took it that their conversation was at an end. He rose to his feet. 'Just one more thing,' he said. 'What do you know about Ascalon?'

The two brothers exchanged glances. Evidently the word meant something to them. It was Konstantin who chose to explain.

'It's a part of the story that no one has ever understood – it may not even be true, but it's been passed down through the family since Pyotr.'

'Go on,' insisted Mihail.

'It dates back to Senate Square in 1712 – just a field then – when Zmyeevich drank Pyotr's blood, and then Pyotr refused to drink his, and Zmyeevich fled. Well, the story also goes that Pyotr took something from him – took Ascalon – and it's for that Zmyeevich hated him most.'

'So you have it – it was passed down?'

Konstantin shook his head. 'What Pyotr did with it, I've no idea. The whole thing may be nothing more than myth. It's said that he hid it – buried it. We don't know what it is, how big it is – nothing.'

'Buried it? Where?'

'Where else would he bury it,' explained the tsar, 'but in his new capital?'

'In Petersburg?'

Aleksandr nodded. 'We don't know the street or the building, but somewhere, perhaps somewhere that you or I walk every day, Ascalon lies waiting.'

News travelled fast. It had been only hours since Iuda had tapped out his message, and now Luka stood before him. Who he might have bribed to gain access to a prisoner in the Peter and Paul Fortress, Iuda did not care to ask. The door slammed shut behind them, locking them in together. Luka walked over and embraced him.

'It's good to see you, Vasya.'

'You too, Luka,' Iuda replied, patting him on the back. They separated and Iuda held him by the shoulders, eyeing him up and down. 'You look well.'

'I wish I could say the same for you,' said Luka. 'It must be hell in here.'

Iuda could not tell how he looked, but he knew he was hungry, so it would not be good. His skin would be wrinkled and dry and his muscles withered. His hair would not have changed colour, but the human eye was happy to see blond as grey when it matched the tone of the skin. It was probably for the best. He had known Luka for over two decades, long enough for the question of his eternal youth to be whispered insidiously by Luka's subconscious.

'No worse for me than for any other comrade,' he said.

Luka nodded. It was hard for Iuda to look at him and not think of Lyosha. The grandson was only a shadow of the grandfather, and yet Iuda feared him, just as Pelias feared Jason – as Pharaoh feared Moses. Luka was the last descendant of Lyosha; the last living descendant – Dmitry did not count. If Luka should ever make contact with his mother and discover the truth about Iuda, then his attitude might be very different.

That was why Iuda had befriended him. After his escape from the cells beneath the Kremlin Iuda had headed for Petersburg. And once in Petersburg he had sought out Luka. He knew the details; Tamara had been an employee of the Third Section and so all the information about her children – the two who died and the one who survived – was on file. Iuda, under yet another alias – though he'd grown to like the Christian name of Vasiliy – made his move. It was a variation upon a theme that had worked well in the past, not least when he inveigled his way into the lives of Lyosha's wife and son, Marfa and Dmitry, so many years before. He worked on Luka's adoptive father first, making a few business deals, then became a friend of the family. Then as the father was away more and more often, thanks to Iuda, he took a special interest in the son, Luka.

It was once Luka had gone to study in Moscow at the Agricultural Academy that he'd shown an interest in politics. He fell under the sway of the radical Sergey Gennadiyevich Nyechayev. Luka didn't speak of it directly, but his occasional references to the lot of the peasants and the need for democracy were enough for Iuda to pick up on. Iuda displayed a little sympathy for the cause and Luka displayed a little more and soon each understood the other; the only hope for Russia lay in the overthrow of the tsar.

Even after Nyechayev had murdered one of Luka's fellow students, the improbably named Ivan Ivanovich Ivanov, Luka's faith in the cause had not been shaken, though he had turned against Nyechayev. Iuda had affected a greater degree of disillusionment, only to draw Luka in more. Before the war against Turkey both of them had been on the peripheries of various underground groups, but the war had changed a great number of things. Many of the revolutionaries, staunch Slavophiles, had gone to the Balkans to protect Serbs and Bulgarians from their Ottoman oppressors. It had thinned out their numbers, but those who returned knew better how to kill. Iuda had marched with the army – though for reasons of his own – while Luka had remained in the motherland. The three years of Iuda's imprisonment had weakened his ties with the revolutionaries, but for Luka it seemed that time had only drawn him closer to their centre.

Today, Nyechayev was Iuda's fellow prisoner, somewhere in one of the fortress's many cells. Messages from and to him travelled through the pipes. He'd been so bold as to ask the People's Will if they could organize an escape, but the reply was curt, pointing out that they had more important things to do. Perhaps Iuda should ask Luka for a similar favour. In his case they might at least give it a try, but in practical terms it was still an absurd idea – and an unnecessary one. Iuda would walk out when he wanted to.

'I heard you were in Petersburg,' Luka told him, 'but I'd no idea you'd been arrested. Have they interrogated you?'

'Not yet,' said Iuda, 'but it will come.' His mind was already racing. How had Luka known he was in the city?

'Do you think you'll be able to stand it?'

'I can only try. Fortunately, I know very little.'

'You know me.'

'Your name will never escape my lips.'

Luka shook his head. 'You don't know what they're capable of.'

'If it came to it . . .' Iuda paused, feigning uncertainty. 'You could smuggle something in for me; something that would mean I could not speak.'

'No.' Luka spoke firmly. 'I'd rather die myself.'

Iuda mentally noted the offer. He changed the subject. 'You said you knew I was in the city? How on earth could you?'

'Through a mutual friend.' Luka grinned. 'Another of your "projects", if I might so describe myself.'

Iuda smiled back. 'You're no project.'

'You know what I mean. I know how you picked me out, in the hope of making something of me. You did just the same with Mihail Konstantinovich.'

'Mihail Konstantinovich?' Iuda's ignorance of the name was genuine.

'Mihail Konstantinovich Lukin. There's no need to pretend, Vasya. He came to visit me.'

'And what did he say?' Iuda's mind stepped through the possibilities. He had encountered a Lukin recently – one of the soldiers in Geok Tepe; a lieutenant. The name had been familiar, but any connection to the long-dead Maksim Sergeivich Lukin seemed unlikely. But if this was the same man who had been there in Turkmenistan then there was only one conclusion to be drawn – that he was working for Dmitry, and therefore, inescapably, for Zmyeevich.

'He told me about how he knew you – how you kept an eye on him after his father died. He said how the two of you had planned to meet here in Petersburg. But he said there was no trace of you. Naturally he presumed you'd come to see me.'

Iuda nodded. It all reeked of Dmitry – he had learned from how Iuda had approached him and Marfa. Who else would know that, and use it to play upon Luka's trust?

'And did Mihail mention anyone else – any other "mutual friends" of ours?'

'No, no one. You're not forgotten though. There are still members of the Executive Committee who remember you and trust you. How do you think your message got to me so swiftly?'

It was true – there were far too many people who could connect him to Luka. Iuda tried to remember faces and names. It could be any one of them – almost anyone.

'So how much did you tell Mihail about me?' he asked.

'Nothing – nothing that he didn't already know.'

Iuda tutted. A clever interrogator could easily make it seem as though he already knew what he'd wheedled out of his subject.

'Did I do wrong?' asked Luka.

'Luka, I've never heard of anyone called Mihail Konstanti-novich Lukin in my entire life.'

'My God!' Luka's hand went to his mouth. 'So he's . . . one of them?'

'We can only presume so. Did he ask anything specific?' Iuda tried to remain calm. It would do no good to puncture the façade of congeniality that he'd created for Luka's benefit.

'Whether I'd seen you. Where you usually stayed in the city. He said he'd tried your club – I didn't know you had one.'

'He asked where I stay? And did you tell him?'

'I'm not stupid, Vasya. I remember what you told me.'

'Have you been there recently?'

'Not for six months – no one had been there.'

'Were you followed?'

There was a flash of anger in Luka's eyes, but it quickly subsided. 'I'm not stupid,' he repeated.

Iuda reached up and touched the young man's cheek, the manacles he still wore forcing him to raise both hands. 'Of course you're not, Luka, but I worry about you – I always have.'

Luka smiled. 'I know you do. But it's you we should be concerned for. We've got to get you out of here. What did they arrest you for?'

'Do they need a reason? They're just fishing.'

'You think you'll be released soon?'

Iuda was sure of it, but he wasn't going to tell Luka his plans.

'I hope so. It always depends on who's running things. I never met the bastard who arrested me before. Chap by the name of Otrepyev – a colonel.'

Iuda studied Luka's face as he spoke, scouring it for a reaction, but none was evident. He could go further and use Dmitry's real name, but Luka wouldn't be ready for that. That all presumed he was lying; Iuda doubted it, but prepared for it.

Luka shook his head. 'I've not heard of him. Must be from Moscow. I'll ask around.'

'You do that, Luka.' It couldn't make things worse.

There was a banging on the cell door and it opened to reveal the scowling face of the sentry. Luka stepped towards Iuda and embraced him once again, whispering, 'Don't worry, Vasya, we'll get you out.' Moments later he was gone, and the door slammed shut.

Iuda slumped to the ground, leaning back against the cold stone wall. It was a shame, but there was no other way. Luka was a useful ally, and if he was to die, Iuda had always hoped it would be in circumstances that in some way punished him for being a Danilov. But he had become too dangerous. He was the only person who knew the location of Iuda's lair in Petersburg – where he kept his real notebooks and his more important blood samples. He hadn't gone to all the effort of luring Zmyeevich and Dmitry to that abandoned cellar under Senate Square only to have them learn of his true hideaway from Luka.

He could have killed Luka there and then. It would have been pleasing to see the surprise on his face, and it would have satisfied Iuda's growing hunger. But he would not have been able to hide the body from the guards, and even they would have guessed what he was. No, Luka must die remotely, by the mere tapping of a cup against pipework.

It was a short message, using codes that Iuda had learned years before when he had first infiltrated the revolutionaries. But on hearing it, no one would be in any doubt. Luka was a spy; an *oprichnik*; an agent of the Ohrana. What his punishment would be was down to the Executive Committee, but their motto had always been '*pour encourager les autres*'. There would be no more risk that Luka would tell what he knew of his Uncle Vasya.

But there was still the matter of Iuda's freedom. There the People's Will would not be called on for help – a higher power was required. Fortunately such a power was just as able to eavesdrop on the tapping of the pipes as any revolutionary. He would start with something simple, but something that would make them prick up their ears. No requests, no demands, just an announcement of who he was. He began to tap again on the pipe.

5,6   2,6 – 1,1 – 2,4 – 3,3

Я Каин

I am Cain

CHAPTER XII

LUKA MARCHED DOWN MAKSIMILIANOVSKY LANE, HIS HANDS deep in his pockets and his eyes fixed on the snowy path in front of him. It was dark now. He had taken a circuitous route back to the apartment, but he'd seen no one following him from the fortress. It hardly mattered – the Ohrana knew about this place anyway. Titov, the *dvornik* – always sitting in his little room at the door, watching who came and went – was in their pay. Luckily, he was in the pay of the People's Will too. That didn't mean he kept quiet to the authorities, but everyone was aware of what he'd told them. At least he was honest in his treachery. Luka preferred that to what Mihail Konstantinovich had done, the way he'd played on Luka's friendship with Vasya.

His thoughts were interrupted by a sharp, penetrating tapping sound, three reports, then a space, then three more, repeatedly. He looked up. The sound was coming from the tavern on the street corner. Someone was at the window, banging against it with a coin or something similar. In a moment he realized who it was: Mihail. Luka returned his gaze to the snow and carried on walking.

He was almost at the door of the house when Mihail caught up with him.

'What do you want?' asked Luka, making no attempt to hide the bile in his voice. He knew that he should string the man along, make him think he was trusted and then use him against his pay-masters, but it was too sickening even to be in his presence.

'I wanted to talk to you again,' Mihail told him. 'I've not been entirely straight with you.'

'Really?' There could be no mistaking the cynicism in Luka's voice.

They had stopped at the door of the building. 'Can I come in?' Mihail asked.

Luka felt the urge to spit in his face, but what good would that do? Perhaps it would be better to take him up to the apartment and then kill him. There was a pistol up there – it would be very easy. But he shouldn't be too hasty. He must report what he had learned to the committee. If Mihail were to die, they would decide and would deal with it safely. If not, they would turn him to good use as a conduit for false information back to the Ohrana. Even so, it would be worth taking him up to the rooms, sitting there with him for a little while to hear him spin out his lies, knowing that the revolver was just a short reach away, hoping that he would force Luka into doing something delightfully rash.

'If you must,' he said.

They went up the stairs and sat down in the living room. This time Luka made no offer of tea.

'So you lied to me,' he said.

Mihail nodded. 'I did, though not entirely.'

'Not entirely?' It was typical of the equivocation of an *ohranik*.

'My connection to you is not through Vasiliy Grigoryevich.'

'You astonish me. Not in that you don't know him, but in that you have the honesty to admit it. But then I suppose you already know that I've been to see Vasiliy. Your spies at the fortress would have told you that. I'm only surprised you heard so quickly.'

'You've found him?'

'Don't play games,' sneered Luka.

'He's at the fortress? The Peter and Paul? A prisoner?'

'A prisoner that you put there – or at least your boss Otrepyev did.'

Mihail's reaction to his colonel's name was evident. He rose to his feet and turned away from Luka, preventing his face from revealing the truth. 'What did Vasiliy say to you?'

'I'm sure there's nothing he could tell me that you don't know already – being such a close friend of his.'

'I've already told you I lied about that.'

'Well then, none of what we said is any of your business.'

Mihail nodded in acceptance. He turned back to face Luka. 'I'm not what you think I am,' he said.

For a moment Luka almost fell for his sincerity. He examined the man. There was not a huge difference in their age – ten years perhaps. They would certainly be considered to be from the same generation. From the way Mihail spoke, he guessed they'd had a similar level of education. Luka was a little taller, though Mihail looked the stronger. What was it that made them different? What event in their early lives had made Luka choose to be a champion of the Russian people and Mihail the acolyte of their oppressor?

'What did you mean earlier?' Luka asked. 'When you implied an association with me other than through Vasiliy?'

Mihail didn't reply. He stood in silence for a full half-minute, looking directly at Luka but deep in thought. When he spoke, the question was obscenely personal.

'Did you ever go to look for your mother – your real mother?'

Luka felt his face redden – in anger more than embarrassment. 'My real mother is the woman who raised me,' he explained coldly.

Mihail gave half a nod. 'Thankfully I've never had to make the distinction.'

'No distinction needs to be made.'

'You think so?'

Luka had thought about it often. 'I am my mind – nothing more. My mind was made by my experience, my parents contributed much to that.'

'As did Vasiliy?' Luka could not account for the cynicism that Mihail managed to inject into his question.

'More so than my birth mother, certainly.'

'But don't you ever wonder about other things, where they might come from? You wouldn't question that your hair or your eyes come from your parents. What about other things, not your whole mind but parts of it perhaps; small parts? Your sense of right and wrong?'

Mihail spoke with a passion that Luka could only admire, enough for him to wonder if, in other circumstances, they might have been friends. And his argument might also serve to answer Luka's original silent question: were the contrasts between them down not to the unique events of their lives, but to difference in their parentage? It was not the way Luka wanted to see the world. He believed that all men were created equal, and moulded as they grew. He had to believe it.

'I told you, my mother went mad. Would you want to inherit that?'

Mihail's lips lost their colour as he pressed them tightly together. His eyes became misty and he turned away from Luka, suppressing an anger whose cause could not be fathomed. He stared down from the window on to the gas-lit street below, his hands clasped behind his back, the thumb of one squeezing so hard on the fingers of the other that they had become white and bloodless. He remained silent for several seconds. When he spoke, it was not to answer Luka's question.

'Shit!'

The emission of the word from Mihail's throat was accompanied by a sudden galvanization of his body – his whole mood. He spun round on his heel.

'What?' asked Luka.

'An *ohranik*,' spat Mihail. 'Out there, on the street.'

Luka glanced involuntarily across the room at one of the faded paintings that hung on the walls. He was not interested in the picture, but hidden there were documents that must not be allowed to fall into the hands of the police. That was where the gun lay too, if needed. In an instant he was looking back at Mihail.

'You're sure?'

'It's Otrepyev, for God's sake!'

So Mihail did know Colonel Otrepyev, just as Vasiliy had predicted. Even so, his reaction was not what might be expected.

'Is he coming up?' Luka asked.

Mihail looked again. 'No. No – he's moving on. He was just talking to the *dvornik*.' Even as he spoke, Mihail was crossing the room, heading for the door. 'Stay here, I'm going after him.'

Luka had no intention of going anywhere. At the door, Mihail paused.

'We still have to talk,' he said earnestly. 'I'll come and find you. I know you don't trust me, but you will, I promise.'

With those words, steeped in faux sincerity, Mihail was gone.

'Where's Luka?'

The question came from Dusya, and was to be expected.

'Don't worry about Luka,' said the chairman sternly. 'He's doing other work essential to our cause.'

Dusya said no more. She was like that. They were all like that – obedient to authority even within an organization dedicated to overthrowing authority. Their only freedom was to choose whom they would obey. But the need to obey someone was what made them, underneath it all, serfs. Most of the aristocrats of Europe were serfs in that sense. Only a select few ruled themselves.

This meeting of the Executive Committee was held in a different apartment, this one on Voznesensky Prospekt, the long, straight thoroughfare that split Petersburg into east and west, meeting with Nevsky Prospekt as they converged on the Admiralty. There was only one item of business. The chairman was not happy with it, but there was nothing he could do. There were some matters over which even he would not be obeyed. He glanced at Sofia and she stood up. She dared look at no one as she spoke.

'As some of you may already have heard, Comrade Kletochnikov has been arrested.'

Gasps filled the room, though not from everyone. For some the name Kletochnikov meant nothing – such was the need for secrecy. Sofia explained.

'For the past two years Nikolai Vasilyevich Kletochnikov has worked as a filing clerk at Fontanka 16, first for the Third Section and now for the Ohrana. In all that time, he has in truth been a loyal member of the People's Will. Some of you may have heard of him as the Protecting Angel. He reported whatever came across his desk that might be of use to us. He's saved many from arrest with his information.'

'But not himself,' said Kibalchich grimly.

'There's been too many arrests recently,' said Bogdanovich. 'Somebody's been talking.'

The chairman raised a finger to silence him. 'Let Sofia proceed.'

'We think you're right,' said Sofia. 'And we think we know who it is.' She looked at each face in the room in turn, as if testing each one to reveal its guilt, though she knew that the traitor was not present.

'Kletochnikov was arrested on Wednesday,' she continued. 'In the early hours of Friday morning another arrest was made, that of a comrade who has been away from Petersburg for many years, but who has always remained loyal. He was taken to the Peter and Paul Fortress. His name is Vasiliy Grigoryevich Chernetskiy.'

A few faces around the room nodded in recognition of the name, as well they might.

'What was he doing back in Petersburg?' asked the chairman, though he would be surprised to receive an answer.

'We don't know,' admitted Sofia, 'but we believe that the reason for his arrest is that he was about to unmask the collaborator who betrayed Kletochnikov.'

'We all know who Vasiliy Grigoryevich would visit first on his return to the city, don't we?' said Zhelyabov.

Sofia glanced at Dusya, but her eyes were glued to the floor.

'We can't make guesses like that,' said Kibalchich. 'Now they're both locked up, we'll never know.'

'We can and we do know,' countered Sofia. 'Kletochnikov is incarcerated where he worked, at Fontanka 16. We won't hear a word from him. But the Pyetropavlovskaya Fortress is a different matter. We received a message from Chernetskiy today.'

'Saying?' asked Kibalchich.

'Saying that Luka Miroslavich Novikov betrayed both him and Kletochnikov.'

'No!' The word came as a whisper from Dusya's throat – more of a prayer than a denial.

'Can we trust Chernetskiy?' asked Kibalchich. 'Especially after so long?' He was addressing the chairman.

'I've never met Vasiliy Grigoryevich,' the chairman admitted, glad not to be forced to make the decision. 'He was before my time.'

'I'd trust him with my life,' said Sofia firmly.

'I too,' added Zhelyabov.

There were general nods of the head from those who knew the man. Only Dusya dared object.

'Can we be sure it *was* Chernetskiy who sent the message?' she asked. 'A prisoner tapping against a pipe has no face.'

'He used a codeword that we recognized, Dusya,' Sofia explained. 'I'm sorry.'

'What was the codeword?' Dusya asked.

'"Susanna".'

Dusya nodded meekly and returned her eyes to the floor.

'So what do we do?' asked the chairman, though he could already guess the decision of the committee.

'We should question Luka,' said Kibalchich firmly.

'And let him tell us more lies?' countered Sofia. 'We can't even risk him guessing we're on to him. We must be swift and brutal.'

'Sofia's right,' agreed Zhelyabov. 'Luka doesn't know our exact plans for the tsar, but he knows all of us. If we deal with him now we may be able to cut out the rot. If he thinks we're about to act, he might have us arrested en masse.'

'What do you think, Dusya?' asked the chairman gently.

'I can't question your reasoning,' she replied. 'And we can't allow sentiment to turn us from our course. If Luka is guilty, he must die. If he is innocent, he would understand the sacrifice he has made.'

The chairman almost sniggered at the perversity of her logic; these people had managed to delude themselves quite thoroughly.

'There's only one thing to do then,' announced Sofia. 'We vote.'

The chairman could not prevent it. 'Very well,' he agreed. There was nothing like democracy to wash the blood from one's hands.

There was only one place to be in Petersburg on that morning, Sunday 1 February: at the funeral of Fyodor Mihailovich Dostoyevsky. He was to be interred at the Tihvin Cemetery at the Aleksandr Nevsky Monastery, alongside Glinka and Krylov and other great Russians, but none so great as him.

Mihail followed the path beside the Yekaterininsky Canal and then turned on to Nevsky Prospekt, named after the monastery to which it led. The road was densely packed, the rich in carriages, the poor on foot – all heading in the same direction; all to pay honour to the same man.

As he walked, Mihail considered his encounters of the day

before; one with his father and his uncle, another – two others – with his brother. Speaking to the tsar Mihail had realized what he should always have known: that it was impossible to surgically isolate his search for vengeance against Iuda from Zmyeevich's vendetta against the Romanovs. Zmyeevich and Iuda might no longer be allies, but their lives were intertwined. Mihail would gladly help the tsar in his fight against Zmyeevich, as long as their two fights were the same.

But there was always another possibility. Aleksandr and Iuda were both enemies of Zmyeevich, and might each not think that his enemy's enemy was his friend? Then where would Mihail be? Would he be able to take on Aleksandr and even perhaps his own father if they sided with Iuda? He would have to, though he prayed events wouldn't come to that. And yet the Romanovs would always do what was best for their dynasty.

He was equally torn over Luka. At their second meeting yesterday he had been on the brink of revealing the truth of their relationship – that they were half-brothers – but had funked it at the last moment. Seeing Dmitry out on the street below had been a shock, but it was probably to the good. Now wasn't the time to tell Luka. It would have been easier if Mihail hadn't lied in the first place. Luka naturally had greater loyalty to Iuda than he would have to a brother he didn't even know existed. But Mihail needed to discover where Iuda was – and in that he'd succeeded. Why Dmitry should have had him locked in the fortress was beyond Mihail's understanding, but he would be safe there for now.

And Luka would come round eventually, however much his politics made him fearful of all those around him, and however much he insisted that the ties of blood meant nothing to him. A brother could not be separated from a brother. All it would take was time, and they had plenty of that.

Mihail's pursuit of Dmitry had been short-lived. By the time he had got to the street the *voordalak* had gone. Mihail had chosen a direction at random, and then another at the next junction, but he wasn't in luck. He wondered what Dmitry had been doing there. Perhaps he'd come to visit Luka but had learned of Mihail's presence from the *dvornik* and changed his mind. It certainly went to prove that there was a connection between him and Luka. It was another thing he would talk to his brother about when the time was right, revealing to him not just a long-lost brother but an uncle to boot; though not an uncle to be proud of.

And there was one other benefit to Dmitry's visit the previous day. Mihail now knew that there was something hidden in that apartment. It might be papers, or explosives, or both. And Mihail knew pretty much exactly where it was. He'd seen Luka's furtive glance at the picture on the wall, wondering if his secret would be revealed. Soon Mihail would find an opportunity to see just what lay behind. Brotherly love was not strong enough to stop him in that.

After the Nikolaievsky Vokzal, the station where Mihail had first arrived in the city, Nevsky Prospekt kinked slightly to the right before heading directly to the monastery. From here Mihail, and those around him, could see the folly of their journey. Not far ahead, the road was packed. Those in carriages had no hope of progress; those on foot might squeeze forward a little further, but would have to fight their way through to get anywhere close to the ceremony, the speeches and the burial itself. There must have been tens of thousands trying to say their farewells to the great novelist. Mihail felt a little pride at being Russian. In what other nation would a man of words instil such affection in the common people?

But Mihail knew he did not need to push his way through the throng in order to mourn – that could be done anywhere. He turned round and headed back towards the centre of town. The crowds quickly thinned as he made his way up Nevsky Prospekt, finally slipping between the Winter Palace and the Admiralty to gaze out on the great white expanse of the frozen Neva. Across the ice the fortress could be clearly seen, the spire of the Peter and Paul Cathedral looming inside it. Somewhere in there, in a deep, dark cell, unlit by the winter sun, lurked his enemy. It was safe enough to leave him there for now, but soon Mihail would have to act.

He turned left and strolled along the quayside. He had been in Petersburg for less than a week, but he was beginning to gain some sense of familiarity with it. Tamara had told him much about the place, and every street he walked down, every river or canal he crossed, he had only to associate with the name that was already lodged in his mind. Soon he found himself on the edge of Senate Square, the place where his grandfather's life had changed for ever – both his grandfathers' lives.

He looked out across the ice again and tried to imagine the precise spot at which Aleksei had shot Iuda, and then cradled him, and then realized that he would not die but become undead. It was close to there too that he had been arrested, to be sent into exile in Siberia for thirty years. It had ruined Tamara's life, but she had forgiven him for it. Mihail saw the man with better perspective – saw his flaws as well as his patriotism – and knew how both existed in Mihail himself, much as he might fight them. It was what he'd been telling Luka the previous day. They were both sons of Tamara and grandsons of Aleksei. Mihail was the lucky one; he was aware of it, but in the end Luka would not be able to elude his destiny.

Mihail looked at his injured hand. There was no need for a bandage any more and there was only a slight scar, which would heal. It still hurt when he flexed his fingers, but like the scar the pain would fade. He was luckier than Aleksei, who had lost two of his fingers when only a little older than Mihail, and then later the tip of a third. He turned inland and tramped across Senate Square. It had snowed recently and his were among the first footsteps to break through the glistering whiteness of what lay before him. Soon he was at the foot of the statue of Pyotr – the Bronze Horseman, as Pushkin had unintentionally named it.

'Not going to the funeral?'

The question was posed in French. Mihail turned. An old man had emerged from the far side of the statue, where he had been hidden from view behind the Thunder Stone. The word 'old' was inadequate. Even 'wizened' did not quite do him justice. He was bent forward and moved his feet by only the smallest amount on each step, though he carried no stick. A thick, woolly *ushanka* was pulled down tight over his head, hiding whatever hair he might have had. He was clean-shaven but for a long moustache of purest white, scarcely paler than the wrinkled skin that sucked into his hollow cheeks. He was almost too old –

like a younger man in stage make-up, though close up Mihail could see that his flesh was quite real. He was certainly eighty – possibly ninety.

'It's too busy,' Mihail replied, sticking with French. Given the age of the man, he might have grown up at a time when that was the first language of the aristocracy. 'Fyodor Mihailovich will be buried well enough without me.' The old man gave a short laugh. 'How about you?' Mihail asked.

'I've stood by enough graves in my time.'

'A soldier?'

'For a while.'

Mihail wasn't in uniform, and didn't feel the need to point out his own, so far insignificant military career. 'Were you here?' he asked instead, on a whim. 'When it all happened?'

'Here?'

'14 December 1825.'

The man shook his head with a tight, rapid motion. 'No, I was somewhere else. But I heard tell of it.' Mihail wondered whether, even now, the old soldier was lying to hide his part in a rebellion against his tsar. 'Three thousand men standing against Nikolai Pavlovich,' the man continued. 'But they didn't have a chance. Nikolai was strong. Just like him, up there.' He nodded towards the statue of Pyotr, mounted on horseback.

'He was a great man,' said Mihail, instantly regretting the platitude.

'Funny way to pose him though – pretending he's Saint George.'

Mihail turned. No one other than his mother had ever mentioned the similarity before. 'How do you mean?' he asked, happy to let the old man share his memories, and curious too.

'Don't you see it? Victorious; on horseback; with the vanquished serpent at his feet. Just like in all those icons. Of course, you see them more in Moscow than round here. And have you noticed how they always show the dragon's tail just curling around the horse's leg, as if he's about to topple George from it, even as he raises Ascalon high in the air to deliver—'

Mihail's heart pounded. 'Ascalon?' he interrupted.

'Ascalon. Nobody remembers. It was George's sword. Like Arthur's Excalibur or Beowulf's Hrunting. Though some say it was a lance, not a sword, but I don't suppose that made too much difference to the dragon, eh?' He emitted a wheezy laugh.

'I suppose not,' muttered Mihail, deep in thought. At last he had a meaning for the word, though it was hard to see how it was connected to Iuda or Zmyeevich. And yet it had come about from a discussion of the statue of Pyotr. It was too much for coincidence.

'I can tell you've had enough of me,' said the old man. Mihail tried to object, but the man raised his hand. 'Anyway, I'm starting to feel the cold. It's been pleasant talking to you.'

Mihail murmured a goodbye and watched as the old man hobbled across the square in the direction of Saint Isaac's, his shadow a long black streak across the snow. Mihail watched him for a little while, then turned back to the statue, pondering what, if anything, he had discovered.

Luka looked at the note once again.

> My dearest Luka,
>   Meet me at two o'clock on the corner of Nevsky and Kalashnikovsky Prospekts. It is urgent. Tell no one; your life may depend on it.
>   With my undying love,
>   Dusya

It was a quarter past now. It was a stupid place to meet, but Dusya had probably not considered the masses that would be attracted to the monastery by Dostoyevsky's funeral. They were close here and the crowds were thick; still slowly trudging along Nevsky Prospekt. Luka tried to examine every face, in search of Dusya, but she was small and might easily get lost among the jostling bodies.

He had seen one face that he knew – the ugly, flat nose of Rysakov, or was it Glazov? One name was genuine, the other an alias, but Luka couldn't remember which. They might both be fake, such was the need for security. They hadn't spoken much recently; Rysakov had been given some covert assignment by the Executive Committee and secrecy was deemed essential; an honour for one so young, only nineteen. It wasn't so surprising to see him there, hoping to pay homage to the great novelist. The revolutionary movement had always been in two minds about Dostoyevsky. Without question they saw him as a writer of genius, a man who understood the heart of the Russian people; and they knew of his younger days as a radical, of how he'd even stood in front of a firing squad for his beliefs, only to be reprieved and exiled to Siberia. But he'd become a reactionary, loving God and, worse, loving his tsar more than he did his fellow man. And he'd grown to hate revolutionaries.

Devils – that's what he called them; made it the title of a novel. It was only a slight exaggeration. Luka had been there, at the Agricultural College in Moscow in 1869. He'd been a follower of Nyechayev, but only on the periphery. Their fellow student, Ivanov, had seen through Nyechayev sooner than anyone else and questioned his authority – and his honesty. Nyechayev and a few of his cronies – not Luka – had murdered him for it. Dostoyevsky had turned it into fiction, but all who read it knew the truth. But it was an exceptional case, not the general rule. Nyechayev was a charlatan – there were a few in the movement, but they were rare. The People's Will was prepared to kill – but it would only be for the good of the people.

Even Dostoyevsky had come to see it, if the rumours were true. His next novel had been planned to follow on from *The Brothers Karamazov*, where the pious Alyosha would leave the monastery and himself become a revolutionary. But Fyodor Mihailovich would not have kept things simple. Who could say whether Alyosha's new calling would be for good or ill? Only one man knew, and soon he would be in the embrace of Russia's soil.

And then through the crowd Luka saw a head of blonde hair that he recognized. It was not Dusya's glimmering flaxen, but a little darker. Beneath it was the unmistakable high forehead of Sofia Lvovna. She of all people was unlikely to come to an event such as this. Luka remembered the words of Dusya's note. '*Tell no one; your life may depend on it.*' By 'no one' she could only mean members of the Executive Committee. Luka wondered what he could have done to arouse their displeasure, but he could think of nothing. It must be a mistake.

He looked again and Sofia was at his side. She held something hard against his ribs. A gun? A knife? He couldn't tell. He heard her voice in his ear.

'Come with me, Luka Miroslavich. Don't make a fuss.'

It was a straightforward enough request. Why shouldn't he just go with her? They would talk. They'd sort things out. All of them were reasonable people. But he remembered what had happened to Ivanov. Things had got worse since then. Sofia was desperate – they all were. He could hear it in her voice. She was afraid, and that meant he should be afraid of her. She wasn't here to talk; she was here to kill – unless he could prevent it. He shoved with both hands and she stepped back away from him. Soon the crowd had enveloped her like waves coming in from the sea. Luka turned down Kalashnikovsky Prospekt and started to walk briskly.

The crowds began to thin. A few figures milled around, looking for a better route to the monastery along a side street, but Luka stuck to the prospekt. He glanced over to the other side of the road and saw that a figure was shadowing him, and realized in the same instant that it was Zhelyabov. Luka quickened his pace, but Zhelyabov's long strides easily kept him level.

Luka briefly turned his head to glimpse what was behind him, and saw three figures that he knew: Sofia and Rysakov, whom he had already seen, plus Mihail Fyodorovich Frolenko. None of them bothered to call out to him, or even to raise a hand in greeting. Conversation was not their intent.

Luka broke into a run. The road itself had become a trap, with the high walls of the Cattle Market meaning he could not turn off to the left. On the right Zhelyabov, now running too, prevented any escape and behind Luka knew that Sofia and the others would be keeping close. His only chance was to move forward. Ahead lay the river. With luck there would be people on it – walking as they did every winter when it was frozen. He was there moments later, but the river was quiet. Not empty, but with none of the swarming masses that there had been on Nevsky Prospekt. He should have stayed there, in the crowd – but even there a silent blade slipped between the ribs would have allowed the assailant to steal away unnoticed.

The bank down to the river was steep; it would take too long to negotiate. Instead Luka turned left, sticking to the wall of the Cattle Market. There was no real path here, just snow-covered, frozen mud. It made for slow progress, but it would have the same effect on the others. He risked turning to look, and saw that they were now some way behind, further hindered by having to move in single file. Luka could count only three of them, but didn't waste time trying to spot a fourth. He pressed on, seeing that the end of the wall was in sight and knowing that there he would be able to turn back inland and perhaps make good his escape.

But then the path was blocked. It was Frolenko. He must have cut through the Cattle Market – closed and abandoned on a Sunday – and found some gateway out to the river. As Luka approached he could see the narrow gap in the wall. He slowed to walking pace and then finally stopped a few paces in front of Frolenko. They were of about the same stature. Luka might get past him, but in the time it took, the others would be upon him. He turned. They were close now; Zhelyabov in front, Sofia and Rysakov at the rear. Rysakov carried a revolver in his hand, but had not raised it.

Now it seemed there was no option but to talk, to try to clear up whatever confusion had led them to this moment. He opened his hands in a gesture of friendship and breathed in, preparing to say he knew not what. But he could see in none of their eyes the willingness to talk. He chose not to speak but to shout.

'Help!' he screamed. He had never produced such a sound before, but neither had he been so close to death. 'Murder!' There were still a few passers-by, walking or skating along the river, trying to get to the funeral by a back route. They were some distance away, but surely they'd hear him.

He felt Frolenko's hand across his mouth and then the full weight of Zhelyabov's shoulder hitting him in the chest, knocking him backwards into the Cattle Market. Frolenko landed underneath him and wriggled away as Zhelyabov moved forward, sitting on Luka's chest and pinning his arms. Luka was winded but still managed to shout and scream, not knowing or caring what words came out of him, hoping only to attract some attention and the chance of salvation.

He felt a hand pressing against his mouth, trying to silence him

– a small, dainty, female hand. He looked up into the eyes of Sofia, but saw only malevolence in them as she pushed down to stop his screaming. He tried to think of the kindness and simplicity in Dusya's eyes, and prayed that he would live to see them again.

He bit hard and tasted blood. Sofia emitted a startled yelp and withdrew her hand. Luka began to scream again, louder even than before. He felt the back of Zhelyabov's fist catch him heavily across the jaw. Now it hurt him to scream, but still it didn't stop him. He kicked and thrashed, but he was no match for the huge frame that held him down. He heard Sofia speak.

'Give it to me.'

He looked and saw Rysakov handing her something – the gun he had been carrying. She held it to the left-hand side of Luka's head.

He heard the sound of the blast in his right ear and felt burning to the side of his face. In the other ear there was nothing – he could sense the absence of sound like a void. He noticed too that he had stopped screaming. He could feel his mouth and his throat, but had forgotten how to command them. He could now only see with one eye, though whether the other was filled with blood or whether he was blind, he could not tell.

He felt Zhelyabov relax his hold, and chose the moment to kick with all his strength. The big man fell sideways and Luka was on his feet. His head was exploding with pain and he could barely see. He ran forward, hoping it would take him back out on the river, where he might get help. The ground vanished and he was slipping down a slope, then he felt hard smooth ice beneath his fingertips. He crawled forward, but then hands grabbed him. He hoped for a moment that they might be friendly, but found himself being dragged brutally along.

Then the ice vanished and Luka sensed cold, flowing water close to his nose. A hand grabbed his hair and pushed his head downwards. His face became instantly numb as the river enveloped it. Cold tendrils of water infiltrated his nostrils and mouth. He pushed upwards and found himself for a moment above the surface and able to breathe. He heard Sofia's voice whisper in his ear.

'Thus perish all traitors.'

At last he rediscovered the ability to scream, but at the same moment the water took him again, absorbing the sound and snatching the air that created it. Luka lay still, his lungs empty, the hands on his back and head preventing any movement. He willed himself not to breathe, and managed it for a few seconds.

But then his body rebelled, his mouth opened and his lungs howled as the icy water hit them.

CHAPTER XIII

LUKA'S DEATH MADE THE NEWSPAPERS ON THURSDAY, THE DAY after his body was found. Mihail had suspected something. He'd called on Luka several times and never found him home. On Wednesday evening he saw gendarmes standing at the door of the house on Maksimilianovsky Lane, and walked on by. On Thursday he learned the truth.

The reports were guarded, but one thing was thankfully clear: Luka had not been killed by a vampire. The wounds did not match up; the bullet to the head was not the ultimate cause of death, but neither that nor the actual drowning could be the handiwork of Zmyeevich, Dmitry or Iuda.

It was only by luck that the body had been found. It should either have been washed out to sea or remained shrouded by the frozen river until spring, but there were always a few holes in the ice, and the corpse had snagged against one of them, just where the Great Nevka split away from the Neva. Whoever had killed him had not wanted the body to be found. To Mihail's mind there were two possibilities: either Luka had been running from the Ohrana and their attempts to capture him had gone too far, or he had been killed by his own side – either rightly or falsely taken for a police informer. They were quite capable of it. Mihail remembered hearing a few years before of a government informer called Gorinovich. They'd lured him to a railway siding in Odessa where they'd stabbed him and then poured quicklime on his face so that he wouldn't be recognized. But he'd survived and staggered to safety, the label they'd pinned to his chest still clear to read: 'Witness the fate of a spy.' If it was the People's

Will who'd killed Luka then they'd been more efficient and less ostentatious about it.

But whatever the direct cause, Mihail could see how convenient Luka's death was for Iuda, eliminating one of the few people who knew anything about him. Iuda was locked away in the Peter and Paul Fortress, but Mihail knew that would be little hindrance to his achieving what he wanted. Luka had visited Iuda the day before his death; he would have spoken of Mihail and his questions. Had it been enough for Iuda to realize the danger that Luka might pose to him?

If that were the case then Mihail was responsible for Luka's murder. In the space of just a few weeks he'd lost a mother and a brother. He searched his heart to find true sorrow at Luka's death, but he could not. He pitied him as a stranger, a man he had met just twice. It went against his point of view, the one he'd pressed when talking to Luka, that blood – the family bond – was the strongest tie in existence. He should have told Luka the truth – told him that they were brothers. Then at least they'd have been able to judge each other fairly. Perhaps Mihail would still have felt none of the affection that one brother should hold for another, but at least he would have been certain.

The Ohrana had spent all of Thursday and most of Friday searching the apartment, preventing Mihail from making his own investigation. Instead, he'd followed up another unlikely lead – the apartment on Konyushennaya Street. The bookshop underneath that Tamara had spoken of was still there, but neither its proprietor nor the new tenants above had heard of Iuda, by any of his names. It had never been likely, but it was best to be certain. Luka's rooms would be of far greater interest.

Now, on the Friday afternoon, all was quiet on Maksimilianovsky Lane. A solitary gendarme stood guard at the door, chatting occasionally to the *dvornik*. It was possible that there were still other police up there, but no one had gone in or out for a very long time.

Mihail walked boldly down the street and then mounted the steps of the building; not of number 15, but number 17, next door. He was in luck. The *dvornik* there was asleep, his snoring wafting gently across the hallway. If he'd been awake Mihail had

204

a story about a romantic liaison worked out, and the bribe to back it up, but it proved unnecessary. The house was the mirror image of its neighbour. Mihail climbed the stairs up to the first half-landing. There, just as he'd expected, was a small window looking out behind the building. It opened easily. Beyond was a tiny yard, the overgrown weeds punctuated only by rubbish from the stacked apartments on all four sides. Everything covered with undisturbed snow.

Mihail stuck his head and shoulders through the small gap and looked right towards number 15. The equivalent window was there, just as he'd remembered it, but the wall between them was flat and smooth, and there was no way he could climb across. He pulled himself back in and ascended two more flights. Here, on the half-landing, was a similar window. Looking out he saw that it was directly above the first, with another in between. He reached into his bag and brought out a rope, securing it to the banister. He threw it out and watched it fall and dangle, just outside the first window.

He crept back downstairs and climbed out, using the rope to support himself, then, hanging from it, traversed across the featureless wall until his toes were perched on the window ledge of number 15. He brought out a knife and eased the sash up a little. It wasn't locked. Soon he had it open and was inside. He pulled the rope in afterwards so that it could not swing back without him. He went down a few steps and peeked round the corner. He could see the gendarme standing in the doorway, performing his duty to protect the building from unauthorized entrants.

Mihail tiptoed up to apartment 7. There was no guard on the door here. In truth, there was not much of a door. The *ohraniki* had evidently taken an axe to it in order to gain access, and had not bothered to replace it.

Inside it seemed they had been thorough but tidy in their search. The chairs and other furniture were roughly where Mihail had seen them before, but the fabric of the divan had been slashed open to allow a hand to delve inside in search of whatever secrets might be found there. Tufts of stuffing were scattered sparsely across the floor. The samovar had been moved to the other end of the table. As Mihail had noted on his first visit, there was quite deliberately little to find in this place.

He looked into the other two rooms. Both were bedrooms. The one on the left was as unlived-in as the main room. There was a bed, but the bedding had been thrown on the floor. It was rumpled, but seemed clean. There was a wardrobe and a washstand, but nothing that hinted of a personal effect. He opened the window. It looked out on to that same yard. From above hung his rope, stretching diagonally down to another window below. It was beyond reach, but not by much.

He went back and grabbed a length of wood from the remnants of the door. It had a nail sticking out of the end which would serve as a hook. Within seconds he had the rope. He pulled it in and wrapped it around his makeshift fishing rod so that it would not fall back. Now he could make a quicker exit, if needed.

The other bedroom was clearly the one that Luka had normally used. The bedlinen smelt of human sweat. There were clothes here too. Some of them were women's; Dusya's, he guessed. How would she be taking the news of her lover's death? As stoically as he himself had, Mihail would have to assume. They both had their hatreds: he of Iuda; she of the tsar. It was an effective immunization against sorrow.

He went back to the living room. He'd expected the *ohraniki* to have done their job thoroughly and so there was really only one place they might not have looked. The pictures still hung on the wall, but they could easily have been removed and replaced. Mihail went over to the one that Luka had glanced at when afraid. It was a watercolour, a cheap copy of a view of Moscow by Alekseyev. Mihail lifted it off the wall.

Behind it the wallpaper had been neatly slashed in the shape of a cross – one vertical stroke, one horizontal. Looking more closely Mihail could see that this was in fact a separate square of wallpaper, of the same pattern that covered the remainder of the room, but pasted over at this point. Behind the flapping corners he could see a cavity in the wall beyond. Luka – or someone else – must have removed a few bricks to create the hole, put whatever he wanted in there and then concealed his work with both the wallpaper and the picture. An alert *ohranik* had not been fooled, but had removed the painting, cut through the paper and uncovered whatever lay within.

Mihail reached inside. It was cold and a little damp in there, but nothing of its contents remained. He looked behind the other pictures in the room, but in each case the wall was solid. He sat down on the same chair he had used when first visiting Luka. So he had been right in guessing where Luka kept his secrets, but had been beaten to the chase. He went over and lifted the picture from the wall again, desperately groping around in the cavity behind in the hope that they – and he – might have missed something. He was about to hang the painting again when he noticed something odd about it.

Instead of the usual cheap brown paper, the picture was backed with wallpaper – the same wallpaper that had been used to cover the hole. He ripped it away and at last found what he was looking for – or at least found something. It was a letter. The envelope was unsealed and unaddressed. Mihail leaned the picture against the wall and pulled out the single sheet of paper from inside the envelope. Handwriting filled one side.

To the manager, Hôtel d'Europe, Saint Petersburg,
As we discussed, please allow the bearer unhindered access to my apartments in order that he may manage my affairs until my return.
Yours faithfully,
Collegiate Councillor Vasiliy Grigoryevich Chernetskiy

Mihail clicked his tongue. It was the only hint he gave of his excitement, both to have a clue that might lead him to Iuda, under whatever pseudonym he went by, and also to have been smarter than the Ohrana.

He quickly checked the other pictures, but none had been similarly used as a hiding place. He sat again and considered. This would be his only chance to search the apartment. Was there anything he'd missed?

His thoughts were interrupted by the sound of feet on the stairs outside. He heard a shout. Perhaps it was not the Ohrana and perhaps they were not coming here, but he wasn't going to stay to find out. He slipped the letter into his pocket and went back to the bedroom, unhitching the rope and clambering out across the windowsill. Already he could hear that they had entered the apartment.

'Someone's been here. How the hell did they get past you?'

Mihail did not wait for the response. He slid down and across and in seconds was at the next-door window, moments later through it. He skipped briskly down the stairs and out of the building. The *dvornik* was still asleep.

Out on the street he looked towards the door of number 15, but even the gendarme had gone – rushing upstairs to be upbraided by his superior. There was no need for Mihail even to run. He sauntered calmly away.

'You're free to go.'

They were evidently not words that the sentry regarded as a part of his duty to recite, and so he made no effort to hide his childish disappointment. Iuda looked up from where he sat on his straw mattress and smiled broadly.

'Colonel Otrepyev has relented then?'

'This came from higher up.'

Iuda had not expected any different. It had taken a few days and countless messages sent and received through the pipes. The People's Will had little idea that their communication system might be shared with at least one quite distinct set of individuals, whose identity they would despise if they knew it. It was foolish of them. Did Alexander Graham Bell think his new invention would be reserved exclusively for the use of himself and his friends?

The deal was done. Iuda received his freedom and in return all he had to do was visit a certain building at a certain time and discuss an arrangement with a certain highly placed dignitary. The deal would be to their mutual advantage, but even in offering it Iuda had ensured his freedom. But there was never a question in his mind that he would fulfil his side of the bargain.

He took one last look around his cell. He had been here only a week, far less than in his previous gaol. He glanced up at the little window, high above. It was dark now. That was thoughtful on the part of the man who had ordered his release. There would be no hanging around just inside the gates of the fortress, looking for excuses to delay his departure. Everyone he encountered, it seemed, wanted to ensure he remained alive. It was not by accident. He could only congratulate himself on having become so indispensable.

He was escorted through Saint Peter's Gate and the Ivan Gate. Only then did they unlock his manacles and allow him to cross the Petrovsky Bridge on his own. He was free. In his head he knew that his first thought should be for safety – not personal safety but the safety of his possessions. Luka was dead – Iuda had heard that through the pipes – but that didn't mean he hadn't let slip some information about Iuda's rooms at the Hôtel d'Europe. There was much there that he treasured.

But he could not deny his nature. He was a *voordalak*, and however much he might insist to himself that he was different and that his brain ruled his actions, he still, like any of them, needed sustenance. He could have taken one of the guards once he was out of his cell, and would still have escaped easily, but that would not have pleased the man who had ordered his liberation. And it would have had to be quick. Much better to slip into the dark streets of Petersburg and hunt at leisure.

Once off the bridge he doubled back on himself and walked along the path beside the Kronversky Channel, separating Hare Island, on which the fortress stood, from the larger Petersburgsky Island. Some former inmates might have tried to get away from the place of their captivity as quickly and directly as possible, but Iuda enjoyed his freedom more for the sight of the building that had contained him. Even so it was soon behind him. He stepped down on to the ice and crossed the Lesser Neva to Vasilievskiy Island. Minutes later he was among the Twelve Colleges, at the heart of Petersburg's university. It was busy here with students – both rich and poor – out in search of an evening's entertainment.

It was nothing compared to Oxford. It reeked of modernity. Iuda had already been forty-one years old when Petersburg University was founded. Oxford was founded before . . . before even Zmyeevich was born. Iuda could not say he had enjoyed his time at Trinity, though he had certainly benefited from it. The young Richard Cain desired solely to learn of the natural world, but in those days that was only just beginning to be considered a subject suitable for gentlemanly study. His tutors had instructed him in languages, divinity and history, all of which would ultimately prove useful to him, but in studying and understanding science he had been forced to teach himself – dragging knowledge from those few dons who possessed it, instead of having it forced into him as with the other subjects.

On graduating he chose to travel, and managed to bluff his way aboard a merchant vessel – the *White Hart* – as an apprentice to the ship's surgeon. They sailed south, then through the Strait of Gibraltar and into the Mediterranean. It was quite unplanned, but there the ship became part of the great battle between Napoleon and Nelson for the possession of Egypt.

The *White Hart* and its crew – Cain included – had been captured by the French frigate *Artémise* which had in turn been sunk by the British at the Battle of the Nile. Cain had managed to salvage his notebooks, and a little of the captain's stash of Louis d'Or, then thrown himself to the mercy of the waves. At the age of just twenty he found himself alone, washed up on an Egyptian beach.

He made his way east, following the path of the Israelites, but rounding the tip of the Gulf of Suez rather than waiting for the waters to part so that he could march straight through. He did not linger in the Holy Land but continued north, noting as he went the remarkable fauna he encountered, quite unlike anything he had observed in England. He arrived at the Black Sea coast in the town of Samsun and there, with little real direction to his wanderings but the desire to learn, found a passage to Yalta on the Crimean Peninsula. It was the first time he set foot on Russian soil, little knowing that the country was to become his second home.

It was his detailed study of wildlife in the Crimea that gained him, on his eventual return to England, his fellowship at the Royal Society. He catalogued several species that were previously quite unknown in the West and provided details of the life cycle of many others. His favourite creature – the vampire excepted, of which he had encountered none since leaving Esher – was the scolopendra. He had seen centipedes and the like in England,

and on his travels, but it was the venomous bite and carnivorous temperament of these creatures that fascinated him most. In later years he heard of relatives from South America that grew to over a foot in length and would devour creatures as large as bats and could defend themselves against tarantulas. In the Crimea he only witnessed them feeding on other insects and once a small lizard. Perhaps his life would have been different if his travels had taken him to that distant continent, but he had no regrets.

It was also on that first visit to the Crimea that he reached Bakhchisaray and climbed up to the citadel of Chufut Kalye to explore its caves. Even then he had remarked how the steep cliffs around it had created what, with a little human intervention, might become an inescapable prison – a fortress built by nature for herself against infection and the hand of war – but he had not then guessed what manner of creature his prisoners might be.

In total he spent six years in the Crimea, venturing occasionally into southern Russia and on one expedition getting as far as Odessa. He spoke Russian almost perfectly, though when later he travelled to the north of the country he realized that he sounded like a yokel, and quickly learned to adjust his accent. Eventually, he craved a return to civilization and began to make his way back west, sailing first from Sevastopol to Constantinople. By the time he arrived, the Ottoman Empire was at war with Russia, and an Englishman who could speak Russian was seized upon as being of enormous potential use to the sultan. Cain was happy to be made use of – for a fee.

The sultan at the time was Mustafa IV, whose reign was to prove brief and to whom Cain never spoke in person. His grand vizier was Çelebi Mustafa Pasha, who negotiated with Cain and quickly dispatched him north to the Danube where he would be able to channel valuable information back to the Porte. Ibrahim Edhem Pasha, who had later betrayed Iuda, was not even born, but Iuda came to wonder if some record of his first visit to Constantinople might have been passed down through the years.

By the time Cain reached the front lines both the grand vizier and the sultan had fallen from power, and the deal they had struck was meaningless, but for the time being it was safer to stick with the small band of Turks he'd been assigned to lead. They soon crossed the Russian lines and were in Wallachia. Only a few days into their mission, when he and his squad had camped high in the hills, he saw his chance and crept away. But he was out of luck. In the valley below he stumbled across a Russian encampment. There was no way he could sneak past, and he had no desire to return to the Turks. His solution was elegant. He simply marched in among the Russians, announced himself to be one of their own and revealed the location of his erstwhile comrades.

A platoon was dispatched, briefed by Cain as to exactly where the enemy was situated, and he retired for a relatively comfortable night's sleep, confident that he would soon be able to give the Russians the slip and head for the Adriatic coast and thence back to England. Outside the campfire blazed, Russian troops sitting around it, chatting and eating. Cain wondered for a moment whether he should join them, but preferred to rest.

It was a little after midnight that the camp was attacked. To begin with all that Cain knew of it was the screams from nearby tents. His first thought was that somehow his Turkish companions had survived the Russian raid and were coming for their revenge. He looked out of the tent and saw silhouettes flitting through the camp in the glowing firelight, running from tent to tent. Guns fired, but he saw no one fall. He had no gun – the Russians had not trusted him enough to allow him to carry a musket. All they had left him was his beloved double-bladed knife, and he doubted that would be much use against even a sword. He looked around him but could see nothing that might be used for his defence, except possibly the pole that supported the tent itself – a thick stake of wood, almost like a lance.

Before he could do anything to get hold of it, he realized that he was no longer alone. He turned and saw a figure standing at the open flap of the tent. The face was instantly familiar – it had not aged or gained one wrinkle, even in fifteen years.

'Honoré,' Cain gasped.

The vampire looked at him, surprised to be addressed by name. An expression of recognition slowly crept across his face.

'Cain? Richard Cain?'

It was an uncomfortable reunion. They could hardly be regarded as friends. How were a prisoner and his captor supposed to behave when reunited, even if one had finally set the other free? And Cain couldn't help but notice the blood on the vampire's lips.

'I should thank you,' he said, 'for keeping your side of the bargain.'

Honoré looked at him quizzically, his head tilted to one side. 'Your father, you mean?'

Cain nodded.

'We were hungry,' said the vampire simply.

'You still are, it would seem,' replied Cain, forcing the implication of the plural from his mind.

'No. This is more for the pleasure of it.'

'You're not alone?' Even though his heart pounded with fear, Cain was still curious. Were these creatures hunting as a team?

'These are the Carpathians,' Honoré explained. 'Here my kind is never alone.'

'What do you mean?'

'Like foxes in England, or wolves in Russia. You may not see us, but we are there.'

'You run as a pack?'

'No, no. We simply gather when we smell food. Many of these creatures I have never met before, nor will ever see again. To be honest, I'm thankful – they've been living too long as wild animals.'

'Not fitting company for a *vicomte*?'

'You understand me.' Honoré's bloodied teeth showed as he smiled.

'So why are you here?'

'One has one's baser side. The Russians don't understand the mountains like the locals do. No Wallachian would ever make camp in a place like this. It would reek to them of the undead.'

There was a scream from outside and then a face appeared at the flap of the tent. White fangs glinted in the lamplight, already stained with blood. Angry red eyes flicked from side to side in search of prey. Honoré turned and snarled at his fellow creature, which paused for a moment in contemplation, then turned away. Cain took a few steps back.

'Thank you,' he said.

'For what?' asked Honoré.

'For saving me from your . . . comrade.'

Honoré emitted a little snort and grinned to himself. 'Yes, I suppose I was saving you,' he said. 'But not in quite the sense you mean. I was saving you' – he paced swiftly across the tent – 'for myself.'

Cain backed away, putting the tent pole between himself and the vampire. The tent only opened at one end, and he would have to get past Honoré for that. To cut open the canvas at the side or to crawl under it would take too long.

Honoré lunged, reminding Cain of when he had tried to escape from the crypt beneath Saint George's. This time there would be no schoolfriend to come to his aid. Cain took a further step back, tugging at the tent pole as he went. The ground was soft and muddy and it came away surprisingly easily, and with a double effect, the first being that Cain now had a weapon in his hand, the second that the cloth of the tent collapsed on both of them.

Cain flattened himself to the ground and crawled backwards, soon finding where the hem of the canvas was stretched tight and level with the ground. It took only the removal of one peg to allow him exit, dragging the pole after him. Honoré did not fare so well. The canvas surrounded him, clinging to him. He scratched against it with his fingers but could find neither a grip nor a gap. The material rose and fell like some stormy sea. Cain held the stake in his hands, ready to thrust, hoping that its legendary effect on a vampire would prove true but unable to make out the creature's shape clearly enough to strike.

Then the movement calmed. Cain could see where two hands had taken a grip of the cloth and were now holding it close to Honoré's mouth. He heard a rending sound as the vampire's teeth cut through the rough canvas and a single eye appeared, angry and searching. Fingertips poked through the tiny hole and pulled it wider, until the whole of Honoré's face could be seen, his teeth gnashing, his eyes wandering until they fixed upon Cain with a ravenous glare.

But now Cain could make out the position of the body. He charged forward, the tent pole held in front of him like a battering ram. The point, which had been sharp enough to pierce the ground, cut through the tent cloth and penetrated Honoré's body within. It was like some conjuror's illusion; beneath the cloth Honoré's body seemed to disappear. His face, still visible at the rent in the canvas, contorted in a moment of agony, and then relaxed in death. But death was not the end of it. His features collapsed into an expression of tranquillity and then continued to dissolve. Cain caught the image of his flesh melting and cascading off his skull, just before the entire structure of his body crumpled. What remained of the head disappeared back down into the tent, which itself dropped gently, expelling the air trapped within until it was flat on the ground, emitting a little puff of dust from the chimney-like hole at the top. At the time Cain had no idea of what happened to the body of a dead vampire, and neither did he care to look. For some time he even considered the possibility that Honoré had been – like Don Giovanni – dragged down to hell.

Unthinking, Cain cast the stake aside and turned to fly. The camp was in a clearing, and the woods were only steps away. Soon he was in them, but he kept running until the campfire was out of sight. Only the moon, casting dappled shadows through the forest leaves, provided any light. He held his breath and realized he was not alone. The sound of heavy, laboured panting, almost sobbing, came from nearby. He walked in its direction and saw a figure slumped against a tree, his face in his hands. By his uniform it was clear he was one of the Russians; a mere *ryadovoy*. Cain recognized him from the camp, though they hadn't spoken. He stood over him.

'Are there any more?'

The soldier looked up, terror showing in his tearstained eyes. 'Please,' he whispered. 'No.'

'What?' hissed Cain.

'You're not . . . one of them?'

Cain shook his head. 'I came to the camp today. I'm Russian.'

'I remember.' The *ryadovoy* still looked wary. 'How did you get away?'

'I was lucky. I—'

'Sh!' the boy interrupted him. Cain was silent. They both listened. The boy's ears were good; they were not alone. As far as Cain could make out, there were three of them approaching from different directions, but there'd be others behind. There

215

was no chance of survival. Cain had no wooden stake now, only his knife, the one he had originally made to mimic the wounds inflicted by a vampire. And after that thought, the idea came to him in an instant. Honoré had said that the creatures did not know one another. The *ryadovoy* had mistaken Cain for one of them. Why not? It was a straw to clutch at.

Cain's knife was already in his hand. He leaned forward, grabbing the soldier by his lapels and lifting him up a little. There was no time for hesitation. He ran the serrated top edges of the blades across the man's neck, knowing that they would cause the messiest, bloodiest wound. The soldier didn't even have time to look surprised. His eyes simply rolled back and his body became limp. Cain returned the knife to his pocket and leaned forward further, forcing his mouth and nose into the gaping bloody mess of the *ryadovoy*'s throat, revolted by the very concept and trying not to taste any blood, worse still swallow it, but knowing that if he was to live then everything must appear authentic.

Soon he sensed he was not alone. Two of the creatures stood close by and the third quickly arrived. Cain raised his head from the tangle of red, glistening flesh and snarled, mimicking the way he had seen Honoré snarl, and hoping that it would convince.

It was a sacrilegious term to apply, but to Cain's mind it could be thought of as nothing other than a miracle; it worked! The creature towards whom Cain had directed his anger straightened and stepped back, then turned away in search of alternative prey. The other two did likewise. Cain had felt the urge to vomit, but had known he must keep up the pretence, burying his face in the soldier's flesh and pretending to relish the bitter, metallic taste of his blood.

Now, in an alleyway behind the Twelve Colleges in Petersburg he found himself in a similar stance, hunched over the dying body of a student, much the same age as the *ryadovoy* he had killed in Wallachia decades earlier. But there were differences. This boy was dying, not dead – that would spoil the taste of the blood. And there lay the bigger distinction: blood which had once been repellent to him, blood which he had let dribble from his lips rather than have a drop of it run down his throat and into his stomach, was now a delight. It was a necessity – and for years after

Iuda had first become a *voordalak* he had pretended to himself that it was only a necessity – but it was more than that too. It was blissful. He tried to recall the sense of revulsion he had felt with that *ryadovoy*, but it was lost to him. He could remember the event, but not the sensation. However much he attempted to bring to mind how he had once felt, the only experience that came to him was the joy of a vampire tasting human blood, and an irritation that the fool of a boy he had then been did not bother properly to drink.

He let the student drop to the ground. He was dead, and Iuda was replete. Now he needed to find somewhere to sleep. It was too late to go to the hotel; it would arouse suspicion. Besides, for the moment he wanted to be nothing other than a vampire – he wanted to sleep with the dead. The Smolenskoye Cemetery was not far; he would spend the day there.

In Wallachia, when he had finally decided his pretence with the soldier's corpse had gone on long enough, he had returned to the camp to find the other vampires there, sitting around the embers of the fire, chatting just as the soldiers had done earlier in the evening. Some chewed on hunks of raw flesh, not bothering to cook them. Hours before Cain would not have been able to control his urge to vomit, but he had already stomached much worse.

He was not the only newcomer. Two or three of the creatures introduced themselves and Cain made up a story for his own arrival, which seemed to satisfy the gathering. Among them was a Wallachian, a priest in life, by the name of Sordin Iordanescu. Over the next few years Cain came to know him well, though later under a pseudonym: Pyetr to Cain's Iuda. During his three years in the Carpathians Cain continued his study of vampires, though not the full-scale experimentation he would later pursue.

But even in the Carpathians the affairs of great men could not be ignored. By 1812 Bonaparte was preparing for his march across Europe and into Russia. It was Iordanescu who told Cain that the vampires of Wallachia were being summoned by the greatest vampire of them all, that they would join forces with Russia and send the French scurrying back to their homeland. Cain was tempted, but feared he would be discovered. In the end his curiosity got the better of him. He'd already heard of this great vampire from Honoré, and of his feud with the Romanovs. It was the creature he would come to know as Zmyeevich. But that was not the name that either Honoré or Iordanescu had used – the Russian form of his name was to come later. The name they called him by was Romanian.

The name was Dracula.

CHAPTER XIV

ITT WAS FRIGHTENINGLY SIMPLE. ALL THAT MIHAIL NEEDED TO DO was go to the Hôtel d'Europe, present the letter and he would be allowed access to Iuda's rooms. But that was what made it frightening. Would Iuda really be so remiss as to allow an intruder such easy access to his inner sanctum? And yet Iuda had been absent – a prisoner in distant Turkmenistan for more years than Mihail could guess. In that time things would have begun to slip out of his control. And even now he was still a prisoner, in the Peter and Paul Fortress. What could he do to endanger Mihail? But Mihail would be circumspect.

The hotel occupied the entire west side of Mihailovskaya Street, stretching from Nevsky Prospekt all the way back to Italyanskaya Street. Mihail chose to wear his dress uniform. It would not make him stand out from the crowd – not in Petersburg – and it might lend him some air of authority if the letter wasn't enough. It was late afternoon by the time he arrived. He'd spent the day in the Imperial Public Library, just a little further down the Prospekt, on the corner of Sadovaya Street. He'd spent most of the past few days there, while waiting for the Ohrana to finish their search of Luka's flat, but hadn't managed to find much that he didn't already know.

The old man he'd met in Senate Square had told him that Ascalon was the sword, or possibly the lance, that Saint George had used to slay the dragon. The documents he found in the library confirmed it, but added little. Ascalon was indeed the name of the weapon, though as to its being a sword or a lance, the tales varied. The earliest reference to the name seemed to be as late as the sixteenth century, though legends of the weapon itself were far older. The name did derive from the city of Ashkelon in Asia Minor. There was also a connection with the Karaite Jews, just as Dmitry had mentioned. The city of Ashkelon had been home to a large Karaite community. There was a famous letter from the Karaite elders of the city, written after the fall of Jerusalem in the First Crusade. It described how they had found money to pay the ransom on captured members of their community, and also for holy relics.

That was all he could discover. It was fertile ground for speculation. Had George's lance been one of those holy relics? Had it first acquired the name, long after its use against the dragon, by virtue of the time it spent in the city – even if it had taken centuries for that link finally to be written down? Had the Karaite Jews of Ashkelon delivered the lance to the Karaite Jews of Chufut Kalye? Iuda had built an entire laboratory in the caves there, but had his purpose also been to take Ascalon from the Karaites? Had he succeeded? And of what interest was it to Dmitry?

There were no answers, and the tenuous links that formed in Mihail's mind were quite without substantiation. He left the library earlier than he had done on previous days, before dusk – he had no desire to encounter any of the *voordalaki* he knew to be in the city. Even in the evenings it was light in the area, thanks to the bright arc lights – Yablochkov Candles – that illuminated Aleksandrinsky Square, beside the library. It was a harsh, unnatural luminance that might at first be mistaken for sunlight, but not for long. Neither was it like the illumination of a candle or a lamp, or any of the various other electric lights that had been invented in recent decades. Mihail had studied them all, and knew their strengths and weaknesses. They would be switched on again in a few hours, but Mihail's work would be done by then.

The hotel lobby was busy when he entered. He had chosen the time carefully, between afternoon and evening, when those whose reason for being in Petersburg was to frequent the pres- tigious boutiques on Nevsky Prospekt were returning, and those whose plans were for dinner or a night at the theatre would be preparing to leave. The busier it was the less likely Mihail would be subjected to serious scrutiny.

He waited until the concierge had finished giving an elderly lady and gentleman directions to the Mariinskiy Theatre, and then approached him. The man looked tired and irritable, but forced a smile as Mihail came near.

'I wonder if you could present this to the hotel manager,' said Mihail, handing him the envelope, and within it the note that he had recovered from Luka's rooms. Underneath was a one-rouble bill, folded up. The concierge smiled as his fingers rubbed across it.

'With pleasure, sir,' he said, turning away. Mihail couldn't see quite how he slipped the banknote into his pocket, but was sure that he had done. The concierge disappeared through a door at the back of the lobby. After two minutes he emerged with another man, who came to speak to Mihail, smiling unctuously.

'It's been some months since we've been privileged to receive a visit from a representative of Collegiate Councillor Chernetskiy,' he said, handing the letter back to Mihail. 'I trust that His High Nobleness is in good health?'

No, he's rotting in a dungeon in the Peter and Paul Fortress. It would not be a helpful response, however much the words would be a pleasure on Mihail's lips. 'He's very well, and sends his regards. He trusts his instructions have continued to be carried out.' It was pure bluff, but Mihail could hazard a guess as to the nature of the arrangement between Iuda and the hotel.

'Absolutely.' As he spoke, the manager guided Mihail towards the front desk. 'His rooms have remained quite undisturbed.' He leaned over and whispered in the ear of one of his staff, who turned to the rack of keys behind him.

'Good. Good,' muttered Mihail.

The key was handed to the manager and the manager handed it to Mihail. 'Would you like someone to show you the way?'

'I'll be fine, thank you.' The number, 215, was clearly stamped on the tag attached to the key.

Mihail followed the direction that the manager had involuntarily indicated, leaving the lobby via a short flight of steps on to a corridor from which a far grander staircase ascended. At the top stood the door to a dimly lit dining room, while the stairway turned and continued upwards on either side. However intent he was on his task, Mihail could not help but be awed by the opulence of the hotel – and the expense of it. He was the son of a grand duke, and yet he would never be able to afford rooms in a place like this. The stairs turned again. Mihail glanced at the room that led off the landing, at the front of the building overlooking the street. Its main feature was a grand piano, finished in colourful marquetry. This was still the level of public rooms. After the third flight of stairs, things became less grandiose, but only slightly. The corridor led off in both directions, but all the numbers began with the figure 1. Now the stairs were more mundane, what Mihail might expect in any large building, constructed of iron and twisting back on themselves to take up the minimum amount of space. He needed to ascend only one more flight. He noted the numbers as he passed: 209, 211, 213. At last he was there. He hesitated, then put his ear against the door. There was no reason to expect the room to be occupied. Iuda was a captive. If Dmitry knew of the room, he could not come here in daylight. Even so, Mihail was cautious. Dmitry could have come here at night, and be waiting inside. He knocked and listened again. There was no response. He could think of no more precautions he could take. The key turned smoothly and he pushed the door open.

Iuda awoke. He had slept well. How a *voordalak* would manage without the tombs of the rich was a mystery. The common man was buried in the ground, but for the rich an ornate chamber was built and the casket was placed within a stone dias so that though it would decay, it would not be food for worms. Iuda lay alongside one such long-departed noble – safe from the sun, comfortable among the dead. He was almost surprised not to find other creatures like himself gathered around the sarcophagus to sleep, like faithful dogs around their master. But there were many graves about the world, and few *voordalaki*. There were two others in Petersburg though, of that Iuda was sure. Where might they be sleeping, he wondered.

He crawled through the narrow gap that had given him entrance to the tomb and emerged into the cemetery. He raised his hand to his face, but could feel no stains of blood upon it. Even so, he picked up a handful of snow and washed himself. He had no mirror to look in, not that it would have helped. He'd stolen the clothes of the student he had killed – but for the shirt, which was drenched in blood. They weren't ideal, but they were better than the ragged garments that he had worn for three years in gaol. They would be enough to get him into the hotel without raising too many eyebrows. There he had plenty of other outfits to choose from. And he would need them. Tomorrow was the appointed day for his meeting. It would not do to be ill-dressed for that.

He headed south, back to the centre of town.

There were three rooms in the suite: a bathroom, a bedroom and a study. The bathroom and bedroom were much as might have been expected in any great hotel, except that nothing had been cleaned or even touched for many months. The windows were shuttered. A thick layer of dust sat upon every surface. The wardrobes and drawers were filled with clothes of every style, from the finest evening dress, through a variety of military uniforms, to peasant outfits. Iuda was prepared for any eventuality – for any disguise he might need to adopt. He had not, it seemed, been prepared for moths. Half of the garments were unwearable, most had one or two holes. But it was not these for which Mihail had come.

The study contained three locked cabinets. Mihail had no qualms about wrenching them open. Within he found what he'd been looking for – and much more. The first cupboard contained notebooks – more than fifty of them, all written in English. Some dated back to the 1810s, the latest was as recent as 1877. Mihail had brought a knapsack for the very purpose, but he could not take all of them. With luck he would have the chance to return for more later, but he could not be sure of it. He skimmed through them, trying to determine which were the most valuable, checking dates and headings and glancing over the body of the text for any words that might shout out at him. His English was good, but he did not read it like he could Russian; each word had to be deciphered and understood, rather than simply recognized as a familiar shape. It took him two to three minutes to scan the first volume. He moved on to the second.

He froze. There it was, written in the Latin alphabet but still unmistakable, his grandfather's name: Aleksei Ivanovich Danilov. Preceded by one and followed by two others that Mihail knew almost as well: Vadim Fyodorovich Savin, Dmitry Fetyukovich Petrenko and Maksim Sergeivich Lukin. The last bore the surname that Mihail had adopted and was still using. There was nothing much to the entry – just a note that they were the four officers who would be liaising with Iuda and the others when they were in Russia. It was dated 27 August 1812. It was the beginning of a story that Mihail knew well.

He quickly worked his way through the notebooks. There may have been other references familiar to him, but if there were he missed them. Everything was in too much detail to be of any real use. These were the day-by-day observations of a scientist; they described the minutiae of what Iuda had seen, but made little effort to explain it. It was only when it got to the more recent volumes, from the 1870s, that Iuda had begun to set down his conclusions about the nature of vampires, drawn from so many years' experimentation. These Mihail slipped into his bag, along with those from 1855 to 1860 – the years that Tamara had been in contact with Iuda, and a few more after that. Mihail was keen to discover how much Iuda had really known about his mother and, vitally, whether he even guessed at Mihail's existence.

The second cupboard contained other papers – not Iuda's own writings but mostly correspondence he had received. Rather than being categorized by date they were divided into folders named after cities: Constantinople, London, Moscow, Simferopol, Saint Petersburg and others – the cities Iuda had been in when he received the letters, Mihail guessed. Again, he had to compromise and took only Moscow and Saint Petersburg. At the bottom of that cabinet there was also money – both paper and coins, some Russian, some from across Europe. The coinage would be too heavy, but he took the banknotes. He wasn't short of funds, but there was a pleasure in stealing from Iuda – a breach of the eighth commandment that served as an aperitif to the violation of the sixth that Mihail would soon commit against him.

The final cabinet was the most securely locked, and on smashing his way into it Mihail understood why. It contained blood – dozens of small glass bottles and vials, each carefully labelled with a name. Some Mihail recognized: Raisa Styepanovna Tokoryeva, Marfa Mihailovna Danilova, Vadim Fyodorovich Savin. It seemed that Iuda collected blood as a child collects postage stamps. From every person – man or vampire – that he had encountered and had been afforded the opportunity, he had taken blood, even before he became a vampire. Of the names Mihail recognized all were dead, or at least so he presumed – hoped. There was one exception: Zmyeevich. His was the largest bottle of all, though it still fitted in the palm of Mihail's hand. He made sure the seal was good, then slipped it into his bag.

He looked at the other samples and wondered what he should do with them. Most, if not all of the donors were dead, but still Iuda might have some foul purpose for them. Even if not, it was disrespectful – particularly for the likes of Marfa Mihailovna, Aleksei's wife – to have the remnants of their corporeal existence here on display long after they had died. Perhaps they should be returned to family members, or buried with due ceremony so that their owners' souls could rest in peace. But Mihail doubted that God would require any such ritualism to help in His judgement of who was and was not righteous. Besides, Mihail did not have room to take them all. Thankfully the newly rebuilt hotel was an exemplar of modernity. The bathroom had running water – both *froide* and *chaude* according to the enamel labels – and a sink that drained directly to the sewers. It was a simple if time-consuming task to empty out every bottle and wash its contents away. It struck Mihail as odd that the stuff hadn't congealed, but evidently Iuda had found a way to keep it as fresh as on the day it had been drawn from the body. No doubt it was described somewhere in all those journals.

At the bottom of that last cabinet there was a small, brown envelope – unmarked. Mihail picked it up. The contents hidden within were small and unyielding – six little lumps as hard as stone. Mihail could make no guess as to what they were. He ripped open the paper and poured the contents on to the table. Now there was no misunderstanding: two distal phalanges; two intermediate phalanges; two proximal phalanges. They were the bones of the smallest two fingers of the left hand of his grandfather, Aleksei Ivanovich, cut from him in a gaol in Silistria in 1809. It was a slight leap of intuition, but Mihail felt confident in it. There was no doubt that they were finger bones, and who else's would they be? How they had come into Iuda's possession was a mystery, but they would not remain there. Mihail returned them to the envelope and placed it in his bag.

It was time to go. Mihail had been in the room for over an hour now. From what he could guess, Luka's duties had simply been to keep an eye on things while Iuda was away. Mihail was playing the role of his replacement, and the manager might become suspicious if he stayed too long. He looked around him at the mess he had made; the smashed cabinets and the pile of emptied bottles. It did not matter. No one would be entering here. The hotel staff was under orders not to and Iuda was safely locked up. It was a shame. Mihail would have liked him to know just how easily this inner sanctum had been penetrated.

He took one last look around the place, then headed for the door.

Iuda turned off Mihailovskaya Street and into the Hôtel d'Europe. It was much as he remembered it: the elegant high ceilings, the bustling clientele, the attentive staff.

'Round the back!'

Iuda felt an iron grip on his shoulder as he spoke. He could have broken the man's arm without a second thought, but he required the goodwill of the hotel and its staff.

'What?'

'If you're looking for work,' explained the concierge, 'it's round the back. Though to be frank, I don't rate your chances.'

Iuda switched from Russian to French, in the hope of making it clear he was very much entitled to use the front door. 'Is Monsieur Kryukov available?'

'Who?'

'Kryukov, your manager.'

'Kryukov's not been here for two years. It's Sazanov now.'

'Well go fetch Monsieur Sazanov, and when you find him, tell him that Collegiate Councillor Chernetskiy is here.'

226

'Chernetskiy?' The idiot seemed to recognize the name. 'But . . .'

'Just go and do it.' Iuda raised his voice a little. It had the desired effect.

Moments later a figure approached, almost bowing as he walked. Iuda presumed him to be Sazanov.

'Your High Nobleness. I should have known. I should have known.'

'Known what?' snapped Iuda.

'That we were to be graced by your presence.'

'Why?'

'Because of your man. You sent him ahead. To prepare the room for you.'

Iuda squeezed his jaws hard together, feeling the muscles tighten. He'd been right to be concerned. Luka had given something away before he died. Iuda should have come straight here and not wasted so much time the previous night.

'I sent no one,' he said firmly. 'When was this?'

'An hour ago. An hour and a half.'

'How long did he stay?'

'He's still up there. He has the key.'

In seconds Iuda had crossed the lobby and was bounding up the steps. He had no trouble remembering the way and the unending flights of stairs did nothing to exhaust him. He recognized the bronze faces that decorated the rails of the final staircase, with snakes in their hair, like Medusa. Soon he was at the door of 215. It was locked. He prepared to put his shoulder to it – it would offer no effective resistance to his strength.

'Sir! Please!' Sazanov was at the far end of the corridor, moving with surprising swiftness for a man of his build, but red-faced and out of breath. In his hand he was waving a bunch of keys. 'Use this.'

Iuda snatched the keys from him, holding the one that had been proffered. 'Go!' he snarled.

'But sir, that's the master key. I can't leave it with a guest.'

'I'll return it when I'm done,' Iuda whispered. Something about his tone convinced the manager, who waddled quickly away. Iuda turned the key and flung open the door to his room.

*

227

Mihail threw himself down on the bed. This hotel was far less grand than the Hôtel d'Europe, but he was happy to be here. His heart was still pounding; not from exertion, not through fear, but simply at the thrill of seeing his quarry – though not at all where he had expected him to be.

Mihail had just turned on to the final flight of stairs that descended into the lobby when he had seen Iuda – not his face, simply the back of his head, but the straight blond hair just touching his collar was clue enough. Then he'd turned and Mihail had seen his profile. They'd met only on one occasion, in that gaol at Geok Tepe, but Mihail had spent the whole time studying him, learning his every feature, so that even at a distance of half a verst he would be able to pick him out, hunt him down and kill him.

Mihail's first instinct was to strike there and then. In his knapsack he carried the simplest of weapons; one that had proven effective against vampires – though never yet in his hand. But to rush down the stairs and attempt to plunge a short wooden dagger into Iuda's heart was too risky. Iuda was strong and fast. The lobby was crowded with people. Even if he succeeded, he would be arrested. And he would have to take Iuda by surprise, and where would be the fun in that? This was to be punishment – an execution. The pleasure would not be solely in Iuda's death, but in the knowledge that Iuda understood he was about to die and the reason for it. Iuda must know regret.

And so it was better to wait. Somewhere on a train between here and Saratov a trunk was being delivered, at Mihail's request. He would be reunited with it soon. Inside he would find far better tools to complete the task, devices he and his mother had worked on together; had tested as best they could. Ideally it would be a slow death – and a painful one – so that Iuda would have time to contemplate. There was a way it could be done – a modern, scientific way. Mihail had seen it with his own eyes. But it would take careful preparation.

He'd slipped back up the stairs and hidden in the room with the piano. Iuda had passed in a whirl of fury and Mihail had not waited. He headed down as quickly as he could. He almost bumped into the hotel manager on the stairs, but the man was so flustered that he did not even notice. At the exit the concierge held the door for him and tipped his hat with a conspiratorial wink. Mihail felt sure the man wouldn't reveal that he had witnessed Mihail's departure, though it would matter little if he did.

Now he was safely back at his own hotel on the other side of the city centre, the bag of loot sitting on the table, tempting him to delve inside and discover its secrets. But he restrained himself; there would be plenty of time for it later. One simple thought possessed him: Iuda was free. It shouldn't have been too much of a surprise. Mihail recalled everything he had seen in Geok Tepe that had been designed to restrain Iuda. There would be nothing like that at the fortress – the troops were unlikely even to know what Iuda was. It might be worth scouring the newspapers for news of the mysterious, bloody deaths of fortress guards, but that would most likely be covered up. No one escaped the Peter and Paul Fortress; a record like that could only be maintained by the occasional editing of the facts.

On the other hand Iuda's liberty did present new possibilities. In the fortress he had been invulnerable. Mihail would have had no chance of getting in there. Now there would be opportunities to creep up on him; to catch him alone. Mihail even knew where to find him, though it was unlikely he would stay much longer now at the Hôtel d'Europe. But perhaps there was some clue as to where he might go in the papers Mihail had taken. He went over to the table.

As he moved, he heard a sound – a light tap against the window pane; then another. He opened the curtain, but could see nothing. The sound came again and this time he caught a glimpse of some tiny fragment ricocheting off the glass. He pulled up the sash and looked down. A figure stood below. In the darkness he couldn't make out a face, but from the build he felt sure it was female.

'Mihail?' The voice was hushed.

'Who is it?' he hissed back.

'It's Dusya. Come down.'

'Why?'

'Please.'

He pulled his head back inside and closed the window. Then he dumped the knapsack in his trunk and hid it under a pile of clothes. He slipped on his coat and went downstairs. Dusya had been at the back of the building – Mihail did not care to pay for a room with a view – but when he emerged from the hotel she was waiting for him.

'How did you know where to find me?' he asked.

'You gave Luka your address, didn't you? You think he wouldn't tell me?'

It was conceivable, but when would he have had the chance? More likely she, or one of them, read it on the card they'd found on Luka's body before they dumped it in the river.

'What happened to him?'

She breathed deeply, as if about to speak, but then her eyes filled with tears and she flung herself forward, burying her face in Mihail's chest. Mihail could do nothing but reciprocate. He put his arms around her and held her. They stood like that for half a minute and then she lifted her head to look up at him, her eyes still glistening. The look suited her.

'I don't know,' she said, her voice choked. 'It must have been the Ohrana.'

It was a convincing show, but it still seemed unlikely. 'Wouldn't they have just arrested him?' Mihail asked.

'You understand what we do. He'd have run rather than be caught. And they'd prefer him dead than free. Punishment is more important to them than justice.'

'So what is it you do?' Mihail had guessed, but he needed to know more.

'Come with me,' she said.

'Can't you tell me here?'

'Please.'

She walked away without looking over her shoulder to verify that he was with her. He had no option but to follow. She led him away from the river and from the centre of town into an area he was not familiar with. He quickly caught up and walked alongside her.

'Where are we going?' he asked.

'Somewhere safe.'

'Why weren't we safe before?'

'They're always watching.'

'Watching me, or watching you?'

'We both spoke to Luka, so they're watching us both.'

She walked quickly for someone of her stature, her eyes fixed on the ground ahead of her. Mihail grabbed her by the arm, forcing her to stop and turn to face him.

'Who are "they"?'

She looked up at him in silence, her eyes, still moist, gazing into his.

'Please,' she insisted. 'It's not far.' She began walking again.

They passed an insalubrious-looking tavern, but didn't go in. Just beyond was an alleyway. Dusya ducked inside, grabbing Mihail's hand and pulling him after her. They were beside the kitchens. Warm air blew out of an open window, making the alley warmer than the street they had come from, and filling it with the smell of pork and cabbage.

'What is it then?' he asked.

She reached up to him and put her hands on either side of his head, pulling him down towards her. She was going to bite him. He had been a fool not to bring a weapon, and not to consider the possibility that she might be a vampire. But he *had* considered it; he always considered it, with every individual he met. That was how his mother had raised him. He had seen Dusya in daylight twice now – on the train and when he had followed her. Any doubts were dispelled when he felt her lips not on his neck but on his own lips, trying to kiss him. He pulled away. It was madness. It was not what he was here for.

'What's wrong?' she asked. 'Don't you want me?' As she spoke, she allowed her overcoat to fall open. She began to unfasten her blouse beneath, revealing more of her pale white flesh with each button.

It was pathetically clumsy; inept and fake. But it was too late. Even as Mihail watched her he sensed somebody behind him and the world went black. He felt coarse material sucking against his mouth as he breathed in and a cord tightening around his neck. He reached up to pull it away, but Dusya's hands grabbed his wrists and held them down with surprising strength. Then he felt a screaming pain at the back of his head, and stars filled the darkness, and then he sensed no more.

CHAPTER XV

IUDA WAS A CAUTIOUS CREATURE. HE HAD BEEN SO AS A MAN AND had become more so as a *voordalak*. He expected problems. He did not always know where they would come from or what their nature would be, but he accepted that the world was unpredictable, and so he prepared. He hadn't known specifically that someone would find his rooms at the hotel and steal the one blood sample that was most precious to him, but he had known that to have only one sample would be the error of a fool.

Had they been trying to hide the fact that they had taken Zmyeevich's blood, he wondered. All those vials, emptied away. Was he supposed to think that Zmyeevich's blood too was now mingling with sewer water and being flushed into the Neva? Where then was the empty bottle with Zmyeevich's name on it? And the greater question remained: who had been in his rooms? The obvious culprits were either Dmitry or Zmyeevich, but the description that Sazanov had given matched neither. Moreover, whoever it was had arrived in daylight, but they could easily have recruited someone to do their work for them. Sazanov – desperate to redeem himself – had mentioned the letter of permission. That linked the whole thing back to Luka. Dmitry had known about him, and might have been able to get hold of the letter. The intruder had worn the uniform of a lieutenant. What about the fellow that Luka said had been sniffing around – Lukin? Sazanov's description could match the man of that name that Iuda had seen in Geok Tepe. It seemed ever more likely that he was working for Dmitry.

It all made Iuda's meeting more vital than ever. The message

232

had been clear; the place, the time, who to ask for. The place was very familiar. Iuda had worked there himself in his early days at the Third Section, before he had moved to Moscow. The time was in a quarter of an hour; eight o'clock on the evening of Sunday 8 February. He left the Hôtel d'Europe for what he suspected would be the last time. All his remaining possessions there – what was left of the notebooks and the money, along with some of the clothes – were crated up ready for transportation to the luggage depot at the Nikolaievsky Vokzal. Where he would have them sent from there he did not yet know.

He walked along the slippery compacted snow of Nevsky Prospekt, heading south-east towards the Fontanka. The moon had not yet risen, but the city was strangely bright. On the main thoroughfares there had been gas lighting for several years, and some experiments with electrification, but the light they produced was weak – helpful to humans, but of little benefit to a vampire who could see clearly even with only the light of the stars to help him. This was different though; a bright, white light that almost mimicked that of the moon. As Iuda walked on, the source of it soon emerged from behind the Imperial Library.

It came from Aleksandrinsky Square. Tall lamp-posts stood there, topped with the sources of this strange, disconcerting light. In the square below, the people seemed comfortable in the glow. Iuda watched them as he walked. His attention as a scientist had always been focused on biology and sometimes, like today, he regretted that he was not *au fait* with the latest developments in the field of electricity, undoubtedly the power source for this strange radiance. He would find out about it. There was a chance it would prove helpful to him, or any vampire, providing a safe form of bright light for those occasions when it was needed, such as for use with a microscope.

But even as he walked by, separated from the square by the wide Nevsky Prospekt, he began to feel uneasy. His stomach knotted and from it spread a sense of nausea that permeated his body. His skin began to itch. He turned his face away from the light and pressed on towards his destination, but even that did not protect him. The glare of the light was reflected back at him undiminished from the snow all around. Worse than the physical discomfort he felt was the unaccountable fear that filled him, itself almost a sensation. It was the same fear that any vampire felt at the prospect of the rising sun and however much Iuda told himself that this was a manmade, artificial light that could do him no harm, still he felt gripped by the urge to run away from it.

He did not, but he walked more briskly than he might have done, and soon he was beyond the square, and the light – along with his unease – began to fade. He tried to push the incident from his mind; he would need his wits about him for what was to come. The prospekt took him across the Fontanka and then he turned north along the embankment. Soon he was outside number 16.

At the guard post he asked for Colonel Mrovinskiy. The man soon appeared and led him along a dark, brick corridor. Iuda tried to remember the layout of the building, but there had been much work done in the thirty years since he had last been here. They came to a door.

'Through here,' said the colonel, holding it open.

Iuda stepped inside. The room was comfortably furnished – at a guess, the office of a civil servant of relatively high rank. There was another door on the far side of the room and near it a chair, in which sat the man who had invited Iuda here. A vacant chair stood near to where Iuda had entered. The only thing unusual about the room was the cage of heavy iron bars that fenced off the section that Iuda was in; to the front, to the sides and above. The only access was by the door through which Iuda had just come, a door which now slammed shut behind him. He heard bolts sliding home.

He had become an exhibit in a zoo, caged and trapped in his portion of the room while others could enter and approach the bars to peer and poke at the strange exhibit, never daring to come too close lest he lash out at them. But the zoo's only visitor – or was he the zoo keeper? – remained seated, gazing intently at Iuda.

'You release me from one gaol just to lock me in another?' Iuda asked.

'You're free to go whenever you like, Cain. These bars are simply for my protection. I'm sure you understand.'

'Why the bolted door?'

'You just have to knock – it will be opened. Now sit down. I'd offer you some refreshment, but I don't think we can cater for your tastes.'

Iuda accepted the offer and sat on the chair. It was soft and upholstered with leather, just like the one on the other side of the room. They could be any two gentlemen engaged in a quiet evening's conversation, but for the bars that separated them. It was a sensible precaution; Iuda had no plans to attack but only a fool would take the risk, and the tsar was no fool.

'I hope you're not simply going to make me the same offer that you made my uncle,' said Aleksandr. 'I'd give you the same answer.'

'You do not desire to become immortal, then?'

'I do not desire to become Zmyeevich's pawn.'

It was an interesting answer. Immortality under his own terms might still be on the table.

'I no longer represent Zmyeevich,' explained Iuda.

It had been fifty-six years since Iuda could say he represented Zmyeevich, but before that they had been close – allies rather than master and servant, though Zmyeevich would not have admitted it. They certainly weren't friends. By then Cain had abandoned the concept of friendship. But before that – back in 1812 when they'd conspired against Bonaparte – they'd worked hand in glove.

After the call had gone out across Wallachia, Cain had made his way with the other vampires, still posing as one of their number, through the mountains to the ancient, ruined castle. Cain never knew if Zmyeevich – Dracula as he had styled himself in his home country – recognized him for what he was. It was unlikely that he cared. He had a mission for Cain – beyond that of helping to rid Russia of the French invaders. Once in Russia, Cain was to go to the tsar, Aleksandr I, and make him a simple offer: immortality, under Dracula's terms. It was a proposition no sane man would refuse. And yet when Cain had finally made the offer, that was precisely what Aleksandr had done.

And now Iuda faced this second Aleksandr. This new tsar did not resemble his uncle physically – not in his face at least, though they were both tall men. What they shared, Iuda suspected, was the same resolution. To a degree it was a sign of stupidity, but it had served the Romanovs well through the years and they saw no need for change; not this generation of them, at least.

'If you no longer speak for Zmyeevich, what can you offer me?' asked the tsar.

'Freedom from his power.'

'He has no power over me.'

'He has the power to make you see – make you see what he sees, even if only in your dreams.'

Aleksandr looked uncomfortable, as if Iuda had read his mind.

'My dreams can't hurt me. Zmyeevich can make me do nothing that I do not wish.'

'True,' replied Iuda. 'But what of the tsarevich?'

'Aleksandr is my son. Zmyeevich will get no further with him.'

'I was speaking of the former tsarevich; your elder son, Nikolai. Which of your sons, do you think, would have better led Russia? Which of the two would have better resisted Zmyeevich?'

Aleksandr leapt to his feet. 'Nikolai would have had no truck with him!'

It was just the reaction Iuda had expected. Now he played his ace.

'Which is why they killed him.'

'What?' Aleksandr could only force a whisper.

'Zmyeevich – and his henchman. They made Nikolai the same offer you think I came here to make you. He refused. And so they killed him.'

'My son' – Aleksandr breathed between almost every word, desperate to remain calm, his face close to the bars – 'died of tuberculosis of the spine. Why the Lord chose to take him early I have no idea, but I can tell you it was not the work of Zmyeevich.'

Iuda emitted a short, sarcastic laugh. 'Believe what you like, Aleksandr Nikolayevich. Whatever the truth is, it is your son Aleksandr who will become tsar. That's very much to Zmyeevich's advantage. If the Lord chose to arrange things in such a way then we can only speculate as to whose side He is on.'

'How,' the tsar asked with deliberate precision, 'is it to Zmyeevich's advantage?'

'You weren't surprised that Nikolai would refuse Zmyeevich's offer.'

'Of course not.'

'Because you raised him to be tsar. You raised him to be wise. You told him that Zmyeevich's offer would come and you told him to reject it. But more than that, you raised him to be a man who would reject any such ignoble offer, regardless of your instructions.'

'Exactly.'

'And did you raise your second son in the same way?'

The tsar grew pale. He walked backwards and fell into his chair. 'Sasha will make a fine tsar,' he muttered unconvincingly.

'I hope he shares your confidence, but he wasn't raised to be tsar, was he? You poured all your attention on to Nikolai, and kept nothing in reserve. Aleksandr was thrust into the role, quite unprepared, at the age of just twenty.'

'There's been time since for him to learn.'

'Zmyeevich had already made his offer.'

'You're lying.' The tsar spoke wearily.

'Tell me' – Iuda was enjoying his opponent's humiliation, though he knew he mustn't overplay it – 'when did your uncle, Aleksandr I, die?'

'You know perfectly well: 19 November 1825.'

'You don't have to keep up the pretence. Your family may have fooled me then, but not for long. I don't know what name he took, but I know for certain that Aleksandr was still alive when you ascended the throne. Now when did he die?' For all his confidence, Iuda was genuinely curious. He had never discovered the full truth of Aleksandr and Lyosha's trickery.

'1864. 20 January.' The tsar's fingers massaged his brow.

'And in scarcely a year your son Nikolai was dead. Zmyeevich may plan for the long term, but he acts quickly.'

'You're saying Sasha was privy to this?'

'Not at all. He loved his brother – you know that better than I. Zmyeevich would play things subtly in making his offer.'

'Why turn on my son? Why not deal with me?'

'You've already answered that; because you'd refuse.'

'So will my son.' It sounded more a hope than an expectation.

'I can ensure that the question need never be asked.'

Silence filled the room. The tsar remained in his chair, his eyes fixed on Iuda, considering all he had said. Iuda had spun a good story, but he was not certain of any of it. But it was what he himself would have done in Zmyeevich's shoes, and that made it likely to be true. He'd long ago heard rumours of Aleksandr Aleksandrovich's acquiescence and now Aleksandr Nikolayevich knew of it too.

'What can you do?' the tsar asked.

Iuda smiled. He scented victory. The Romanovs would pay well for their salvation. They would give Iuda the protection he needed. And Zmyeevich would know once and for all that he was bested.

'You're aware, I take it, that Zmyeevich can only exercise his sympathetic influence on the Romanov bloodline once in each generation?'

'That's what I've been assured. That is why Aleksandr Pavlovich's feigned death trounced you so thoroughly. It kept his brother safe as tsar.'

Iuda did not relish being reminded of how he had been tricked, but he let it pass.

'Exactly,' he said. 'That is why Zmyeevich must be careful. He could not attempt to influence each of your sons in turn until he found one who would comply. The first failure would be a failure for all. We can exploit that.'

'I will not sacrifice one of my sons to save another.' The tsar had cottoned on quickly.

'To save your entire dynasty?' Iuda asked.

Aleksandr shook his head.

Iuda had expected as much; he was prepared. 'What, might I ask, is Your Majesty's opinion on the sanctity of marriage?'

The tsar shuffled in his seat. His infidelities to his wife were well known.

'Nature, I assure you,' Iuda continued, 'is quite indifferent to the institution.'

'Meaning?'

'Meaning that what applies to your legitimate heir would equally apply to a bastard child. They all carry Romanov blood.'

238

'I love all my children.' Aleksandr thought a moment before adding, 'And I have no bastards.'

Iuda laughed out loud. 'Oh, come on! What about all those kiddies that have sprung from the Dolgorukova girl?'

For the first time in their conversation, the tsar lost control of himself. He stood and strode towards Iuda, but regained his composure before speaking. Iuda decided it would be better not to goad him too much.

'Princess Yurievskaya, as she is now titled, and I were married last July,' he explained. 'In secret.'

'I apologize; I hadn't heard. I've been rather out of touch.' Iuda was genuinely ignorant, though there was much more that he could have said, not least to comment on the indecent haste with which they had wed – Aleksandr's first wife, Maria Aleksandrovna, had died only in June. He might also have mentioned that it was common knowledge that there were other children by other mistresses. He couldn't legitimize them all.

But Iuda held his tongue. The suggestion that the tsar should sacrifice one of his own children was not Iuda's main thrust. He had suggested it merely to guide Aleksandr to the correct conclusion, to make that conclusion more palatable by comparison. Now he made things explicit.

'The child in question need only be of the same generation as Aleksandr Aleksandrovich,' he explained. 'They do not have to be siblings.'

The tsar fell silent, deep in contemplation. Iuda studied his face, imagining his thoughts as his mind wandered over each of his nephews and nieces, dismissing those he loved, dismissing all who had a title, and then considering those born out of wedlock – pondering those of whose existence Iuda was not even aware. For his part, Iuda had no specific individual in mind – any of them would do.

'How distant can they be?' he asked. 'Pyotr must have descendants all over Russia by now.'

'True, but there is the question of certainty. There have always been pretenders to the Romanov name – look at the False Dmitrys who plagued your predecessors in the Time of Troubles. If we attempt this on someone who does not, in truth, carry Pyotr's blood then Zmyeevich will detect our ruse and will not fall for it a second time. The closer our subject is to you, the safer we shall be.'

Aleksandr lapsed into silence again. For over a minute there was no sound in the room. Then he looked up.

'I shall consider what you have said. Come back to me, here, in two weeks' time. I'll let you know my decision.'

He turned and made for the door. Before leaving, he tugged on a bell pull. Then he was gone. A moment later Iuda heard the bolts being drawn on the door behind him. He smiled. He had achieved all he could hope for. Aleksandr would come round, he felt sure of it. Even so, a fortnight was a long time to wait. Given all that Iuda had heard about the activities of the People's Will, His Majesty might be dead within days.

The cowering body was dragged before the committee. He still wore the hood that had been used in his abduction, tied at the neck so that he could not remove it and might fear strangulation, though there was no real danger of it. They'd stripped him to the waist so that the cold would weaken him too. And then they'd left him – for almost a day.

Now he would be ready to answer their questions.

'What do we know of him?' asked the chairman.

Sofia replied. 'We're reasonably certain that he is the same man as the sapper who worked on the undermining of Geok Tepe. He was born in Saratov and studied at the Imperial Technical School in Moscow. While in the army he is not known to have expressed strong political views in any direction. However, he did with apparent spontaneity assist Yevdokia Yegorovna with her cover story when she was transporting explosives from Rostov.'

As Sofia spoke the chairman noticed how she nervously rubbed the outside edge of one hand with the other. Beneath her fingers he could see the red scab of a crescent-shaped lesion: a bite mark – caused by a human rather than a *voordalak*. It was too deep a wound to have been inflicted by Zhelyabov as part of some sexual frolic, but the chairman could take a good guess as to the terrified individual whose teeth had inflicted the injury.

'You think he was aware of what she was doing?' he asked.

'She'd been careless,' interjected Kibalchich. 'I'd have been able to spot what she was up to. I'm sure he would.'

Sofia continued. 'We also suspect that he was the man that Rysakov and I witnessed accosting Konstantin Nikolayevich as he left the Marble Palace. He was arrested and taken to Fontanka 16, but released the following day. He then made contact with the traitor Luka Miroslavich.'

'Let's begin there then,' said the chairman, nodding at Zhelyabov, who gave Lukin a hefty kick in the ribs. Lukin fell on his side.

'Why did you visit Luka Miroslavich?' demanded the chairman.

'I'd heard his name.'

'When?' asked Sofia.

'When I was a prisoner – at Fontanka 16. I overheard that Kletochnikov had been arrested, and then they mentioned Luka.'

'So you knew he was a traitor?'

'No. I thought they were going to arrest him too. I went to warn him.'

'Why would you care what happened to him?'

Lukin didn't answer. Zhelyabov kicked him again and he coughed, but then spoke. 'I thought he'd be grateful; let me help him.'

'Help him to do what? Betray our entire group?'

'I didn't know that!' Lukin shouted through the bag. 'I wanted to help you to . . . to change Russia.'

'Change Russia how?' asked Sofia.

Lukin's mumble was inaudible. Zhelyabov kicked him again. 'By any means necessary,' he said.

'So why had you already made contact with Dusya?' asked the chairman. 'You expect us to think that was a coincidence?'

'There are no coincidences. I helped her because I had sympathy for her. I'd help anyone who was up against the Ohrana.'

'Helped her because she's a pretty girl, too, I expect,' said Sofia.

Lukin seemed to shrug, though it was hard to tell without seeing his face. The chairman scowled at her; the comment was a distraction. 'That doesn't explain Luka,' he said.

'I tried to ingratiate myself with one revolutionary on the train to Moscow. In Petersburg I tried again with another. The two knew each other. Is that a coincidence?'

'What do you think of the tsar?' asked Sofia.

'He's a tyrant.'

'What about his reforms?'

'He enacted his will – that still makes him a tyrant.'

'You'd prefer if there were still serfs?' asked the chairman.

'I'd prefer to be a slave of the people than the servant of a king.'

There was silence. It was a powerfully simple statement, though that didn't mean it was spoken with any sincerity. The chairman glanced at Kibalchich, who took up the questioning.

'You're a sapper,' he said.

Lukin nodded.

'You understand explosives?'

Again a nod.

'Why is nitroglycerin a better explosive than gunpowder?'

'With nitroglycerin the ignition front travels faster than sound. It explodes. Gunpowder just burns.'

Kibalchich looked at the chairman and nodded, with a hint of excitement in his eye.

'So what's the problem with nitroglycerin?' he continued.

'It's unstable. It's as likely to blow you up as . . . as whatever you're using it for.'

'What's the solution?'

'Mix it with something; sawdust, clay. I've used ground-up sea-shells. Nobel uses kieselgur, which is much the same. They mine it in Simbirsk.'

Again Kibalchich seemed satisfied, but he had more questions.

'How much did you use at Geok Tepe?'

'Just over 2,000 kilograms; that's around 5,000 pounds.'

'Let's move on to tunnelling. At what separation should you place your props?'

Lukin laughed. 'That depends on a dozen factors. The width and height of the shaft; the nature of the earth.'

'And what's the earth like in Geok Tepe?'

'Sand, sandstone.'

'And here in Petersburg?'

Lukin laughed again. 'In a word – mud.'

'That's hardly specific.'

'Enough!' The chairman's interruption cut through the room.

'I'm confident the lieutenant knows his job. The question is where his loyalties lie.'

'How can we know?' asked Sofia. 'It's not worth the risk. If we take him in we'll all be arrested within days.'

'So what?' asked Kibalchich. 'If we kill him we'll all be arrested in weeks anyway. This organization is on the brink of collapse. The question is what we do in that time.'

'What can we do?'

'If we can get that tunnel completed, the tsar could be dead before the month is out. I think this man could get it done.'

'He's army,' said Zhelyabov. 'He should be with the Fighting Services Section, not with us. He'll be more use *after* the tsar is dead, when we need to take control.'

'We're too short of people to worry about that,' pressed Kibalchich. 'Since they got Goldenberg to talk the arrests haven't stopped. There's more of us in the Peter and Paul than out.'

'It's still a question of trust,' said Sofia.

'It's a question of whether he'll do it,' said Bogdanovich, speaking for the first time. It was a good point.

'So let's ask him,' said the chairman, bored with the prevarication.

'Wait,' said Sofia. 'I want to see his face when he speaks.'

The chairman considered. It would not only allow Lukin to be seen, but to see. Did it matter? Did it really matter whether he lived or died? Did it matter if the tunnel was ever completed? None of it was relevant.

'Very well then,' he said. 'Take off the hood.'

He leaned forward so that his face was just inches from Lukin's. Lukin knelt, his hands tied behind his back. Zhelyabov held him by the shoulders as Sofia began to loosen the cord around his neck. Moments later, Lukin's face was revealed. He blinked, becoming used to the lamp-lit room after a day in darkness. He turned his head, exercising his stiff neck. As his eyes adjusted he began to take in his surroundings. He glanced from face to face, trying to link individuals to voices, until his gaze settled on the one that was directly in front of him. His eyes met the chairman's and he blinked again. His face showed surprise.

Surprise and, just as the chairman had expected, recognition.

CHAPTER XVI

I T WAS DARK AND COLD AND DAMP AND MIHAIL'S HEAD THROBBED. But he was alive. Twenty-four hours before, that had not seemed like a probable outcome. Better than that, he had now been accepted – albeit tentatively – into the People's Will. And he had discovered something that he had never expected: the identity of the chairman of their Executive Committee.

It was Dmitry.

Conversely, Dmitry had recognized him, but that – so Mihail hoped – mattered little. To Dmitry he was simply Lieutenant Lukin, the man who had so ably assisted his cause at Geok Tepe. There was no reason why Dmitry should have discovered his true identity. On the other hand, to Mihail Dmitry was in fact Colonel Otrepyev of the Ohrana, but clearly Dmitry did not fear being denounced. Why should any of them believe him? And why should Dmitry really care? Mihail doubted whether the assassination of the tsar was his primary concern.

The important thing was that for Mihail the trail was hot again.

He sat up and put his hand to his head. They had knocked him out a second time and he'd found himself here in the street. The last he had heard they were going to discuss him, but evidently the decision had now been made; otherwise he'd be dead.

Dmitry's had not been the only face he recognized. There was the man who had greeted him at Luka's flat, with the pince-nez and the battered top hat, and also the big man who had been keeping an eye on Dusya on the train. And then there had been the woman with the large forehead who had been watching Konstantin's coach, who today had a strange semicircular wound to the side of her hand. How many more of the souls that Mihail had walked past on the city's streets might also be connected with the People's Will? Aleksandr should be afraid.

Mihail looked around and tried to work out where they had dumped him. It was a quiet back street; it could be almost anywhere in Petersburg. He pulled himself to his feet, his head still throbbing, and began to walk. The road sloped a little and he chose the downhill path; the key to navigating this city was to find a river or a canal. It wouldn't be long before he came to one.

His senses gradually returned to him as he walked, and it was only a few minutes before he realized that he wasn't alone. Someone was shadowing him, travelling on the other side of the street, always hanging a little way behind. He thought about breaking into a run, or doubling back around a block of buildings, but none of it appealed to him. If he was being tracked by an *ohranik*, then what did he care? If they arrested him he could simply appeal to his father for help. If he was being followed by the People's Will, they would still learn nothing. And why should they bother? They'd only just let him go.

He continued along the road and then turned left, where the way sloped more steeply. Soon he hit a river that he could only guess was the Fontanka. He was south of it, so he followed its curve round to the right. Eventually he found himself on familiar territory, and headed north towards his hotel. Still his pursuer shadowed him and still he didn't care. By now he felt confident as to who the diminutive figure was.

In twenty minutes he was back at the door of his hotel, but he didn't go in. Instead he turned and marched swiftly towards where the tail stood watching him. He covered the distance between them in seconds, but there was no attempt to evade him. When he was close, he saw what he had suspected. It was Dusya. He hadn't heard her voice during his interrogation, but when the hood had been removed he'd caught a glimpse of her, at the back of the room, her lips pressed tightly together and her eyebrows pinched.

'Why don't you come in?' he asked.

She lowered her hood so that he could see her face more clearly, but shook her head.

'So you're just going to stand out here all night?'

'I just wanted to see you safely home,' she said.

'They're dangerous stairs. I might still not make it.'

She smiled. 'I'd better make sure then.'

They walked back across the street side by side and went in. Mihail spoke briefly to the porter to ask him to send up some refreshments, then he and Dusya went up to his room. It was not the kind of establishment that asked questions concerning its residents' guests. It would have been a quite different matter at the Hôtel d'Europe. Mihail still had the key to one of their rooms. Would Dusya be impressed by such splendour, he wondered.

'I'm sorry,' she said as soon as they were alone.

'I'm not,' he replied. This was no time to drop his guard. He was still being interrogated, simply in a more charming manner.

'What do you mean?' Dusya was removing her coat. She was an attractive girl, but tonight she looked something special. It took Mihail a moment to realize; she was wearing make-up. He'd never seen that before. It fitted his concept of why she was here.

'Your freedom, your lives depend on you making sure that you can trust the people you work alongside. And if I join you, then my life depends on it too. So it's nice to know just how seriously you take security.' He too began to take off his overcoat. 'That sort of peace of mind is worth a few bruises.' He winced as he spoke, perhaps a little theatrically, but it hardly mattered.

'Is it very bad?'

'Nothing broken – I don't think.'

She stood and went over to the washstand. 'Take off your shirt,' she instructed, dipping a flannel into the cold water.

He sat on the bed and complied.

'And I'm sorry about last night – about tricking you,' she said.

'It was the smart thing to do. You couldn't just invite me over for a chat; it would have given me time to work out my story.' He glanced up at her and smiled. 'If I'd needed to.'

'I didn't have to . . . you know. They told me it would distract you.'

'It worked,' he said with a laugh which he cut short, genuinely in pain.

She drew her breath over her teeth. 'Those don't look too pleasant.'

He turned and tried to see, lifting his arm. He could feel each point at which Zhelyabov had kicked him, more to his back than his side. He stretched to see further.

'I wouldn't if I were you,' she said, then began to dab at him with the flannel. He relaxed and let her get on with it. The cold water stung at first, but then began to ease the pain.

The People's Will had been right to grab him and take him by surprise for just the reason he had said. But then they'd made the mistake of leaving him alone for twenty-four hours. The idea, he presumed, was to make him sweat, and he'd done that for the first two or three, until he'd realized just where he was and why he was there. Then he'd had plenty of time to think – to do exactly what he'd said and get his story straight. He guessed they were unsure of him, seeing him as a possible ally. He worked out what they might know of him. What he had said to Dusya; what he had said to Luka. If Luka had revealed all then Mihail was doomed, but he'd not had long between speaking to Mihail and his death – and it seemed more likely that he would have reported to Iuda rather than to the others. Mihail's only fear was if they had any inkling as to what had happened within Fontanka 16. Konstantin had told him of one spy they had just uncovered there; there could be others, but Mihail's continued survival indicated not.

'So is it true what you said?' she asked. 'About why you spoke to me, and then Luka?'

'You're asking me if I just lied to the Executive Committee?'

'No, but . . . I thought there might have been another reason.'

She was more likely to mean in regard to herself than Luka. 'I was brought up to be a gentleman. You were a lady in distress.'

She went back to the bowl and rinsed the cloth. Mihail could see his blood mixing with the water. He thought about the bathroom in the Hôtel d'Europe, and the blood he had washed away. In his trunk was Zmyeevich's blood, and more besides. Much as he wished she'd go, so that he could examine it, he sensed she was here to do more than wash his wounds.

'So what happened to Luka?' he asked.

'What do you mean?'

'I read about it, Dusya. I'm not stupid. I can guess who did it.'

'He was a traitor. He paid the usual price.' She began tending to his wounds again.

'I got the impression that the two of you were close.'

'At times we were. But we don't hold to the view that a man and a woman should be exclusively faithful to one another.'

'We?' asked Mihail. 'So Luka agreed with the idea?'

'He did, but I meant "we" in a broader sense; our movement. Marriage is a vehicle for the state to control us, just like poverty. Sex belongs to us, the people, the same as the land does.'

She turned as she spoke, placing her hand on Mihail's and squeezing it. There was passion in her eyes, but he suspected it was not the personal attraction of one human being for another. Her fervour was for the idea; to her he was not a man but an audience.

'I'd have thought any affection would be a distraction from the ultimate goal,' he said. 'Wouldn't it be better to postpone it till afterwards?' It was a question he had asked himself often, though the goal he was speaking of was quite different from hers. His conclusion was that it did no harm, as long as it became no more than a distraction.

'That could be a long time to wait.'

'Not from what I heard today. It sounds like the end is very close.' Again, he hoped that it applied to his own quest.

'I'm not supposed to talk to you about that,' she said.

'Ah! And what are you supposed to talk to me about?'

She grinned. 'All done,' she said, returning to rinse the cloth once again. 'I hear you studied in Moscow.'

'That's right.' So this was what they were meant to discuss.

'We have a lot of supporters at the Imperial Technical School.'

'I know.'

'And yet you weren't one of them?'

There was a knock. Mihail raised a finger to his lips and then put his shirt back on. He went over to the door and opened it a crack. It was only a boy with the food he had ordered. He took the tray and handed back a few kopeks. He put the tray on the table and poured two glasses of the red wine, then grabbed a piece of bread and began to gnaw on it. It had been over a day since he had eaten.

'Do have some,' he said after a minute or so, through a mouthful of cheese.

'I'll let you have what you want first,' she said. She sipped at her wine.

In the end, Mihail ate everything, leaving only an apple for Dusya out of politeness, though he would still have liked to devour it. He hadn't realized how hungry he was. She ate it at his insistence, but he guessed that she too was being polite.

'You were telling me about Moscow,' she said.

'Don't think I was,' he replied, 'but I can if you want.'

'So why didn't you get involved at the institute? From what we hear, you kept your head down.'

'I mistrust youth,' he said.

'What?' she laughed.

'Even in myself.' He leaned forward, speaking intensely. He was being honest, even though his purpose was to deceive. 'Think about it. At the institute half of them, maybe more, claimed to oppose the tsar. Not openly – that was the fun of it. It makes them important – makes it clear to everyone that they care about something; really care. And that makes them popular. Then others see it work and copy; not just the action, the belief. But there comes a point where it's obvious that it's just a fashion and so there's others – the richer ones generally – who have to react against it and say how much they love their tsar. But how many really keep their beliefs, on either side, as they grow older? They'll pay lip service to them, to prove they're not hypocrites, but in the end they just get on with their lives as best they can and hope the Ohrana don't have their names on file.'

'But that's not you.'

'No, but I thought it might be. How was I to know? I remember thinking to myself, if I still believe this at twenty-five, then I'll know it's right.'

'And now you're twenty-five?'

'No, I'm twenty-three, but I bumped into a pretty girl on the train and I realized it might be my only opportunity to get involved.'

She smiled, averting her eyes. 'And you think that I'm one of those who'll grow up and forget it all?'

'How old are you?'

'I'm twenty-six.'

'Well if I'm old enough, then you are.' He noticed a twinkle in her eye and realized the other meaning of what he'd said. 'You're old enough to let the man you loved die,' he added.

She leaned forward. 'Does that bother you so?'

Mihail tried to hide his reaction. It was so preposterous a thing to say, and yet she believed it so sincerely – more than that, she expected him, and presumably the rest of the world, to see it in the same way. They called themselves the People's Will, but they had no understanding of the people, no comprehension that such clinical decisions as to what was best meant nothing when stood up against the sense in men's hearts of what was right. Though who was he to judge? He had no idea – nor very much interest – as to what lay in the hearts of ordinary men, but he felt pretty sure it wasn't what Dusya stood for.

And yet for Mihail specifically, she was right. It didn't bother him that Luka, his half-brother, was dead any more than it bothered her that Luka, her lover, was dead. Mihail had a singular destiny to fulfil and so did Dusya – and the rest could go hang. They were made for each other. He felt a sudden attraction to her. It was mostly physical, but also the realization that they were kindred spirits. That was probably a rarer thing for him to find than for her.

'If it did, do you think I'd be here?' he asked.

She leaned forward and kissed him lightly on the lips. He pulled away and put his hand to the back of his head, which was still bruised.

'I know what happens next,' he said. 'I don't want another bang on the head.'

She giggled and leaned towards him once more. 'Not this time.' She kissed him again.

'You don't have to, you know, just because they've told you to.'

She looked at him intently. 'Just because they told me to doesn't mean I don't want to.'

Mihail gazed back. Where would be the harm? It would

make her – and therefore her comrades – more trusting of him. It wouldn't hinder his search for Iuda in any way. And she was attractive and willing and . . . here; and it had been a long time. But however pleasant it might be, it riled him that this opportunity to exercise his passions came at the behest of the Executive Committee of the People's Will. Christ, they'd probably even taken a vote on it!

A chuckle escaped him.

'What?' she asked.

'They told you to say that too, didn't they?'

The slap to his face was well deserved, but it didn't make what he'd said untrue. Now she was on her feet and putting her over-coat back on.

'I'm sorry,' he said.

'Don't be,' she replied. 'You were right.'

'Does that make a difference?'

She looked at him, puzzled, giving him one last chance.

'Please don't go,' he said. It was only when the prospect of her departure had become a reality that he realized how much he wanted her, and feared that he had pushed her too far.

She considered, then took off her coat again. It was inevitable now. Mihail lay back on the bed, feeling content, but detached from his normal life – from his quest. She sat beside him, with her back to him. He ran his finger down her spine through the cloth of her blouse, enjoying the fact that she allowed him to more than the sensation itself. It was better that he had pushed her – better that they knew where they stood, each aware of the other's insincerity. She reached to the table beside them and extinguished the lamp, leaving them in darkness.

'Don't stop,' he heard her say.

He reached out again and this time only her bare skin stood between his fingertips and the ridges and valleys of her vertebrae. She turned and he managed to remain in contact with her, so that now he could feel the smooth flesh of her belly. Her lips pressed against his, and he silently thanked the Executive Committee for their efforts.

*

When Mihail awoke he was alone. He tried to think what had roused him, then he heard the sound again – a knocking at the door. It was only the maid, bringing hot water. Mihail washed and dressed. Looking in the mirror as he shaved, he noticed how broadly he was smiling, as memories of his night with Dusya played through his mind. He glanced over at the rumpled bedding. It was no surprise that she had gone – to have stayed might have suggested a depth to their relationship. She knew where her loyalties lay, but even so Mihail wondered whether he might in future gain some slight advantage if she had to make a choice between him and her beliefs. She pretended to be stalwart, but she was still human. As was Mihail. He knew that he too must take care that affection for her did not cause his determination to waver. But already he felt the urge to be with her again, if only to test that determination.

But that was for later. What was he to do next? He felt both energized and helpless. Now that he knew of Dmitry's connection with the People's Will, he felt sure he was a step closer to Iuda, but he knew also that there was little he could do but wait. He had, it seemed, been accepted into the organization. If he started investigating they would become suspicious – take him for an *ohranik*. But they would come for him. They needed him. He would uncover what he needed to know, but at their pace, not his.

Besides, he had another line of enquiry – perhaps a better one, but one that he had not had a moment to examine.

He went over to his trunk and opened it. He found the knapsack where he'd left it, underneath his clothes. He looked inside. The blood sample was still there, undamaged; Zmyeevich's blood. He knew full well the power that it gave him. He could simply open the curtains and throw it out into the sunlight and Zmyeevich, wherever he might be in the world, would experience the most unimaginable pain. But the moment would be short-lived. There were better uses to which he could put his treasure. He grabbed the shirt he had been wearing the previous night. It was in a sorry state anyway. He ripped off a sleeve and used it to wrap the vial safely, then pushed it back among the clothes in the trunk.

Then he moved on to the papers he had taken. Iuda's journals were written in English, as he had expected. The other documents were in a variety of languages, French and Russian mostly, but some English and even a few in what looked like Italian, which Mihail had never studied. He began to skim through the folder marked 'Petersburg', but did not learn much. Most of the Russian material related simply to Iuda's rooms at the Hôtel d'Europe, some of which was new to Mihail – such as the fact that Iuda had first settled there on 6 December 1876 – but was of little value.

He was interrupted by a knock on the door. It was the maid again, this time offering him a note.

Dear Mihail Konstantinovich,
There is a basement shop on the east side of Malaya Sadovaya Street which sells a fine selection of cheeses from around the world. Please meet me there at 10 o'clock this morning.
Yours,
Yevdokia Yegorovna Nikonova

Mihail looked at his watch. It was after nine. For a moment he hesitated. The last time he had been lured away by Dusya it had ended in a great deal of discomfort for him. He believed he had been accepted into the People's Will, but could he ever be sure? If they were to discern one tiny extra fact about him, it could change their entire attitude; and they would not hesitate to deal with him as brutally as they had Luka. What if he had talked in his sleep? But if he didn't go, they would come and find him anyway, and worse, he might forfeit the opportunity to gain the knowledge he craved.

He packed the papers away and set off. The direct route was to head towards the Admiralty and then turn down Nevsky Prospekt. This would take Mihail past the Hôtel d'Europe. He wondered for a moment whether it might be tempting fate to go so close to where he presumed Iuda still resided, but he dismissed his fears. It was a sunny winter's day. Iuda would be sleeping. Even if not, he wouldn't dare even peek out of the window, and anyway those windows looked out of the back of the hotel, not the front; a *voordalak* would seldom ask for a room with a view. The thought of his pilfering of Iuda's hotel rooms brought to mind the fact that he too could easily become victim of a similar manoeuvre. Dusya knew where he was staying, and therefore undoubtedly Dmitry did too, as chairman of the committee. There was no reason for him to search Mihail's rooms, but if he did he would be overjoyed at what he found. Mihail would have to find himself a new den – for those stolen possessions, if not for himself. Another room in another cheap hotel would suffice. He had Iuda's money to pay for it, and he could always sell that final sapphire. It occurred to him that it might already be too late – that Dusya's letter had drawn him away from his rooms with the express intent of allowing them to be searched. There was no time to go back, but Mihail cursed his stupidity.

There was a little snow in the air as he pressed on down the street. He buried his hands in his pockets to keep them warm, wishing he had worn his uniform, but knowing that civilian clothes would be more appropriate for the day ahead. He passed the corner of Mihailovskaya Street and the hotel without incident and carried on past the frontage of shops and bars and the gateways that led to courtyards within the blocks of buildings. A break appeared in the façade, allowing access to a little blue and white church, set back from the street, behind the buildings. Mihail quickly realized what it was: the Armenian Church. His mother had often said that it was a place he should visit if he ever went to Petersburg, but as in everything to do with her there was a sadness to the truth behind it. She had always promised to take her other children there – Mihail's half-brothers and sister – but it had never happened. Only Luka had survived into adulthood, and now he was gone too. Had he ever fulfilled his mother's wish, Mihail wondered. He made a vow to himself that he would one day go in there and look around – but not today.

He pressed on across Sadovaya Street and finally turned into Malaya Sadovaya. It stood right opposite Aleksandrinsky Square and beside it the library where Mihail had been studying just two days before. The 'Malaya' of its name evidently referred to its length rather than its width. It spanned only one block, between Nevsky Prospekt and Italyanskaya Street, but for that short length was broad enough for perhaps six carriages to run side by side, without even taking to the pavements. About a third of the way along, Mihail saw it.

Склад Русских Сыров – Е. Кобозева
Russian Cheese Store – Y. Kobozev

The sign was at the level of his knees. Beneath it a set of stone steps with an iron railing led down to the basement shop. Barred, arched windows peeped just over the level of the pavement. As he descended Mihail noticed in one of them an unlit votive candle in front of a small icon depicting Saint George. He smiled; another connection to Zmyeevich – another coincidence.

He went inside.

He was immediately assailed by the aroma of cheese. Looking around, it was easy to see that the source of the smell was everywhere. Behind the counter stood a young woman, about the same age as Dusya and just as attractive. She gave Mihail a furtive glance, though he did not recognize her face. Over by the shelves stood a more familiar figure – Mihail had noticed him during the brief period he'd had to take in the members of the Executive Committee. He was explaining the merits of a particular cheese to another man who was a stranger to Mihail – presumably a customer. Soon the shopkeeper had cut a piece and had taken it over to the counter for his assistant to wrap and charge for.

'Good morning, sir,' he then said to Mihail. 'And what might I interest you in?' There was not a flicker of recognition in his eyes.

'As it happens, I was looking for something French,' replied Mihail. On his journey there he had not considered the possibility of putting on a show like this; his knowledge of the subject would rapidly dry up.

'Soft or hard, sir? Or perhaps blue?'

Mihail rubbed his chin and narrowed his eyes to gaze at the range of cheeses in front of him, without the slightest idea what country they might hail from. With relief he heard the door close behind him and footsteps ascending, but he was wise enough not to turn and check they were alone. The shopkeeper, however, had a clear view.

'You don't know much about cheese, do you?' he said.

Mihail grinned. 'I'm afraid not.'

'Neither do I, really. They call me Yevdokim Yermolayevich Kobozev – at least they do when I'm in here. Truth be told, it's Bogdanovich. This is my "wife", Anna Vasilyevna.' He indicated the woman. She nodded at Mihail. He conceded a smile, noting that this revolutionary shared a name and patronymic with his father's mistress. Whatever the other inequalities, names were common property to rich and poor in Russia. She turned and went to the window, lighting the candle in front of the icon with a match.

'If it's lit, the place is clear,' explained Bogdanovich. 'If not, just walk on by. The chairman's idea.'

'You certainly take security seriously,' said Mihail.

'That's nothing.' He glanced at Mihail's cheek. Mihail could feel that there was a bruise forming there. 'Did we do that?' Bogdanovich asked, with a hint of concern.

'Afraid so.'

'Sorry. It must hurt. You should slap a bit of Brie on it.'

'Does that help?'

Bogdanovich laughed. 'God knows. It's the sort of stuff I tell customers; seems to keep them happy. We'd be ruined if an *ohranik* came in who was a real expert.'

He led Mihail to a door at the back of the shop and opened it, but didn't go inside. 'That's just a storeroom,' he explained. 'Some of the barrels really contain cheese, but we also keep the earth in here until we can shift it somewhere else. Through here is where the real action happens.'

They went across the shop to another door, which this time they went through. The room was smaller than the shop itself, and furnished with a table and a few chairs. On the table a ledger lay, with similar books on the shelves behind. Next to it stood a samovar and a parcel wrapped in newspaper. On one of the chairs a cat lay curled in sleep. On their arrival it looked up and then leapt on to the table, sniffing at the parcel. Bogdanovich shooed it away. The high windows did not let in much light, but afforded glimpses of feet passing on the pavement above. Beneath was the only unusual feature of the place: a gaping hole in the wall, two-thirds of Mihail's height, leading out in the direction of the street. Mihail considered making a joke about them having trouble with mice, but guessed they'd have heard it from every newcomer who came down here.

Bogdanovich leaned forward and called softly, his hands cupped around his mouth. 'Nikolai!'

The next instant the head and shoulders of a man popped out of the tunnel and into the room. The face was familiar, not least from the pince-nez perched on its nose. Mihail had seen it at Luka's flat and again at his interrogation. The man didn't bother to emerge fully, but held his hand outstretched from where he was. Mihail took it.

'I'm Kibalchich,' he said. 'Nikolai Ivanovich.' Mihail recognized his voice as that of the man who had asked the technical questions. 'I'm very much hoping you're going to be able to help us with a few problems.'

'I'll do my best.'

'Come on in,' said Kibalchich, before disappearing again.

Mihail bent forward and followed. The tunnel was surprisingly well lit. A string of electric light bulbs – of the Edison or Swan type – trailed along its low ceiling, fastened to the regular wooden struts, giving enough light to see to the end where Kibalchich was crouched, not very far away. The whole place stank. In the shop Mihail had put it down to the cheese, but here it was stronger, and fouler.

'Very impressive,' he said.

'The lighting?' replied Kibalchich, with a hint of pride in his voice.

Mihail nodded.

'A little bit of showing off, I'm afraid. We don't use them most of the time; the batteries wouldn't last. Generally it's just oil lamps.'

'I'm surprised you've room for any batteries at all,' said Mihail.

'Ah! That's what you're supposed to think.'

Kibalchich reached out in front of him and for the first time Mihail noticed that the floor at that point was not mud, but a sheet of wood. Kibalchich levered it up to reveal a narrow vertical shaft. It was not a rough structure like the one they were in, but lined with brick.

'We thought it was a well at first,' explained Kibalchich, 'but it turns out there was someone here before us.'

He sat with his legs dangling in the hole and then pushed himself forward. Now he stood in it with the floor at the height of his chest and began to descend more slowly. Evidently there was a ladder beneath him. Mihail gave him a few seconds to get to the bottom and then followed.

The passageway below was far more spacious than that above and far better built, reminding him of the change at Geok Tepe from roughly hewn tunnels to the stonework of the corridors that led to Iuda's prison cell. Here the floor was paved with flagstones and the walls were of brick, curving to an arched roof that supported the weight of the earth above. The ladder and the shaft upwards were at the end of the corridor. Kibalchich was already making his way in the opposite direction, which Mihail judged went out under the street, but at an angle.

The path ended with three archways, one at the end of the corridor and one to either side. In each hung a rusty iron gate, but only the one on the end was closed. Beyond it there was no further light. Mihail could just make out a pile of collapsed stonework, but nothing more.

'That one's locked,' said Kibalchich. 'We could get through, but what would be the point? We're not here for archaeology.'

He went through the doorway on the right. It led to a small cellar, constructed in the same style as the corridor outside and full of clutter. A figure whom Mihail could recognize even from behind was unpacking one of the crates.

'He's here,' said Kibalchich.

Dusya turned and smiled at him. He reciprocated. There was nothing in her face to indicate what had happened between them the previous night. 'You got my invitation then?' she said. The hint of something in her voice could have been genuine or purely his imagination.

'This is where we keep the majority of the batteries,' Kibalchich explained, casting a hand across the room. 'Most are like this one' – he indicated a Leclanché cell on the workbench – 'but we have lead-acid accumulators too. I'll show you what we've got and then we'll go back up and look at the tunnel.'

'Security first,' said Dusya, her coldness contrasting with Kibalchich's enthusiasm. Mihail looked at her plaintively. She gave him the slightest shake of her head and pressed a finger briefly to her lips, so that only Mihail would see. Her need for reticence was not clear; perhaps she was in truth far more diffident about her liaisons than she'd made out. But that was not important. The simple act of secrecy itself was enough to make Mihail feel close to her.

'Of course,' said Kibalchich. 'First a quick observation test. In the living room up there, what was on the table?'

'Ledger. Samovar. Parcel.' Mihail reeled off the items quickly. 'And a cat,' he added after a brief pause.

Kibalchich smirked. 'Very good. And most of those items are just what they seem. The parcel, however, contains nitroglycerin – without any stabilizer. Just inside the entrance of the tunnel there's a revolver.'

'A dangerous combination,' Mihail observed.

'But a necessary one,' Kibalchich countered. 'If there's a raid at least they won't take us alive – and we'll take a few of them with us.'

'Who makes the call?' Mihail asked.

'Whoever's nearest.' Kibalchich saw the expression on Mihail's face. 'Terrible waste, I know.' He picked up a saucer and offered it to Mihail. In it sat half a dozen hazelnuts, still in their shells. 'Care for one?' he asked.

'No thanks.'

'Good answer.'

He put down the saucer and picked up a single nut, turning it around in his fingers until he had it in the orientation he wanted. He pointed to it. 'See there – that little blemish?'

'Just about.'

'That's where we drilled it. Then we scrape out the kernel, fill up the shell and seal the hole with a bit of clay. Ingenious, eh?'

'Fill it with what?' asked Mihail, bewildered.

'Prussic acid,' Kibalchich happily explained. 'Cyanide.'

'And why do you do that?' Mihail asked, though he could hazard a guess.

'Again, it's if we're caught. It's not something you'll need every day, but there are times – you know – if you're carrying a gun, or a bomb. Just keep one of these under your tongue or in your cheek and when they arrest you all you have to do is bite on it. It's better than being tortured and hanged.'

'Be quick about it though,' interjected Dusya. 'They know about them. They'll try to stop you.'

Mihail shot her a look of distaste that he hoped she could tell was in jest.

'We wouldn't want you to suffer,' she said, hiding a smirk.

'Take one,' said Kibalchich.

Mihail complied, slipping the nut into his pocket.

'I'd say take two but it would be . . . superfluous. Though some of us like to have one under the tongue when we're digging the tunnel. If there's a cave-in and you're buried it'll be – well – quicker.'

'You think of everything,' said Mihail.

'You haven't heard the half of it,' replied Dusya.

Both men looked at her, puzzled, before Kibalchich's face revealed an understanding of what she meant.

'Oh yes. One last thing,' he explained. 'We'll need an obituary. Yours, I mean.'

'What?'

'We have our own newspaper – underground, of course. And if one of the heroes of the revolution dies we like to print something of the life that has led to such an act of noble sacrifice. But by then, of course, it's too late. We don't need anything now, but have a think.'

Mihail smiled ruefully. They really had thought of everything. Kibalchich was momentarily thoughtful, but quickly returned to his more familiar enthusiasm, which seemed almost as if projected to hide his fear.

'But that's enough of that,' he said. 'Let me show you our problem.'

Back in the corridor, he gestured towards the other cellar. 'That's just used for storage,' he said, then led Mihail back along the corridor and up the ladder to the tunnel. The stench was stronger again, and Mihail recognized it as sewage rather than cheese. They walked along it a little way. It was low and tight, and neither of them was able to stand upright. Mihail was reminded of Dmitry, stooped in the tunnels beneath Geok Tepe.

'Not much room down here,' he said. 'That chap who inter-rogated me – what's his name? – I bet he's not too comfy down here.'

'Chairman Shklovskiy, you mean?'

Mihail nodded, pleased to have discovered Dmitry's alias so easily.

'He doesn't come down here much,' Kibalchich continued. 'Not since we uncovered those cellars. But you're right – it's a bit cramped for him.'

It wasn't long before the tunnel came to an end. Mihail recalled the width of the road above. As far as he could reckon they'd barely got beyond the pavement. From the mud wall ahead of them a curved wooden surface protruded. In the centre of it was an ugly mound of dirty rags, mixed with some sort of glue. The smell was strongest here, and a little dark fluid still dripped from the bottom of the rags.

'A sewer?' Mihail asked.

Kibalchich nodded. 'Pickaxe went right through it.'

'What's the plan?'

'We can't go around. If we go over we'll be up in the street. So we have to go under.'

'Tricky,' said Mihail.

'Why?' Dusya had come up behind them.

'Because we'll have to dig away the earth supporting the sewer,' explained Mihail. 'It might snap.'

'That's what we're worried about,' agreed Kibalchich. 'Do you think it can be done?'

'Why don't you just use one of the cellars down there?'

'Too deep. We'd have to dig up and that's harder than digging across, especially since that brickwork might be structural to the street. And at that angle it would be difficult to judge when the carriage went over.'

'Carriage?'

'You don't need to know,' said Dusya, sternly. 'It's this tunnel we want you to fix. Can you do it?'

Mihail shrugged. 'Get me a pencil and paper. I'll work it out.'

They headed back to the shop. Kibalchich fetched some paper from a drawer and Mihail began his calculations.

'How far does it need to go?' he asked.

'Twenty feet should get us to the middle of the street.'

'And that's where the carriage will be?' Mihail asked, following on from what Kibalchich had said earlier.

'That's no business of yours.' It was Bogdanovich who spoke, echoing Dusya's words. 'Not yet at least.'

Mihail returned to his work. The question had not needed answering. He'd been here before, or somewhere very like it. This was on a smaller scale, but the basic plan both here and in Geok Tepe was the same. First you dig a tunnel, then you lay your dynamite, then you blow it up. There the intent had been to bring down a city wall. It didn't take a genius to guess what the plan was here.

CHAPTER XVII

KIBALCHICH COULD HAVE WORKED IT OUT FOR HIMSELF, BUT he lacked the confidence. His understanding of mathematics and engineering was far greater than Mihail's, but having done all the calculations he couldn't look at his numbers and then look at the tunnel and say to himself, 'That feels about right.' Mihail had more experience to fall back on, and had never been allowed the luxury of doubting himself; there had always been an impatient officer at his shoulder, demanding he get on with it.

Not long ago, that officer had been Dmitry, in the guise of Colonel Otrepyev. Why, Mihail wondered, had not Dmitry in the guise of Chairman Shklovskiy exerted the same pressure upon Kibalchich? He began to piece together an answer.

Once they had decided upon a course of action, then digging began again. Almost everyone pitched in – the women as well as the men – though as far as Mihail could tell, Dmitry never came down. Zhelyabov never dug, though he did help out. Like Dmitry, he was too big to be able to employ his great strength in the enclosed space.

Over the following days Mihail began to get to know his comrades, to admire some and despise others. Sofia Lvovna he liked least of all. He wondered even if she might be mad, her dedication to the cause so eclipsed every other consideration. It was a madness he knew well, though his cause was different and he was forced to keep it hidden, but it helped him to fit in well with them. Where they said 'Aleksandr' he had merely to think 'Iuda' and he became indistinguishable in his hatred from those

263

around him. And even as he pretended to be one of them, their attitudes began to rub off on him. Each night he would lie awake thinking about it; it worried him to admit it, but more and more he could imagine himself remaining quiet – not warning the tsar, his uncle, of the plans against him.

Dusya did not often come to the cheese shop, and when she did her slight build made her little use for digging. Even when she was there she and Mihail spoke little. They exchanged occasional glances and smiles, but had few opportunities for private conversation. Their nights together were quite different. Since the first time they had lain together in each other's arms there had been only two occasions when he had heard her tapping at his door and let her into his room and his bed. In the darkness it could almost have been anybody, but he quickly grew to know every detail of her using only the four senses that remained. As planned, he had rented another room in another hotel, but never stayed there – it served purely to store his precious booty. Neither Dusya nor any of them knew of its existence, as far as he could tell.

He never asked her again whether the Executive Committee was aware of their relationship; he had no desire to offend her, or more importantly to lose her. He would assume that they were and hope that they were not. It was hard to imagine her speaking of it to anyone. In the presence of the others she seemed very different from the brave girl who had couriered dynamite halfway across the country, or the passionate one whose nails and teeth left their marks on his back and chest, or the thoughtful one he spoke to in the darkness afterwards. When with them she willingly placed herself in their shadows, particularly when it came to Sofia. She wanted to be like her but, Mihail was happy to observe, she could not achieve it.

It was with Kibalchich that he formed the strongest bond. It was unsurprising; they both understood engineering and they found themselves working side by side every day. The chances were that they would either despise one another or become friends. If Kibalchich had possessed any true dedication to his cause, it might well have proved to be the former, but he was one of the type that Mihail had spoken to Dusya about. His dedication today was just an echo of the radicalism of his youth, but he dared not admit it – not to himself and certainly not to his comrades. But it was obvious to anyone that Kibalchich now had a new passion towards which to dedicate his great intellect, and that passion was science.

They had been speaking, as all the group often did, of the world to come – a world in which Russians were freed from the Romanov tyranny. But Kibalchich's view of the future had little to do with politics.

'In our lifetimes,' he said earnestly, 'men will walk on the moon.'

'You think so?' Mihail replied.

'Why not? And they wouldn't just walk. They would run faster and leap higher than any man has dreamed – Olympian gods compared to those left on Earth.'

'How come?'

'You'd weigh less. About a seventh of what you do here. Look.'

Kibalchich had shown him the calculations. There was no principle that he invoked of which Mihail was unaware, but Mihail had never in his whole career thought of applying his knowledge to so impractical a question as what a man would weigh on the moon. But Kibalchich was not a practical man.

'And how would you get there?' Mihail asked.

'Aha! You'd need a rocket.'

'You mean like a firework, or a Congreve Rocket?'

'Exactly, but bigger of course, with some kind of vessel for the explorers.'

'It would be impossible.'

Kibalchich had proved him wrong, with a few lines on a scrap of paper. It was a tricky formula; the more fuel you carried, the more fuel you needed to lift its own weight, along with that of the men and equipment on board. But it was calculable and finite. The amount required was enormous, Kibalchich was happy to concede it, but it wasn't so large as to be unattainable within a few decades.

'I've already started work on a design,' Kibalchich explained.

'To go to the moon?'

Kibalchich's face fell. 'Small steps, Mihail. We'll start by travelling between cities first, then continents. These things take time.'

'You have your plans here?' Mihail asked.

Kibalchich glanced around furtively and lowered his voice. 'No. I'm not sure I'd trust everyone here. They wouldn't understand. But I have them at home. I'll show you some time and see what you think – get a practical viewpoint on them.'

Mihail never saw Kibalchich's rocket designs, and doubted he would have understood them if he had, but he secretly imagined the two of them as old men, themselves too decrepit to take that fateful flight, but able to stand and watch others depart for the moon in Kibalchich's machine.

In the evenings he would read through Iuda's papers, sitting on the scruffy, uneven chair that along with the bed made up the sole furnishings of his second hotel room. He would not sleep here – if he did, how would Dusya know where to find him? – but he had brought his more unusual possessions here. He placed the hazelnut that Kibalchich had given him on the window ledge and would glance up at it as he turned each page. It was a reminder of just how dedicated these people were, and reaffirmed how dedicated he would have to be to defeat Iuda. He imagined his teeth pressing down on the shell and feeling the liquid inside spill on to his tongue and roll down his throat, wondering just how much pressure his jaw would have to exert to break it. He thought about slipping it into his mouth and resting his teeth lightly against it, allowing fate to decide if it would shatter or not. But he never did.

From Iuda's books on vampires he learned of new weaknesses and new dangers of which he and Tamara had never been aware. Even in these later volumes where Iuda had begun to summarize his years of work there was too much for Mihail to remember every detail, and he could not know now what might one day be of use to him. The other correspondence, he hoped, would be of more help in locating Iuda, but there was nothing. The most obscure collection of letters dated back to the 1830s and were signed Auguste de Montferrand, a name with which Mihail was unfamiliar. The letters discussed issues of architecture, sometimes in general, sometimes very specifically, particularly with regard to the positioning of windows – an issue over which any *voordalak* would be concerned. It would seem that de Montferrand was taking advice from Iuda – whom he addressed as Vasiliy Innokyentievich Yudin, an alias which Mihail knew – on the design of some building, but there was no clue to its location, save for the fact that the documents were in the folder marked Petersburg. In all of it there was thankfully no indication that Iuda knew where Tamara had fled to in 1856, nor that he had any inkling she had borne a son.

The strangest thing he found was a single sheet of paper, not part of any of the notebooks, but placed between the pages of one of them. It could have been put there as a bookmark or for safe keeping. In any event it was a peculiar thing for a creature like Iuda to have in his possession: a charcoal drawing of a woman's breast. The artist had talent and Mihail mused as to why it had been drawn. It was more than an anatomical diagram; it seemed to have been crafted with love, though not with lust. It lacked the exaggerated perfection that might come from a lascivious imagination. And yet it was not so mundane that it did not raise desire within him. It was initialled and dated:

S.M.F. 22.iv.1794

It could be another of Iuda's aliases, though he would have been young judging by the date. It was hard to conceive that such a thing could have been created by Iuda's hand. Mihail lingered over it for a while, then continued on through the journals.

The other possible trail that might eventually lead Mihail to Iuda had gone cold. Dmitry never came down to the cellar of the cheese shop, and Mihail found no opportunity to make contact with him. The name of Shklovskiy came up occasionally in conversation, and Mihail did his best to uncover more about him, but he dared not appear too inquisitive. It seemed that at first, before he had gone to Geok Tepe, Dmitry had been most concerned with what lay beneath the cheese shop. But once the digging had begun, once those older cellars had been unearthed and explored, he had lost interest.

The location of the cheese shop had one further advantage as far as Mihail was concerned: it was close to the Hôtel d'Europe. On travelling to and from his subterranean work there was ample opportunity for Mihail to keep an eye out for Iuda, either entering or leaving. He even managed to exchange the odd word with the concierge, who, in return for a few roubles, would tell him what he had seen.

But whether it came from the concierge's mouth or from Mihail's own eyes, the conclusion was the same. Iuda had not returned to the hotel.

Iuda looked out across the frozen river. The icy surface hid the turbid currents beneath. More than once those currents had clutched at him and carried him where they would. But they were all duplicates of the Berezina, where Lyosha had held his hair and thrust him beneath the surface. He didn't remember how he'd escaped – he'd been unconscious and so whatever it was that had allowed him to live on, it was not his own wits. He had washed up and marched west with the pathetic vestiges of the Grande Armée. It was only in Warsaw that he had managed to get away from them. He was desperate and alone and with only one thought in his mind: to go home. It was another four months before he found himself in England and once there he realized that Esher meant nothing to him. There was only Oxford, where at least a few people remembered him.

And there his life had met a turning point. The letter had been waiting for him for almost a decade. His father's brother, his uncle Edmund, had died and named Cain as the sole beneficiary of his will. The estate at Purfleet was worth thousands, and there were other assets to boot. It all belonged to Cain. He let the property to tenants to get an income, and bought himself a house in London, on Piccadilly, but still he spent much of his time in Oxford, writing a thesis based on what he had learned on his travels. He soon understood he could do little without his original notes, and so he had to return to where he had hidden them, in Petersburg. There he had reacquainted himself with Lyosha's wife, Marfa, and with his son Dmitry. It was then he had realized how much he loved Russia – loved the naivety of its people and their potential for exploitation – and had known he would return there.

But there were other matters to attend to. On returning to England his thesis on the fauna of the Crimea gained him a doctorate and, with the addition of later work, a Fellowship of the Royal Society. But it all meant so little; the property, the wealth, the accolades. Still he craved only knowledge, a knowledge for which he would be laughed out of the Royal Society even for mentioning. He wanted to know of the *voordalak*. One day perhaps London would accept such a paper for the work of genius that it was, but that was not where he would do his research. From his uncle he had money, from Oxford he had an education. Both would help further his studies, but they would take place in Russia, in the Crimea, in the caves he had seen beneath Chufut Kalye. It was more than most scientists could dream of.

Was this, then, the fate for which he had been destined? Was this the proper life of an FRS – to lie on his stomach on the bank of the Neva, spying upon his enemies? But he knew he must watch them, even though the more he watched, the more he despised them. They were like gypsies, occupying property that did not belong to them and then treating it as their home. In Zmyeevich it was understandable; he hailed from the same part of the world as they did – it was in his blood. For Dmitry there was no excuse. Iuda had watched them for several nights, ever since he had discovered the invasion of his rooms at the hotel. He could no longer sleep there, and couldn't return to the cavern beneath Senate Square – Zmyeevich and Dmitry already knew of it. But he'd little thought that they would choose to make their own nest there. Iuda himself continued to rest in the same tomb in the Smolenskoye Cemetery that had had been his home since his first night of freedom. From there it was only a short walk, at dusk, down to the northern bank of the Great Neva, from where he could look out over the river, across Senate Square and to the entrance of Saint Isaac's. By the second night he'd acquired – unpaid-for – a pair of binoculars from a shop on Nevsky Prospekt, and could clearly identify the two figures that slipped from the cathedral as night fell, and returned before dawn. He had little doubt as to where they went once inside the building.

Some of the time he kept watch on the Hôtel d'Europe. He had removed his remaining journals from there on his first visit, so there was nothing more to be taken, but there was always the chance that Lukin might go back there, or even Dmitry or Zmyeevich, but there was no sign of any of them. Whatever his suspicions, Iuda was well aware that he had no clear evidence linking Lukin to the two vampires, but what other reason the lieutenant might have for searching his rooms he could not imagine. He could still only deduce that the connection was through Luka – the one person who knew about the Hôtel d'Europe – so there remained other avenues to explore.

But for now his main concern was what Dmitry and Zmyeevich were planning. They wanted to take back Zmyeevich's blood. In that they might already have succeeded. Lukin had certainly taken it and could well have handed it over. Could Zmyeevich sense that there was yet more of his blood out there, safe and far away? In his experiments Iuda had not discerned that ability in any other vampire, but Zmyeevich was a special creature in ways that even Iuda could not imagine.

The other thing they wanted, more even than Zmyeevich's blood, was Ascalon – or at least the fragment of it that had once been in Zmyeevich's possession and which Pyotr the Great had stolen. They did not have it – of that Iuda was quite certain. But they had discovered much about where Pyotr had hidden it. Why else had Dmitry – under the name of Shklovskiy – ordered the mine that was to kill His Majesty to be dug at quite so precise a location in the city.

Iuda peered through the binoculars again. Dmitry had already returned to the cathedral to sleep, but Zmyeevich was still out there, somewhere. It had been like that on several nights, and Iuda had been forced by the rising sun to return to his own tomb before catching sight of the great vampire. He felt uneasy; vulnerable. There was no reason to suppose that they knew of his presence, but seeing Dmitry alone made him wonder whether Zmyeevich might even now be watching him. In a fair fight between them, Iuda did not rate his chances – but fair fights were not his style.

He needed to learn more. He had to hear them, not just see them. He dared not go back into the cellar itself – he would be too easily trapped – but he could at least get into the cathedral safely. It was a building he knew very well indeed. After all, he'd helped to design it.

'Is this the sort of thing you meant?'

Mihail handed over the single handwritten sheet and returned to sipping his tea. It was Friday now – his fifth day of working on the tunnel, and they'd made good progress. They'd got under the sewer and propped it up safely. It sagged a little, but Mihail was sure it wouldn't break again. Now they had only another eight feet to go. There was room for two men at most at the digging face, so they worked in short shifts of just an hour. They left it to the women to clear away the displaced earth and mud, shovelling it into barrels in the storeroom. Currently Bogdanovich and Mihailov were doing the digging. The sound of their work could be heard in the living room where a small group of them sat drinking tea: Mihail, Kibalchich, Zhelyabov, Frolenko and Sofia. The cat, recently discovered to be pregnant, snuggled quietly in Sofia's lap. In the shop beyond Anna Vasilyevna kept an eye out for customers. Dusya had gone out a few hours before, and had not yet returned.

Kibalchich glanced over the obituary that Mihail had scribbled down the previous evening. There was nothing in it that was very far from the truth. It spoke of his youth in Saratov and of his mother, though identifying her as a member of the Lukin family. It referred to his years in Moscow at the Imperial Technical School and then his life in the army. Those occasions when he had mixed with radicals, particularly in Moscow, were emphasized. His exploits in the army and his commendation at Geok Tepe were told in terms of love of country, not love of the tsar. He had no doubt that what Kibalchich had said was the genuine reason behind it. He'd read the underground newspaper and seen the same done for others. But equally he understood that whatever he told them might be checked out, to ensure that he really was who he said he was. It was unlikely they'd discover the truth. He'd taken steps to hide the name Danilov from a far wilier enemy than these.

'Seems reasonable,' said Kibalchich, handing it over to Zhelyabov, who skimmed over it before folding it and putting it in his pocket.

271

'Any last words?' asked Sofia.

'Charming!' Mihail laughed.

Zhelyabov smiled. 'Sofia Lvovna can be very direct. We generally like to print something short and personal to round it off. "My heart lies with the Russian people" or "He laid down his life for freedom".'

'But a little less vomit-inducing,' added Frolenko. Zhelyabov glanced at him sternly, then tried to conceal a smile.

Mihail already had an answer. '"He sought revenge,"' he said. He looked round the faces in the room. Most nodded with approval, but Zhelyabov was an exception. His mouth was twisted, as though eating a lemon. 'Problem?' asked Mihail.

'Is revenge really what we're all about?' replied Zhelyabov.

'We're going to kill the tsar for what he's done,' said Frolenko. 'That sounds like revenge to me.'

Mihail's words had nothing to do with His Majesty, but the debate could apply equally to Iuda, so he listened with interest.

'For what he's done to whom, though?' continued Zhelyabov. 'To ourselves or to the people?' he looked around, expecting an answer, though none came. 'If it's for ourselves, then yes, this is mere revenge. But our business is not vengeance; it's punishment. We've seen what Aleksandr has done to the people. We calmly judged him on their behalf – at Lipetsk. If this is revenge then it is the collective revenge of the entire people. Isn't that the very definition of punishment?'

Mihail's mind wandered back to when he had been a little boy and he and Tamara had gone through the process of trying Iuda. Neither the verdict nor the sentence came as a surprise. But Mihail still knew in his heart it was revenge, and was not ashamed of it. True, as with Aleksandr, it was in part on the behalf of others, but it would be a personal pleasure he took in killing Iuda. He doubted that any of the others here felt differently about their own quest, but it was better to keep his head down and leave it unmentioned.

Thankfully Kibalchich had been thinking along similar lines. 'But it's personal too, isn't it?' he said. 'We are all victims ourselves. I mean, I'm not saying we're wrong, but we're hardly neutral in this.'

'All victims?' asked Mihail.

'Most of us here have spent months in prison, if not years,' explained Zhelyabov. 'You remember the trial of the 193? Me, Sofia, Anna Vasilyevna and 190 others. That's how a lot of us met.'

'You were acquitted,' said Kibalchich with a hint of competitiveness in his voice.

'Which makes it worse. They kept me locked up for almost a year only to decide I'd done nothing wrong.'

'I was in prison for 969 days,' said Kibalchich, more passionate than Mihail had ever seen him or imagined he could be. 'You know how long the actual sentence was? One month – for lending a banned book to a peasant. The rest was waiting for trial.'

'I don't know what you're all complaining about,' announced Frolenko. 'I for one enjoyed my time in prison.'

Kibalchich and Sofia both smiled and Zhelyabov emitted a brief laugh.

'What?' asked Mihail.

'Frolenko saw the other side of prison life,' Zhelyabov explained. 'He was a guard.'

'Seriously?'

'Not quite as you imagine it,' said Frolenko. 'It was back in '77, when Stefanovich, Deutsch and Bohanovskiy were in prison in Kiev. I got myself a job as a warder in the hope of breaking them out. But first we had to get rid of the head warder.'

'A notorious drunk,' added Zhelyabov happily.

'Indeed,' continued Frolenko. 'So we lured him away with the offer of a job at a distillery. I'd been such a good boy that I got promoted to fill his shoes. And my first duty as head warder was to escort those three dangerous subversives out through the prison gates and onwards to freedom, never to return. It was only when the old head warder found there was no distillery and came back begging for his job that they realized anything was up.'

Even Sofia laughed as the story came to an end, but the good humour subsided as first Bogdanovich and then Mihailov emerged from the tunnel exhausted, their bodies plastered with mud. Their hour was up.

Sofia was on her feet in an instant. The cat dropped to the floor and then looked up at her reproachfully. 'I'll get you some water,' she said.

The two men stood, stretching their aching muscles. It was Mihail and Kibalchich's turn next. They both stripped down to only their trousers; it was easier to clean flesh than cloth.

'Any problems?' asked Kibalchich.

'Nothing special,' replied Bogdanovich. 'Slow but steady.'

Kibalchich bent down and crawled in first, followed by Mihail. Today the tunnel was lit only with oil lamps which the two previous diggers had left close to the entrance, and which Kibalchich and Mihail now carried as they made their way out under the street.

'There was something I meant to ask you,' said Mihail, addressing Kibalchich's wobbling backside as it led the way.

'What?'

'Who's Auguste de Montferrand?'

Kibalchich gave a little chuckle. 'You're not from these parts, are you?'

'No. He's big then, is he?'

'One of the city's great architects.'

'What, back in Pyotr's day?' Mihail realized as he spoke the stupidity of the question. The dates on Iuda's letters were much more recent.

'No. Under Aleksandr I and then Nikolai.'

'Was he any good?'

Kibalchich stopped and turned his head. He raised a hand towards the city above them. 'Next time you're up there, look around you.'

'Anything in particular?'

'There's the Kazan Cathedral, just up the road. And he did various rooms in the Winter Palace – though I think we undid a little of his good work there.' He emitted a brief snort.

'Anything else?'

'Saint Isaac's, of course. And the Nikolai Monument behind it. And the Aleksandr Column in Palace Square.'

'Busy chap.'

Kibalchich nodded. 'Died the year they finished Saint Isaac's.'

There was no further for them to go now – they had reached

the tunnel's end. Even in the time since Mihail had first been here it had almost doubled in length, but there was still more to be done. They picked up the shovels that Bogdanovich and Mihailov had left for them and began to dig.

On leaving the cheese shop, Mihail once again made straight for the library. It was easy to rule out some of the buildings that Kibalchich had mentioned. De Montferrand's letter to Iuda had described windows. There were none of those in either of the monuments to emperors past. He also dismissed the work at the Winter Palace, at least for the time being. Even for Iuda, that would be too audacious. That left the two cathedrals: Saint Isaac's and Kazan. In broadest terms they matched what Mihail had read in the letter.

Of course, it might be none of the more famous examples of de Montferrand's work that had been under discussion. Or it might have been something built outside the city. After only a few minutes' research Mihail discovered that he had also done a great deal of work on the design of the park and buildings at Vyborg, over a hundred versts away. But he had to start somewhere. He soon found the information he needed. The Cathedral of Our Lady of Kazan was built during the reign of Aleksandr I and completed even before the start of the Patriotic War. That was too early for the letters.

Saint Isaac's, on the other hand, fitted perfectly. It had taken forty years to construct, spanning more than the entire reign of Nikolai and reaching into that of both Aleksandrs. When Aleksei had stood with the Decembrists in Senate Square it was scarcely begun. The letters from the '30s were bang in the middle of the period. Mihail tried to recall their detail. What he could remember now began to make sense in the context of what he knew, but he still couldn't be sure.

He walked briskly through the snowy streets. As so often he was grabbed by the fear that someone would have broken into his room and taken the papers and the blood, but once again they proved to be safe. He read through the letters voraciously, nodding as each statement suddenly made sense in the context of the cathedral. The last lines he read had originally been the most bewildering of all with their reference to 'the toes of Saint Paul', but now Mihail began to have some idea of what it might mean.

He itched to test out his theory, but it was dark now. Only a fool would go hunting vampires at night. Even by day, in the dark passages that he guessed he would discover beneath Saint Isaac's, it could be dangerous. Thankfully, just that morning, a delivery had arrived for him from Saratov.

Mihail chose midday to visit the cathedral. The sun was rising higher in the sky now as winter drew gradually to a close. The days were over ten hours in length and gaps were beginning to appear in the ice sheet that covered the Neva. Saturday was a busy day at the cheese shop – remarkably, for the purpose of selling cheese. Thus they did not dig on Saturdays out of fear that they'd be overheard.

Mihail walked from his hotel along the English Quay and then turned across Senate Square to approach the cathedral. It was built to impress, and it succeeded. The great golden dome, gleaming in the sunlight, was visible from all over the city but seemed designed to be most imposing from just about this distance, close to the Bronze Horseman. Across the water the spire of the Peter and Paul Cathedral was still the tallest structure in the city, but it had none of the fat, squat authority of the dome, itself stolen, in some sense, from both Saint Peter and Saint Paul.

Mihail had only ever seen them in pictures, easy to find during his researches at the Imperial Library, but the similarities with Saint Peter's in Rome and Saint Paul's in London were unmistakable, particularly with regard to the latter. De Montferrand had even managed to incorporate the Greek Cross floor plan that Wren had been refused permission to use.

But he was not here to admire the building's exterior. He began walking again towards the steps, noticing how the whole edifice seemed almost to shrink as he moved closer, away from the ideal viewing point. As he approached he noticed a hunched figure emerge through the massive bronze doors and walk gingerly down to street level. Mihail recognized him as the old man he had met in the square on the day of Dostoyevsky's funeral, almost two weeks before – the one who had first told him what

Ascalon meant. He hurried his pace so as to intercept him and offer a greeting, but once on the pavement the man moved with unexpected sprightliness and was soon heading towards the Admiralty. Mihail chose not to be distracted from his quest.

Inside the cathedral was quiet, but not empty. It was bright, but the sun was high and Mihail guessed that there would be more light still when the morning or evening sun shone through the tall, arched windows. Two or three people knelt facing the iconostasis, praying. Others simply stood, their necks bent back and their jaws hanging loosely as they gazed up at the painted interior of the dome, or at the walls, or the columns. Almost every surface displayed artwork, either statues or paintings or mosaics, each depicting an individual or scene of the holiest nature. A *dyachok* pottered about the place, tending to candles and incense, as was his duty. Mihail stood among the gawkers, and studied the decoration, with a specific interest in just one adornment that he knew was somewhere inside the building, but had no idea quite where; an icon of Saint Paul.

He found it quickly enough, just outside the Nevsky Chapel in the north-eastern corner of the church. He checked around him, but no one would see him if he was quick. He reached out and rested his thumbs against the saint's big toes, precisely as de Montferrand's letter had suggested. At first there was no response. He began moving the tips of his thumbs in small circles of widening diameter, searching the nearby area. The letter had said that if either button was pressed on its own there would be no discernible movement. Only when both were pushed would the mechanism release. It made it safe, both from accidental activation and from what Mihail was now attempting. But he was determined. Within a minute he felt a slight depression beneath both his thumbs as tiles of the mosaic yielded, and the whole icon felt suddenly loose, pressing back on him as it tried to swing open.

He checked around him again. A man and woman were emerging from the side chapel, arm in arm, but still their mouths were open and their eyes upraised. Mihail could probably have made it through the doorway without them even noticing, but he chose to wait. He moved his hands across the icon until they were side by side, in front of him, still holding the panel in place.

He closed his eyes, as if drawing strength from the apostle. He heard footsteps and when he looked around again he was alone. It took him only a second to pull open the door, climb up into the passageway beyond and shut himself inside.

It was utterly black. Mihail reached into his bag and fetched out a paraffin lamp. Once this was alight he could see more clearly. He examined the door he had come in by, feeling in the corners where it met the walls until he found a catch. He tested it and the panel sprang open again, just a fraction of an inch. It was enough for him to know he had an escape route. He looked ahead. The passageway was not long, but he couldn't make out how it ended. He reached into his bag again and pulled out his favourite weapon of the many he knew could kill a vampire.

At his side he had his military sword, which he could use for beheading. Under his coat he carried the short wooden dagger, with which he could stab through the heart. But both were close-range weapons. This was something rather different, arrived from Saratov just the previous morning.

It was an *arbalyet* – a crossbow. He'd been developing it since he was a boy. The device itself was standard enough, an eighteenth-century German *Armbrust* that he'd found rotting in a barn. The problem had been the bolts. The short drawback and high tension of a crossbow meant that it needed a dense bolt to receive the maximum kinetic energy. That was why iron was the traditional material. Wood though, not iron, was what was needed to kill a *voordalak*. But a wooden arrow fired from an *arbalyet* was liable to fly off in any direction, and even when it hit its target it had little penetration.

In the end Mihail settled on a hybrid: a core of iron or, better, lead, wrapped in a wooden sheath, almost like a pencil, but whose sharp tip was of wood. It was accurate and penetrating – Mihail had successfully hunted wild boar with it more than once. Neither he nor Tamara had seen any reason that it should not be fatal to a *voordalak*, but they had never tested it on one. There had been only one opportunity for such an experiment, and they had chosen to exploit their single chance in a different way. Five glass cylinders safely wrapped in straw had been delivered in the case from Saratov too. Mihail knew just what a potent weapon they could be, but they needed preparation and stealth – and a source of power. But he had seen the effects with his own eyes. The *arbalyet* was a different matter; theoretically sound, but untested. Perhaps soon, very soon, Mihail would discover the truth.

He pulled back the lever, tensioning the bow, and then inserted a bolt. He carried on along the short passageway. Already the splendour of the cathedral seemed far behind. The corridor ended in a descending spiral staircase. Mihail made his way down the stone steps, the lamp held high in his left hand, the crossbow outstretched in his right. Before long the steps brought him to a long, straight corridor, its end further than the lamplight could penetrate. He continued forward, nervous but determined. The narrow passage meant that attack could only come from ahead, and he was ready for that. Besides, however dark it was down here, it was still noon above. Any *voordalaki* he encountered were likely to be sleeping; likely, but not certain.

The passageway ended in a door. Mihail could see a keyhole and an iron ring for a handle. If the door was locked, then he would have to abandon his search, at least for today. He had no explosives with him, and he didn't relish the idea of slowly breaking down the door and giving whatever lay beyond ample time to prepare for his entrance.

The handle turned and the door swept noiselessly open. Beyond was a vaulted brick chamber. Along one wall were a number of cupboards, much like the ones in Iuda's rooms at the Hôtel d'Europe. All were closed and one, at the far end, was locked shut, the handles tied together with a far greater length of chain than was necessary, fixed with a sturdy padlock. It served only to intrigue Mihail.

In the middle of the chamber, among the brick columns that supported the ceiling, was some kind of ornamental pond – perhaps a font. The water in it was still and a few slivers of ice floated on it. It was cold down here, but warmer than on the surface. In the shadows towards the back of the cellar Mihail saw almost what he had been expecting to see. There were two coffins; he had anticipated only one.

It was not unthinkable that Iuda had acquired a companion. When Tamara had encountered him, he had hunted and killed alongside Raisa. Tamara had described her discovery of their two coffins, side by side, just like these two. Mihail wondered if he would be familiar with Iuda's vampire companion. Would it be someone he had seen at night in the streets of Petersburg? Or someone he would recognize, unchanged, as an acquaintance of years before?

On the other hand, two coffins did not necessarily mean two vampires. It might not even mean one. Iuda had known of this place for at least fifty years, when he had somehow persuaded de Montferrand to build the passage down from Saint Isaac's. At some time in that long history he might have slept here with a companion, but that did not mean he did so now. Mihail could not even be sure that Iuda himself slept here. Perhaps he should have waited – watched the cathedral just as he had been watching the hotel. But he was impatient for revenge. He felt his heart beat faster. It might be just moments away.

He went closer. Both coffins had their lids in place. Mihail looked around and found a hook on one of the pillars from which he hung his lamp. It rocked a little from side to side, making the shadows waver. He held the crossbow out in front of him, like a pistol. It would be more accurate if he squeezed the stock tight against his shoulder, but at this range accuracy should not be a problem. He had tested it held close to the carcass of a dead pig; the result had been spectacular. The only thing to remember was not to hold it too close. The bow had to be given time to transfer all its energy to the bolt.

He reached forward with his left hand and curled his fingers under the lid of the first coffin. It did not resist. Once he had raised it an inch he slipped his toe under it, allowing him to straighten up and take better aim. He reached into his pocket and withdrew another bolt. If there were two of them he would have to reload and take aim again quickly.

He gave a kick and the coffin lid slid from its position and hit the brick floor with two hollow thuds, as first one edge and then the other made contact. Mihail's finger tightened on the trigger, but he did not fire. He wanted Iuda to be conscious; wanted him to know.

The coffin was empty. Mihail stepped quickly over it to the

second one, afraid that the noise had disturbed whoever slumbered within, expecting to see the lid begin to rise and pale fingers to creep around the edge and take a grip.

All remained still.

Mihail repeated the process of lifting the lid, first with his hand and then with his foot. This time he scarcely heard the noise of its landing. His mind was occupied with what he saw.

This coffin was not empty. The tall figure that filled the wooden box lay deathly still, his eyes closed, his arms by his sides. Mihail's finger relaxed a little on the trigger and his arm dropped a few inches. He forced himself to raise it again. He had rehearsed this moment so many times in his mind; how he would feel; how he would wake Iuda; how he would say the words, 'My name is Mihail Konstantinovich Danilov, son of Tamara Alekseevna Danilova, daughter of Aleksei Ivanovich Danilov'; how long he would wait to see the look of understanding in Iuda's eyes before he finally pulled the trigger.

But this was not Iuda. It was a *voordalak*, of that there was no doubt, and one that Mihail instantly recognized, but one that he had not expected to find here.

His thoughts were interrupted. A shudder ran through the vampire's body and his chest began to rise and fall. Air scraped in and out of his throat. Mihail's mind raced, wondering whether he should flee, or just kill the creature where it lay.

But it was too late. Dmitry opened his eyes.

CHAPTER XVIII

'ON'T MOVE,' SAID MIHAIL, HIS VOICE CLEAR AND STEADY IN the enclosed space.

'Why shouldn't I?' replied Dmitry.

'Because I have this aimed at your heart.' He jerked the *arba-lyet* a little so that Dmitry would know what he meant.

Dmitry eyed the weapon, but did not move. 'I take it this is more than revenge for our encounter the other day,' he said.

'Much more.'

'And that our paths crossing both here and in Geok Tepe is more than simple coincidence.'

Mihail nodded. Dmitry thought for a moment, giving Mihail time to do the same.

'Please, may I at least sit up?' Dmitry asked.

'Very well, but don't stand,' Mihail replied. The extra seconds it might take Dmitry to rise to his feet could mean the difference between life and death. Mihail backed away a little, so as to be too far for Dmitry to lunge at. He felt something against his thighs, stopping his movement, and realized it was the walled side of the pool. He took a few steps sideways, so that he could see both Dmitry and the door, then leaned back against one of the closed cupboards, making himself a little more comfortable. Meanwhile Dmitry had raised his body and pulled his knees up. He had nothing to lean back against, so he hugged them for support. Despite his stature he looked small and pathetic.

'You didn't expect to find me here, did you?' said Dmitry, suddenly a little more confident.

'Why do you say that?'

282

'Because this is not my home. You came here for just the same reason you went to Geok Tepe; for the same reason I went there – to find Iuda.'

'That's very astute.'

'Thank you.' Dmitry smiled and shifted his position a little. Mihail raised the *arbalyet* an inch or two, just as a reminder that it was still there. 'The question is,' Dmitry continued, 'are you a friend or an enemy of Iuda?'

'The question is, are *you*?'

'How can you ask that? You saw what happened at Geok Tepe.'

'You're a vampire. Your allegiances can change with the flicker of an eyelid.'

'You seem to know a lot about my breed.'

'I've been studying for a long time. I know enough.'

'So why don't you simply kill me?' Dmitry asked.

'I'm considering it.' Mihail realized that he was losing control of the conversation. It should be him asking the questions. 'Whose is the other coffin?'

'It's just a spare.'

Mihail shook his head. He already suspected the answer, but still he needed it confirmed. 'No. In Geok Tepe you spoke of "we". So whose is it?'

'So you understood us; you speak English.'

Mihail said nothing. Dmitry thought for a moment more before speaking.

'That means you also heard our conversation concerning Luka Miroslavich; which would explain why you sought him out . . . though not how you found his address, or even that he lived in Petersburg.'

'You didn't cover your tracks very well,' said Mihail. It was an unnecessary bluff; he would have done better to say nothing. 'I'll ask again, who's with you?'

Dmitry completely ignored the question. 'Have you any idea where Iuda is now?' he asked instead.

'In the Pyetropavlovskaya, where you left him.' Mihail deliberately understated his knowledge, hoping to tease something out of Dmitry.

'I wish that were the case, but I'm afraid he was freed. He must have friends in some *very* high places. We've no idea where he is now.'

'There's that "we" again.'

'You really don't want to know.'

'I don't suppose you actually call him a friend.' Mihail looked for a flicker of reaction, but saw nothing. He tried goading Dmitry. 'It's been, what, a quarter of a century you've been a vampire? You can't have made many friends. An entire human lifetime, and how many vampires have you met? How many that you can trust? Two? One? None?'

Dmitry's eyes narrowed and his lips pressed hard together, becoming pale. For a moment Mihail thought that he'd got to him, but again he seemed to regard himself as in control.

'Mihail Konstantinovich Lukin – that's your name, isn't it?' he said, peering closely at Mihail. 'My father had a friend called Lukin. He was killed by Iuda – well, killed by Iuda in the way that we all were; me, Raisa, Papa. He causes it to happen, but he keeps his hands clean. Anyway – Maks died a long, long time ago. You're not a relative, are you?'

Mihail said nothing.

'No, I don't think you are,' Dmitry continued. 'Not of Uncle Maks, anyway.'

'No,' said Mihail, 'not of Uncle Maks.' He guessed where Dmitry was leading, and did not mind.

'I remember,' said Dmitry, speaking more loudly, as if this were an entirely new topic, 'sitting in a restaurant in Moscow, many years ago – eating blini, as I recall. And I looked into the eyes of the woman opposite me – brown eyes, just like yours. She had red hair too, like yours, but brighter, more vibrant. Anyway, I looked at her and in an instant I just knew that she was my sister – a sister I hadn't even known existed until that moment.'

Mihail kept his silence, trying not to show any reaction.

'Tamara – that was her name.' Dmitry looked Mihail square in the eye. 'How *is* your mother?'

'How's yours?' asked Mihail, brutally.

Dmitry burst into loud, mocking laughter. 'Touché, Mihail. That would really hurt, if I cared any more about my mother than I do about yours.'

'You cared about your father.'

'What makes you say that?'

'You didn't want him to know what you had become.'

'I didn't want him to hear it from Iuda's lips.'

'So why are you pursuing him now?' asked Mihail. 'Aleksei is long dead.'

'Does it really matter? Your reasons for finding Iuda are so much better, so much more noble, more human. You do it out of pure hatred.'

'I don't deny it.'

'And that's why you'll succeed. For my part . . .' Dmitry suddenly stopped, as though he had forgotten what he was going to say. He looked confused; deflated. Then he spoke with sudden resolve. 'I'm going away.'

'Away?'

'From Russia. From Europe. To some undiscovered country. There's a new world out there. America. Africa. Australia. America, I think.'

Mihail was astounded. 'Why?' he asked.

'It's a nice long way away,' Dmitry said simply.

'From Iuda?'

Dmitry's mood changed again. 'I'm quite indifferent to Iuda. But we need what he has. That's why we hate him.'

It was a bizarre contradiction, but it seemed like a chink in the armour.

'And what does he have?' Mihail asked.

'He has our blood,' said Dmitry.

'Your blood?'

'Yes!'

'*Your* blood?' Mihail switched from the plural to the singular form of 'your'.

'No.' Dmitry shook his head irritably.

Again, it made little sense, except somewhere deep in Dmitry's mind. 'And what about Ascalon?' Mihail asked.

Dmitry looked up at him eagerly. 'Does he have it? Do you know where it is?'

'You think he has it?'

Dmitry paled suddenly. His eyes flickered across every corner of the cellar. 'He's coming,' he said. 'You must go.'

'Who's coming?'

'Zmyeevich. He mustn't find you here.'

Mihail was unsurprised by the revelation; he'd always suspected it to be the explanation of the 'we' that Dmitry had used. He was more puzzled by Dmitry's strange clairvoyance. 'How do you know?' he asked.

'Just go!' screamed Dmitry. As he spoke he rose up from his coffin and flung himself towards Mihail. Mihail flinched and tried to back away, but found only the wall behind him. Instinctively his finger tightened on the trigger of the crossbow and the bolt was released. For a moment he felt a pang of sorrow – he had not intended to kill Dmitry, or at least not yet decided to. It didn't matter. He had not been aiming and the bolt embedded itself in Dmitry's arm. His hand went to it and he pulled it out with little effort.

'Go,' he shouted again.

Dmitry's conviction was compelling, his terror infectious. Mihail stood in momentary confusion, then turned and fled, fumbling to load another bolt into the *arbalyet* as his feet carried him involuntarily across the floor. It was only when he was in the dark tunnel that he realized he had left his lamp behind, but he dared not go back. He knew that Zmyeevich might already have entered that same passageway from the other end and if so he was trapped. He hadn't realized that he and Dmitry had talked for so long, and that above it was now dark enough for Zmyeevich to make his way through the streets and back to his bed.

He stumbled and fell. He was at the stairs. He heard the bolt spill on to the floor, but made no attempt to find it. He scrambled up the hard stone steps, his free hand waving the crossbow in front of him, even though it was no longer loaded, ever turning to the right with the spiral of the steps. Soon he was in the upper corridor and moments later at the door. His fingers fumbled for the catch and eventually found it. He stepped out into the cathedral.

He was back outside the Nevsky Chapel. A monk was kneeling in prayer. He turned at the sound of Mihail's arrival, but did not notice where he had come from. Mihail breathed deeply, and quickly hid the bow in his bag. There was no sign of Zmyeevich. Mihail walked briskly into the main body of the cathedral and then out on to Senate Square.

It was only then that he realized his fears had been groundless. It was still daylight. Zmyeevich could no more have been returning to the cathedral than Mihail could have flown to the moon – Kibalchich's rocket notwithstanding. Dmitry had been mistaken. But then Dmitry had begun to behave very strangely indeed. It was a weakness that Mihail would exploit, if he got the chance.

'Oh, it's you!' Colonel Mrovinskiy's tone was of surprise rather than disdain.

'Yes,' replied Mihail. 'Expecting someone else?'

'You want to see him?'

'As soon as possible.'

'It won't take long; he's in town – they both are. Meet me in an hour in Palace Square.'

Mihail was there ten minutes early. He stared up at the angel that topped the monument to Aleksandr I, designed like Saint Isaac's by Auguste de Montferrand, in this case in honour of the present tsar's uncle. Mihail stopped himself; that was an odd way to put it. Mihail's own great-uncle would be a more direct way to describe him, though it was still difficult to see him that way, even after meeting Konstantin. Mihail's uncle on his mother's side was a more pressing concern. He'd tried to piece together what he had learned.

It was no great revelation that Dmitry and Zmyeevich were working hand in glove. It had always been a likelihood; Mihail remembered when he had first raised the possibility to Tamara. Both vampires had reason to hate Iuda; that would be enough to draw them together. Mihail shared that common purpose, and so it might be that he too would inadvertently join that alliance. But he would be wary of Zmyeevich, even more so than of Dmitry. Dmitry had not harmed him in that chamber beneath the cathedral, but it meant nothing. Dmitry's behaviour had been erratic; bordering on madness. Mihail tried to fathom a reason for it, but there was no explanation. He knew that he could not count on his safety next time – and yet there had to be a next time.

He saw Mrovinskiy emerge from the Winter Palace before the colonel caught sight of him. He strode over and Mrovinskiy stopped and waited. They entered by the door through which Mrovinskiy had come and he led Mihail along a narrow back corridor that seemed to run for half the length of the building. They turned left and up a flight of stairs and the passage opened up into a hall that was filled with scaffolding. No men were at work, but Mihail could see that the whole room was being repainted – in places the wall was being rebuilt.

'This is thanks to the bomb last year,' said Mrovinskiy. 'Eleven good men dead – others maimed. I hope your friends are pleased with themselves.'

Mihail felt the urge to protest, but there was little point. He noted that his activities were known of in these circles. Konstantin and even Aleksandr might understand the reasons for what he was doing, but others did not, and without their protection he could easily suffer whatever punishment befell any other member of the People's Will. He did not relish following in Aleksei's footsteps and spending the next thirty years of his life in exile – or worse.

At last they came to a room on the far side of the palace, overlooking the Neva. Mrovinskiy left Mihail there alone. He wandered nervously, looking first out across the frozen river and then examining the artwork – if that was the word for the panoply of erotica that bedecked the walls. One particular painting caught his eye: a young woman reclined on a bed, the top of her head towards the viewer so that her face couldn't be seen, the curls of her hair falling across her neck and shoulder, her breasts splayed by the force of gravity, but still pert. A hunched, muscular figure bent over her, leering at those breasts. He pushed her legs up close to her, bent double, with a hand on her buttock as he entered her, though the details of that were not visible. The dark hue of his skin contrasted with the milkiness of hers. His nose was sharp and pointed, as was the angle of his eyebrows, all aimed at the object of his desire. The oddest thing about him was his ears – pointed like a bat's. For a moment Mihail thought of the woman as Dusya; there was some resemblance in the blonde curls of her hair, but Dusya's body was more petite. Perhaps Sofia would have made a more fitting model, although Mihail could not find it in him to see her as an object of man's desire. For no good reason, the male figure made him think of Iuda, and he tried to push the thought from his mind.

'Engaging, isn't it?'

Mihail turned. It was Konstantin.

'It has a certain . . . curiosity to it,' said Mihail, returning his attention to the picture.

'It's by Zichi – the Hungarian. It's called "The Witch and the Devil".'

'Her identity is the less obvious.'

Konstantin chuckled.

Mihail turned to him. 'I can't say I share your tastes.'

'My tastes? Good Lord, no. This is Sasha's private study.'

'It must be distracting.'

Konstantin had no time to either confirm or deny the suggestion; at that moment the tsar himself entered.

'Your Majesty,' said Mihail, bowing. Aleksandr gave a brief nod of acknowledgement.

'You have news?'

'I do. Zmyeevich is in Petersburg; I'm sure of it.'

'You've seen him?'

'No, but I've spoken to someone who has.'

'You know where he's made his nest?'

'No.' Mihail realized only at the last moment that he should lie about it. Aleksandr's concern – that of the whole Romanov dynasty – was with Zmyeevich. If Mihail told him of that chamber beneath Senate Square he would rush in there with a squad of specially armed men, intent on dealing with Zmyeevich once and for all – and would very likely succeed. But it could send Iuda scurrying in fear, and Mihail might lose track of him for years, if not for ever. Aleksandr might have some desire to assist Mihail in his quest, but for him it was a side issue. 'But I'm working on it,' he added.

Aleksandr eyed him, but if he doubted Mihail's word there was little he could do.

'Can we help in that?'

'Not as yet. Your help with Iuda would be of greater value.'

'You've found him?' asked Konstantin.

'I had. He was in the Peter and Paul Fortress, but not any more. I'd like to know who ordered his release.'

'We'll look into it. What name was he using?' said Konstantin. At the same time Mihail noticed Aleksandr nervously straightening his moustache with his fingers. It would seem that he already knew plenty of what Iuda had been up to.

'He had rooms at the Hôtel d'Europe under the name Vasiliy Grigoryevich Chernetskiy, but he has other aliases.'

Konstantin noted it down. '*Had* rooms?' he asked.

'I don't think he'll go back there, but it may be worth asking a few questions. Has Zmyeevich tried to make contact in any way?'

'No,' said the tsar guardedly, 'but I have some idea of his plans.'

'What?' This was evidently news to Konstantin.

'How?' asked Mihail.

'You forget – I can see parts of his mind.'

'So what is his plan?' asked Konstantin.

'I think he's given up on me,' explained the tsar.

'After a hundred and seventy years? I very much doubt it.'

'Given up on me, not on us. He thinks he stands a better chance with my son.'

'Does he?' asked Mihail.

The tsar remained silent. Konstantin filled the gap with 'Of course not,' but there was little enthusiasm to it.

'But if that's his plan,' said Mihail, 'then his only interest in you would be to see your death.'

Aleksandr paused. His face was grey. His brother took a step towards him, but Aleksandr waved him back. At last he spoke, but it seemed to have nothing to do with the matter at hand.

'Fifteen years ago I visited Paris. I was the guest of the emperor, Napoleon III. He was not to remain emperor for very long. It was just a year since my son Niks died. A year too since Lincoln was murdered, after he'd freed *his* slaves. I was walking in the Tuileries Gardens. There was a gypsy there and she read my palm. She was very honest – perhaps she didn't understand who I was. She told me that she foresaw seven attempts to murder me, that six times my life would hang by a thread and that the seventh attempt would be the last.'

Mihail said nothing. He began to count the number of times they had attempted to kill Aleksandr, but the tsar provided the answer for him.

'So far there have been six plots – shootings, bombings – but all with the intent of seeing me dead.'

'The next attempt will come soon,' announced Mihail. 'They're digging a tunnel underneath Malaya Sadovaya Street.' Even as he spoke, he was realizing the full meaning of what he had witnessed there. 'They're going to fill it with nitroglycerin and blow you up as you ride over.'

'Then that,' replied the tsar, 'will be seven.'

Iuda looked down into the cathedral, in precisely the opposite direction to most of those who came to view its architectural splendour. They would strain their necks to look up at the dome from the floor below, whereas he was perched among the gilded angels that ringed the lower reaches of Saint Isaac's central tower, and could look down and see all who came and all who departed. He had arrived here soon after dark on Sunday evening, mingling with the congregation who came for vespers before slipping up one of the many staircases that were hidden within the church's thick stone walls. The people had left and then the priest had left and all had become silent.

The two figures had emerged from the corner beside the Nevsky Chapel; one tall, the other taller still. Zmyeevich and Dmitry. They slipped out of the cathedral and into the darkness. Iuda waited. He had last fed the night before, so he was neither distracted by hunger nor drowsy with satisfaction. He spent some time wandering around the quiet, empty building, remembering his conversations with de Montferrand and how he had needed to couch the necessities of his modifications in terms of the aesthetics that would appeal to the architect's mind. But what Iuda had planned was beautiful, regardless of its function – anyone would see that, when the sun shone.

He skulked back to his perch to wait. In the small hours Zmyeevich returned, alone. Iuda guessed that Dmitry would not be far behind, but he was wrong. Soon dawn began to break. Beams of light cut across the geometric patterns of the marble floor as the earliest rays of the sun entered from the east through the building's long windows. To the south and east he had opened every door, every shutter and every gate to ensure that the sun should fill the space inside. A cathedral should be a place of light – that's what he'd said to de Montferrand. But a cathedral should be a place of shadow too, and knowing the paths of shadow through the light could be of great benefit to a vampire.

He waited a few more hours. It was Monday, and the church would be quiet for most of the day, and he would be safer if the sun was allowed to get a little higher – the ideal inclination had been calculated with utmost precision. At about ten o'clock he began to move. He would not confront Zmyeevich down in the cellar below – that would be suicidal. But it would be simple enough to lure him up to the cathedral, where light would be Iuda's friend.

And then came a slight perturbation to Iuda's plans. The northern door of the cathedral creaked open and in walked a figure that Iuda had scarcely paid attention to when first they met, but who had thwarted him since. It was the lieutenant from Geok Tepe – Mihail Konstantinovich Lukin – now, so Iuda had learned, an enthusiastic recruit to the People's Will. It was no surprise that Lukin was working for Zmyeevich, alongside Dmitry, but it was pleasant for Iuda to have his speculation confirmed. And it made no difference to his plans. Lukin could be easily disposed of – he was only human, as his comfortable stroll across the sunlit floor of the church demonstrated. It took him just moments to find the hidden switches in Saint Paul's toes and disappear behind the icon. Iuda would deal with him before he could even reach his master, somewhere in the dark of the tunnels, where Iuda would be at his strongest and Lukin at his most vulnerable.

He lowered himself from the pedestal of the statue behind which he hid, and began to climb down into the nave.

Some might call it foolhardy, but Mihail could think of no other option. He had to speak to Dmitry again. The cathedral was quieter today than when he had last come here – empty. He quickly crossed to the icon of Saint Paul and within moments was in the passageway. He proceeded slowly, but with a little more confidence than on his previous visit; he knew what lay ahead. At least he did in terms of the geography – whether in the chamber below he would find Dmitry or Zmyeevich or both or neither he could not be sure.

He was at the steps. He began his stealthy descent, always turning to the left, never able to see beyond the curve of the wall, but he found no one on the stairs. Soon the dark gap of the lower corridor appeared as a tall black rectangle. His lamp shone against the wall, and with each step, light penetrated further along the passageway, although Mihail knew that the door at the end was too far away to be seen with such dim illumination.

He continued along the corridor, out under Senate Square, lamp still held high, *arbalyet* gripped and ready to shoot. He turned back to check behind him, and saw the slightest of movements, but realized it was nothing but the dancing shadows cast by the rough, uneven walls. He reached the door and put his lamp on the ground, using his free hand to try the handle.

It was locked.

This time, though, he had come prepared. In his bag was a crowbar. It should be easily strong enough to break through. Before he could reach for it he heard a sound, back up the corridor behind him. He turned, raising the lamp again. Still there were only shadows, but at that moment he realized his mistake. The walls on his last visit had not been uneven. They bulged a little with age, but generally he had been impressed by the quality of their construction.

He stepped forward, holding the lamp close to the passage wall to maximize the length of the shadow as he moved ever nearer to the indistinct shape. He was only paces away when he at last saw the figure, pressed into the shadows of the stone wall, motionless and invisible when viewed from the front, but casting a shadow once the light was beside it. Mihail should have been prepared for it – he knew how vampires chose to conceal themselves.

Mihail froze and the *voordalak* moved, aware that he had been seen. He stepped out from the wall and his body filled the corridor. It was not Dmitry. There was no real doubt as to who it was: Zmyeevich. Mihail had never seen him in the flesh, and yet he seemed so familiar. Even Tamara had not met him; her description came from Aleksei, and the few short hours that he and the arch vampire had spent in each other's company, seventy years before.

Zmyeevich had not changed one iota. He was an impressive man. His age could have been anywhere between fifty and seventy. A domed forehead was underlined by thick, bushy eyebrows which topped a thin, aristocratic nose. Arched nostrils were almost hidden by a long moustache of dark iron-grey, which contributed to a general air of unkemptness.

It took Mihail only an instant to take all of that in, and then he raised his crossbow and squeezed the trigger, not even pausing to relish the moment – this was not Iuda. The bolt cut the air, faster than Mihail's eyes could track it, but Zmyeevich's movement was faster still. His hand was in one place and the next instant in another. If he had been bothered he might have snatched the bolt from the air in mid-flight, but that was unnecessary. He merely brushed it aside with a casual blow of his hand and it slipped past him, level with his heart, but inches to the right. Mihail heard the scraping sound of its ricochet from the wall and moments later the clatter as it hit the floor.

Zmyeevich said nothing. He approached calmly, his lips forming into a smile which spread into a grin, revealing his fangs. Mihail thought to reload, but realized it would be useless – the crossbow had failed once, why should it succeed on a second attempt? He understood how ill-prepared he was. All that remained were his swords. He drew them both – the sabre in his right hand and the short wooden dagger in his left. There was not much room to wield the longer weapon down here, but Mihail felt more comfortable with it. Despite the hours of daily practice in how to use the little dagger that his mother had forced upon him, the army had trained him better with a more conventional blade. And anyway, he doubted he would have the chance to plunge the wooden blade into Zmyeevich's heart whichever hand it was in. He would feel happier to die defending himself like a soldier.

The *voordalak* continued to walk forward and Mihail felt the hard wood of the door at his back. There was no choice but to stand his ground. Zmyeevich took another pace and Mihail saw his chance; he lunged forward, aiming the wooden dagger straight for Zmyeevich's heart, but again the vampire was too quick. He clasped the blade in his right hand and with a sharp twist wrenched it from Mihail's grip, casting it on the ground behind him. Now Mihail had only his sabre.

Then from over Zmyeevich's shoulder, far down the passageway, there was a glimmer of light. Zmyeevich perceived it too. He turned away to look, presenting his back to Mihail. Beyond him Mihail could see the flickering flame – most likely a candle – sway from side to side as whoever was carrying it approached, but did not waste a moment in trying to make out who was coming. He raised his sabre. His only chance was to behead Zmyeevich, but there was no room to make the broad horizontal swing that might have achieved it. Instead Mihail could only bring the blade down diagonally.

It caught Zmyeevich just at the point where his shoulder curved into his neck, embedding itself a few inches and drawing blood. Its only effect was to enrage Zmyeevich. He turned and in the same motion swung his arm, catching Mihail's jaw with the back of his hand and sending him flying into the door behind. The sword fell from Mihail's hand and his head slammed against the wood. He slid to the ground, scarcely conscious, and stared upwards. Zmyeevich towered over him, considering, preparing to deal the final blow.

But instead the *voordalak* turned again to face the advancing figure, his body blocking it from Mihail's view.

'You!' snarled Zmyeevich.

'Why not?' The voice was instantly recognizable – it was Iuda.

'I'm surprised you dare.'

'Remember, Țepeș, I am the master here.'

'The years have taught you nothing,' said Zmyeevich. He set off down the corridor towards Iuda, walking but at a tremendous pace. Mihail heard Iuda's feet moving quickly, the rapid patter of them climbing the spiral stairs. Zmyeevich was relentless in his pursuit. Soon both were gone. Mihail forced himself to his feet. His head swam but he knew he must move. If either one of them were to return then down here he would be vulnerable, but up there in the cathedral it was light – the domain of the living, not the undead.

He moved quickly, picking up lamp, sabre and *arbalyet* and only pausing a little way down the corridor to grab the wooden dagger from where Zmyeevich had cast it. Soon he was at the foot of the stairs, but then he stopped. The fact that there was daylight in the cathedral might mean something else – that the two vampires would remain in the corridor. Mihail had no choice but to go on, but he would at least be prepared. He returned his sabre to its scabbard and the dagger to his coat, then he reloaded the crossbow. However ineffective it might have been before, he'd be a fool to abandon it. He pressed onwards.

Even as he reached the top of the stairs, he perceived that it was getting lighter. Once in the upper corridor he saw that, at the end, the doorway behind the icon was open. Evidently there was enough shade for them to step out into the cathedral. For Mihail, it meant a chance of freedom. He ran forward, but paused as he reached the doorway. He peeked out from behind it.

Zmyeevich stood a little way ahead, to the side of the Beautiful Gate and looking into the centre of the nave, leaning against a pillar. He was in shadow, but even the ambient light was bright. Iuda stood directly beneath the dome, upright and confident. Around him, beams of light cut through the air, entering through the tall windows in the walls of the church and coming down from the dome through the windows there, making the space far brighter than Mihail had known it to be in any other cathedral. But somehow, Iuda had found himself a safe place to stand, at a point where he seemed certain that no light would hit him.

'You begin to understand why I led you here,' Iuda was saying, addressing Zmyeevich. He had not seen Mihail.

'You led us here?' said Zmyeevich.

'Don't pretend, Ţepeş. It should be obvious enough from the fact that I escaped you within minutes of our arriving here. Do you think that I didn't know my house in Moscow had information that would bring you here? Do you think I failed to understand what you'd see in that mirror down there?'

'But still you came back.'

'Of course I did, because there's more to this – much more.'

As he spoke, Iuda began to walk, almost dance across the floor, weaving between the sun's rays as they cast a pattern that Mihail could only guess he knew by heart. Zmyeevich remained motionless. He was not trapped by the light, but there was no obvious safe path to reach Iuda. All he could do was wait.

'All you seem to have is a means of temporary protection from me,' said Zmyeevich, 'but it will soon fade. You cannot leave here until darkness falls.'

'I assure you I can.' Iuda continued his motion as he spoke, sometimes leaning so that his body was parallel with the sun's sloping rays, allowing him to closely avoid them. At one moment a wisp of smoke rose from his ear as it brushed against the light, but it did not perturb him. 'I know of more dark tunnels leading out of here than the one you just crawled from.'

'So,' said Zmyeevich, 'you are safe from me. And equally I am safe from you. In that case, what was the point of you coming here?'

'To talk.'

'Talk then.'

Iuda paused, and then began. 'I don't want to be your enemy, Țepeș. You know that.'

'You want to be my equal. I cannot allow that.'

'Oh, come on! How could I ever be the equal of the great Count Dracula?'

'You couldn't,' said Zmyeevich simply, 'but you still desire it. I should have guessed it the moment we met. But then you were merely human.'

'Well if I can't equal you, you have nothing to fear from me. Surely you'll allow me the fantasy of my forlorn hope?'

'You're nothing, Cain,' said Zmyeevich. 'If I allow you to live, it is because I have better things to do with my time.'

'Such as ruling Russia?'

Zmyeevich was silent.

'We worked together on that once,' said Iuda. 'We could again.'

'You can assist me?'

'No, but I have the power to hinder you, and I can choose not to use it.'

'What power?'

'I have your blood, Țepeș.'

'With it you can cause me pain, nothing more.'

'If a Romanov were willingly to drink your blood, and share your mind, then he would free his entire generation from your influence. If that Romanov were of little consequence, then he would free the tsar.'

'He would have to do it willingly,' said Zmyeevich, 'and even then, there will be future generations.'

'If he were to die, with your blood in him, he would become a *voordalak* – your vampire offspring. You would control him. And yet your chances to influence *any* other Romanov would cease. Your fox would have been shot, as we say in England.'

Zmyeevich considered for a moment. 'You don't speak as someone who does not want to be my enemy.'

'I'm being honest with you, Ţepeş. That is what friends do – or had you forgotten?'

'It's still a better reason to see you die than to let you live.'

'Currently that's not an option for you, though, is it?' Iuda waved a hand lightly in the air, reminding Zmyeevich of the sunlight. He did a little pirouette and moved to a different patch of shade. Mihail noticed him looking at the floor, with its intricate mosaic of checks and spirals, as he moved. Was there some map embedded in them that allowed him to know with such confidence where he would be safe?

Zmyeevich remained silent.

'I can of course offer you Ascalon,' said Iuda, 'if that would sweeten the deal.'

'Ascalon?'

'Oh yes, I know all about that, Ţepeş.'

'Pyotr tore it from where it hung around my neck, even as his blood was on my lips.'

'What do you care?' asked Iuda.

'It made me what I am. I unearthed it – four centuries ago. The dragon's blood still stained it. I tasted it. I became . . . me.'

'And if it is destroyed you believe you will return to what you were before?'

Zmyeevich stiffened, disconcerted by the depth of Iuda's understanding. He nodded slowly in agreement.

'Superstition!' exclaimed Iuda. 'Claptrap!'

'You say I don't know my own history?'

'You have a medieval mind, Ţepeş. How could a primitive like you be expected to understand the processes which control his own body? But then who am I to question a man's beliefs, when I can exploit them instead. I can offer you Ascalon. Or I can destroy it, and we'll discover which of us is correct about its power. I do hope I'm proved wrong.'

'You do not have Ascalon,' said Zmyeevich. 'Pyotr entrusted it to the Armenians. They buried it – and soon we shall unearth it.'

Iuda smiled tightly – confidently. 'Then it seems there is nothing I can offer you,' he said.

Zmyeevich stood upright, moving away from the pillar. He took a few cautious steps, eyeing the beams of sunlight. Mihail took the opportunity to scurry forward a little, finding a new hiding place close to the entrance to the chapel, where he was bathed in the sun's protective rays.

'You're wrong,' said Zmyeevich. 'You do have something I want – and that I will take from you. You have your life.'

Iuda chuckled, but there was no hint that Zmyeevich had spoken with anything but the utmost conviction. The arch *voordalak* took a deep breath and seemed to tense himself, like someone about to dive into water that they knew to be cold. Then he took a pace forward.

The sunlight enveloped him.

Mihail gasped and Iuda's face fell into an expression of genuine bewilderment. Both waited to see the vampire's body reduce in seconds to powdered ash, but the transformation that did take place was far less spectacular – and infinitely more surprising.

Zmyeevich aged before their eyes. He became wizened. His skin grew thin and wrinkled, sucked in at his cheeks. He began to stoop forward, his spine curving. The hair of his head, and even his moustache, grew white. For Mihail, the metamorphosis transformed Zmyeevich into a familiar figure – the old man to whom he had spoken as they stood at the foot of the Bronze Horseman, the man who had first told him about Ascalon. Mihail had stood there in broad daylight, conducting a conversation with Zmyeevich himself. And – because it was broad daylight – he had never for a moment suspected.

Iuda simply gawped; his confidence evaporated, his arrogant goading silenced.

It was Zmyeevich who spoke first – the sound still resonant and grinding, unaffected by the sunlight. Clearly when he had been speaking to Mihail he had been disguising his voice to be in keeping with his physical appearance.

'Who are you to presume to understand my body?' he asked. 'Do you think that after four hundred years I'm unaware of my own capabilities?'

'But . . .' Iuda's terror robbed him of the power of speech. 'Every vampire . . . I experimented . . . They all . . . None of them could face the sun . . . They burned.'

'They were young,' said Zmyeevich. 'I have had time; time to learn how to face the pain; time to expose myself, and recover, and expose myself again.'

'But your blood. When I threw that into the sun you screamed in agony.'

'The skin protects the blood,' explained Zmyeevich. 'But even then I was not as able to endure the light as I am now. I was not as confident of my strength. The sun weakens me, as you can see, but it does not kill.' As he spoke he straightened up, stretching his shoulders, as if becoming inured to the light. 'I wonder if you can boast of the same.'

With that he paced across the cathedral floor, heading directly towards Iuda, slower than if he had been at the zenith of his strength, but fast enough to reach his goal. Iuda turned and fled and although he was quicker, he was forced to follow a far more circuitous path as he dodged the splashes of light that had so recently been his allies. Zmyeevich was soon upon him and flung himself forward on to the marble floor, grabbing Iuda's ankle in his hand. Iuda fell and turned as he went down. His left hand was flung outwards into a pool of sunlight and erupted with smoke and steam.

Iuda screamed and snatched his hand away, but now Zmyeevich was crawling towards him. Zmyeevich was still weakened by his exposure to the light, while Iuda remained strong but was compelled to stay in the shade. He kicked at Zmyeevich's face with his free foot, and kicked again. Zmyeevich was forced to let go. Iuda rolled on to his stomach and in moments was back on his feet, running, his injured hand cradled against his chest. He made for an archway in the south-east corner of the nave, still dodging from side to side to avoid the light. Soon he disappeared and Mihail heard his feet pounding against stone steps. Zmyeevich was only seconds behind him.

Mihail stepped out into the nave, feeling strangely elated by this turn of events. All his life he had wanted the pleasure of killing Iuda himself, but to see his foe so thoroughly outwitted and humiliated was almost as gratifying. The sounds of the two vampires' footsteps faded, but Mihail had no intention of pursuing them. Instead he stared up at the dome above him, hoping that he might catch some glimpse of their continuing battle.

He was not disappointed. Iuda appeared first and Zmyeevich moments later. Somehow they had found their way to opposite sides of the circular gallery that ran around the inside of the tower at the foot of its windows, just above the heads of the golden statues. They locked eyes for a moment, each wondering which direction the other would take, but it was Zmyeevich who moved first, setting off clockwise. Iuda did the same, but as he ran past each of the windows the light caught him and another cloud of smoke rose above him.

After three windows he could take no more pain. He stood with his back pressed against the outer wall of the gallery, where at least he was in shade. Zmyeevich quickly followed the path of the semicircle which separated them and soon he was face to face with Iuda. He reached out, ready to drag his enemy into the light.

Iuda leapt. Mihail's eyes followed him as he descended through the gallery, past the twelve gilded angels and down towards the floor of the nave, his eyes wide, his arms flailing, his legs kicking against the air as though he thought to swim up, away from the ground.

The sound of his impact with the floor came from a mixture of sources, the breath being knocked from his body, the cracking of his bones, the squelch of his less rigid body parts splayed against the marble. It did not kill him, but his body lay as an unrecognizable jumble in the middle of the church, with arms and legs sticking out at all angles, like a broken puppet. He was lucky to have landed in shade. Only his leg caught the sunlight, and where the cloth of his trousers had been pulled up the flesh of his ankle began to burn. He pulled his leg away, but the booted foot remained where it was, its contents smouldering to nothing, leaving the boot empty.

Above, Zmyeevich began his more controlled descent. He had swung himself over the railing of the gallery and was clambering down one of the four great pillars that supported the tower. It was an eerie sight. Unlike any human climber, he descended head first, his body pressed close to the stonework. His fingers grasped any corner or crevice they could find, moving downwards with enormous speed. Mihail was reminded of a lizard traversing a wall. In seconds he was at floor level. He took no notice of Mihail, but strode over to Iuda's crumpled body, grabbing him by the collar and dragging him across the marble. The look on Zmyeevich's face was one of impatient anger – he wanted to be rid of Iuda and rid of him quickly.

Mihail had not noticed until now, but in the iconostasis in front of the altar the Beautiful Gate had been opened. It was unusual in any church. Iuda must have done it himself to allow more light in, when he thought it would protect him. What was revealed behind, above the altar, was a spectacular stained-glass window, depicting the Saviour, dressed in an orange robe. In his left hand he carried a tall cross and he formed his right into the symbol of the *troyeperstiy*, the two smallest fingers folded into the palm, the thumb touching the tips of the middle and index fingers, in preparation for making the sign of the cross. It had never occurred to Mihail before, but it suddenly reminded him of his grandfather, Aleksei, and his two missing fingers.

The sun, low in the eastern sky, shone brightly through this image of Christ, casting its light, altered in colour by the glass, through the Beautiful Gate and on to the church floor. Even there, a little of the coloration could be discerned, though the main impression was of simple brightness. Zmyeevich flung Iuda into its glow, and pressed his foot down on his enemy's chest, so that he could not crawl away. Whether by luck or design Zmyeevich had arranged things so that Iuda's body was not entirely subject to the sun's glare. His head and left arm and shoulder remained in the shade. It would mean he experienced every last ounce of the pain that the burning of his body might inflict upon him.

Mihail wondered with bitter irony whether Iuda would take the opportunity to draw knowledge from this final great experiment in which he was the specimen. Did the fact that the sun's rays were coloured by the glass reduce his torment? Did the fact that it was the image of Our Lord that was projected upon him increase it? Mihail had nothing to compare it against, but Iuda seemed to take a little longer to die than Mihail might have expected from what he had heard, and his screams seemed to echo a little more loudly than Mihail had hoped. The only disappointment was that Iuda's death was at the hands of Zmyeevich. It would be some recompense if he could be looking into Mihail's eyes as he died. There would be some small chance of recognition.

Mihail took a few steps to the side, removing Zmyeevich as a block to his view of Iuda – what was left of him. He had stopped screaming, not because he experienced no more pain, but because he had no more lungs with which to breathe, no more diaphragm with which to force the air across his vocal cords. He was not even a torso – just a head, an arm and enough of a chest to join the two together. And soon there would not even be that much of him left. Above all, Mihail wanted Iuda to see him now.

At the same moment Iuda somehow found the strength to raise his head, but he stared not into Mihail's face but at the image of the Saviour in the window, through which shone the light that was destroying every cell of his body. Mihail realized Iuda did not need to see him, he merely needed to see that image of Christ and to be reminded – as Mihail had been reminded – of the significance of the *troyeperstiy*. Mihail breathed deeply. The sound of his voice filled the cathedral.

'Remember the three-fingered man!'

Whether Iuda heard the words or was even capable of doing so, Mihail could not tell. Zmyeevich most certainly did. He turned. He took one last look at Iuda and saw he was finished, and so focused his attention on his newest prey – Mihail.

'Who *are* you?' he asked.

Mihail looked at him. In appearance this was the same old man he had spoken to beneath the statue of Pyotr. How much more his knowledge of Ascalon meant now. But the malevolence in Zmyeevich's eyes was not that of an old man – or perhaps it was that of a man older than old. Four centuries, he had mentioned. How much hatred could accumulate in that space of time?

Mihail could think of no response to the question.

'It matters not,' said Zmyeevich. He bared his fangs once again and descended upon Mihail, who had no defence. His crossbow had already proved ineffectual; his wooden sword was in his coat and would take too long to draw. All he had was his sabre, which he drew as a matter of instinct rather than calculation. And then he remembered Zmyeevich's own words: 'The skin protects the blood.'

It was a slim chance. Mihail raised his sword and slashed at Zmyeevich's face. It caught him under his high, noble cheekbone. In a man it would have left a scar that would have made the ladies swoon, but it would not have slowed the attack. In a vampire it would normally have been a wound of little consequence. But as the blood oozed from the neat horizontal cut, the sunlight caught it and it began to smoke and smoulder and then burn.

Zmyeevich screamed, as loudly as Iuda had been screaming just moments before. He raised his hands to his face to block out the sunlight and then staggered backwards, falling upon his *voordalak* instincts and searching for shade. For Mihail it might have been an opportunity to move in for the kill, but terror took him. He raced to the great bronze cathedral doors and struggled to push one open. Eventually he was out in the cool air of Senate Square, gasping for breath, feeling protected in the morning sunlight, but knowing he was not.

He ran – across Senate Square, past the Bronze Horseman and on to the Neva. Only when his feet slipped from beneath him and sent him sprawling out of control across the frozen water did he stop and look around and see that he was alone. Zmyeevich had not followed. Mihail was safe.

More importantly, Iuda was dead.

CHAPTER XIX

AGONY. PAIN. ABSENCE. MISERY – NEW EXPERIENCES, OR LONG-forgotten ones. More than merely a physical sensation, a tenderness of the spirit – of the soul. But a good thing. Agony brought strength. Pain brought malice. Absence brought growth. Misery brought the desire for revenge.

Strength first though. Movement. Fingertips curling, finding the tiniest crevice, like climbing, but along, not up. Once the fingers grip the arm can pull – so little to pull. But the fingers must not lose their prize. Suffocating – unable to breathe the air all around. Creeping, inch by inch. Not far. A dark gap – enticing. Close now. Closer still. Drowsy, but no rest, not yet. Metal, iron bars for the fingers to grip and pull against; yielding, engulfed by darkness, falling. Weightless like before, but falling into darkness. Then the ground below, far below, hard, still. New pain consumed by the old, but dark.

Dark now. Sleep. Grow.

It was not the blissful state of being that Mihail had been anticipating, and it did not last long. There had been only a moment to check as he fled the cathedral but he had looked back and seen no trace of Iuda, just a few smouldering fragments of his clothes. It should have been preposterous to conceive that any vampire could have survived such an exposure to the sun's rays, but in the moments he had seen Iuda die Mihail had seen Zmyeevich live through just the same circumstances, with little sign even of discomfort, except for that last moment when his blood had been let.

Mihail needed certainty, and he knew where to find it. But even as he strode along the streets of the capital his pace slowed to an easy saunter. He was right to be careful, to make sure, but whatever his need for proof he still had a belief, and his belief was that Iuda was dead. Mihail's first thoughts were of Tamara – of her measureless need for vengeance. If only she could have lived just a few more months, long enough to learn of Iuda's death. How that might have changed her. Mihail had seen when a boy the relationships that other children had with their mothers and had yearned for it, but had understood it could never be. Iuda had to die, he had known that for as long as he could remember. It was a fact, as fundamental as the fact that his name was Mihail, that eating dispelled hunger, that falling over caused pain. Those things remained as true as ever, but Iuda no longer had to die. Iuda was dead. It was as revolutionary a change as if he had discovered that he no longer needed to eat; that he could defy gravity.

What would have been the effect on Tamara though? Would she have seen herself as free? Would she have carried on happily into her dotage? She was a woman who lived by her obsessions, Mihail knew that – for half her life to find her father, for the other half to avenge his death. As far as he could tell she had been truly happy for only one brief period of her life, when she had been married to the man she loved, and lived with him and her three children. It had not lasted long, and Mihail had not been one of those children. Would news of Iuda's death have returned her to that happiness, or would she have been forced to find some new mania to sustain her? Or would she have died anyway, with no reason left to live – not even her son Mihail. It was better not to know.

He was close to his room – the room where he stored his collection of bizarre curios, not where he slept – when he realized that his journey might be unnecessary. He stopped and reached into his shirt, pulling out the two pendants that lay always against his chest. He looked into the eyes of the Saviour. The face in that icon, intended to be a depiction of Christ, had always reminded Tamara of her father, Aleksei. Mihail hadn't thought of the connection until now, but remembered that he had made the same association looking at the stained glass of the cathedral. It was a reminder of Him who should really be thanked for Iuda's death. He kissed the icon and offered up a silent prayer of gratitude.

But the icon had not been what he sought. The other item that hung around his neck was a locket. He flipped it open with his thumbnail. Within still lay the dozen coils of hair, as blond as the day they had been plucked from Iuda's head. It was inconclusive. Had they withered now, it would show that Iuda was dead, but they had been taken from Iuda before he became a vampire and any human hair might have survived as long as they; there was no reason to suppose that their immortality depended on him.

He pressed on, with greater determination now, greater eagerness for certainty. Minutes later he was kneeling in front of his trunk, having carefully drawn the curtains to allow no sunlight to fall upon what he was about to examine. He unlocked it. Inside nothing had been touched. The second *arbalyet* and its bolts, some batteries, the Yablochkov Candles, Iuda's books and all the other paraphernalia that Mihail regarded as so precious were just where he had left them. He piled the books on the floor, revealing among the heaped clothes a silk handkerchief, folded to hide what lay within.

Even as he lifted it out of the trunk, he knew. He could tell by the weight, by the slight rigidity. He placed the handkerchief and its contents on the table, with a reverent gentleness for which he could find no reason. He unfolded the four corners and saw the contents plainly.

It was just as when he had last looked: a white crescent of flesh, internally bloodless but externally bloodstained, the intricate curls and folds that were somehow necessary to funnel sound to its centre perfectly preserved. It was Iuda's severed ear. The hairs from his head might have been able to survive his death, but this more recently separated slab of flesh could not. If it lived, so did he. Aleksei had seen it in the vampire skin that covered Iuda's notebooks, and the notebooks themselves described it. Mihail and Tamara had seen it with their own eyes – a severed hand that decayed to dust in the same moment that its owner did, even though in a different building.

Mihail picked up the ear and hurled it against the wall. It hit the paper with a splat, sticking for a moment before peeling away and falling to the floor, bouncing off the skirting board to land a little way from it. Mihail walked over to it, anger filling him. He laughed briefly at the thought of the thanks he had given to God for Iuda's death. Even then he had wondered what had taken the Lord so long, but now His utter indifference revealed itself once again.

Mihail stamped on the ear with the heel of his boot and then again, hoping that wherever he might be Iuda would feel it, but doubting that it would add much to the agony he must be suffering. He would have carried on, but he knew that he could do damage – the ear would not heal like its owner – and he would need it again. He would need it one day soon to verify that which was the whole purpose of his existence, what he had hoped would be verified today.

But the evidence before him was irrefutable. Iuda lived.

Time passed, but could not be measured. Wounds healed, but did not make whole. Respiration returned, but not breathing. The lungs were the first organs to begin their slow reformation; before even the heart, what little there was left of it. If nothing had remained, he would be dead. One chamber had survived, one of the atria, though whether the left or right he could not tell. It still pumped feebly, but alone could not cause the blood to flow. And what would be the point of pumping blood if the blood had no oxygen to carry? So the lungs would grow first. He did not know how he knew that – did not even know his own name, not clearly; there seemed too many possibilities.

Even to say that his lungs were reforming was to give dignity to his status. A hash of alveoli hung from somewhere beneath his neck and remaining shoulder. There were no bronchi to feed into them, no diaphragm to draw fresh air in and expel it once it grew stale. He remembered the terms, the structure, so clearly. He had seen it all, in frogs – where the lungs were very primitive – in rats, in pigs and in men. He'd eventually seen it in creatures such as himself, whatever that might be. He knew he was neither frog nor rat nor pig nor even man, but that was not the same as knowing what he was.

In truth at the moment he was more like a fish. He did not have

308

lungs but gills, exposed to air rather than water, at the whim of the currents that carried the precious oxygen to him. He was glad he could not see himself, sprawled – if the little that was left of him could sprawl – in that foul, dark sewer, the horrid mess of his nascent lungs spilling out from him, giving him his only chance of life.

And indeed they had. They were enough to save him – enough at least to keep him conscious. But no more. That in itself was a cruelty that tempted him to ponder whether there might be a god – the wrathful, vengeful god about whom his father had preached from his pulpit in . . . wherever it was. No – pulpits; there had been three of them, each closer to heaven than the last. He remembered the grass and the trees and the rolling green hills. 'The Downs' – that's what they were called. God had made those, he had been told as a boy – that same God who had put him in this state; alive, conscious, but too weak to recover any more. He was in a perpetual limbo, able neither to die nor to revive. There was much that could tip the balance in one direction, to kill him, but only one thing would restore him. He needed . . .

He could not remember what it was he needed, much as he yearned for it. He could taste it on his lips and tongue, and feel it cascading down his throat, but he could not name it. It was warm and vital and corporeal and . . . Was it milk? His mother's milk? No – that could not be. He had killed his mother much as he had killed his father. Someone must have fed him, but no, he was sure; milk was not the fluid he craved.

And even if he could drink, it would be of little sustenance. He had no stomach. Somewhere among the slime that was his lungs lay the end of his oesophagus, where anything he drank would spill. But he would absorb some tiny part of it; through his mouth, through his gullet, just as his lungs – though pathetic shadows of what they should be – could absorb a few molecules of oxygen. He would heal by the tiniest fraction, and on the next sip there would be a little more of him with which to absorb the nourishment, and then a little more still. But for now even that first sip was only a dream.

Then a light. At first he feared it. Light had made him what he had become, but this was not the great celestial orb that brought death to his kind. This was the flimsy, guttering flame of a candle, still far away, but coming towards him. He heard footsteps and the light came nearer. Then they stopped. There was a gasp. A face loomed close.

He tried to remember, but memory was still unclear. He knew the face. It made him feel safe, comfortable, secure. Faces he had known ambled through his mind and he tried to recall names. Then one matched.

'Raisa?' he said. But he did not say – he did not even whisper. He still did not have the organs to force breath across his vocal cords. But his lips moved sufficiently for him to be understood.

'No,' said the face, 'I'm not Raisa.' A hand stroked his hair.

He thought again, and now he was certain. This time he did not even attempt to speak, but merely mouthed the name.

'Susanna?'

'No, I'm not Susanna.'

He thought again, but there was no other possibility. He knew he was right.

'You must be,' he mouthed. 'You must be Susanna.'

The face smiled. Then nodded. The hand continued to stroke his hair.

'All right then, yes,' she said. 'I am. I am Susanna.'

They met as they had done each evening of their vigil under the low, vaulted ceiling of Wulf and Beranger's café on Nevsky Prospekt. They both drank tea. On the table between them sat the remains of a plate of chocolates – Georg Landrin's finest – which she had got through with unexpected gusto.

'Who is it you suspect?' asked Dusya.

'I can't say,' Mihail replied. 'I'm not sure I even know. Why? Have you seen someone?'

She shook her head. 'No one like any of the three you described.'

She could not know that he had in fact described to her two men, not three, but one of those would appear quite different depending on whether she saw him by day or by night. Mihail had given her both descriptions of Zmyeevich, the old, doddering man of the day and the impressive strong creature of the night. He had no reason to suppose that Zmyeevich had any concept

310

of the connection with the Hôtel d'Europe, but his real motive in asking Dusya to watch it – apart from having an excuse to meet regularly with her – was in case Iuda returned. His was the third description Mihail had given her, though he had little idea what Iuda might look like at present, given his state when Mihail had last seen him. Mihail himself had been keeping watch on Saint Isaac's, thinking that the more likely location to see either of them, or Dmitry. There had been no need to describe Dmitry to Dusya; if she saw him she would immediately recognize him – as Chairman Shklovskiy. His suggestion that the reason for watching the hotel was that there might be a spy in their midst was purely an invention, but it would fit well with Dmitry's arrival. Even so she might hesitate to mention it, which prompted Mihail's next question.

'And no one from . . .' He glanced around the salon. Any one of those present, quietly drinking coffee or tea or enjoying the café's famous confectionery, could be an *ohranik*. He rephrased the question. 'No one we know?'

'Oh, lots of them. It is Nevsky Prospekt – just around the corner from you know where.'

'You've seen some? Going into the hotel?'

'Not going in – just passing.'

'Who?'

'Let me see. Frolenko a couple of times. Bogdanovich. Zhelyabov. Sofia, of course.'

'Why of course?' asked Mihail.

'Because if you see Zhelyabov you're bound to see Sofia. Well, usually. I've seen her alone a couple of times. She's been very strange.'

Mihail couldn't give a damn about Sofia. 'No one else?'

'No. And I guess I can cross all of them off my list.'

'What list?'

'My list of the people you think could be the traitor. You're clearly not interested in any of them.'

Mihail smiled. 'I might be bluffing,' he said.

'There was one other person,' she added.

'Who?'

'I paid him particular attention.'

'Why?'

'Because he's very pleasant to look at.'

Mihail racked his brains. 'Mihailov?'

She grinned. 'You, you idiot. I saw you chatting to the concierge.'

Mihail smiled back. 'He's my man on the inside.'

'I don't know why you can't watch the place yourself and leave me out of it.'

'It's not their only rendezvous. Besides, I wouldn't get to sit and have tea with you if I didn't need to find out what you've seen.'

'You see me most nights,' she said, her eyes flashing momentarily at him, then returning their gaze to the window beside them. It was true, during the past few days, now that the work on the tunnel was almost complete, she had become an even more regular – and more passionate – visitor to his bed.

'I don't deny it,' he said. 'But that's not the same as having tea.'

'You're so bourgeois,' she replied, neither as a joke nor an insult.

'Because I like to drink tea?'

'Because you like to dress up what we do to each other at night with displays of conventionality like this. It's not for your benefit, and you know it doesn't impress me, so who's it for?'

Mihail offered no answer.

'Them!' she said, waving a hand around the room, her voice raised. A few eyes glanced towards them, but they could not have heard the bulk of what she said. She lowered her voice again. 'And they wouldn't even suspect that you were screwing me if you hadn't brought me here. You're showing me off – a trophy.'

So vulgar a word on her lips both shocked and thrilled him, but still he wasn't convinced of her logic. 'So I meet you here both to disguise the fact that we're lovers and to announce it?'

'A typical bourgeois dichotomy. Like ordering a huge meal and then only picking at it. You're showing the world that you can, even though you don't.'

'Not something you'd see very much in Russia,' said Mihail.

'Absolutely. You're really quite an advanced specimen.'

'But not as advanced as you?'

'What I do is to please myself, not others.'

As she spoke she leaned forward, hunched over the table, her eyes fixed on his. Beneath it he felt her hand on his thigh, her fingers caressing his flesh through the cloth of his trousers, working their way up. Though the action was hidden from them both by the table top, anyone else in the room who cared to look would see it. He grinned and decided to call her bluff, copying her action, his fingers pressing into her thigh through the material of her dress, searching for a gap. Still their eyes remained locked.

'My arms are longer,' he whispered.

She pulled away, sitting upright. Her hands came up to the table, allowing her to push her chair back a little.

'Now who's bourgeois?' he asked.

'It's not that,' she said, 'but we have a higher duty. We can't raise suspicion.'

It might have been true, but her flushed cheeks indicated more embarrassment than revolutionary ardour.

'But come the glorious day . . . ?' he said.

She reached across to him, above the table, and held his hands in hers.

'I don't think we have to wait *that* long,' she smiled.

Whatever his expectations might have been, Mihail spent that night alone. Before he and Dusya could leave the café, Sofia had entered, her face pale, her eyebrows knitted. She had summoned Dusya over to speak to her in private and then the two women had left together. Of all of them, it was Sofia that Mihail feared the most. She was the most fanatical, the most driven, the most hardened. If anyone were to expose him, it would be she.

And yet what was there to expose? That in reality he had no interest in blowing up the tsar and that his real purpose was to destroy a vampire that had persecuted his family through the generations? If she doubted him, it wouldn't be because she suspected him of that. There was the fact that Konstantin was his father, and that Aleksandr was therefore his uncle – that would certainly be a black mark against a member of the People's Will. But that would seem even less likely than his vampire hunting. No; he felt safe; safer still in the sense that he had Dmitry on his side. Since they had spoken, Dmitry had apparently made no attempt to denounce him. That did not make him an ally, but it meant that the two were locked together within the People's Will. They had a shared secret and neither would betray the other for fear of betraying himself.

But it was not simply that Dmitry had not denounced him. No one had seen Dmitry for several days. Mihail's surveillance of Saint Isaac's had yielded nothing, and neither had Dusya's at the hotel. All had gone cold – nothing of Iuda, nothing of Dmitry, nothing of Zmyeevich. Those latter two were chiefly of interest in that they might lead to Iuda, but Mihail knew that if the chance came to act against Zmyeevich, he would take it. The world would be a better place without him, but more than that, with Zmyeevich out of the picture Aleksandr would have no reluctance in helping Mihail with his true quest. But there was a greater motivation; it was what Aleksei would have done. There was little point in avenging him if Mihail could not live up to his image. But all that hinged on finding Dmitry and Zmyeevich.

He thought back over what he knew – not recent discoveries, but the things his mother had told him, the things Aleksei had told her. Any connections there might be to Dmitry in Petersburg – anywhere he might go. There was the apartment on Konyushennaya Street where Dmitry had grown up, but that had come to nothing. He tried to think if there might be any remaining military connections with the city, but it was unlikely; the comrades of Dmitry's days fighting in the Crimea would be old men now. He would not have been able to keep in touch with them, or they would have commented on his eternal youth.

Dmitry had no children, at least not that Aleksei had known about. But then, what would he know? He had been in exile for the best part of Dmitry's adult life. He and Dmitry had not communicated with each other – or at least the attempts they had made to communicate were intercepted by Iuda. It was quite possible that there were children – other Danilovs – Mihail's own cousins. But where to start?

Then he realized how stupid he was being. The answer was obvious, and it was valid regardless of whether Dmitry had fathered children or not. He had been married. Tamara had visited the woman. Svetlana – that was her name, though there was little more that Mihail could bring to mind. It did not matter.

He leapt to his feet and went over to his trunk. Tamara had been an obsessive woman, not least when it came to this. In it were all the notes she had written down, every fact that she could remember; she had told him – but had recorded it as well. It was almost as if . . . well, she *had* known, known about the thing growing in her lungs, known that it would kill her. It was just a question of when.

He leafed through the pages. They were not well organized, but he could recall seeing what he wanted, high on a left-hand page, about a third of the way in. He soon found it.

> *Svetlana Nikitichna Danilova,*
> *Apartment 4,*
> *Fontanka 134*

Mihail was familiar enough with Fontanka 16, the Ohrana headquarters, but Fontanka was a long thoroughfare, following the entire path of the river from which it took its name. He didn't know quite where number 134 stood, but he would easily find it.

He returned to his bed. It was a fragile straw, but he gladly grasped at it. Svetlana Nikitichna might be long dead. She might have moved away. Even if she were there, why should she know anything of a husband she had buried twenty-five years before? But for the first time since he'd looked down at Iuda's severed ear, intact and undamaged, Mihail went to sleep with some sense of hope.

CHAPTER XX

NUMBER 134 STOOD ABOUT HALFWAY ALONG THE FONTANKA'S seven-verst arc through the city, on the southern bank. The river split from the Neva to the south just a little way downstream from where its far mightier sister, the Great Nevka, split to the north. It rejoined the main river just at the point where the Great Neva discharged into the Gulf of Finland.

Mihail looked up at the nondescript building. His mother might have described it to him, but he had forgotten. There were many like it in the city. This was one of the better appointed ones, but as with them all, a *dvornik* sat in his little room, close to the door.

'I'm looking for a woman named Danilova,' Mihail explained. 'Svetlana Nikitichna. She used to live here, I believe.'

The man grunted. 'Still does, if you can call it living.'

'What do you mean?'

'She's a bit . . . you know . . . in the head.' He pointed to his own head in case Mihail still failed to understand.

'Does she accept callers?'

'No one ever tries. I take up her food but she's not a good tipper.' His hand came out as he said the final word.

Mihail slipped him five kopeks. 'It's number four, isn't it?'

The coin vanished. 'That's right. First floor.'

Mihail went up. The door was much the same as the others on the staircase, but as he approached it he could sense an unpleasant smell. It was nothing too stomach-churning, but not what he would have expected in a block like this one.

He knocked.

There was no answer, so he knocked again. This time there

came an indistinct shout from within – a woman's voice – but still no one came to the door. He tried the handle; it wasn't locked.

The smell was stronger inside: unwashed clothes, an unwashed body, rotting discarded food, perhaps even rotting flesh – a rat that had died and not been cleared away. He looked around. Nothing had been cleared away in here for a long time. Dust and cobwebs hung everywhere. Beneath them Mihail could see the remnants of a once well-decorated set of rooms; but that had been a long time ago.

He was in a small hallway. Stairs ascended to another floor, and three doors led off.

'Madame Danilova?' he called.

'*Ici!*' She spoke in French. Was that because of the way he had addressed her, or a throwback to a time when ladies of her stature spoke only that language? Mihail was reminded of the old man he had met in Senate Square, and who he had turned out to be. He was not expecting to encounter a vampire here, but in his bag he still carried the *arbalyet*.

The voice had come from the door straight in front of him. He went through. The room beyond was in much the same state as the hall. Even his feet falling on the carpet threw up a cloud of dust that caught his nostrils and gave him the urge to sneeze. At least in here, it was bright. Tall windows stood along one wall, unshuttered, looking out on to the street and the river, though no sunlight fell directly into the room. It faced north, slightly to the west. Perhaps it would receive a smattering of the sun's rays, on summer afternoons.

At the far end of the room, close to the window, sat the apartment's occupant. She was thin – almost childlike in build, though it was hard to judge her height. Her hair was long, straight and lank. He remembered Tamara had told him it was blonde, and perhaps she had kept that colour. More likely it had turned to white, and the grease that mingled with it had returned it to its former hue. It was difficult to discern any individual strand. Instead the hair was matted into a single block, glistening slightly. Mihail was reminded of rancid butter. Her skin was thin, but not excessively wrinkled. There was no colour to it, but for the blue of her veins.

'Come closer,' she said, still speaking French.

Mihail walked across the room and stood a few feet away from her. She looked him up and down. He had worn his uniform, hoping that it would impress.

'Come on then,' she said. 'Tell me.'

'Tell you what?'

'You have news; from Sevastopol. Why else would you come? It can't be good. He's dead, isn't he?'

'Dead?'

'My husband!'

Mihail had been warned by the *dvornik*. Svetlana was not well in her mind. She was living in the past. Momentarily he pictured a different life for himself. This was just an elderly eccentric aunt who as a child he had been forced to visit and now did so out of sympathy, but rarely stayed long. Such visits would be commonplace for many families, but a closed door for Mihail. He allowed himself only a moment's regret.

'That's right,' he replied. 'He died bravely.'

'I knew it. I knew it when she came to see me.'

'When who came?'

'That woman, with her questions.' Svetlana leaned forward in her chair. There was even less to her frame now that it could be seen clear of the upholstery. 'You look like her. Are you related?'

'My name is Mihail Konstantinovich Lukin,' he told her. 'I'm a lieutenant.'

'In Dmitry's regiment.'

'No.'

'Then why have they sent you?'

Mihail could provide no answer.

'What's the date?' she asked.

'19 February.'

'What year? What year?'

'1881.' He could not lie to her.

She sat back, a look of surprise on her face. 'He's been dead a long time, then,' she said simply.

Mihail nodded, hoping she was returning to reality. 'Twenty-five years.'

She looked up at him, her eyes suddenly seeming to plead with

318

him. 'I coped,' she said, 'for a while. I was even courted. I could have done well for myself. But he wouldn't leave me alone.'

'Who wouldn't?'

'Mitka. He walked past in the street.' She pointed out of the window. 'He never even bothered to look up, but it was him. I told them, and they said they understood. They didn't believe me, so I made sure they'd listen. Then they didn't come back.'

'When was this?'

She waved a dismissive hand. 'Oh, years . . .' She paused. 'Then he stopped walking past, and there was just me. I preferred it when he was there.' She raised her head towards the ceiling. Her irises disappeared under her eyelids and Mihail could see only the blank whiteness of her eyeballs staring at him. Then her head dropped and she looked at him more normally. 'You think I'm mad, don't you?'

'I think . . .' Mihail had no answer. If she was mad she had been driven mad. Her husband was undead – it was quite conceivable that she had seen him, but what was she supposed to make of it?

'I wish I were,' she moaned. 'When I was mad, I believed it when I saw him. Now I'm sane, I know he's not real, even when I do see him.'

It was an unfathomable contradiction, but she was bound by no law that insisted she should make sense.

'You still see him?' asked Mihail eagerly.

'Don't tease me. I know he's not real.'

She pushed down hard on the arms of her chair and rose unsteadily to her feet. Mihail noticed a faint peeling sound as the fabric of the dress separated from that of the chair, as if she had not moved for a very long time. She walked, taking the smallest of steps, over to a high table, or perhaps a dresser, in the corner of the room; it was impossible to clearly discern its shape. A sheet had been thrown over it, now thick with the ubiquitous stratum of dust, and it was covered with rags and junk. The journey took half a minute, during which neither of them said a word. She was purposeful in her motion and Mihail did not want to distract her.

When she reached the table she lifted the sheet and reached beneath it, her fingers stretched. A sound emerged and Mihail realized he had been mistaken. It was neither a table nor a dresser, but a piano – unrecognizable among the furniture and rubbish that had been piled around it and on it. The tune she played was mournful, made even more deathly by the instrument's untuned strings. It was Chopin's *Marche Funèbre*, though Svetlana was playing only the melody. Even so, she managed to invest the short, repeated phrase with far more melancholy than Mihail had ever heard in it before.

'He loved Chopin above anyone,' she said. 'Even me, I think. I wonder if he still plays.'

'Where do you see him?' asked Mihail.

Svetlana raised her hand from the piano and the tune stopped. She turned and made the same slow, steady progress as before; this time towards the window. Mihail walked over to join her, arriving long before she did. The foetid smell was stronger when she stood beside him.

'He walks along the embankment, just here,' she said, pointing to the street below. 'You'd think he'd look up, just for old times' sake, but he never does.'

'Where does he go?'

'He crosses by the Egyptian Bridge, but then I lose sight of him.'

'This is in the evenings?'

'Of course,' she said, with a casual certainty that made Mihail suspicious. To him the fact it was evening made perfect sense, but there was no reason it should for her. Did she guess?

'And does he come back?' Mihail asked.

'I wait up until I see him safely return. He usually does, but not always.'

'When did you last see him?'

'He stopped for a while, but then he started again.'

'Recently?'

She began to nod, but then her head came to a standstill. She turned to him and gave a puzzled frown. 'Pardon?'

'When did you last see him?' asked Mihail.

'Who?'

'Dmitry Alekseevich – your husband.'

'My husband's dead,' she said and turned away. She resumed

her slow shuffle back towards her chair. When she reached it she turned and sat down, emitting a small, contented sigh. Then she looked up, as if catching sight of Mihail for the first time.

'You have news?' she asked. 'From Sevastopol?'

Mihail left without another word.

Blood – that was what he craved. Not milk. Blood. And she gave it to him. He could not understand why, nor did he care. He needed blood and Susanna provided it. She had wept when she saw him and he had tasted the salt of her tears on his dry lips. He'd still been unable to recall the word, even to mouth it let alone utter it, but she had understood. She had removed her coat and undone her blouse so that the smooth white expanse of her breasts was revealed. He remembered a time when that had interested him, a stolen moment when Susanna had first persuaded him to touch her, but now it meant nothing. She revealed her bosom only as a consequence of revealing her throat. That was what concerned him now and she knew it.

She leaned over him, pressing her hands against her chest so that her breasts did not brush against his delicate exposed lungs. She raised her chin, stretching the skin of her neck close to his lips, but much as he craved to lift his head and taste her, he could not; he did not have muscles or bones to do it, even if he'd had the energy.

She understood and pressed closer, so that his lips gently kissed her flesh. He could feel the pulse of the blood in her veins, just the thickness of human skin away from him. He parted his jaws and bit, but the glorious, warm satisfaction of flowing blood did not cascade into his mouth. He tried again, but still there was nothing. His teeth did not even have the strength to pierce the delicate skin of this fragile, willing girl.

She straightened up. He tried to keep his lips pressed against her, but was still unable to move.

'You poor thing,' she said, still with tears in her eyes. She unbuttoned her left cuff and rolled up the sleeve. It was wrong; he despised drinking from there, though he knew it would still nourish him. But he could not complain; Susanna was in complete control. From her bag she took a small knife – an ordinary thing

321

with a single blade. She cut across the inside of her forearm, close to the crook of the elbow. She let out a little grunt.

The blood flowed fast, spilling on to the stones and running, wasted, into the sewer. She moved quickly, holding her arm above his face so that the blood began to splatter over it. Even that was nourishing. Every cell of his body craved it, and in the absence of better means, would assimilate it directly. But it would be most effective in his mouth. She moved her arm until the blood flowed between his open lips, trickling off the tip of her elbow. Now he could taste it. Memories came flooding to him, each recalling the pleasure of consuming human blood. He did not swallow, but allowed the warm liquid to fill his mouth, surrounding and caressing his tongue, until it overflowed and ran down his cheek.

Then he opened his pharynx and the liquid flowed down his throat. It was not really swallowing – he was not yet capable of that. It was simply the removal of a hindrance, allowing gravity to do its work. The blood did not have far to go, spilling out on to the ground beneath him from his incomplete oesophagus. Even there though he felt himself drawing nutrition from it, as the intricate folds of his half-formed lungs proved capable of absorbing more than just oxygen from their surroundings, sucking up the spreading blood like a mop cleaning dirty, spilled water.

Susanna pushed her arm down towards him and his lips sealed around the wound. He played at it with his tongue, hoping to inveigle more blood out of it. She yelped – which he enjoyed – but then pulled her arm away.

'Gently,' she murmured, then returned her arm to his mouth. He did not disobey her.

After a few minutes, she pulled it away again. Still he tried to move his head and still he could not. He watched as she bandaged her wound with a strip of cloth from her underskirt.

'No more,' she said. 'Not today.'

'Please,' he mouthed. It was not an easy word for him at the best of times.

She shook her head. 'Where would you be if you took it all?' she asked.

She stood and departed. He lay still. Even the little blood she had given, which he had so feebly absorbed, had done him good. He closed his eyes, trying to sense the shrivelled extremities of his own body. It was working, he could feel it. Morsel by morsel, cell by cell, his body was renewing itself.

It was on the fourth night of watching that Mihail finally saw Dmitry taking the path that his wife had described. He'd hidden himself on the northern side of the Fontanka, where Nikolskiy Lane joined Great Podyacheskaya Street. As he arrived, just before dusk, he noticed he could look along Podyacheskaya Street and see in the distance the dome of Saint Isaac's, perfectly aligned as though the road had been built to point at it. He had been wise to abandon his post at the cathedral and take up this new position. Tonight, a little before midnight, he gained his reward.

Dmitry came from the south, emerging from Izmailovsky Prospekt and turning left along the embankment. As he passed beneath the windows of his former home Mihail thought he perceived a flicker of movement at them, but Dmitry did not look up, just as Svetlana had been so keen to point out. As she had described, he crossed the river via the Egyptian Bridge and carried on north. It would be too risky to follow his path directly, so Mihail too headed north, along a parallel street. Soon he found himself at the corner of the square containing the Saint Nikolai Cathedral, its blue and white plaster and small golden domes making it a quite different style of building from Saint Isaac's, but Mihail had no time to take it in. Looking along the stretch of canal that bordered the square, he saw that Dmitry had now turned east, and was heading towards him.

Before Mihail could make a move, Dmitry turned north again along the far side of the square. Mihail paralleled his movements and both of them reached the top of the square at about the same time. Dmitry pressed onwards, oblivious to Mihail's presence. Mihail continued to shadow him a block away and soon found himself in a broad, open square. Ahead and to the left he could see the multi-tier green stucco of the Mariinskiy Theatre, sitting in the square like some squat wedding cake. Mihail flung himself back into the shadows. Dmitry was approaching along the theatre's southern wall, evidently no longer able to continue his journey north. Mihail cursed himself for his lack of knowledge of the city's layout, but his luck held; Dmitry did not see him.

Instead Dmitry kept close to the theatre, turning into the square as soon as it was possible and then finally stopping at a small wooden door, some way from the main entrance. Mihail heard him knock and then there was a pause. Dmitry knocked again. This time he got a response. A few moments later the door opened. There was a brief conversation which Mihail could not hear and Dmitry disappeared inside, the door closing behind him.

Mihail scampered over, but the door was already locked. He considered knocking, but it seemed unwise. Dmitry had been welcomed in, so whoever was in there was on his side. Even if Mihail could gain access, he would be walking into hostile territory. Better to wait. This was not Dmitry's new lair; it was too early for him to be returning home and anyway, Svetlana had said she usually saw him make his way back along the route by which he had come. Mihail had little doubt as to what Dmitry had come there for – he wanted to feed – though why the theatre should be an appropriate place for it, he could only guess. Perhaps there were ballerinas in there who would sell their blood to vampires, just as there were those who sold their bodies to rich noblemen. His father Konstantin's mistress had begun her career in that very theatre.

It was none of Mihail's concern. If there were girls in the ballet who would take such a risk then they were fools and got what they deserved. Mihail was interested only in Dmitry – and through him Iuda. Dmitry would have to emerge at some point; with luck through that very same door, or at least one nearby.

Mihail crossed the square, to a point where he could see that entire side of the theatre, and settled down to wait.

Dmitry trotted eagerly down into the theatre's cavernous depths. It had cost him five roubles to bribe the nightwatchman, but it was money well spent. And what did money mean to him anyway? He could always steal more from his next victim.

He held a single candle to light his way, included in the price of his admission. The old man had been surprised to see him on his first visit since returning to Petersburg, three weeks before. His journey to Turkmenistan in search of Iuda had meant he had not been in the city since the end of the previous year. While away there had still been opportunities to indulge himself, but they were stolen and infrequent, and he knew of few places in the whole Russian Empire where he would find a creation of such elegance and beauty as what lay here beneath the stage of the Mariinskiy Theatre.

Soon he came to the door with which he was so familiar. This was his fifth visit since returning to Petersburg. He was over-indulging himself, but who was to stop him? Zmyeevich laughed at him but offered no objection. How could he? He had his own vices of which Dmitry was well aware.

He almost felt the urge to knock before entering, though he would receive no granting of admission. Perhaps crossing himself would be a more appropriate act of deference, but coming from a *voordalak* it would be a worthless sham. He knew he was just delaying the moment, aware that the anticipation was almost as thrilling as the act. Almost.

He opened the door. The room was lined with mirrors so that the dancers could watch themselves as they rehearsed. Dmitry could never, therefore, be a dancer. He crossed the floor, but no image was reflected in any glass. He might have expected to see the candle floating mysteriously in mid-air, supported by his invisible hand, but even that was gone. He was by now used to the phenomenon, but had no way of explaining it. No doubt Iuda had conducted some foul experiment to determine the mechanism, but Dmitry did not care. Who knew where such exploration might lead? Dmitry shuddered. He did know – he had seen it in that strange mirror beneath Senate Square. At least these reflected nothing.

Thoughts of Iuda filled his mind once again, but he felt no sense of relief at the death of the creature that had once been his mentor. Zmyeevich had assured him that Iuda was no more, but even as he spoke there had been doubt in his eyes. He had witnessed Iuda's body burned to almost nothing, but had been distracted. Together they had searched Saint Isaac's and found no trace of Iuda – but what did that tell them? Raisa, lurking somewhere at the back of Dmitry's skull, remained unconvinced. But she had no mind of her own. Her suspicions were a reflection of Dmitry's. She merely told him what he hid from himself. He pushed them all – Raisa, Zmyeevich and Iuda – from his mind. They were not the reason he was here.

At the far end of the room stood the object of his desire: a piano. It was probably not the finest in the theatre; that would be upstairs where it could be heard in the auditorium. This was merely for rehearsal, but all the same it was a wonderful instrument: a Bösendorfer – only around five years old, regularly tuned. He fixed the candle to the floor behind him with a drop of its own wax. He did not need to see in order to play, but it would help him in finding his way out. He would not risk placing it on the beautiful instrument itself and seeing the hot wax dribble down on to the smooth, polished wood.

He sat and lifted the lid.

Music no longer filled his mind as it had done when he was human – right up to the very moment of his death. He could still bring to mind a melody, but not in the same way as before – there was no orchestra filling his skull. A tune was just a tune, like a word on a page rather than a word spoken out loud. Worse still, every tune he could bring to mind was one that he already knew; one that had been created by someone else. When a man, the orchestra had played madly and creatively and he had known that the music could only have come from him. That part of his mind was gone, sucked from him in the same moment that Raisa Styepanovna had taken his blood and his life. Perhaps that part of him was his soul.

But at least he could still play – in some ways better than he had before. His fingers possessed greater dexterity and greater strength. He could truly perform Chopin's *Valse du Petit Chien* in the minute prescribed by its mispronounced English title. He knew that it must sound awful but – and this was the worst of it – it did not sound awful to him. His abilities – to play loud or soft, fast or slow, staccato or legato – were all of the highest degree. But his taste – the judgement as to when each was appropriate – was lost. If he hit a wrong note, which he rarely did, then he could hear that, but if his performance lacked passion, then he was not to know. The best he could do was to imitate. He had once heard Anton Rubinstein, in Warsaw, play Liszt's piano sonata in B minor and heard all in the audience proclaim it a performance of genius. Dmitry could reproduce it perfectly, in all its genius, except that he did not know what made it good. He could even vary the performance, but he had no idea whether each slight change he made was for better or for worse. It wouldn't be long before someone invented a machine that could do as much. But it wasn't such a curse. All but the most attuned human ear had as little skill in judging a great performance as he did. And he would never truly know how badly he played, since he could not judge. He was like a man who had been blind since birth; how could he know what he was missing? Except that Dmitry had not always been like this.

Today he chose to play something modern. He'd come across the piece in a music shop on his brief stay in Moscow, and had learned it there and then. It was by Brahms – his Rhapsody in B minor. This was the hardest test of all for him – to play what he had never heard played by human hands, but seen only on paper. That little semiquaver run in the first bar, echoed by the left hand in the fifth, was marked as a triplet, but mightn't a great pianist choose to play it faster, as an acciaccatura, slipped in quickly before the following D natural? Dmitry could certainly play it fast; he had tried it both ways, but had no clue as to which was better.

He began, sticking strictly to what had been written and playing the notes as a triplet. The piece progressed and he began to enjoy himself, for reasons he could not fathom. It was a pretence – a pretence that he was what he had once been. He'd heard once of an Austrian prince who would stand in his box at the theatre and conduct the orchestra and at the end of the performance the audience would rise and applaud him. But all in the theatre – the prince included – knew he had done nothing. The real conductor stood in the pit, doing his job as usual. The musicians kept their eyes on him and took their time from his motions. The prince was following them, not the other way round. And yet he happily took the applause. Dmitry indulged himself in a similar delusion.

He turned and looked into one of the mirrors. He could see the candle now that it was not carried by a creature of confusing invisibility. The reflection of the piano was clear in the dim light. It stood, quite still. Naturally, there was no pianist sitting at the keyboard, but more than that, even the keys themselves did not move. It would have been pleasant to see – a visible reflection of Dmitry's skills.

But that did not matter. It was only the music, the sound that mattered, and that filled the room. Dmitry closed his eyes and let it fill him too. If nothing else, it drove Zmyeevich from his mind.

Dmitry stayed for about two hours. He re-emerged from the same door by which he'd entered. Mihail had crept over to the theatre to take a further look around and by luck he was close to the main entrance when Dmitry appeared. He pressed himself into a doorway and listened to what was said.

'That was very beautiful, sir,' said one voice, not Dmitry's.

'Really?' That was Dmitry. It was no casual response – more of a plea.

'God, yes! You could get a job here, if you wanted, easily.'

'Not here, I don't think,' replied Dmitry sadly. 'Not in Russia.'

'Follow in the steps of Rubinstein, then? Take America by storm. Make your fortune.'

Dmitry chuckled, but there was no pleasure in it. 'Perhaps,' he said.

He set off back the way he had come. Mihail knew his route well enough, at least as far as the Fontanka, and so was able to make his own way there, reaching the river bank before Dmitry emerged and managing even to cross ahead of him. The streets were virtually deserted now and the gaslight mingling with the half-moon cast strange shadows across the frozen water.

Once across, Mihail ducked troll-like back beneath the bridge, waiting for Dmitry to pass over. Looking up he could see one of the towering obelisks that gave the bridge its Egyptian flavour, and a sphinx sitting patiently on its plinth at the end of the balustrade. As Dmitry crossed, the bridge began – as tradition suggested – to sing. His footsteps caused the walkway to vibrate, which in turn ground the chains that suspended it against their brackets and a strange ululation filled the air, each stretch of the chain, with a slightly differing length and tension, contributing its own pitch to the cacophony.

The singing continued for a minute after Dmitry had left the bridge, but Mihail did not stay to listen. As soon as his quarry had disappeared down Izmailovsky Prospekt Mihail set off for the junction. There he could see that Dmitry had turned left and then right. He was now on the long, straight Zabalkansky Prospekt, stretching south to the outskirts of the city. There was no chance now for Mihail to lurk in the side streets, and so he had simply to follow at a distance, hiding in the shadows whenever he feared Dmitry was about to turn and look back towards him. But whatever was on Dmitry's mind, it was not the possibility of pursuit and Mihail found his task remarkably easy. After ten minutes they crossed the Obvodny Canal, officially marking the edge of the city. Ten minutes later still Dmitry disappeared. He could only have turned off the road, to the left. Mihail made a note of the point, and soon reached it, looking at what lay to the side of the road.

Ahead of him stretched a vast, flat expanse, punctuated only by the jagged silhouettes of gravestones, tombs and sepulchres. This was the great Novodyevichye Cemetery, resting place of so many of the city's wealthiest dead. A plot here could cost hundreds of roubles; many bought their own grave before they died, for fear that their relatives would find a better use for their inheritance.

The tall figure of Dmitry was still visible in the moonlight, making his way between the graves. Mihail stayed by the road. If this was merely another leg of Dmitry's journey, then there was the risk of losing him, but Mihail doubted it. One of those graves – or more likely a larger tomb – would be where Dmitry settled for the night, either alone or with Zmyeevich. Mihail moved a little to one side until Dmitry's path aligned with two unmistakable statues of angels or saints that marked points where the dead rotted below. Now he would be able to follow the path Dmitry had taken. It was after about a minute that Dmitry came to a halt and looked around him. Mihail ran – on tiptoe so he would not be heard and ducking down so he would not be seen – until Dmitry's position aligned with another pair of reference points; this time a tall cross and a tree. Now he had two lines for his triangulation. They had taught him the technique at the technical school and he had used it often in the army, but never heard of its use in hunting a vampire.

Dmitry was gone. Mihail waited a few moments in case he had

simply stepped behind some monument, but there was no more movement. Dmitry had gone to ground – gone *into* the ground. Mihail drew and loaded his crossbow, then checked again to make sure he could identify all four of his markers. He stepped forward into the graveyard, following the path laid out by the second pair, the cross and the tree. He kept an eye on the first two statues, initially far apart in his field of view, but converging with each step he took. He had not run far between his two triangulation points, fearing that Dmitry would be lost from sight, and so he knew that the process would not be hugely accurate. While there was still quite a gap between the two statues, he slowed his pace and began to look for more direct signs that he had reached the correct spot.

The evidence came to him in the form of the orange glow of a lamp, spilling from the doorway of one of the largest tombs in the whole cemetery. It was the size and shape of a shed, but built of stone rather than wood. Two urns sat atop pedestals on either side of a heavy bronze door that stood ajar. Above the doorway a typical Byzantine cross was carved into the stone, with its three crossbeams: at the top the plate on which would have been written the letters INRI; in the middle, the longest, where Christ's arms would have been spread, suspended by His nailed hands; the bottom was the beam on which He could rest His feet, allowing Him, if He so desired, to prolong His torment. That lowest beam was tilted to an angle, one end pointing towards heaven for the righteous, the other directing the wicked to hell.

Mihail followed the path of the sinful, and peeped around the open door. The tomb was deceptive – bigger on the inside than it appeared. Rather than housing the burial chamber, the upper building was merely the cover to a flight of steps leading down into the earth. Mihail could not see to the bottom, but he heard the sound of murmuring voices. He dared not descend, as his feet would be seen long before he could see what was in there. Instead he lay down flat on his front, his head just level with the top of the flight, one hand still clutching the *arbalyet*, the other underneath him, ready to push him to his feet if he needed to flee. It was an uncomfortable pose and he could not see everything, but he could see enough.

Dmitry and Zmyeevich were both there, sitting as if on opposite benches in a railway carriage, though in fact the objects upon which their weight rested were their own closed coffins. Zmyeevich was stripped to his waist, revealing a sturdy frame of which any man of his apparent age might be proud, except for the fact that his flesh sagged a little. He was not fat, but it was as if the skin were weak – tired. Dmitry had removed his coat and jacket and sat in his shirtsleeves. Zmyeevich was speaking.

'Do not deny yourself,' he said.

Dmitry looked at him and then reluctantly began to unbutton his shirt, like a girl hesitantly succumbing to her seducer. Soon he was in the same state of undress as Zmyeevich. Zmyeevich reached over to his coat, beside him, and withdrew a tiny object that glinted silver in the lamplight. It was a knife – some kind of scalpel. Zmyeevich placed his left hand flat against his chest, covering his nipple, and used his right to draw the blade across his skin just below it, leaving a horizontal line of red blood which oozed out and began to slither unevenly down his chest and towards his stomach. Despite his being a vampire, the wound did not seal itself, though a look of intense concentration appeared on his face as he prevented the healing process from occurring.

He handed the scalpel to Dmitry, who gazed at it in fascination, twisting it in the air so that both steel and the droplets of blood that clung to it gleamed as they caught the light. He opened his mouth and moved the blade towards it, stroking first one side of it and then the other against his tongue, as though he were buttering bread. When he was done, the knife was clean of the blood that had once stained it.

But it did not stop there. Now Dmitry mimicked Zmyeevich's action, down to the smallest detail. He held the flesh of his breast taut with one hand and cut across it with the other. Again his faced strained, not from pain but as he focused his mind on keeping the wound open. He did not mirror Zmyeevich, but imitated him exactly; both their wounds were to the left. A moment later Mihail discovered why.

Dmitry lay back so that his body was now in the appropriate orientation with regard to the coffin on which he rested, except that he was above it rather than within it. His arms dropped limply to his sides and hung loosely, his knuckles just brushing against the ground. Zmyeevich moved forward, kneeling beside Dmitry and looking over him like a concerned nurse. He shuffled round so that he was now hovering over Dmitry's head.

Then he leaned forward and his lips found the gash in Dmitry's chest. They sealed over it and Mihail saw Zmyeevich's Adam's apple move up and down as he began to swallow. Dmitry was breathing faster and more deeply. He raised his head towards Zmyeevich's chest, but could not find what he wanted.

'Left,' he whispered.

Zmyeevich adjusted his position a little, still keeping his lips clasped to Dmitry's flesh. Now Dmitry's own lips could reach what they desired. He first licked at the blood that had smeared across his companion's skin and when that was gone he pressed his mouth against the wound and began to drink, imitating Zmyeevich exactly. A little blood seeped out from beneath his lips, but he was too intent on his task to care.

Mihail studied the scene. A sense of revulsion and nausea filled him as he looked. He knew that now was his chance. Never again would he find the two so vulnerable. Zmyeevich's back was turned to him, his mind focused on the obscene ritual they were performing. Mihail could plunge his wooden dagger into the creature's heart and still be able to deal with Dmitry using the crossbow. But he felt unaccountably sickened. Why the thought of a vampire drinking the blood of another vampire should revolt him so, he had no idea. He must steel himself to his task.

But then his gaze fell upon Dmitry again and he knew he was too late.

Dmitry's eyes were open, and stared directly at Mihail. There was no doubt that he saw him, but he made no acknowledgement of it. He simply continued consuming the blood of the monster that lay upon him, and enjoying it too. And the worst of it was – Mihail could see it in his face – that the whole thing was made more pleasurable by the very fact that they were being watched.

Mihail would not give them the satisfaction. He pushed himself up on to his feet and fled.

CHAPTER XXI

NOW HE COULD DRINK AS HE SHOULD – FROM THE THROAT. HE had the strength in his jaw for his teeth to pierce her skin and he had begged her and at last she had succumbed. He had lungs now too, which he could fill with air thanks to his diaphragm. Below that, it was still an obscene hash of half-formed organs; something that might become a stomach, a few lengths of intestine, not yet comprising a whole. When she left him alone he would watch as they formed and developed, the half-grown parts never seeking one another, but somehow knowing when they touched and joining into something greater. Even his other arm was beginning to lengthen and grow stronger, but still he did not have an elbow.

It was all down to her – to her blood. Each night she gave him a share of what was hers, and each day she found some way to recuperate. Her friends must suspect she was pregnant, the amount extra she would have to eat. It was much the same process: she ate and produced blood, which she used to nurture a creature that she loved, a creature that grew each day and would soon be reborn. The only difference was that she needed no umbilical cord to transfer to him the blood that he craved.

Once she had been persuaded, she was pleased to do it. She unbuttoned her collar as before to reveal her neck, and then leaned over him. There was no need now for artificial blades to break the skin, his teeth were enough. As her flesh yielded she pulled away, not out of want of love for him, but from an instinctive human fear that deep down knew the nature of a vampire. He was ready; his one working hand held her by the back of her head, its fingers caressing her blonde curls and pulling her back down to him.

She squirmed and moaned as he drank, but did not pull away again, though she was still stronger than him. Now that he had the beginnings of organs that could properly digest it, each mouthful of her blood did him so much more good than before. But that did not concern him – his desire was solely to slake his thirst. Nature made him enjoy drinking so that he would be nourished, but he was not yet well enough for such rationality to prevail. He would drink and go on drinking until she was dry and lay dead, her body sprawled across his torso. It would be the end of him, since he would no longer have her to feed from, but he did not care.

Thankfully, she did. She was his conscience and his salvation. All too soon he felt her pull away from him. He tried to hold on with his single hand, but he could not. Even if he had cast aside the precious object he had held in his palm for as long as he could remember, he had no strength to hold her. In an instant he could see her again, kneeling above him, her hand clutching at a bandage which she held to her neck. She looked pale and faint, but she would survive.

'Please,' he said softly, more softly than was necessary, considering the new strength of his lungs. But he knew humility was more likely to persuade her.

She shook her head, rubbing her neck against the bandage and causing a little blood to ooze from under it. 'Next time,' she said.

He smiled meekly and nodded, thinking of next time. Involuntarily the stump of his growing right arm twitched. She saw it too, and understood his thoughts – as he drank she had shared a fragment of his mind. Next time, he would be strong enough to hold her.

Mihail was bewildered. He could not make sense of what he had seen. What he knew of the *voordalak* he knew from folklore, and from what his mother had learned – both first-hand and from Aleksei – and from what they had discovered from their simple, rudimentary experiments. And of the idea that one vampire should ever choose to drink the blood of another he knew nothing.

But there was a greater experimenter than either he or Tamara, and he was a meticulous note-taker. Mihail scoured Iuda's journals for an explanation of what he had witnessed. The books were not indexed, but were divided into chapters, one of which, though by far the longest, also seemed to be the most apposite.

On Vampires and Blood Magic

Iuda began with an immediate apology for the title, firmly asserting that there was no magic involved, merely the laws of science, but that the broad set of phenomena he was discussing was regarded both by vampires and by their adversaries – typically men of the church – as being magical.

Mihail read on avidly. Much of what he saw, he knew already. The first subtitle was 'On Induction'.

It featured a long discussion of the situation in which the Romanov family found itself, with references to similar observations in less august bloodlines. The basic facts were simple. Because of the blood Zmyeevich had taken from Pyotr, any one of Pyotr's descendants was at risk. If he – or she – should drink Zmyeevich's blood and die with it in his body, then he would be reborn a vampire. Like any vampire, he would have a mental link with his creator, Zmyeevich. But in facing a mind as strong as Zmyeevich's he was more likely to become the vampire's slave than his brother.

Even before that, the mental link was there, but only in one direction. Zmyeevich could project the influence of his mind towards any carrier of the Romanov blood. He could not force that Romanov to act against his will, but he could communicate with him, influence him, scare him. Thus it had been that Zmyeevich had persuaded Aleksandr I to travel to Taganrog, and thence to Chufut Kalye. The only good news for the Romanovs was that this power could be exerted only once in each generation. His manipulation of Aleksandr meant that his brother Nikolai, even when tsar, was quite free of it. It meant Zmyeevich must choose carefully.

The last comment of the section was an example of why such care was needed. The current Aleksandr's eldest son, Nikolai, who would one day have become tsar, had died young. If Zmyeevich had begun to work on him, his efforts would have been wasted and he would not be able to redirect them towards the new tsarevich, Aleksandr Aleksandrovich.

Here Iuda had scribbled a footnote, short but chilling.

I now have reason to believe that Z. deliberately brought about the death of N.A.R., knowing he will have better luck with A.A.R.

The initials were easy to decipher.

The next section was far shorter. Mihail skimmed through it quickly. It did not seem to apply to the current situation, however intriguing the subtitle might be.

On Anastasis

I have recently heard of a legend not uncommon among Wallachian vampires, though less widespread elsewhere, which, if true, would add another level to the bond between a human and a vampire in the circumstances of the Romanovs and Zmyeevich, or indeed any other pairing where the human's blood has been drunk by the vampire, either directly or through descent, but for whom the process of induction has not been completed. I have long known that if the vampire were then to die there is still the possibility (as I am living proof) that induction may be achieved, but equally the human, if left unmolested, may go on to experience a natural death. However, it seems that under certain conditions the human may be susceptible to drinking the vampire's blood not to the end of themselves becoming transformed but of bringing about a form of parousia with regard to the dead creature. This seems to be a very ancient story, going back to before the time even of Zmyeevich's human existence as Țepeș and I can find no vampire who has been eyewitness to it. However, it is an intriguing possibility and clearly an apt subject for experimentation, when circumstances next permit.

The final section contained what Mihail wanted, and explained the bizarre behaviour he had witnessed the previous night. Here the title was 'On Assimilation'.

Mihail read it through three times. Iuda began with the basics, describing the revulsion that any vampire had for the taste of the blood of its own kind. He described the flavour in great detail, writing from personal experience, though adding how he had grown to regret his actions as he learned the biology behind it. He went on to explain that, as with any unpleasant experience, such as pain or nausea, there was a good reason for it to occur; simply put, it deterred the creature – be he man, vampire or beast – from behaviour which could be damaging to it. Sunlight inflicted pain upon a vampire to persuade him to return to the shade where he would not be burned. The taste of vampire blood was foul to dissuade him from drinking it and suffering consequences perhaps worse still than being roasted in the sun.

Iuda went on to describe how he had been puzzled by the eleven creatures that accompanied him to Russia back in 1812. He referred to them as *oprichniki*, just as Aleksei did, though acknowledged that he had not coined the term himself. It had always been puzzling to him why they and other vampires that he had met in Wallachia were such feral creatures compared to others of their breed who might pass themselves off in the best of human company. He mentioned the first vampire he had ever encountered, a French aristocrat by the name of Honoré Philippe Louis d'Évreux, whom he described as an intelligent and entertaining interlocutor. That description could certainly not be applied to the *oprichniki*. But it came down to the exchange of blood between vampires.

When Mihail had finished he understood it all, and realized that in his knowledge he now had a wedge to drive between Zmyeevich and Dmitry. If he could gain Dmitry's acquiescence, or even his assistance, then it might be possible to blunt Zmyeevich's power over the Romanovs. What he would then do with Dmitry he did not know. It depended how far things had gone.

Even so, taking on Zmyeevich would be absurdly dangerous, but Iuda's journals had provided Mihail with an idea as to how he might save not just his own soul. He went over to the windowsill and picked up the cyanide-filled hazelnut that Kibalchich had given him. The People's Will had made suicide its ultimate defence against its enemies. Maybe that wasn't such a stupid idea after all.

A pretty one would be better, but she didn't have to be anything special. Someone who would willingly do what he told her, and then pretend she did it unwillingly. Halvard Karlsson had been travelling for weeks. His captain had planned to make it into Petersburg before the Gulf of Finland froze over, but there had been delay after delay and they hadn't even reached Tallinn when winter set in. But the cargo had to get through, so they'd hired sleds and loaded the goods on to them and the sailors – Halvard among them – had swapped navigating the sea for navigating the ice. But at last they had made it, delivered the cargo and been handsomely paid. Halvard did not know whether he would try to return overland to the stranded ship, or wait until the thaw came. But for now he was in the city, he had money and he had one thing on his mind.

The single word of Russian that he knew covered it: *shlyooha*. He knew the equivalent in several languages. He said it to one of the men at the docks, who'd gabbled on in Russian but managed to convey vague directions that Halvard should head south, across the river. He said it to a few others when he got lost. Some had frowned, one man had tried to hit him, but at last he'd met a man who spoke a little German and had told him, with a wink, to follow the canal until it started to curve down towards the Haymarket. Around there, on the embankment or in the side streets, was where he would find them. When he did find them, he was spoilt for choice; some young, some older, all eager once he showed them his purse.

There was a problem though. Halvard liked to talk. You could show them what you wanted them to do, but it wasn't the same. These girls all spoke Russian – a few of them French, but that was no help to Halvard. He did find one who said she was born in Göteborg, and he believed it from the accent, but that had obviously been a good few decades ago. He'd got the money to do better than that.

Then he saw one that really took his eye. She was older than some, in her mid-twenties, but as long as they were half his age Halvard wasn't going to make a fuss. She was dressed more soberly than the other girls, with only a pretty scarf tied snugly around her neck providing any adornment. It was the gleaming blonde hair that made him think she might even be Swedish, but when he spoke to her she didn't understand a word. He was about to move on but she was a real treat, so he tried again in German. She knew enough to name a price, to which he eagerly agreed.

'Where shall we go?' he asked. In some cities the whores would do their business in an alleyway, but not in Petersburg – not in winter.

'I know a place,' she said.

'Nearby?'

'A little way.'

She led him away from the canal, along a grubby street. As far as he could tell they were heading back towards the docks. Soon the way was blocked by another canal – the city was full of them – and they turned to walk alongside it.

'How much further?' he asked.

'Not too far.' She glanced at him, worried that she might lose the business. She stopped. 'Don't worry – it'll be worth it.' She grabbed his hand and pulled off his mitten, then thrust the hand inside the flap of her coat, down between her legs. He squeezed, but there was nothing much to feel beneath the layers of clothing. Even so, it showed willing, and the glint in her eye as she held his hand there for a few seconds showed that she knew what she was about.

They carried on walking and soon the street opened out into a broad, paved square. At its centre was a monument – a tall, round stone plinth topped with a bronze soldier on horseback. This wasn't the statue of Pyotr the Great – Halvard had seen that. There was an inscription on the plinth, but he wasn't going to waste time looking at it. The girl led him onwards, across the square towards an even more impressive construction – a great cathedral with a shining golden dome, grander than that of Hedvig Eleonora in Stockholm – more like Saint Paul's in London.

She led him towards the cathedral, but avoided mounting its

steps, instead going around the side of them. Finally she stopped, in a corner shadowed by the building.

'Here we are,' she said.

'I thought you said somewhere warm,' he grumbled.

'It is.' She pointed downwards and beneath her feet he saw an iron manhole cover. She stepped back and pulled it open on a hinge, revealing a set of steps. 'It's lovely down there.'

It was not tempting. 'Sod this,' he growled and made as if to go, but she grabbed him and kissed him hard on the lips. He felt her hand rubbing his crotch and felt himself respond. He let her continue for a few seconds, imagining how her hand would feel against his naked flesh, knowing now that he wouldn't be going back to find an alternative. He grinned at her. 'All right,' he said. 'I can tell you want it.'

He went down first and she pulled the cover closed after her. A lighted lamp hung from the wall – clearly she kept the place ready. And she was right, it was warmer down here. He began to unbutton his coat. She kissed him again, and her fingers unfastened the laces of his shirt, pulling it open. Her hands caressed his chest and neck.

'What's your name?' he asked.

She looked at him for a moment, and then smiled. 'Susanna,' she said. It was obviously a lie. He did not mind. It was a nice name – the same in Swedish as in Russian.

'You got a mattress or something down here, Susanna?'

She nodded. 'That way. And grab the lamp.'

He did as he was told. There was a slight smell of the sewers, but it wouldn't put him off. He began to imagine what was to come, what he would do to her, picturing the little body that was hidden beneath all those clothes.

And then he saw it.

At first he thought it was a corpse, half covered in a blanket so that nothing showed below the waist. But he was wrong. Nothing covered the body's legs – there simply were no legs. It was a man – as well as Halvard could guess. The chest showed no hint of breasts, but the genitals were malformed – either mutilated or undeveloped. It was impossible to make out what they were supposed to be. The upper body was fine, the head with its blond hair; the left arm. The right arm was not quite there – the hand had been cut off – blood, sinew and bone were visible at the wrist.

Further down he seemed to have been roughly hacked through at about the level of his waist, but at an angle. There was the stump of one thigh, but on the other side his hip and belly were not complete. Halvard could see the organs within, intestines and more that he could not name, which churned and seethed as the man drew breath.

Jesus Christ! He was alive. Compassion and revulsion tore Halvard in two, but it was compassion that won. He knelt down, leaning over the man's face.

'What's happened to you?' he asked, only to realize there was little chance that the man understood Swedish. Even so, the pathetic figure pushed its head up, trying to speak, reaching out with its good arm. Halvard leaned closer.

Then he felt a shove from behind. He had forgotten about Susanna and now it was too late. He fell forward and felt the wretch's arms around him, pulling him closer. Then he felt a terrible pain in the side of his neck as the creature bit. The sound of his own scream, echoing in the sewer, filled Halvard's ears.

It was mid-afternoon when Mihail returned to the Novodyevichye Cemetery, a day and a half since he had followed Dmitry there. He was as prepared as he would ever be. Even in daylight it was tricky to find the sepulchre until he was almost upon it. Fortunately, he still remembered the landmarks by which he had navigated.

The door was closed. Mihail could see no lock or handle by which he might open it, nor anything on which he could find purchase. He reached into his knapsack and brought out a crowbar, slipping its tip into the crack between door and frame. If he had not previously seen the door ajar he would not have known which side was hinged and which opened. There was no resistance to his leverage and soon the great slab of bronze had moved far enough for him to curl his fingers around it and pull it ajar. Light spilled inside, which was a good thing, but he did not want it to go too far. He wanted to talk to Dmitry – not kill him.

The stairs he had seen before were now covered with a sheet of grubby tarpaulin held in place by stones. Evidently the tomb's inhabitants also feared light accidentally spilling upon them. Mihail quickly moved it aside. Below, the chamber was much as he remembered. The two coffins lay parallel, pointing away from him – one open and empty, the other closed. That was to the good. If the slumbering occupant of that one coffin was Zmyeevich then it would be Mihail's best chance to deal with him; if Dmitry, they would have an opportunity to talk. The sunlight just clipped the foot of the closed casket, but penetrated no deeper. With the sun now past its zenith the light would get no further. Mihail unpacked what he needed from his bag and went down the steps. He tentatively lifted the coffin lid.

Inside lay Dmitry. Mihail let the wooden lid fall to the ground with a loud clatter, then sat back on the steps, safe in the sunlight, his loaded *arbalyet* in his hand, his two swords – of steel and wood – at his side.

Dmitry did not move. Mihail took his sabre and poked Dmitry in the leg with it. Still there was no response, so he jabbed harder. He suspected Dmitry was only feigning sleep, but either way the vampire began to stir. Mihail raised the crossbow and aimed it, but he doubted he would need to shoot.

'It's you,' said Dmitry once he had sat up.

'It's me,' Mihail confirmed. He stared at Dmitry. There was only one reason he had come here – one topic that he wanted to discuss – but now he shied away from it, almost embarrassed. Of all the foulness that had ever been perpetrated by Dmitry, this seemed a matter that was above all his own private concern. And yet as he looked into his uncle's face Mihail saw a reluctant expectation of what was to come. He could only be direct.

'I saw you and Zmyeevich,' he said, 'saw what you were doing.'

'I know.' Dmitry's voice expressed none of the pride that Mihail had seen in his eyes while the events were actually taking place.

'Do you know what you were doing?' Mihail asked.

'Having fun,' replied Dmitry, bitterly.

Mihail shook his head. 'Perhaps Zmyeevich was, but not you. Or if you were, then you're a fool – and I don't believe there are any fools in our family.'

'What would you know?'

'More importantly, what would Iuda know?'

'What?'

'I've read his journals,' explained Mihail. 'I've stolen his knowledge. And he understands more of vampires than even Zmyeevich – at least he thinks so.'

'He didn't know Zmyeevich could walk in daylight,' scoffed Dmitry.

'No, that's true. Zmyeevich has kept things from both of you.'

'What do you mean?'

'You remember the *oprichniki*? At least, how your father described them.'

'Of course; brutish creatures.'

'Not like you, or Zmyeevich, or Kyesha, or a dozen others I'm sure you've met in your time. You ever wondered why?'

'It's a big world,' said Dmitry. 'I've known humans who were as base as the *oprichniki*.'

'But they've not always been so. Take Pyetr, for example, their leader. According to Iuda he was a priest in his former life – an intelligent and well-read man. And as a *voordalak* he remained the same. Until he met Zmyeevich.'

Mihail paused, allowing Dmitry to consider his own existence since he had formed his partnership with Zmyeevich.

'Go on,' said Dmitry.

'Iuda wasn't able to find out about all of them, but there were similar stories for many. You're right; some of them started out as peasants – but they *all* ended up like that. And then, of course, Iuda was able to conduct experiments.'

'He was a monster before he became a vampire.'

Mihail could not disagree, but for once Iuda was not his primary concern. 'How long have you known Zmyeevich?' he asked.

'Almost two decades.'

'And when did you begin to exchange blood?'

'It wasn't like that.'

'Like what?'

'It's complicated.' Dmitry would not look Mihail in the eye.

'Do you like the taste?'

'Of course not.'

'Do you think it's right?' Mihail fired the questions off quickly now, pressing his advantage.

'Right?'

'Morally.'

'A *voordalak* has no God – why should he have morals?'

'What does your gut say? Does it tell you that this is what you should be doing rather than drinking down the fresh, living blood of a human?'

'Of course not!' Dmitry shouted. 'That's what makes it . . .' His voice petered out.

'What?'

'That's what makes it fun.' Dmitry was calmer now. 'Doing something that's wrong – just for its own sake.'

Mihail pressed on with his interrogation. 'And it was soon after – after you and Zmyeevich first exchanged blood – that you started to feel . . . different?'

'Yes.' Dmitry gazed down sullenly, then looked directly at Mihail. 'How did you know?'

'You're an orphan, aren't you, Dmitry – in vampire terms?'

'If you mean the vampire who created me is dead – murdered – then yes.'

'Murdered?'

'Raisa – she was killed by Iuda.' He spoke in a growl, suppressing a visceral anger.

That wasn't how Mihail had heard it. His mother had witnessed Raisa's death, and it was the hands of Domnikiia – Mihail's grandmother – which had forced Raisa's head into the path of the train's wheels. But ultimately Mihail could not disagree that Iuda was to blame for it all. For now though, it was a distraction.

'Being an orphan, apparently, makes it easier,' he said.

'Easier?' asked Dmitry.

He was vulnerable enough now to hear the truth. 'When you became a vampire and exchanged blood with Raisa, the two of you formed a mental bond. You knew each other's minds.'

'That's right. That's how a newborn vampire learns.'

'And when you exchange blood again, with a different vampire, don't you suppose that a very similar process occurs?'

'I . . . I don't know.'

'I think you do. You share a part of your mind with Zmyeevich.

344

You could tell he was returning the other day when we spoke beneath Saint Isaac's. How could you know that?'

'I won't deny it. We share. It's useful. We're partners.' There was a reluctant pride in his voice that had not been there before.

'But who has the stronger mind, Dmitry? You or he?'

'I'm not a fool.'

'Pyetr was not a fool, but his mind rotted through sharing his blood with Zmyeevich. Look at all the *oprichniki* – mindless animals whose will was sucked out by Zmyeevich. How do you think Zmyeevich has grown to be so old and so strong? How do you think he can walk in sunlight?' Mihail was speculating now. He saw a defiant smile forming on Dmitry's lips, but he continued to press the point. 'Feeding off humans is no longer enough for him; he must feed off vampires too – not their blood but their minds. All that's left is base animals who crave flesh and do his will. I don't know how long it will take, Dmitry, but one day, if Zmyeevich has his way, that will be you.'

As he spoke, Mihail watched carefully, trying to gauge the reaction as Dmitry began to understand the degradation into which he was descending. But with each word Dmitry seemed to grow stronger and more confident, as if succoured by an external presence. When he spoke, he was a changed man.

'And why should I care?' he asked, his voice cold and calm. He was no longer looking at Mihail but above him, up the steps and out to the graveyard. Mihail stood and turned.

Silhouetted in the doorway stood a familiar hunched figure; pale wrinkled skin, a white moustache, hollowed cheeks. Mihail knew just how dangerous Zmyeevich could be even in daylight, but he was now at his weakest. Mihail raised the crossbow, at the same time noticing that while he had been talking to Dmitry the sun had moved on and he himself was now in shade.

It was too late. Dmitry's arms clasped Mihail around the chest – pinning his hands to his sides and knocking his weapon to the floor. Had Mihail misjudged just how far Zmyeevich's power over Dmitry had developed? Or was this simply a rational decision of Dmitry's own free will, deciding that it was still best for him to side with his master? It made no difference to the position in which Mihail found himself.

Dmitry dragged him backwards across the tomb; away from the light. Mihail's heels flailed uselessly against the flagstones until eventually they came to a halt, Dmitry's back pressed against the wall. Zmyeevich slowly descended the stairs. Before reaching the bottom he had stepped into shadow and his transformation into a younger man began. By the time he was standing between the two coffins his back was straight, his skin was taut, his moustache and hair were iron-grey. His eyes blazed.

'So – the last surviving Danilov,' he said. Then he smiled. 'I'm sorry, Dmitry. The last *living* Danilov.'

'Dmitry told you who I am, then,' said Mihail.

'As you've so ably deduced, he did not need to. I know his mind.'

'You don't rule him yet.'

Zmyeevich remained silent for a moment, considering Mihail. Then his eyes flared and at the same moment Mihail felt Dmitry's grip upon him tighten, squeezing a little of the breath out of him.

'You see?' said Zmyeevich. 'Our relationship is a sound one. We need go no further.'

'You won't be able to stop yourself.' Mihail spoke through gritted teeth, his words more for Dmitry's benefit than Zmyeevich's. 'And why should you? Once you've used up Dmitry, there are plenty of others out there.'

'And how do you know all this?'

Mihail said nothing.

'Ah, yes,' Zmyeevich continued. 'Because you've read Cain's books. Where are they?'

'Somewhere safe.'

'I would dearly like to see them.'

'What? There are things that even the great Dracula doesn't know?'

Zmyeevich winced at the sound of his Romanian name. Mihail had learned it from Iuda's notebooks.

'You're right, of course,' said Zmyeevich. 'I have no need for Cain's knowledge. But he has other trophies that rightfully belong to me.'

'Your blood, you mean? Or Ascalon?'

'You don't have either.'

'I have his books – why shouldn't I have his other possessions?'

'He's bluffing,' said Dmitry from behind.

'I'll trade you them for my life.'

Zmyeevich chuckled. 'I'm afraid my reputation means you would not trust me to keep my side of such a bargain. It's a curse I have learned to live with.'

'You're prepared to lose Ascalon?' asked Mihail.

'If you had even *touched* Ascalon, I would know,' spat Zmyeevich. He looked over Mihail's shoulder at Dmitry. 'I take it you know where he's staying?' he asked.

'Zhelyabov will know – and will tell me.'

'Then we shall search there, once we have dealt with him.'

Mihail felt Dmitry's grip on him tighten again as Zmyeevich spoke, leaving him incapable of almost anything but speech.

'Dealt with me?'

'Your grandfather, Aleksei Ivanovich, thwarted me in my attempts to persuade Tsar Aleksandr I to join me. His grandson will have no opportunity to do the same for Aleksandr III.'

'The third? Aren't you missing a generation?'

'The reign of this generation of Romanovs will soon be coming to an end. Dmitry's friends will see to that.'

'And then nothing will stop you,' said Mihail.

'Nothing, indeed. If need be, I'll be free to dig up the whole of Petersburg in search of Ascalon.'

'There's nothing you or anyone can do,' added Dmitry.

'I do wish Aleksei Ivanovich were alive to see this,' Zmyeevich continued. 'His beloved son, my closest acolyte, assisting me as I drain the life from his only surviving grandson, holding him still, pinning him so that he is exposed and defenceless, allowing me to take my pleasure, to pierce his skin and drink, oh so slowly, until the last drop of blood is drained from his body.'

Zmyeevich opened his jaws wide, revealing his great fangs, and descended towards Mihail's throat, his eyes still fixed on those of his victim. Mihail knew it was time to act. He used his tongue to slip the hazelnut from his cheek where it had nestled since his arrival and held it for a moment between his incisors, so that Zmyeevich could see it plainly. Then he let it fall back between his molars and bit down hard, feeling the liquid inside spill into his mouth, its foul, metallic taste washing across his tongue.

He made sure a little of it escaped his lips, just so there could be no doubt as to what was going on, and then swallowed the rest, spitting out the crushed shell. Then he let his mind open, inviting in anyone who cared to come. He stared back at Zmyeevich victoriously. Zmyeevich's own expression was one of confusion. He could see the blood on Mihail's lips but would not yet understand its import, or even guess whose blood it was. He would search around for an explanation, using all his senses, and then . . .

And then Mihail felt it: Zmyeevich's own impression of puzzlement. The vampire's mind had searched for understanding and had, inescapably, locked on Mihail's. Mihail knew that he had a far greater feeling of Zmyeevich's intellect than the vampire would have of his, but it was enough. Within moments, Zmyeevich understood.

He stepped back. Dmitry's grip on Mihail relaxed as Zmyeevich's will receded, and then strengthened again under Dmitry's own volition.

'No,' said Zmyeevich thoughtfully. 'Let him go.'

Dmitry took a moment to consider it, but obeyed. Mihail stepped away from him and sat on the side of one of the coffins. Zmyeevich eyed him, with a curl of disgust on his lip. Dmitry simply looked bewildered. Mihail himself felt nausea at the blood he had swallowed, and at the flashes of Zmyeevich's repellent mind that flickered through his own. He tried to push them away. They were no use to him now.

'Dmitry told me you were a Danilov,' Zmyeevich said. 'But he failed to mention that you are also a Romanov.'

'A Romanov?' Dmitry's voice revealed that he had no idea of the fact, let alone its implications.

Zmyeevich waved a dismissive hand at him. 'How long has it been, I wonder, since Cain took that blood from me? Fifty, sixty years? Was it still fresh?'

'It tasted as foul as I'd expected,' said Mihail, making sure that Zmyeevich would perceive the laughter in his voice. 'And it was as effective as if it had come straight from your veins.'

'*How* are you a Romanov?' Zmyeevich asked.

'My father is Grand Duke Konstantin Nikolayevich.'

Zmyeevich thought for a moment. 'So you are of Aleksandr Aleksandrovich's generation.'

Mihail nodded. 'The tsarevich is my first cousin. It's becoming quite a family tradition. My grandfather plucked Aleksandr I from your grasp, and I shall do the same with Aleksandr III. All of my generation are safe.'

Zmyeevich roared. His arm swung across the room and his hand caught Mihail on the jaw, knocking him to the ground. He was quickly upright, squatting, rubbing his cheek. He glanced around the tomb, noting where his knapsack lay, and more importantly his crossbow.

'All are safe except for you,' sneered Dmitry.

'And how would killing me help you?'

Dmitry laughed. 'It wouldn't, but it would still be just. It would serve as a lesson to others. And it would be a pleasure.'

Mihail suspected he was speaking to impress Zmyeevich, but it would not work. Zmyeevich was a long way ahead of him.

'So are you going to kill me, Ţepeş? It would be so very easy. I'm your prisoner. Perhaps you'll even allow Dmitry the honour.'

'Gladly,' said Dmitry.

'No,' said Zmyeevich curtly. 'That would be the worst outcome of all. If he dies, with my blood in him, then he will become a vampire – one of my many offspring and sway to my will. It would be a fitting punishment, but not worth the price.'

'What price?' asked Dmitry.

'Tell him, Ţepeş,' said Mihail.

'That fate can befall only one Romanov,' Zmyeevich explained. 'Pyotr owed me his soul, and only a single soul can redeem that debt. If it were the soul of this pathetic creature, this bastard Romanov – a man of no power or value – then I should lose my chance of ever ruling Russia. It would be a self-indulgence that would do me no benefit. What shall it profit me, to gain one soul and lose a whole nation?'

Mihail stood up, reaching out for his knapsack as he did so. His crossbow lay on the floor at Zmyeevich's feet. Did he dare take it, or would the *voordalak*'s wrath subsume his good sense, and would he claim pyrrhic vengeance? And yet Mihail did not want to leave without it. He allowed himself a momentary glimpse into

349

the creature's mind, and knew he would be safe, at least if he did not try to press his meagre advantage. He bent down and picked up the weapon.

'You're just letting him go?' asked Dmitry in astonishment.

'What can we do?' asked Zmyeevich.

Mihail smiled broadly. He felt like a hero. Better than that, he felt like his grandfather. What Aleksei had done to save Aleksandr I, Mihail had recreated in this new generation. He mounted the steps out of the tomb, his knapsack dangling from one hand, his *arbalyet* clasped in the other. About halfway up, when he was just at the border between light and shadow, he turned and looked back down on Zmyeevich and Dmitry, who stood in glum silence. His heart thumped in his chest. He was astounded to still be alive, but he knew he had pushed his luck far enough. He would deal with them another day.

'I'll be seeing you,' he said. Then he walked up and out into the sunlight.

CHAPTER XXII

AT LAST IUDA WAS WHOLE AGAIN – BOTH IN BODY AND IN MIND. He'd done experiments, years before in Chufut Kalye, to establish just how much of a vampire's body could be consumed by sunlight before it would be unable to restore itself. He knew that his own wounds had taken him close to the point from which recovery was impossible. But he'd never thought to question the specimens upon which he had experimented as to their state of mind. It had been remiss of him, but it afforded him the pleasure of surprise as he experienced his own delirium and his eventual happy return to lucidity.

But he couldn't shake off one simple conclusion: his survival was in only a small part down to his own wits. He had been lucky. True, much of the luck had been of his own making. He'd helped in the design of Saint Isaac's and he'd known the location of every exit – concealed or otherwise – from its interior. But it was luck that he'd had time to drag himself, with his one remaining hand, across the floor to that tiny hatch that led down to the sewer; lucky that Zmyeevich had not noticed and stopped him; lucky that his body had been so shrivelled that it could fit through such a slight gap between the stones. Lucky that she had come looking for him – and had found him.

Why had he mistaken her for Susanna? There was some superficial similarity, of course, but then the same could be said of Raisa. He paused in his train of thought. Was his relationship with either woman just coincidence? He doubted it. Had he, throughout his entire life, been trying to make amends?

After that first kiss, outside the deadhouse beside the little church in Esher, Iuda – then just Richard Cain – had been suspicious of Susanna, or at least suspicious of himself in his feelings towards her. It had not been a cause of great concern and his capture of Honoré had given him something far more enthralling to occupy his time and his mind. He paid Susanna little attention.

It was his first, quite accidental lesson in how to handle women. The less of his attention she received, the more she was desirous of it. She would creep into his room at night and talk to him, distracting him from his books. To start with she kept the conversation very girlish, talking of fashion and dancing and of books quite unlike the kind that Richard was interested in. Then, realizing she was getting nowhere, she changed her tune. She clearly remembered the conversation they'd once had about sex. That had been over a year before, but now she returned to the subject often.

It irritated Richard both because it distracted him and because it interested him. Worse, Susanna could tell it interested him, however much he attempted to hide it. Why else would he blush so when they talked?

But still he liked to kiss her – and the kiss at the end of an evening together was always more enthralling than the one at the beginning. In his dreams, and sometimes when awake, he imagined her body, free of the layers of clothing that even one so humble as a housekeeper's daughter was expected to wear in order to preserve her dignity. He had never seen a woman naked. He tried to extrapolate from the anatomy of animals, but his own body was so far removed from those of the animals he'd dissected that he imagined any guesses he took with regard to a woman's form would be laughable.

Instead, he would ask Susanna questions. He did it subtly, so he thought, but in the end it was precisely what she expected of him – for which he hated her. The most pressing point of his inquisitiveness was on the most obvious difference between the sexes and, from what little he could gather, between woman and other female animals – the breast.

She giggled when he first raised the issue, but then tried to describe what she had hidden beneath her cotton bodice. Words were not her forte, but it was then that Richard discovered a hitherto unknown talent in her: she could draw. The following night she returned to him with a piece of paper. At first she would not show it to him, asking what he would give her to see it, but in the end he snatched it from her. It was a charcoal sketch; a reproduction of a single female breast. He became very silent and, he could tell, blushed profusely. She left him alone, but he gazed at the picture for hours before going to bed.

The next night she visited him again, but neither spoke of her drawing. He had learned now not to appear too keen. Eventually, she broached the subject.

'Didn't you like it?' she asked.

'What?'

'My picture.'

'It was very informative.'

'How do you rate me as an artist then?'

'How can I tell?' he asked.

'What do you mean?'

'Well, you could have drawn me the Acropolis or the Colosseum – I've never seen either. How would I know if it was any good?'

He looked back down at the paper, waiting for her to react.

'You're such a silly,' she said. By the time he looked up, she had already begun to undo the dozens of hooks that held her clothing in place. Soon she was naked to the waist. 'You could have just asked,' she said in a whisper.

Richard held up the drawing, as if to compare, but his eyes were fixed on the reality, not the image.

'Well?' she asked.

'Very accurate,' he said, his mouth dry.

'I did it in front of the mirror.'

He continued to stare.

'They're much better than a drawing,' she said.

'Why?'

'Because you can touch them.'

'I suppose so,' he replied.

She tutted. 'I said you can touch them.'

Richard blushed deeper still – partly at the prospect, partly at his own obtuseness – but he did as he was told.

It was around three weeks later that they finally had sex, for the first and only time. They had both known since that moment that it would inevitably happen. Richard wanted to perform the act within the church itself, at the foot of the altar, but it was a step too far even for Susanna. Instead they chose the privacy of the Chamber Pew, the secluded extension housing four enclosed benches, reserved for the Duke of Newcastle, his brother and their respective servants. Both were long dead now, but their families maintained the privilege of using it. That afternoon, though, Richard and Susanna put it to another purpose. They would be seen by no one, unless Thomas chose to climb to the highest pulpit to practise his sermon.

Richard was in no way ashamed of his performance. At the time he had nothing to compare it against, but looking back as a wiser and older man he decided that he had done well. He could not be accused of misremembering. After he had left the church and returned to his room, he had written down all that had happened in his usual detached manner. Susanna had certainly seemed to enjoy the experience. He remembered looking up at her grinning, glowing face and hearing her offhand but complimentary words.

'We must do that again some time.'

They never did, for the simple reason that in one other aspect of sexual congress Richard had performed very well indeed. Two months later Susanna told him she was pregnant.

If he had been only a few years older Richard would not have cared enough even to attempt to keep the event secret. He would simply have moved on, leaving mother and child to their fate, or told them to go hang and see what society would make of their story. But then he was young, and lacked confidence, and understood what the English gentry would take him for. He was still dependent on his father for everything that allowed him to live. He would not risk it. It was not that Susanna made any demands of him. She promised she would not reveal who the father was. In fact she didn't even promise it; she merely said it, and assumed Richard would take her at her word.

Whether he did or did not mattered little. The people of Esher were not imbeciles; they would put two and two together. He half formed a plan of getting his father blamed for it, but he was not sure Susanna would be able to lie convincingly. Moreover, if

Thomas Cain should lose his position and reputation, what good would that do his son Richard?

There was never any real doubt as to how he would solve his dilemma. Honoré had been a captive beneath the church for almost a year – perhaps he had even overheard the exertions above him as Richard and Susanna conceived their child. Richard could not sacrifice too many of his schoolfriends without suspicions being aroused. He put the offer to Honoré directly, supposing that the vampire would have a greater interest in the blood of a beautiful young female, if only for the sake of variety, but Honoré claimed that it did not matter a sou what the age, sex or appearance was, as long as they were healthy enough to produce rich, wholesome blood. Richard noted it down, but was to discover that the same indifference did not hold for all vampires. For some reason, he could not bring himself to tell Honoré of the child that grew within Susanna.

'I have something to show you,' Richard said on that final Sunday of Susanna's life. It was night. Evensong was done, and he'd arranged to meet her in the churchyard.

'Something I'll like?' she asked.

'Something that will fascinate you.'

'Like what you showed me in the deadhouse.'

'A bit.'

He felt her hand slip into his and squeeze. He squeezed back and led her to the church door, drawing out a stolen key to unlock it.

'Just the two of us, in the church again,' she said, leaning forward to kiss him. 'We still can, you know,' she added.

'Sh!' he said, putting a finger to his lips.

He led her across the nave and to the three-tiered pulpit.

She giggled. 'That doesn't look too comfy.'

He descended the steps and opened the low wooden door to the crypt.

'What *is* this?' she asked. 'You've never shown me this before.'

'It's the old crypt. No one else knows about it.'

'Do you bring all the girls down here?'

'Just you.'

They had come to the iron gate. As usual Richard held up

his lamp to check that Honoré was not lurking close, ready to pounce, but the place was quiet. He unlocked the barrier and swung it open.

'You first,' he said.

She looked at him with an intrigued curl to her lips, then stepped through. Richard hung back by the gate, unwilling to close it but knowing that he must. She looked back at him.

'Are you coming?'

'I want you to see it on your own,' he said.

She smiled at him and then walked further into the darkness until he could just make out the white blur of her dress, ghost-like against the black. He pulled the gate quietly to, but did not lock it in case she heard. He knew that at some point she would discover he had betrayed her, but he did not want to see her face when she did.

She called back to him, out of the darkness. 'There's someone here!' Then quieter, 'Who are you?'

Richard heard Honoré's voice.

'*Je suis Honoré Philippe Louis d'Évreux, Vicomte de Nemours.* Welcome to my home.'

There was a yelp and a thud. Richard locked the door and hurried away. That night he cried for the last time in his life.

Since then he had on occasion known a handful of women who would offer him that same unblinking trust that Susanna had shown. Raisa was one – though with time she had grown to realize that Iuda's interests would always lie with himself. Perhaps Susanna would have understood the same, had she lived. Perhaps she did understand it in those last seconds of her life.

And now there was Dusya. She had come looking for Iuda. She knew of his hideout beneath Saint Isaac's and of all the tunnels and sewers around there. She had searched every inch of them until she had found the sad remnant of what had once been his body. Some women might have fled in revulsion at the sight of him, but she was made of sterner stuff. She had nursed him, fed him, fetched others for him to feed on. As he had been growing back to his full strength he had felt grateful towards her, but that had passed. She needed no thanks, no reward. All that she had done confirmed it. She'd even meekly accepted that, in his delirium, he had called her Susanna, though she had no idea what the name meant, except as a codeword he sometimes used to identify himself to the Executive Committee.

They had met through Luka. Within days of his first falling for Dusya, Luka had been eager to introduce her to his old friend and mentor Vasiliy Grigoryevich Chernetskiy. Iuda instantly saw the potential in her, just as he had done in Raisa when he took on the role of her tutor in Kiev. But there must be more to it than that. Why did he never see that same potential in a girl who lacked the blonde ringlets that reminded him of Susanna?

Dusya had immediately warmed to Iuda, simply by virtue of Luka's gushing recommendation. Iuda had wondered if he would need to seduce her to fully win her loyalty, but it had proved unnecessary. What fascinated her about him was his fanatical dedication to the cause of the Russian people and the overthrow of dictatorship, which he expressed, he thought, with great authenticity. Then he had revealed the truth about himself – a sad tale of a good man afflicted by a horrible disease – the disease of vampirism. She had wept for him, but understood that it did not change him as a man. He still loved Russia and loved the working people. He still, he told her, loved *her*. When it came to it and she had to choose between him and Luka – when he had sent his message of denunciation from prison – he had been in no doubt as to whose side she would be on.

Now all that work was repaid. She had saved him. They sat facing each other, her hand clasped in his, in the sewer beneath Saint Isaac's. He felt he was ready to leave now. His body was complete; he even had clothes – the foul garb of a Swedish sailor, but it would do him until the chance came to change. But he still needed to know what had been happening in the world above.

'You were lucky to find me,' he said.

'When you weren't at the Hôtel d'Europe, I worried. This was the only other place I could think of. When I saw you I thought . . .' Her voice cracked and her eyes filled with tears. He squeezed her hand.

'Don't think of me like that. Think of me now – as you've restored me. Think of your blood, in me, giving me life.'

She nodded. 'I'd gladly give you more,' she said.

'But why were you at the hotel?'

'Mihail asked me to watch it.'

'Mihail?'

'Mihail Konstantinovich Lukin – the one you said broke into your room there.'

'To watch for me?' asked Iuda.

'For you and a couple of others – one old, the other middle-aged. He described them to me.' She gave the description and Iuda nodded. She could only mean Zmyeevich – both by day and by night. Lukin had seen Zmyeevich's astonishing ability and had seen Iuda's own fate – or thought he had. Lukin was clearly far more than a lieutenant who had stumbled upon Dmitry and Iuda's encounter at Geok Tepe.

'What else has he been up to?'

'He's trusted by the Executive Committee. He's helping Kibalchich with the digging and the explosives, but it's almost done. Zhelyabov and Sofia are desperate we should act soon. Sofia thinks the organization has been infiltrated; they might arrest us all within days.'

'Who does she think is the traitor?'

'Shklovskiy.'

Iuda nodded. Dusya had already described Shklovskiy to him, and he had no doubt it was Dmitry under another name – that coupled with his peculiar interest in the tunnelling. 'And what about the cellars under the cheese shop?'

'They didn't do much with them; too deep for the explosives. Shklovskiy searched them and then said they led nowhere.'

That was a shame. It meant that Dmitry and Zmyeevich were a step closer; but only a step – there were many more they would have to take.

'Good,' he said. 'Go now. Find out what else is happening.'

'Do you want me to bring you . . . are you hungry?'

He raised his hand to touch her cheek. 'I can fend for myself now, thanks to you.'

'You'll be here though?' she asked.

'Some nights, but it's safer to move around. I will find you.'

They kissed briefly and then she was gone. He sat for a moment, considering what he should do now. A thought danced at the back of his mind, irritating but important: despite losing his fight with Zmyeevich, there was something he had gained, something precious. He held his hands open in front of him and looked into their palms, then realized that it must be the left that mattered – the right was only days old. But whatever he had grasped so urgently in that hand was no longer there. He glanced around the floor until something glinted in the dim light. He picked it up. It was a ring; the figure of a dragon, with a body of gold, emerald eyes and red, forked tongue. Zmyeevich's ring. Iuda had managed to rip it from his finger as they fought inside the cathedral. There was no magical power to it, at least as far as Iuda was aware. It was not Ascalon, but it was a small emblem of victory in the midst of Iuda's defeat. Somehow he would find a use for it. He slipped it into the pocket of his grubby sailor's jacket.

He stood up, flexing the limbs of his new body. They did not feel new – they felt old and stiff and as he stood a wave of dizziness hit him. He would have to move carefully, but more importantly he would have to feed.

'They've arrested Zhelyabov.' Sofia Lvovna blurted out the words quickly, as though it might make them less true.

Mihail eyed the room, judging the reaction of each person in there. Kibalchich, as ever, seemed distant. He would be thinking about the implications of the news, but would not show it on his face. Frolenko threw his hands up to the sides of his head and turned away, as if covering his ears to prevent Sofia's words from penetrating. Rysakov opened and closed his lips rapidly but silently. A few others emitted groans. Not everyone was there. Some were at the cheese shop, others had not been able to make the meeting. He was not surprised by Dusya's absence. Last time he had seen her she had looked pale and cold, a scarf wrapped around her neck even indoors. She would have been wise to stay in bed. There had been no urgent reason for any of them to be here. This was no emergency response to events, simply a regular status report. But events had overtaken it.

'Are you all right?' asked Rysakov.

Sofia's eyes flared at him. 'Of course I'm all right,' she spat.

'Where's Shklovskiy?' asked Frolenko.

'I wish I knew,' said Sofia.

'So what happened?' It was Kibalchich who asked this most obvious of questions.

Sofia shrugged. 'We left our apartment together and took a droshky. We got off at the Imperial Library. He noticed another cab pull up and three men got out. It was obvious they were *ohraniki*. We weren't too worried, once we knew they were there. We'd been planning to split up anyway, so he kissed me goodbye and I went on my way. One of them stuck with me and I presume the other two tailed him. I was meant to be going to the shop, but I changed my route completely; headed out towards the Haymarket and then doubled back along the canal. By the time I got to Nevsky Prospekt I'd lost him. I've no doubt Andrei managed to lose his two as well.'

'They wouldn't have stood a chance,' interjected Frolenko.

Sofia nodded and gave the tiniest of smiles. Whatever she might claim, the arrest of her lover had affected her deeply. She managed to continue. 'From what I heard later, that must be how it was; I knew he was planning to visit Trigoni and he would never have gone there with an *ohranik* on his heels.'

'Trigoni?' exclaimed Kibalchich. 'He's supposed to be in Odessa.'

'He was,' said Sofia, 'but we've been calling everyone back to the capital. We need every pair of hands we can find. Trigoni's been here for a few weeks. I knew Andrei was going to see him, so when he didn't come back I went down to Trigoni's apartment. It was obvious from the buzz that there'd been arrests even before I got there. I asked a few of the neighbours I knew. It wasn't Andrei's fault; it was Trigoni's. The place was under surveillance – *ohraniki* disguised as workmen. Seeing the two of them together was too good an opportunity for the bastards to miss. They took them both.'

'Will he talk?' asked Mihailov.

'Not quickly,' replied Sofia. She looked up, sensing the scepticism in the room. 'I truly believe that,' she said.

'Me too,' said Kibalchich. 'He's a strong man.'

'What about Trigoni?' asked Mihail.

'He doesn't know much,' explained Sofia. 'Certainly not about the shop.'

'But they'll put two and two together,' Kibalchich continued. 'They've seen Zhelyabov with you and you with me and the rest of it. They'll soon link one of us to the cheese shop.'

'They must know already,' said Frolenko.

'They'd have made a move,' Sofia replied.

'Just because they know we use it, doesn't mean they know what for,' suggested Mihail. 'They can't guess what we have down there.'

'Maybe someone's told them to hold back,' said Rysakov, 'wait till they can catch us red-handed.'

'Someone?' asked Mihail.

'If they think that, they're fools,' said Sofia.

'Why?' asked Mihailov.

'Because the tsar will die on Sunday.'

'This Sunday?'

'The day after tomorrow,' said Sofia. '1 March.'

'We're sure where he'll be?' asked Mihail.

Sofia explained. 'Every Sunday, when he's at home, Aleksandr leaves the Winter Palace and goes by coach to watch the changing of the guard at the Manège. The ceremony begins at one in the afternoon and lasts approximately forty minutes. He then returns. On his return journey he travels along Italyanskaya Street and then turns into Malaya Sadovaya in order to cut across to Nevsky Prospekt. His carriage won't have picked up much speed when it passes over the mine.'

'That's certain?' Mihail pressed.

'We didn't choose the place by accident. We've been watching his movements for months.'

'Are we ready?' asked Frolenko.

Sofia turned her head towards Kibalchich. 'Nikolai?' she asked.

Kibalchich shrugged and forwarded the question. 'Mihail?'

'I'd say so,' replied Mihail. 'The tunnel's complete. We just need to place the dynamite.'

'I can work overnight to get the rest of the explosives ready,' said Kibalchich.

'We've got more than enough,' replied Mihail.

Kibalchich winked. 'Just to be on the safe side.'

'That's settled then,' said Sofia. 'Mihail, you go—'

'What does Chairman Shklovskiy have to say on this?' interrupted Rysakov.

Sofia glared at him. 'If he were here we could ask him. In the meantime, I'm in charge.' Rysakov said no more. Sofia resumed what she had been saying. 'Lukin! Frolenko! Go to the shop and start laying what explosives you have. Kibalchich, take Rysakov to Telezhnaya Street and finish your work.'

'I don't need help,' snapped Kibalchich.

'I don't care. From now till Sunday everyone remains in the company of at least one other comrade. That way we can be sure what's going on.'

There was no further protest and Mihail set off with Frolenko to begin their work. Sofia's message was clear but unspoken. From now on they could trust no one – not even each other. Mihail couldn't help but fear her suspicion was directed at him.

Iuda had fed again and felt all the better for it – better in that his body was now strong, but better also to know that he was no longer reliant on the help of Dusya. He'd also procured a change of clothes. It was odd to choose a victim on the basis not of the quality of the blood, nor of the pain he might inflict on them and their loved ones, but merely because of the skill of the man's tailor and his proximity in build to Iuda.

Now, though, he was at a turning point. Zmyeevich had defeated him – almost killed him – and all because of a failing in what Iuda regarded as his greatest asset: his knowledge. He had never carried out an experiment which demonstrated that a vampire could withstand light, never heard tell of it, and yet now he had seen it with his own eyes. What else might Zmyeevich be capable of that made him greater than the common *voordalak* – greater than Iuda? Iuda was not fool enough to do anything but fear Zmyeevich more for what he had discovered, but to what would that fear lead? Would he make himself safe from Zmyeevich by putting as much distance between them as possible? Or would he make himself safe by destroying Zmyeevich once and for all?

However powerful he might be – whatever further abilities he had acquired that Iuda could not even guess at – here in Russia Zmyeevich was at his weakest. He was far away from his

Carpathian homeland, with only one ally at his side. He was in a city run by a family sworn his enemy for a hundred and seventy years. If Zmyeevich could be defeated then surely it was here and now in Saint Petersburg.

But that one word nagged at him. If.

A cool breeze blew past, ruffling his hair. He was familiar with it – the opening of the manhole leading up to Saint Isaac's Square made the cold winter air blow down into the sewer. It meant that Dusya was returning. Would she have something to tell him, or was she just here because she wanted to be near him? She was quickly becoming tiresome.

He heard the cover close and the sound of her feet on the iron staircase. It was only when the footsteps began to move across the flat stonework that he realized they belonged to an individual far heavier than Dusya, and with a longer stride. Simply from what he could hear, Iuda took a guess at who it might be that had come to pay him a visit. When he turned to look, he was proved right.

It was Dmitry.

CHAPTER XXIII

'**N**O ARMY TO ASSIST YOU THIS TIME, MITKA?'
'An army couldn't help me,' Dmitry replied. He
looked Iuda up and down. He had been anticipating
this moment for weeks, ever since he had understood that it was
Iuda who had caused Raisa's death. There had been one opportunity for Dmitry to be avenged, but some part of his mind had
held him back – he knew now it was Zmyeevich's power over
him. One part of Dmitry's mind, that fragment of Raisa that still
lingered, wanted Iuda dead – craved it like he sometimes craved
blood. That part hated Iuda, but Dmitry did not. A greater part,
Zmyeevich, needed him alive – or at least had done for a while.
Now Zmyeevich was at best indifferent. At Saint Isaac's he had
been toying with Iuda. He would kill him if the opportunity
arose, but he did not require Dmitry to do it. The worst of it
was that Dmitry's own mind was an irrelevance. The desire
for vengeance was the more noble cause – if nobility had any
meaning for a vampire – but it still made Dmitry the proxy for
another's wishes. To be ruled by Raisa was no better than being
ruled by Zmyeevich. Dmitry needed to be free, to act from his
own desires, and only one man could advise him how. Vengeance
would have to wait.

Dmitry's former mentor appeared his usual self; calm and
strong. His surroundings were not the most salubrious, but a
voordalak did not always have the choice. 'You look well,' Dmitry
continued. 'Zmyeevich told me you were dead. He lied to me.' It
was not the only lie his master had told.

'Not a lie, I think,' said Iuda. 'An exaggeration born of his optimistic nature. It was a very close thing. How did you find me?' He moved to the new topic without pause for breath.

'Sofia Lvovna is suspicious of everyone and has them followed. She reported that Dusya was spending her time here. Only I could guess why.'

'You knew about Dusya and me?'

'I had my suspicions. She and Luka – you and Luka. One only had to complete the triangle.'

'You came alone?' asked Iuda.

'Zmyeevich doesn't know I'm here.' It was probably true. Dmitry was making a great effort to exclude any intrusion into his mind.

'Why should I believe that?'

'Believe what you will.'

'So why have you come?'

Dmitry leaned back against the hard brick wall of the sewer and slid down to the ground, his hands covering his face. He breathed deeply and tried to work out what he had come to say. It was hard to know how to begin. The best he could come up with was 'I miss you, Vasya.' It had always been true, even while he had hated him.

Iuda laughed. 'Don't be an ass, Mitka. You're not capable of it.'

Dmitry looked up. 'I miss having someone who seemed to know the answers. I miss having someone I trusted.'

'You have Zmyeevich.'

'I can't trust him. As you say, we're incapable of it. Now I know that it's a wise state to be in. It saves us from being tricked – being treated like a *prostak*.'

'Can I take it that the great Count Dracula has duped you in some way?' Iuda sounded delighted, as well he might.

'That's what I've come to you to find out.'

'And you trust me.'

'I trust that you know more about vampires than anyone on the planet.'

'Tell me what you want to know then.'

Dmitry breathed deeply and then began. 'A few nights ago a man came to speak to me. His name's Lukin.'

'Mihail Konstantinovich?'

Dmitry nodded. 'You remember him. He was at Geok Tepe. A remarkable man.'

'Really? How so?'

'Anyone who can steal from you must have a certain distinction. He's seen your journals – or says he has.'

'*Says* he has?' asked Iuda cautiously.

'That's what I want you to confirm – or, please God, deny if you can.'

'What?'

'I know what happens when a vampire and a human exchange blood – obviously I do.' Dmitry paused, hardly able to bring himself to speak of what he had done. 'But what if two vampires were to do the same – to exchange their moribund blood?'

Iuda smirked. 'But what vampires would do such a thing? The very concept would be repugnant to them.'

'Not so repugnant to deter you from carrying out experiments on it,' shouted Dmitry, deflecting attention from his own foul behaviour on to the fouler things that Iuda had done to dozens of their brethren.

'Knowledge must be advanced.'

'Just tell me what would happen.'

'To begin with,' Iuda explained, 'the effect would be much the same as between human and *voordalak*: a sharing of minds. The difference of course is that there would be no bodily change of one – the human – into the form of the other. Instead a mental transformation takes place. The mind of one would be subject to the will of the other and those parts of it that were no longer used – replaced by the other's mind – would wither, like an unused limb.'

It was much as Mihail had said. Dmitry had not doubted it. 'Which mind would wither?'

'The weaker, of course. The most notable case I have seen *in vivo* is with Zmyeevich and his Wallachian cohorts. Through exchanging blood with him they became little more than animals, useful only to do his bidding. Those that he sent to Russia with me were typical specimens. I'm sure Lyosha described them to you.'

He knew – or at least he guessed. And why shouldn't he? Why

would Dmitry be asking if the circumstances did not apply to him.

'Is this what Lukin told you?' Iuda asked.

'Pretty much.'

'Then the man is a genius – or he has read the work of a genius, which is more likely.'

'Can the process be reversed?' asked Dmitry.

Iuda shook his head. 'I don't think so. But it can be halted. Complete separation of the two vampires involved – if it has not gone too far.'

'Too far?'

'There comes a point where the weaker *voordalak* has lost his will sufficiently that he is beyond hope. However much he resists, the stronger can put into his mind the desire to return and exchange blood once again. It's a vicious circle. I've known vampires so far gone that they attempt to claw their way through rock to get back to their master.'

'I see.'

There was a long pause. Dmitry stared at the ground, but he could feel Iuda's eyes bearing down upon him.

'For what it's worth, Mitka, I think you still have a chance.'

It was worth nothing, but why would Iuda lie about it? Did he even need a reason?

'Now tell me about this Lukin,' said Iuda briskly. 'What's he after?'

Dmitry swallowed. He did not want to tell Iuda the whole truth – that Lukin was his nephew, Aleksei's grandson. Iuda might discover it soon enough for himself, but it gave Dmitry some last vestige of defiance to keep the secret for now. Besides, the boy had far more illustrious antecedents than that. He laughed weakly before replying. 'You'll never guess it, Vasya, but he's a Romanov – the bastard son of Konstantin Nikolayevich.'

Iuda's laughter was more hearty. 'You're sure?'

Dmitry could not help but smile. 'Zmyeevich is – he can tell, of course.'

'He can?'

'In this case at least. Lukin drank some of Zmyeevich's own blood, right in front of us. So Aleksandr Aleksandrovich is safe from Zmyeevich, and he couldn't do anything – if he killed Lukin, the whole lot of them would be free.'

Iuda seemed intrigued. 'Indeed they would. When did this happen?'

'Wednesday,' said Dmitry.

'Two days ago,' mused Iuda. 'I take it you're not going back to Zmyeevich.'

'No.' Why not, just for a little longer? 'No,' he added more firmly.

'And what about Zmyeevich himself, will he stay in Petersburg?'

'Why should he? There's nothing he can do to the Romanovs now until Aleksandr Aleksandrovich dies and Nikolai Aleksandrovich becomes Nikolai II.'

'You speak as though the current tsar were already dead.'

Dmitry managed a laugh. 'He's as good as. You know what's going on.'

Iuda nodded. 'That though was not the only thing that brought Zmyeevich to the capital.'

'Ascalon, you mean?'

Iuda said nothing.

'It's gone,' said Dmitry. 'If it was ever there.'

'It was there.' Iuda seemed confident.

'You found it?'

'Long ago.'

'And where is it now?'

Iuda emitted a mournful sigh and then began to speak in English:

> 'This royal throne of kings, this sceptred isle,
> This earth of majesty, this seat of Mars,
> This other Eden, demi-paradise,
> This fortress built by nature for herself
> Against infection and the hand of war,
> This happy breed of men, this little world,
> This precious stone set in the silver sea,
> Which serves it in the office of a wall,
> Or as a moat defensive to a house,
> Against the envy of less happier lands,
> This blessed plot, this earth, this realm, this . . .'

Iuda came to a halt, gazing wistfully into nothingness, but Dmitry completed his words.

'England?' he said. He might have guessed simply from the language that Iuda had spoken, but he had taught himself English over the years, and what better way to learn it than by reading Shakespeare? 'That's where you've taken it?'

Iuda smiled. 'I still have some property there. An estate in Essex. A house on Piccadilly.'

'And in which have you hidden Ascalon?'

Iuda laughed. 'Who says it's in either? England may not be Russia, but it's big enough to hide a little fragment of stained wood – and more.'

'More?'

Iuda's mood suddenly darkened. 'I think you should go now, Dmitry.'

Dmitry felt suddenly alone. He realized he had been enjoying himself. Talking to Iuda was not like talking to Zmyeevich. In neither case could he say he was regarded as an equal, but unlike Zmyeevich, Iuda was a show-off and he saw Dmitry as a worthy audience. It made him better company. Dmitry doubted if he would ever be able to kill him, however much the latent spirit of Raisa begged it.

'Why?' Dmitry asked. 'Couldn't I come back later?'

'I won't be here later.' Iuda paused and looked down at him. 'Mitka, you're a danger to me, you know that. Even if you don't want to, you'll tell Zmyeevich what you know. You don't even need to tell him. He knows your mind. He knows you're here. He knows *I'm* here.'

'What if I refuse to leave?'

Iuda gave a curt smile. 'Goodbye, Mitka.' He turned and walked away, not towards the steps by which Dmitry had entered, but along the tunnel of the sewer. Dmitry could listen to his footsteps long after his figure had become enfolded in the darkness, but soon even they faded beyond the limits of perception.

He was alone.

Mihail walked swiftly along the dark streets. He looked around. He was somewhere to the north-west of the city, on Vasilievskiy

Island, but he couldn't tell precisely where. He couldn't recall how he had got here. All was quiet. It was late and cold and few souls had the desire to be out. But some would, and it was those – one of those – that Mihail sought.

There was a noise ahead, coming from a side street. Mihail froze, surprised that he had been able to perceive so slight a sound, but pleased by it too. He pressed himself against the wall, becoming a part of it, his arms spread wide, following the line of the brickwork. He prayed that he wouldn't be seen, but at the same time knew that there was no need for prayer. The sound grew louder; footsteps in the snow – two pairs of them. He only needed one, but the other would prove little hindrance.

They turned the corner and came towards him, unaware of the figure that stood in perfect stillness against the wall and watched them. They were workmen and they were sober, which indicated they were heading out to whichever factory employed them, not returning home. They didn't speak. They walked past Mihail – inches from him – and still didn't get any hint that he was there. Mihail felt pleased – proud even – at his ability to become invisible, but he didn't dwell on the emotion.

One man was half a pace behind the other, and Mihail struck. It was a heavy blow with his fist to the back of the man's head. Mihail felt the skull fracture and compress under his knuckles. A cosh would not have done as good a job. The man crumpled silently. He might be dead already, but he certainly would not survive even a few hours unconscious in the freezing Petersburg night. His friend sensed that something had happened and began to turn, but Mihail was ready for him. He took only a moment to relish the expression of horror in the man's eyes before clamping one hand over his mouth and pushing his head firmly backwards, though not so firmly as to break his neck – the victim had to be alive.

With his free hand Mihail ripped away the thick scarf that kept the man's throat warm and cosy in the night air. Beneath it was a high collar, but Mihail easily tore that away too, revealing pale, taut skin. He didn't delay. He bared his fangs and thrust his head forward, enjoying the slight popping sensation as the skin first resisted and then yielded to their sharp points. Then he enjoyed even more the warmth of the blood that flowed into him, nourished him.

He would get used to this.

Mihail awoke and sat upright in a single instant. He was cold, but covered in sweat. He forced himself to salivate and smacked his lips, trying to cleanse his mouth of the repellent taste, but the flavour had gone already, left as part of his dream. But the fear lingered. It was not the first time he had seen through Zmyeevich's eyes in the days since he had drunk the monster's blood, but it was the most vivid.

And yet he couldn't be sure even of that. Had Mihail genuinely perceived what Zmyeevich perceived as he stalked his prey through the night streets, or was it as simple as a dream – a creation of Mihail's own mind, reacting to the awful knowledge of whose blood he had consumed? Either way, it was a price worth paying for the victory Mihail had won over the vampire. And there might be further benefits too if Mihail could learn to control this second sight, and thereby discover Zmyeevich's secrets.

Mihail looked around him and quickly remembered where he was. He had slept at the cheese shop, in the living room. In the far corner Kibalchich was asleep in a chair. They were adhering to Sofia's rule that no one should be alone, and it made sense that the two men who best understood the engineering of what was being done should stay closest to it.

In truth there was little more that needed to be done. Kibalchich had fetched dynamite from its hiding place, wrapped in sailcloth and then sunk into the Neva where it could easily be retrieved using a rope attached to a tree on the bank. It was perfectly dry, but even if it had got damp its explosive potential would have been undiminished. Mihail laid it in place and ran the wires back along the tunnel. Then he and Kibalchich had sealed up the chamber where the dynamite had been placed, first with wooden boards, then piling loose earth in behind. In the end the tunnel was only a little shorter than it had been. The shaft down to the cellars below was still easily accessible – that was important, at least for Mihail. The only clue that there was anything beyond was the two thin wires emerging from the compacted dirt. He carried them back, feeding them through his hands to avoid any chance of twisting, and left them just inside the tunnel entrance where they would be hidden even if someone entered the living quarters of the shop. He set up the switch, but connected only one of the wires.

In the army he would have used a magneto, but this approach, described to him by Kibalchich, was just as effective and could produce sufficient electromotive force to ignite the blasting caps from just a single Leclanché cell. The trick was to wire in a Rumkorff coil. The switch was held closed for just a few seconds, allowing the current to stabilize. Then it would be released, the circuit would be broken and the sudden drop in current would induce much higher tension in the other half of the coil, enough to cause detonation. The added benefit was that if the operator were to be interrupted or even shot, he would still release the switch and would in death complete his task.

Through the drawing of straws that task had fallen to Frolenko. They'd moved the table over to the wall on the street side so that he could stand on it and peep through the top of the window to watch as His Majesty's carriage rolled past. It would mean that he could both time the moment of his action and see its result, though it might do him better to throw himself to the floor at that point, to avoid the shards of window glass that would be impelled towards him. After that he'd have a good chance of escape. There would be confusion and it would take a few seconds to connect the bomb with the cheese shop, especially as all in his entourage clustered around the body of the dying tsar.

None of it would come to pass.

Aleksandr knew already. He'd known even before Mihail had told him, thanks to the Ohrana and his wily Minister of the Interior, Loris-Melikov. The tsar would continue with his Sunday routine of travelling by coach to see the changing of the guard at the Manège, but the route would not take him down Malaya Sadovaya Street, not until the People's Will had been smashed, and that would only happen when they had gathered enough information to arrest every member they could. Mihail doubted it would be very long.

But the People's Will knew none of this. Their greatest fear was discovery. With the arrest of Zhelyabov and the absence of Shklovskiy, Sofia Lvovna was completely in charge, and she had become obsessed with security. On cold reflection Mihail realized it was unlikely that she suspected him individually, but she was wise to be circumspect. There was no opportunity for them to leave and no excuse for it. Food was brought in for them – and even if it hadn't been, there was plenty of cheese.

Mihail checked that Kibalchich was still sleeping, then climbed down to take another look at the lower cellars – the ones that Dmitry had so conveniently unearthed. He went back to the ancient dank corridor and along to where it ended at those three rusty gates. Only one remained locked. No one had attempted to open it up or explore further. What would be the point? Beyond, it was clear to see that the stone roof had collapsed and the pathway was impenetrable. Somewhere it must connect to one of the buildings above, but it had long fallen into disuse.

Of the two chambers, the first was still used as a workshop, but was filled with clutter. There were over thirty Leclanché cells there, along with wires, picks, shovels, incandescent bulbs, Rumkorff coils and everything else that a sapper might need to send a city wall crumbling to its foundations. All of it was surplus to requirements. The other chamber was tidier, but still a number of accumulator cells and reels of wire were stacked up against one wall. It too had an iron gate, but this one had been unlocked, assuming it had ever been locked – there was no sign of a key. Inside it was featureless, but for a simple alcove, about a foot high and at eye level, set into the wall. It was empty, but on the stonework above it was an inscription, written in an alphabet that Mihail could not comprehend.

Ասկադրն

No one else could make out the language, neither did they seem to care. Their minds were set on the explosion to come. It was late on Friday now; still a day and a half until the tsar's carriage was due to roll past, though Mihail knew it never would. And even if for some reason the tsar did change his plans and come this way, he would be in little danger. How difficult would it be for Mihail simply to reverse two wires and render the entire trap ineffective? Wiser not to do it yet, though. Kibalchich could come down at any time and check that everything was in order. Sabotage was best performed at the last minute.

Even so, it would be preferable to get out and warn the tsar. More than that, Mihail had his own trap to spring – and this place was perfect for it. It would take only a little preparation, and he himself would be the bait, but bait would only lure its victim if the victim knew of its existence. That was why Mihail sought the opportunity to break free and speak to the tsar. There was no doubt that Aleksandr would help; Mihail had saved him, in a far greater way than by warning him of the plot against him. Mihail had drunk Zmyeevich's blood. It might mean that he would be haunted for ever by those terrible dreams, but it had made the tsarevich immune. There was nothing that His Majesty wouldn't do for Mihail when he heard the boastful but utterly irrefutable words, 'Your Majesty, I have saved your dynasty.'

'Your Majesty, I have saved your dynasty.'

'I find that very hard to believe,' Aleksandr replied.

'I assure you, I'm speaking the truth.'

'An assurance from a creature such as you, Cain, means nothing.'

Iuda considered. He looked around him. Once again he was trapped like an animal in the zoo, in a cage that protruded into the tsar's more comfortable portion of the room. It was not a position of power, but at least Aleksandr had agreed to see him – that demonstrated he still regarded Zmyeevich as a threat.

'What proof can I offer?' Iuda asked. 'Your family's happy survival for another century?'

'That would be a start. You would still be around to receive payment.'

'You would not be around to give it.'

'My descendants would honour my word,' said the tsar.

'I wouldn't trust *you* to honour your own word.'

'I am a Romanov.'

'Ha! So your word is as good as Pyotr's was to Zmyeevich.'

'So it seems neither of us trusts the other,' said Aleksandr.

'Then neither of us can benefit.'

'I must contradict you. You say you have saved my dynasty – if that is true, then I have already benefited.'

Iuda smiled in acknowledgement of the tsar's trap. 'I overstated my position,' he said. 'I have it in my power to save your dynasty.'

'How?'

'I have found the bastard we require.'

Aleksandr sat down, rubbing his moustache. 'Whose child?'

'The child of your brother, Konstantin.'

'He'll never agree.'

'He need never know.'

Aleksandr considered, remaining silent for several seconds. Iuda tried to follow his thought processes, but he was a difficult man to fathom. When he spoke, it revealed a concern for the practical rather than the moral considerations. 'You propose to go to Pavlovsk and just kidnap the child?'

'It is not one of his acknowledged sons,' Iuda explained.

'Who is it then?' snapped Aleksandr.

'His name is Lukin – Mihail Konstantinovich Lukin.' As he spoke Iuda looked for any flicker of expression in the tsar's face that might indicate he was aware of Lukin's existence, but he saw none.

'How do you know he's Kostya's boy?'

'I know he's a Romanov, and what's more Zmyeevich knows it too.'

'How?'

Iuda decided that it was best to come clean. 'Because he has already drunk Zmyeevich's blood. In doing so he has saved your son Aleksandr Aleksandrovich. It will take only a little more effort for your whole family to be saved.'

'By killing him?'

'By killing him.'

'And why should we need you to do it? There are dozens of men in this very building who would kill at a single word from me. Better still, I could do the thing myself.'

'Would they know how? Would you?' asked Iuda. 'Would you know how to deal with him, once dead? Would you be able to find him before Zmyeevich's blood left his body? Would you know how to determine whether or not it had? Would you be able to feed him more of the blood, if necessary? Would you—'

Aleksandr halted him with a wave of the hand. 'You've made your point,' he said. 'And then what – how would you prove what you'd done?'

'I'd bring him to you. It would be easy to demonstrate that he was a *voordalak*.' Iuda imagined the moment even as he spoke. There was another side to this that had nothing to do with the Romanovs. Iuda would have in his power the vampire offspring of Zmyeevich – a creature who shared the great vampire's mind. What power might it give Iuda over his former ally? But that was for another day. 'Then you would give me payment.'

'But at that point you'd have done your work. Why should I need to pay you?'

A lesser man than Aleksandr would not have made the case against his own trustworthiness, but the tsar knew very well that Iuda would have got that far already.

'And at that point I would take Lukin and present him to your brother. I'm not sure just how deep the rift it caused between you would be, but hardly worth it for the little I ask.'

Aleksandr considered. 'Very well,' he said at length. 'Do what you will with him. Then bring him here and show him to me.'

He turned to leave, but there was something else he needed to be told; there was no point in dealing with a dead man. 'One more thing,' shouted Iuda. 'As a sign of my good faith.'

'What?'

'Don't take your coach along Malaya Sadovaya Street this Sunday. They've dug a tunnel under it and they plan to blow you to kingdom come.'

Aleksandr gave a knowing smile. 'I'm well aware of that,' he said.

'I see,' said Iuda. 'Then you probably know something else that should mean you won't shed too many tears over the fate we have planned for Mihail Konstantinovich.'

'And what's that?'

'He's helping to dig it.'

*

Why, Dmitry wondered, did he continue? This was no question of, with Shakespeare still on his mind, '*Bitj ili nye bitj.*' Dmitry did not seek death, nor did he know whether a *voordalak* was capable of suicide. The question was less profound. He knew he must get away from Zmyeevich, just as Iuda had told him, so why did he remain here in Petersburg? Why did he continue to pose as Shklovskiy? Did the success or failure of these fools, the life or death of Aleksandr, really matter at all to his existence? It did not – but it mattered to Zmyeevich and the fact that Dmitry continued to play his role simply demonstrated just how deeply in thrall to Zmyeevich he was.

'You've done well in my absence, Sofia Lvovna,' he said.

'We were unable to communicate with you. I think I made the decisions that you would have.'

It was a small meeting – just the inner circle of the Executive Committee, those that hadn't already been arrested: Sofia, Bogdanovich, Kibalchich, Rysakov. The only surprising face was Dusya's; she'd never seemed anything more than a foot soldier in the organization. But when generals were dropping – or being arrested – left, right and centre there would be many a battlefield promotion. Her new-found status would be a boon to Iuda.

'Is everything ready for Sunday?' Dmitry asked.

Sofia nodded. 'Aleksandr will not escape.'

What did it matter now? Not to the few gathered here, but to Zmyeevich? Aleksandr Aleksandrovich was lost to him, thanks to Mihail, so what would be achieved by his father's death? Was that to be just the start? Would Zmyeevich go on to engineer the death of the new tsar, so that the boy Nikolai could take the throne, under Zmyeevich's control? The people here would gladly help with the first step of that, though they didn't expect there would be any need to remove a second tyrant once the first was eliminated; the people would see to that – so the theory went. On the other hand, might Zmyeevich use this threat to the current tsar's life as one final inducement to persuade him to become a vampire? Dmitry did not care, but Zmyeevich cared on his behalf.

'Any news of Zhelyabov?' Dmitry asked, still feigning interest.

'Were you expecting any?' Sofia's tone was a little pointed.

'I think we'd know by now if he'd talked,' Dmitry replied.

'And how would we know that?'

'Because if he had talked, none of us would be here to discuss it. We'd all be under arrest.' It was straightforward reasoning and Sofia should have understood too. Dmitry suspected that there was something more to her question.

'Perhaps he's only told them what they know already,' said Sofia.

'By other means,' added Dusya.

Dmitry noticed how he had become the focus of everyone in the room. True enough, he was the chairman of the committee, but that role had never previously drawn such attention. He chose to play the innocent.

'Andrei's clever like that,' he said, nodding. 'But eventually they'll realize he's not giving them anything new – and then we'll have to act fast.'

'I'm sure you'll be the first to know,' said Dusya.

'Just as you were the first to learn of his arrest,' added Rysakov, 'long before the rest of us – before it even happened.'

Dmitry grinned. It was now abundantly clear what this meeting was all about. He glanced at Sofia and saw she had a revolver trained on him. Kibalchich had moved to lean against the door, blocking it as an escape route. All eyes were on Dmitry.

'Go on then,' he smiled. 'Tell me what you've got.'

'Not yet,' said Sofia. She nodded to Rysakov who walked over to Dmitry, caressing a coil of rope in his hands. He went behind the chair and flipped a strand of the rope over Dmitry's head and across his chest before tying it tightly. Dmitry's arms were pinned to his sides and to the back of the chair. He gave the vague impression of struggling against his bonds, but he didn't try too hard. That was best left as a surprise.

'Now we can hear the evidence against you,' said Sofia. 'Dusya?'

Dusya stood. 'I saw you,' she said simply. 'I saw you outside Trigoni's apartment. The gendarme spoke to you before they went in to make the arrests. You'd gone before they came out.'

It was all a fabrication, and Dmitry could guess that it came at Iuda's behest. There was no point in denying it – they had clearly made up their minds and anyway he had no desire to remain with them a moment longer. But even so, he'd rather his denunciation was based on the truth than a lie.

He turned to Dusya. 'Are you sure it was you who saw me, or was it Vasiliy Grigoryevich Chernetskiy?'

'Vasiliy Grigoryevich is a prisoner of the tsar, as you well know,' snapped Sofia. 'And even if he were free, I'd happily take his word over yours.' The gun in her hand trembled, but didn't falter in its aim towards his heart.

'Vasiliy Grigoryevich was released three weeks ago,' countered Dmitry, 'on the personal orders of the tsar.'

'Rubbish!' said Dusya. 'But if anyone would know, you would, wouldn't you, Colonel Otrepyev? You're the man who put him there.'

Dmitry shrugged. 'That I won't deny.'

'You admit it?' asked Bogdanovich.

'I admit it. Otrepyev and I are one and the same.'

'Do they know about the tunnel?' asked Sofia.

'They?'

'The Ohrana – or whoever you're working for.'

'I work for no one,' said Dmitry, wishing it were true. 'Certainly not for you.'

'Then you're an enemy of the people.'

Dmitry laughed. 'The people? The people whose will you claim to represent? When it comes to it, you'll find out just how little you understand the people.'

Sofia shook her head and smiled. 'It's a shame you won't live to see it,' she snarled, 'but it will happen. A brave few of us will begin it. We'll kill the despot and yes, the people will be shocked, and saddened, but they'll pause to think and then they'll understand what has happened and the chance they've been given. And they'll grab that chance with both hands and they'll follow us. They will take the reins of power and we will guide them to a new future – free from hunger, free from tyranny. Free from monsters like you.'

Dmitry's nostrils flared. He breathed deeply. For the first time in many years he felt passionate. She knew nothing, none of them did, but he would tell them.

'You brave few? Brave? Your brave plan is to skulk in tunnels like rats. You'll wait for Aleksandr to come past so that you can kill him without having to face him. Then you expect the people to rise up and do the real work for you, and if they fail, you'll stay hidden and let them take the blame. Brave?'

'What would you have us do?'

'Act like men, if you can. Stand up and shout what you believe, like we did on the *quatorze*, on 14 December 1825. Three thousand stood in Senate Square to end Nikolai's tyranny before it could even begin. Three thousand faced canister and grapeshot as the tsar ordered his men to fire upon their comrades.'

Dmitry knew that he was forgetting so much: forgetting that he was a vampire and should not care about such things; forgetting the fact that he himself had walked away from the square before the guns had begun to spit death. But he had not been a vampire back then. He was talking with the voice of the man he should have grown to be instead of the creature into which he had descended, and he enjoyed the deception, not least because he was deceiving himself.

'They failed,' sneered Sofia.

'As you will fail. But at best, your failure will be forgotten. All the *people* will remember is the tsar's bleeding corpse, ripped to tatters by your bomb. He will be a hero and his son – fool that he is – will bask in their mourning. If you go down in history at all it will be as cowards, as killers, as assassins. But we'll be remembered. We who stood up to be counted, we who faced our oppressor and looked him in the eye even as he cut us down, we will inspire the future. We will have the streets and squares named after us. You will achieve nothing but death because you understand nothing but death. We deal in hope while you wallow in terror. We are Bonaparte – you are Robespierre.'

Sofia laughed, quite genuinely. 'You are Bonaparte?' she shrieked. 'You are mad! The Decembrists achieved nothing. They demanded nothing but an easier life. They stood for themselves, not the people. And yet you talk like you were one of them. Did you stand there in your mother's arms, suckling at her teat as the guns opened fire? Did you toddle up to Nikolai, tug at his coat and mewl at him until he granted a constitution? You're living a fantasy. You yearn for a past that never existed, like all who oppose change. You say we understand nothing but death? You'll understand it soon enough.' She raised the pistol to eye level.

Dmitry breathed deeply. He did not know where his words had come from. However rambling and idealistic they were, he was proud of them. But he feared – he knew – that his predictable, pathetic self would return to him before long, and so he relished the moment all he could.

'I was there,' he said slowly. 'I was eighteen years old. I stood on Senate Square with my father and we faced the guns together.' Lies! Lies! All lies! Whose was the voice in his head that screamed? Zmyeevich's? His own? He did not care, as long as he could ignore it for just a few seconds more.

'Quite, quite mad,' said Sofia, a hint of sympathy in her voice.

Dmitry stood, spreading his arms to rip through the rope around him. The flimsy wooden chair collapsed under the strain and Dmitry hurled its fragments across the room. Sofia's jaw hung open in limp surprise, but she held the gun steady. Dmitry took a step forward and it went off. The bullet hit him somewhere in the chest, passing right through, but he scarcely noticed it.

'My God!' whispered Sofia.

Dmitry took another step. Bogdanovich and Rysakov threw themselves forward and grabbed Dmitry's arms, but he cast them easily aside. Kibalchich looked on with detached fascination. Dusya failed to hide an appreciative smile. Had Iuda told her that Dmitry was a vampire when he had told her to denounce him? Had she come with a more appropriate weapon than a revolver? It seemed not. Iuda did not want Dmitry to die – he merely wanted to demonstrate his power.

Sofia raised her aim a little higher and fired twice more. She was a good shot. The bullets hit Dmitry's face barely an inch apart. He felt blood on his cheeks and heard a gurgling, snorting noise when he tried to breathe through his nose. Sofia dropped the gun and raised her hands to her face, covering her silent scream. Only Dusya failed to show any shock. She grinned salaciously, relishing the moment.

Dmitry could have killed them all there and then. Perhaps five minutes later he would have, but it would be an ignoble way to end his fine speech, wallowing in the death he had just condemned.

He made for the door, against which Kibalchich still leaned. Even his veneer of detachment could not disguise his horror, but he had not lost his presence of mind. As Dmitry reached forward to drag Kibalchich out of his way, the young man stepped aside, opening the door with one hand and almost offering Dmitry an exit with the other. It seemed to mock Dmitry's oratory, but he chose not to punish it.

Moments later he was out of the room, down the stairs and running through the cool, dark night. He slowed to walking pace and laughed loudly, but soon fell into silence. His mind began to fill with unwanted intruders: the true memories of what had happened in Senate Square, a hunger for blood, and the presence of Zmyeevich, probing his thoughts, commanding his will. He knew that those first two interlopers would never be far from him, but Zmyeevich could be escaped. There was nothing in Petersburg for him now. Nothing in Russia, nor even in Europe. But it was a big world and Dmitry would travel across it until he was far away – far from Zmyeevich. He would seek out a new world, or a new continent at least. And when he set foot on it he would make it his home. He would live in a land that was what Russia should have been. And he would be free.

CHAPTER XXIV

KIBALCHICH WAS SMOKING A CIGARETTE. IT WAS FORBIDDEN anywhere near the tunnel, and therefore even in the living room – a rule that Kibalchich himself insisted upon, knowing full well how easy it could be to set off the nitroglycerin. In the shop itself it was allowed. Mihail had declined the offer to partake, but he enjoyed the smell of the fumes; it reminded him of his mother. There were two smells he associated with Tamara; one pleasant, the other foul. Both had the same cause.

The pleasant one was what he experienced now, the smoke in the air, whether it wafted from the tip or was expelled from Kibalchich's mouth and nose. Mihail breathed it in deeply, enjoying the way it tugged at his throat and lungs, a pale echo of the sensation he remembered from the few occasions when he had taken in the smoke directly from a cigarette. It had never become a habit for him, in no small part because of that other smell: the smell of his mother when she was *not* smoking; the stale, dirty stink that clung to her clothes, her hair and even her body. When she lit a cigarette the scent of the fresher smoke managed to hide the underlying stench, but added to it as well. Mihail always knew that it was there. When Tamara coughed he knew that her lungs were as filthy as her clothes. When she coughed blood he understood that such stains could not be washed away.

That same stale stench clung to Kibalchich most of the time, but it was only noticeable when he and Mihail were close – when they were together in the tunnel. Up here it was masked by the aroma of cheese, but when a cigarette was lit, its smell obscured everything.

Kibalchich was on his second now. There'd been scarcely a pause between stubbing out the first and lighting a new one. Mihail noticed how his hand shook. He'd seen the same in his mother, but only until those first clouds of smoke hit her lungs.

'Nervous?' he asked.

'Of course not!' Kibalchich snapped.

'You seem on edge.' It was not just Kibalchich. Sofia and Bogdanovich were the same.

'Excited.' It sounded like bravado.

'Anything come up at the meeting yesterday?'

Kibalchich looked at him suspiciously. 'Why should it?'

He seemed terrified, but Mihail did not press it. 'Was Dusya there?' he asked.

'She was. But don't worry. She's all right.'

Mihail looked at him, puzzled, wondering why she might not have been all right. They fell into silence for a while. Kibalchich continued to smoke, but seemed to become calmer.

'You're happy to be here tomorrow?' he asked at length, holding a lungful of smoke and then expelling it through his nostrils.

'One of us has to be,' Mihail replied.

'So why did Sofia choose you?'

Mihail could guess. He didn't want to hurt Kibalchich's feelings, but the reason was obvious. 'You're a man of thought, Nikolai, not of action. I'm a soldier, remember. I've done this sort of thing with enemy shells raining down above me. If you were here, you might suddenly see something – a rat nibbling at a bit of cheese – and you'd have an idea. You'd start wondering – I don't know – whether rats could be trained to carry explosives, or whether cheese would be the best foodstuff for men travelling to the moon. And lo and behold, the tsar would have paraded past and you'd have missed your moment.'

'Frolenko's the one who's actually on the switch,' protested Kibalchich, but with little enthusiasm. He flicked his cigarette butt to the floor and stubbed it out with a twisting motion of his foot.

'True. But you know what I mean.'

'So when that rocket goes to the moon, it'll be a man like you on board, and a man like me sitting and watching, hoping his calculations were correct.'

'Getting distracted by rats eating cheese,' Mihail added.

Kibalchich laughed. 'And you get all the fame?'

'You want the fame for this?' Mihail nodded in the direction of the tunnel.

'I don't know what I want from this – but no, it's not fame.'

'I think you're going to be disappointed,' said Mihail, 'whatever happens.'

They were interrupted by footsteps on the stairs and then the ringing of the bell as the opening door caught it. The scenario had been discussed and practised many times. Neither Mihail nor Kibalchich turned to see who had entered. They peered intently at the truckles of cheese on the shelves, occasionally taking a sniff. What else was there that customers in a cheese shop would do?

'This one has a little more pepperiness to it, don't you think, Nikolai?' Mihail said.

Kibalchich nodded in agreement. Mihail desperately tried to avoid catching his eye, knowing that it risked sending them both into fits of laughter, despite his comrade's nervousness. He ran his fingers across the rind of the sample in front of him and then sniffed them, rubbing them together to release more of the aroma. The silence was discomfiting, but neither of them could do anything about it. Perhaps this would be his opportunity to get away.

Bogdanovich emerged through the door from the storeroom, appearing smooth and unruffled. He was far better at this sort of thing than most of them, certainly better than Mihail or Kibalchich; that's why he'd been chosen for the role of shopkeeper.

'You two gentlemen still all right?' he asked as he passed Mihail and Kibalchich, turning his head a little towards them.

'Still trying to decide,' said Kibalchich. 'You have quite a choice.'

Bogdanovich carried on towards the newcomer, still out of Mihail's line of sight.

'And how can I help you, sir?' he asked.

'Are you Yevdokim Kobozev?' said a gruff, familiar voice that Mihail could not quite place. He turned to take a glance. It was Mrovinskiy, the colonel through whom Mihail arranged his meetings with Konstantin, though today he was not wearing his uniform. He did not look in Mihail's direction.

'Indeed I am,' replied Bogdanovich. 'I take it that my reputation precedes me.'

'I don't think anyone would be proud of the reputation that put us on to *you*.'

Mihail and Kibalchich both turned to look. Bogdanovich had managed to maintain his calm exterior, but it seemed impossible that this did not mean the end for operations at the cheese shop.

'From what I hear,' Mrovinskiy continued, 'anyone swallowing a mouthful of cheese from here is likely to spend the next few evenings in the latrine, crapping their guts out.'

For the smallest fraction of a second an expression of relief appeared on Bogdanovich's face, followed immediately by one of professional indignation. His cheeks reddened. He spoke through gritted teeth.

'I would ask you then, sir, to get out of my shop and take your custom elsewhere.'

'I think not,' replied Mrovinskiy. He presented Bogdanovich with his papers, explaining himself at the same time. 'My name is Mrovinskiy – from the Department of Sanitary Engineering. I'm here to perform an inspection.'

He stepped back towards the door and opened it, signalling up to the street. Two men thudded heavily down the steps to join him. They moved quickly. Mrovinskiy thrust the door to the storeroom open and one of his men went through. Another went across and into the living room, emerging moments later with Anna Vasilyevna.

'Who's this?' Mrovinskiy barked.

Bogdanovich didn't waver in his performance. 'This is my wife. We run the shop together.'

'Anyone else?' asked Mrovinskiy.

'No, sir,' said one of the men, with a little more of a clipped, military tone than might have been expected from a sanitation official.

'Begin the inspection.'

The men started to search the shelves, removing truckles and looking behind them. One took a pencil and began to poke at the cheese with it to see if there was anything hidden within. To Mihail it seemed obvious that the quality of the shop's hygiene was not the true goal of the search, but he had the advantage of knowing who Mrovinskiy was. On the other hand, given how much was already known about what the shop was being used for, it was hard to understand why such artifice was needed. Why else, though, would Mrovinskiy be there?

Having finished with the shop and the storeroom the inspectors moved on to the living quarters. Mihail glanced through and saw that all was in order. The usual planks were covering the entrance to the tunnel and a barrel had been pushed in front of them. On top of that was a cheese. Mihailov and Frolenko had been in there, but there was now no sign of them. They must have hidden in the tunnel. One of them would have the revolver clutched in his hand. If they were discovered he would shoot, first to kill whoever it was that had uncovered the tunnel and then at the parcel which still lay there, filled with nitroglycerin, destroying everyone in the place. If it came to it, Mihail would have to shout a warning, even though that in itself might be enough to trigger the suicidal act; best for now to remain silent. He wondered if any of his comrades had cyanide-filled nuts poised between their teeth, preparing to bite down if discovered.

'Bit of a stink in here,' observed Mrovinskiy. The stench from the broken sewer still lingered, even though Mihail and the others had grown used to it.

'An inevitable consequence of the trade we ply,' explained Bogdanovich, raising his hand to indicate the cheeses surrounding them. It seemed to satisfy Mrovinskiy, though a genuine health inspector might have shown far more interest in the precise nature of the odour.

One of the men lifted the large round cheese off the barrel and the other tipped it away from the wall behind. Mrovinskiy peered at the vertical slats of wood that were all that protected them from their undoing. Mihail saw Anna Vasilyevna glancing desperately towards Bogdanovich, but thankfully no one noticed. Bogdanovich himself remained perfectly calm.

'What are these?' Mrovinskiy asked.

'It's the damp,' explained Bogdanovich. 'That whole section of the wall is sodden. You'd be able to smell the mildew if it wasn't for the cheese.'

Mihail looked back towards Mrovinskiy, who must have guessed the true reason for the planks but was evidently keen not to discover anything untoward. Again Mihail could only wonder why he had come at all. It was a game of bluff which one side was bound soon to lose.

Assistance came from an unexpected source. At that moment the cat leapt down from one of the shelves and began to rub herself against Mrovinskiy's legs. He bent down and held his curled finger to her nose, allowing her to rub her whiskers against it. Mrovinskiy nodded at his subordinates to move the barrel back into place. Mihail felt the urge to laugh at the amateurishness of it, but he was relieved. Bombs did not need to be exploded; poison did not need to be swallowed. Mihail tried not to relax, or give any hint as to a change of his mood – any suggestion that the inspectors were getting colder or warmer. Mrovinskiy's attention was still occupied by the cat. He reached under her belly to pick her up, but stopped when he felt the unusual bulges within.

'She's been careless with her affections,' said Anna Vasilyevna lightly. 'We don't know who the father is.'

Mrovinskiy smiled and stroked the cat, who straightened her tail and curled her back in response. He stood upright and took a last brief glance around the room before returning to the shop. Mihail and Kibalchich had moved over to the main door now, eager not to appear interested in what was going on. Mrovinskiy's eyes passed briefly across Mihail's face, but he was as good an actor as Bogdanovich and showed no hint of recognition.

'This all seems in order, Mr Kobozev,' said Mrovinskiy. 'I'm sorry to have disturbed you. Obviously someone has made a malicious report. Your sanitation certificate will be in the post.'

He opened the door as if to leave and for the first time looked Mihail in the face.

'After you,' he said, indicating the exit with an open hand.

At last Mihail understood the single, simple reason for the entire charade: himself. He had been looking for an opportunity to get away from the others and now he was being presented with it.

'Thank you,' he said. He stepped through the door and trotted lightly up the steps to the street, looking back when he reached it. If Kibalchich left too then his freedom would mean nothing;

he needed to be alone. Mrovinskiy seemed to have anticipated the problem, and was engaging Kibalchich in conversation. Mihail did not wait to hear more. He pressed on down the street, with no doubt as to where he was heading. Mrovinskiy's involvement could mean only one thing: Mihail had been summoned.

'Cain has been to see me.'

Mihail nodded. It came as little surprise. Iuda was Zmyeevich's enemy, as was Aleksandr. At some point one of them would attempt to form an alliance. Mihail's plans assumed it – relied upon it. The only new information was that Iuda had evidently recovered from his ordeal at Saint Isaac's. But if Iuda's visit was predictable, the tsar's reaction to that visit was quite unknown. On it hinged everything.

'You should have kept him here for me,' said Mihail. 'It would have been my pleasure to kill him for you.'

'I would not have shared that pleasure.' The tsar spoke with slow caution.

Mihail looked up. Aleksandr's face was inscrutable. He turned towards his father, but his gaze was not met. Konstantin rubbed his forehead and hid his eyes.

'Explain,' said Mihail.

'This is nothing personal,' Aleksandr was at pains to point out, 'but you must understand that our enemy – my family's – *Russia*'s enemy – is Zmyeevich. When Cain acted for him, he too was our enemy. But now . . .'

'What did Cain say?'

'He said that you . . . that you had saved my son. Is that true?'

'I've saved him from Zmyeevich's power. I can't save him from death.'

'Why did you do that?' asked Aleksandr.

'For God's sake, Sasha,' Konstantin interrupted. 'What kind of question is that? Why do you think he did it?'

'Do you love your tsar that much, Mihail?' asked Aleksandr.

Mihail paused. It would be easy to say yes, but it would not be true. 'I love my grandfather,' he said instead. 'It's what he would have done – what he did.'

'Aleksei loved his tsar.'

'My grandfather was the same as me.' Mihail did not know how he knew it, but he believed it. 'If he loved Aleksandr Pavlovich it was as his friend, not as his tsar.' The difference was that Mihail had no friends.

'I hardly think it matters,' said Konstantin. 'It's what Mihail has done that counts.'

Aleksandr nodded sombrely. 'And what he can yet do.' Konstantin looked away again.

'What do you mean?' asked Mihail.

Aleksandr's answer was obvious enough – almost too obvious given the tone of what he had said. 'I'm talking about the terrorists. When do they plan to attack?'

'Tomorrow,' said Mihail. 'As you return from the Manège. They'll explode the mine under Malaya Sadovaya Street as your coach travels along it.'

'Tomorrow?' said Konstantin. '1 March 1881. It will go down as a historic day for Russia.'

Aleksandr gave half a smile. 'Yes. Yes indeed.'

'Not if we can stop it,' said Mihail.

'Not that,' said Konstantin. 'Tell him, Sasha.'

The tsar took a deep breath. 'Tomorrow,' he said, '*before* I go to the Manège, I shall sign documents establishing the beginnings of a constitution – two assemblies with powers to make law; elected, after a fashion.' Tears formed in his eyes as he spoke – he was proud of what he had planned. 'Konstantin, Loris-Melikov and I have been working on it for months. It won't quite be England, thank God, but it's a step. That's all one can do – make small steps. This is what Aleksandr Pavlovich would have done, if it hadn't been for the war.'

Mihail tried to take it in. It seemed like very little, but in a sense it was revolutionary. Even when the serfs had been emancipated it had been done at His Majesty's command. He was still the unfettered autocrat, enforcing his will upon the nation. This, by the sound of it, would be different. If what Aleksandr implied was true, then he would no longer be the sole source of authority in Russia. It was hard to believe. Perhaps Mihail should go and tell Sofia Lvovna and the others that their plans were no longer necessary, that they would get what they wanted without the need for bloodshed. It would be a slower transition than they desired, but a peaceful one. He tried to picture the joy on their faces as he explained it to them, but it was laughable to imagine that they would welcome the news. They no longer sought liberty; they were too far gone. For them the means had supplanted the ends and the tsar's death had become an end in itself; the goal towards which they struggled and for which they would lay down their own lives and the lives of others. For them reform was as much to be feared as for the reactionaries in the tsar's own circle. Neither would flourish if the people were appeased.

'And if you die tomorrow?' asked Mihail. 'Will the tsarevich enact your plans?'

Konstantin emitted a short, sharp laugh which Mihail took as a 'no'.

'I shall not die tomorrow,' said the tsar. 'I shall change the route of the carriage, as I have done before. After the changing of the guard I'll visit my cousin the Grand Duchess Yekaterina Mihailovna. I'll be nowhere near their mine.'

'Even so,' said Mihail, 'I plan to go back there, presuming Mrovinskiy hasn't had everyone arrested.'

'Why?'

'Because of Cain.'

'Ah. I think this is where we came in.'

'Indeed.'

'He told me of what you have already done for my family; of how much more you can do.'

Aleksandr turned away as he spoke, walking towards his desk. Mihail looked at his father, but still his gaze was not returned.

'You said that before.'

'He told me that you are now the focus of Zmyeevich's attention, but that this is not a permanent state of affairs.'

'It will protect your son – all your children – as long as they live.'

'I have grandchildren. I have a grandson Nikolai. He will be tsar one day. He will need protecting from the curse on his family's blood.'

'I can't help him,' said Mihail. He doubted he would even if he were able.

'Zmyeevich's blood is still in you?' Aleksandr still had his back to Mihail.

'I believe so.' Mihail had read Iuda's notes, but he could only guess.

'In that case you can help him a great deal.'

'How?'

The tsar turned swiftly, raising his arm to shoulder level as he did so. Mihail found himself looking directly down the barrel of the tsar's revolver and saw his knuckle tighten around the trigger.

Clearly Aleksandr understood everything. 'You can die,' he said simply.

It was almost midnight now, on the last day of February. Already the signs of winter were fading. The ice on the Neva was no longer a solid, flat, white sheet. Gaps had appeared in the middle where its waters flowed freely, eating away at the ice that lingered. There was still snow on the ground, but it was mostly old. During the days it melted a little and soon no more would fall to replace it. In just over a week it would be the vernal equinox, and after that there would be more day than night. It would happen throughout the northern hemisphere, but here in midsummer daylight would last for almost nineteen hours. For a *voordalak* Saint Petersburg was a winter retreat – nineteen hours of darkness were more than enough to hunt – but in summer it was too bright.

It was time to be leaving the city, but there was still one thing that remained for Iuda to do. It was no great matter, merely the salvation of the Romanov dynasty. Most of the work had already been done. All that was required was for Lukin to die. But on that issue time pressed. The time in which Zmyeevich's blood would remain in his body was impossible to calculate. It was almost a certainty that it lingered now, but in a week, two weeks – who could tell?

And so Lukin had to be found. There was one obvious source of information; someone who had a greater interest even than Iuda in ensuring Lukin's death. The information should have come by now. He'd been standing here on the Admiralty Quay gazing out over the river for half an hour and he felt uncomfortable. It was too close to where Zmyeevich had stayed – to where Zmyeevich knew him to have stayed. He'd chosen the spot at which he waited with escape in mind. The Admiralty was at his back, but ahead was the expanse of the river. The ice was still strong enough to take his weight in most parts, though even then it might be better to escape beneath the water – as he had done before.

But all that assumed that Zmyeevich came alone. What if Dmitry had returned to him? Between them the two might easily capture Iuda, and this time Zmyeevich was sure to make certain of his death. But it seemed improbable. Dmitry – fool though he was – was not fool enough to go back to Zmyeevich. If he did, it was unlikely he would ever have the strength to leave him again.

Along the quayside, at the corner of the Admiralty, a figure appeared. It was neither Zmyeevich nor Dmitry; that was clear enough. The man approached and soon Iuda could see it was who he had been expecting. Moments later they were side by side.

'Colonel Mrovinskiy,' said Iuda.

Mrovinskiy did not acknowledge the greeting.

'You have the information I requested?' Iuda continued.

'I've consulted with His Majesty. I have what you want.'

'Well?'

'Lukin will be in the shop in Malaya Sadovaya Street tomorrow – or beneath it,' Mrovinskiy said.

'At what time?'

The colonel shrugged. 'At whatever time he chooses to go there. His Majesty's coach is scheduled to pass by between one and two.'

'You're certain of this?'

'It comes direct from the tsar. What more do you want?'

'Very well,' said Iuda. 'You can go now.'

As Iuda had intended, Mrovinskiy hovered uncomfortably. He didn't want to seem to be obeying Iuda's instruction, but neither did he have any reason to remain. He stood for a few seconds then clicked his heels and walked away. Iuda waited until he had disappeared, then began to move.

To have Lukin down there in the cellars would be ideal. It would be dark and safe for Iuda, and Lukin would have far greater concerns. What mattered most was that thanks to Dmitry's excavations, Iuda had an alternative way in.

It was still hours until dawn, but Iuda had already eaten. He would go there and prepare himself, get some rest, but first there was one visit to be made. The journey took him away from his final destination on Nevsky Prospekt and to the south-east, into the huddled, small, cheap apartments that provided accommodation for the city's burgeoning industrial workforce. As far as he could make out, half of them were occupied by revolutionaries, not just from the People's Will but from a dozen other organizations with similar aims, whose hatred for the tsar was surpassed only by their hatred for one another.

The *dvornik* scarcely looked up as Iuda went by, despite the late hour. He climbed the steps quickly up to the third floor and then rapped softly on the door – just like Susanna used to knock on his bedroom door, so many years ago.

There was no response. He knocked louder, but still there was nothing. It was a pity, but it would make little difference to his plans. He took out a scrap of paper and wrote a short note which he slipped under the door. If it was read before tomorrow, all the better; if not, he could manage very well alone.

He made his way back across town, to the east. He felt wary of the direct route, along Nevsky Prospekt, past the Hôtel d'Europe where, if anywhere, Zmyeevich might be on the lookout for him. He could head south and come to Nevsky Prospekt from the other direction, but that would involve going through Aleksandrinsky Square with its unpleasant bright lights.

In the end he chose to take Surovskaya Lane, bringing him out on to Nevsky Prospekt close to the hotel. He walked in the opposite direction and soon the gap between the buildings appeared. He turned off into the little square that housed the blue and white stucco façade and dainty cupola of the Armenian Church of Saint Yekaterina. It was no coincidence that Iuda had chosen rooms in a hotel so close to this building, nor that the tunnel had been dug nearby; Dmitry had been careful in his choice of location. For anyone interested in the fate of Ascalon, this church was at the heart of the city.

Iuda had no key. It had been with his possessions in the cellar beneath Senate Square, and he'd had no chance to retrieve it as he fled – nor had he foreseen the need. It did not matter. He began to climb one of the great neoclassical columns of the portico, the third from the right, and was soon clawing his way over the triangular bas-relief on the pediment. Then he was up on to the tower that supported the diminutive dome. This was nothing to match the grandeur of Saint Isaac's, but then Iuda had played no part in its design. That did not mean that the entire building had not been laid out with just as much guile and to a far more singular end than the Orthodox cathedral.

Iuda smashed one of the arched glass windows of the tower and slipped inside, remembering how years before he had done much the same to get into the Peter and Paul Cathedral, only a couple of versts away. On both occasions his business had concerned the death of a Romanov; then with Tsar Nikolai, to confirm it – now with Lukin, to ensure it.

The tower did not open on to the nave. Inside there was a false dome, suspended lower than the one outside. Iuda remembered the way down. A flight of steps led to a gallery at the western end of the building. From there it was easy to climb down into the nave. The decoration was sparse compared with an Orthodox church – certainly when set against Saint Isaac's. Even so they'd still managed to find room for that ubiquitous image – George killing the dragon. Here it was a separate painting rather than being etched on to the fabric of the building itself, but the message was clear. It was a message repeated throughout the city – throughout Russia. Iuda headed towards the altar and then to a side chapel, where a door he knew well stood waiting. It too was locked, but that would not stop him for long. He took a step back and prised up the flagstone on which he had been standing. It was too heavy to be lifted by a single human, and why would they bother? It had lain there for over a century, or at least so they thought. In truth it had been disturbed just once, by Iuda, in 1872 when he had hidden two keys there.

He raised the stone to the vertical and then looked beneath. There they were, just as he had left them. He picked them up and dropped the slab back into place. The only risk now was if they had changed the lock, but the key turned smoothly and easily. Iuda locked the door behind him and descended. Beneath was a maze of corridors and passageways, but he knew the route. He found his way to a long, eastbound corridor, its entrance blocked by an iron gate, much like the one that opened on to the crypt beneath Saint George's in Esher. This time he used the second key and though it fitted, it was harder to turn. No one had been this way for many years – he was probably the last. Finally the lock gave way and the grille swung open. Iuda went through, again locking it behind him. The tunnel stretched out ahead of him, under the buildings and under Sadovaya Street. He walked on until the way was blocked by stone and rubble. The roof had collapsed. It had not been like that when he was last here. It might have taken a man hours or even days to clear a path through, but for Iuda it was a matter of minutes. Soon there was enough of a gap for him to squeeze through and continue along the passageway. It ended with another gate.

Beyond that the two small cellars stood on either side, with similar gates standing open. The corridor continued a little further, ending in a wooden ladder which led up to the cheese shop above. There would be someone there even now, on guard, so he knew he must be quiet. The same key should fit this lock as the last one, and so it did, offering similar resistance but again yielding eventually. He had merely wanted to test it. For now there was no need to go any further.

He locked the gate again and crept a little way back up the corridor, behind the pile of rubble, settling down in the darkness to await Lukin's arrival.

CHAPTER XXV

Sunday 1 March 1881

Aleksandr did not fire his pistol. He had, he explained, merely been demonstrating what a different man in the same circumstances might have done. It was a display of magnanimity.

Mihail wasn't so sure. Konstantin had backed his brother up, but that was to be expected. Mihail trusted neither of them. Aleksandr had explained what Iuda had told him, how killing Mihail might save the whole Romanov dynasty, by making him Zmyeevich's one and only Romanov offspring. He'd said that Iuda had wanted to do the killing himself. But then he had lowered the gun and laughed – said he would never allow such a fate to befall even a bastard Romanov. But when Mihail announced that he needed to confront Iuda and asked Aleksandr to help lure him down into the cellars beneath Malaya Sadovaya Street, His Majesty had agreed with little hesitation. He evidently thought that such a confrontation would be decisive, but was it Mihail or Iuda whose prospects he favoured?

It didn't matter. Whether Aleksandr thought that he was luring Mihail or luring Iuda, it would still end up the same, with the two of them down there alone. Nobody would guess just how well prepared Mihail was. The one disappointment was Konstantin. Mihail had hoped his father would love him more than that. But did even Konstantin truly know what was in his brother's mind?

Mihail spent the night in his hotel. He didn't sleep much – he was too busy thinking, planning, preparing. Dusya slept soundly beside him. He hadn't been expecting her – they'd not spoken the previous day and since his sudden departure from the shop he had not seen her or any member of the People's Will – but she had crept into his bed some time after midnight. She had been more passionate than usual, thrilled, he guessed, at the prospect of the day to come. He could feel no such excitement – not at the death of the tsar nor even with regard to his own plans – but he forced himself to emulate her feelings. Now was not the time to stumble in his pretence of support for her cause. Neither of them had bothered to light the lamp, or even to speak to any greater degree than a few whispered entreaties.

At some time in the small hours he must have fallen asleep and when he awoke he was alone. He'd suspected that her reason for being there was to ensure his safe arrival at the cheese shop, but apparently not. It made his life easier; there were several items he needed to take with him that it would be better she did not see.

The trunk that had arrived from Saratov a few weeks before contained much that might be of use, but he chose carefully. He could only take what would fit into his knapsack and even then he had to worry that he might be searched. They would be suspicious of him after yesterday's inspection and his departure. But what would they make of what they found in there? There was nothing that could be of much danger to them – the crossbow, perhaps, but if he was planning to start shooting, why not carry a gun?

He stepped out into the street. It was cold and gloomy. Clouds hung low in the sky. The piles of shovelled snow had a sheen where their surface had melted and refrozen. Underfoot the compressed flakes were slippery, but Mihail's shoes had studded soles which found a good grip. It would be the same for everyone in the city, excepting a few foreigners who didn't understand the Russian weather. Those who knew the cold knew how to adapt to it.

He arrived at the cheese shop just before noon. In the window the icon of Saint George still stood and the candle was alight. All was safe. Today Mihail would not quite be Saint George – he had no plans to deal with Zmyeevich – but he did intend to kill a monster. He descended the steps and went inside. The decision had been made that the shop would remain open even as they waited for Aleksandr to pass by. Anything else would have aroused suspicion. Anna Vasilyevna was inside, a smouldering cigarette clasped between her fingers. The smile which she set to welcome a customer soon fell as she saw who it was. Without greeting him she went and knocked on the door to the living room. Moments later the face of Sofia Lvovna, with its large, unmistakable forehead, appeared.

'What the hell were you playing at?' she asked.

'What do you mean?' Mihail understood her perfectly, but it would be better to feign a degree of ignorance.

'You were meant to stay here.'

'What was I supposed to do? I was just a customer. If I'd not left he'd have been suspicious.'

'And why should a health inspector care?' she asked.

'Oh, come on! You really think he was from the Department of Sanitary Engineering?'

She paused, her lips pressed tight together. 'Probably not,' she conceded.

Mihail stepped into the living quarters. Bogdanovich was pacing nervously; Kibalchich and Frolenko stood still. Kibalchich looked like he needed to smoke, but was succeeding in obeying his own rules. The entrance to the tunnel was in plain view. 'What happened after I'd gone?' Mihail asked.

'He chatted a bit more,' explained Bogdanovich, 'mostly about the cat. Then they just left. We'd passed the inspection.'

'But Mihail's right,' growled Sofia. 'It stinks to high heaven.'

'I'm not sure,' said Bogdanovich. 'If they know what's going on, why leave us be?'

'So that we'll incriminate ourselves a little further?' suggested Sofia. 'So that they can humiliate us in our failure?'

Mihail shrugged. 'Maybe so, but I'm prepared to gamble a little humiliation, even for the tiniest chance of success.'

'Hear! Hear!' said Bogdanovich quietly.

'Possibly,' said Sofia. 'Anyway, it's too late now. We're heading off. Anna will close up at the last minute. You make sure everything's ready for Frolenko.'

'Where are you going?'

Her nostrils pinched. The stress of command was clearly

affecting her, but she managed to remain calm. 'Someone's got to keep an eye on which route he takes.'

With that she and Bogdanovich left, leaving Mihail, Frolenko and Kibalchich alone. Mihail crouched down to peer into the tunnel. The switch and its trailing wires sat there just where he had left them.

'You came back,' said Kibalchich.

It was an odd thing to say, but Mihail took it in his stride. 'Of course.'

'Let's get ready then.'

Frolenko clambered up on to the table. His eyes were just level with the street as he peeped through the window.

'Won't it be suspicious if they spot you?' Mihail asked.

'Maybe, but how else am I going to see the coach? Anyway, I'll keep down until I hear it coming.'

Mihail nodded. He bent forward and picked up the switch and its wires from the tunnel mouth, then handed it to Frolenko.

'You know what to do?' asked Kibalchich.

'I've practised a dozen times.' He held the little wooden box in his hand, then pressed the small lever on the side to horizontal. His lips silently counted to four, then he released it, allowing it to spring back to the vertical. Mihail and Kibalchich both glared at him. 'Don't worry,' he said. 'I know it's not connected.'

Kibalchich took out a small length of wire and touched its ends against the switch's terminals to short out any charge that remained from Frolenko's action. Then he connected the second long wire to the spare terminal.

'It is now,' he said grimly.

'One final check?' suggested Mihail.

'I'll do it,' replied Kibalchich.

He crawled out along the tunnel, out under the street, and soon returned. 'All OK there,' he said.

'Good,' said Mihail.

'What are my chances?' asked Frolenko.

'We've shored up the area around the explosives to force the blast upwards,' explained Kibalchich, 'so you won't get anything back through the tunnel. The bigger problem will be through the window, so I suggest you duck. I can't make any promises though.'

'I wouldn't hold you to them if you did.'

'That's about it, then,' said Mihail.

Kibalchich and Frolenko embraced, then Mihail and Kibalchich went through to the shop. Anna Vasilyevna was waiting, ready to close up. Hugged to her chest she held the pregnant cat.

'She can't stay here,' Anna explained. 'Even if she survives the blast, no one's coming back to feed her.' She opened the door and gently placed the cat about halfway up the steps, giving it a brief shoo to get rid of it. Then she closed the door. 'All ready?' she asked.

Mihail nodded. He and Kibalchich in turn kissed Anna on the cheek, then faced each other. Kibalchich offered his hand and smiled. 'I wouldn't bet on us seeing one another again – but I hope we do. Good luck in . . . in whatever you need luck with.'

Mihail grasped his hand. 'You too,' he said.

Kibalchich climbed the steps up to the street and was gone. Anna followed him. At the top of the stairs the cat waited, peering down. Anna bent over and picked up a pebble from the ground, then hurled it at the cat. The creature squealed and ran. Anna turned back to Mihail, a look of irritation on her face.

'It's for her own good,' she said. 'It's just a shame she can't understand that.'

Mihail smiled and Anna made her way slowly up to the street, but he doubted if she could read his mind. It seemed to him that what she had said would have made a fitting motto for the People's Will. 'She' was Russia.

He went back to the living room. Frolenko was sitting quietly in a corner.

'How long have we got?' he asked.

'An hour or two,' replied Mihail. 'I'm going to make a few last checks.'

He crawled into the tunnel. It took him only moments to un-twist the connection between two essential wires. Aleksandr might have been planning to change his route, but there was no point in taking risks. Afterwards it would be easy to reconnect them, and no one would be any the wiser.

Then he descended the ladder, down into the old cellars that

Dmitry had been so keen to uncover, and began his own personal preparations.

Iuda awoke. He knew in an instant that it was a little after midday. Somewhere above him, through layers of mud and brick, the sun was high in the sky – or at least as high as it ever got in Petersburg at this time of year. From beyond the locked gate he could hear sounds – male voices – from the shop above. One was probably Lukin, but Iuda had only ever heard him speak a few words and didn't know the voice well. Soon they fell silent. After a little while someone descended the stepladder. There were vague sounds, but Iuda did not need to know the details of what was going on.

It was still early. It could be Lukin out there, but it could be someone else. All he knew was that Lukin would be there by one o'clock. Even then he would wait. When everything was ready, he would be summoned.

The weather was an advantage. Zmyeevich could survive a bright sunny day; certainly here in the north, though he might not risk it closer to the equator. Even so, direct sunlight weakened him – pained him. Today it was cloudy, and though the filtered sunlight – which would be more than sufficient to obliterate a normal vampire – made him weary, he could easily tolerate it. Today would be a historic day for Russia, and he wanted to be there to witness it.

Dmitry was no longer his ally, but his mind was still a presence in Zmyeevich's, and would be whenever they were geographically close. At the moment Dmitry was moving away, if slowly. Zmyeevich could hear what Dmitry heard: waves lapping against wood; the straining of ropes and canvas; the creaking of masts and yardarms. All that Dmitry knew was known to Zmyeevich.

He knew therefore that the People's Will had chosen today to assassinate their tsar – he knew how, where and when they planned to do it. Zmyeevich would be there, or close by at least. The tsarevich, Aleksandr Aleksandrovich, was lost to him, but perhaps there was still some slight chance with the tsar himself, Aleksandr Nikolayevich – a deathbed conversion, as it were.

Zmyeevich also knew of Dmitry's conversation with Iuda, and their talk of Ascalon. There was little news in it. They had already discovered that Ascalon was no longer buried beneath the Armenian Church – that was the whole reason for Dmitry's directing the digging there. Cain claimed to have taken it to England, which had equal probabilities of being the truth or a deception, but at least it was a start. Perhaps there would even be the opportunity to reclaim the ring that Iuda had stolen from him as they fought, but it was as nothing compared with Ascalon. But all of that was for the future. Today was about Russia.

He set out around noon – challenging the sun to do its worst – and mingled with the crowds on Nevsky Prospekt. The best place to be, he reasoned, was outside the Imperial Library. There the royal entourage would turn off the prospekt and on to Malaya Sadovaya, if that was the chosen route. Otherwise it would continue and take the next turning towards the Manège. He knew from Dmitry that there was no certainty to Aleksandr's route, and that there were plans for all eventualities.

A little before one, a great cheer arose from the people – those same people whose will was about to be enacted – as the coach and its retinue came into view. Six mounted Cossacks came first, one of them shouting to clear the few pedestrians who had not moved out of the street. After them came the coach itself. Another Cossack sat on the perch, to the left of the driver. As the cavalcade continued past, Zmyeevich got a glimpse inside. Aleksandr was alone. He looked sullen and thoughtful, barely bothering to raise his hand in acknowledgement of the ovation of his people.

Then his eyes lit upon Zmyeevich and his face fell in horrified recognition. He and Zmyeevich had never met face to face, but the tsar would have heard descriptions. Moreover, the tsar could sometimes see through Zmyeevich's eyes – though how would that help him? Zmyeevich could not look upon his own face in a mirror. But at this moment Aleksandr could see himself riding past, as seen through Zmyeevich's eyes. Was it that which told him the old man watching must be his nemesis? And what further horror would he feel to discover that Zmyeevich could walk in daylight?

The moment had passed. Aleksandr's coach had continued

down the street. More importantly, it had not turned into Malaya Sadovaya. The tsar would live, if only for another hour. Behind the coach came two sleighs, packed with soldiers and gendarmes. His Majesty was protected from the front and the rear. It was a pity no one had considered how to defend him against an attack from beneath.

Once all had passed, Zmyeevich crossed the road and began to make his way to the Manège. The ceremony would not take long and then Aleksandr would be on his way again, travelling along those dangerous roads. Zmyeevich's route took him along Malaya Sadovaya. He did not know precisely where the shop was, but it was obvious once he saw it. Even through the low windows the racks of cheese inside were easy to see. He imagined what lay beneath his feet – and what had once been there. Then it had been Ascalon, before Iuda had carried it away. Now it was an enormous bomb. When it was detonated it would cause the cobbled street to erupt into the air, taking the tsar and coach and guards and their horses with it and then hurling them to the ground.

It would be quite a spectacle.

Mihail looked up from his work. He heard the sound of feet on the ladder and then on the stone floor. Thankfully, all was prepared. He stepped out of the cellar and into the corridor to find Frolenko nervously glancing around.

'There you are.'

'What's happened?' asked Mihail.

'Nothing,' said Frolenko petulantly. 'Aleksandr's gone past. He didn't come down the street. He must be at the Manège by now.'

'Damn,' said Mihail. He doubted he was at all convincing.

'There's still another chance,' said Frolenko, 'on his return.'

Mihail nodded sombrely. 'And if not?' he asked.

Frolenko shrugged. 'You sure you'll be safe down here? When it goes up?'

'I helped design the tunnel and the bomb. The blast will go upwards. I'm as safe as you are.' It would have been true anyway – the additional fact that the switch was no longer connected to the detonators did not need mentioning.

'I guess you know what you're doing. I best get back up.'

'How long do you think now?'

'Half an hour,' said Frolenko, 'maybe a little more.' He looked around as if seeking a reason to remain with Mihail, but he could find none. He gave a brief smile and then climbed up to the shop to continue his vigil.

Mihail went back along the corridor, all the way to the rusty locked gate. He looked out into the dark tunnel beyond, but saw only the rubble that had always been there. Perhaps it had been moved a little – that was no surprise. He returned to the ancient cellar where he had been working and sat down. It was clearer in here now that he had rigged some electric lights – nothing much, just the dim, incandescent bulbs that Kibalchich had so proudly shown him when he first came here. They didn't use too many cells and he'd stacked the remaining jars of lead plates dipped in acid against the wall. The ones that really mattered were in the other room. He stared up at the strange writing above the alcove, clearer in the electric light, and tried to make sense of it. He made no progress, but it passed the time. For Mihail as for Frolenko, all that remained to do was wait – though what it was that the two men were waiting for was quite, quite different.

Zmyeevich stood at the corner of the square outside the Mihailovskiy Manège. It had been over half an hour since the tsar's cortège had driven in. He had watched as other carriages with other dignitaries arrived: the tsarevich; two of the tsar's brothers – Konstantin and Mihail. They arrived separately and would leave separately, all too aware of the dangers they faced from their own people, and wise enough to understand that their dynasty could survive the death of one, but not of all. After that, it had gone quiet, but for the distant sound of orders barked from within, carried by the wind.

Then suddenly there was movement. The gates at the side of the building opened and the six Cossacks rode out, followed by the tsar's carriage and the police sleds. But they did not turn down Malaya Sadovaya. Instead they sped off along Italyanskaya Street. It could only be that they planned to go to the Mihailovskiy

Palace. It meant that the tsar would not be riding over the mine that had been so carefully prepared for him that day, but it did not matter. Zmyeevich knew that the People's Will had another card up its sleeve.

'Still here?'

Mihail looked up. It was not the voice he had been expecting. Dusya stood in the doorway to the cellar, her hand resting on the iron gate.

'Where else would I be?' he asked, standing and walking over to her. He put his arm around her waist and bent forward to kiss her. She did not resist, but neither did she respond. All the passion of the previous night, and of every night they had been together before that, was gone. He stepped away from her.

'It's all over,' she explained.

'Over?' Mihail did his best to feign surprise. 'What's happened?'

'Aleksandr changed his route. He's gone to the Mihailovskiy Palace to visit his cousin. He'll be leaving there soon for the Winter Palace, but he won't come this way.'

'You saw?'

She nodded. 'I told Frolenko to go. He said you were still down here.'

'I'd better make the bomb safe,' he said.

'Why?'

'So that we can try again next Sunday, or the Sunday after. We only need to get lucky once.'

'There won't be any need,' she said with a smile. She was acting strangely. She seemed smug, almost victorious, though Mihail could see no reason for it.

'We're not giving up?' All he could do was stick to his role.

'Not at all. There's no need because the tsar will be dead within a few minutes.'

'What?' Mihail felt cold. 'But you just said – he went a different way.'

'You don't really think this was the only plan, do you?'

'There's another tunnel?'

'Nothing so sophisticated,' she replied, but Mihail wasn't

listening. He leapt to his feet. There was still time. He did not know how long Aleksandr would linger at the Mihailovskiy Palace, but it was only a few streets away. Mihail could easily reach it and warn him.

'Where are you going?' Dusya asked him, all too innocently. She stood blocking his exit, one arm raised above her head, resting against the doorway. In other circumstances it would have been an alluring pose.

'To warn him. Now get out of my way.'

She did not move. 'Warn who?' she asked. Again she seemed to be overplaying her naivety – it was almost as if she were gloating.

Mihail pushed her aside and charged out into the tunnel. In moments he was up the ladder and in the living quarters of the shop. He went to the door, but could not open it. Normally the key was left in the lock, but today it was gone. Dusya must have taken it. He charged twice at the door with his shoulder, but it would not yield. He leapt up on to the table where Frolenko had so recently stood, but the windows were too small for him to get through. He might shout and attract the attention of a passer-by, but it would take too long. He had to get the key from Dusya. She clearly knew now that his plan was to save Aleksandr, but it didn't matter. If she did not give him the key, he would beat it out of her.

He dashed back to the tunnel, down the ladder and into the passageway where he had left her. She was not there, but Mihail was not alone. At the far end of the corridor the iron gate that no one had been able to unlock was open and in the archway stood a figure. Mihail had been expecting him, but at this moment it was the last creature on earth that he wanted to see.

It was Iuda.

Zmyeevich was more observant than any human – more even than most vampires. It was a predator's instinct. He could look upon a crowd of people – potential prey – and not simply understand their individual movements but sense how they moved as a group, how the action of one member might lead to a specific response in another, even though ordinarily that response would be indistinguishable from the random jostling of the crowd. It was the same as the way that a wolf could watch a flock of sheep and see one of them bleat in panic, and know which of the others would run towards the waiting pack.

And thus it was that, only moments after the tsar's procession had disappeared through the gates of the Mihailovskiy Palace, Zmyeevich noticed a young woman with an unusually prominent forehead reach into her pocket and pull out a white handkerchief which she allowed to flutter in the air for a little too long before applying it to her nose. To any observer who knew his business this was an obvious signal, but it would only be someone of Zmyeevich's skills who would have been able to pick out from the crowd the three young men – the furthest at the other end of the street – who began to move in response, almost as a single entity dispersed through the crowd.

From there it was a matter of no talent whatsoever to notice that each of those three men carried – tucked under his arm or clutched against his chest – a parcel wrapped in newspaper. Each package was the same size and shape as the others. There was no question as to what was going on.

The woman had already moved on ahead. The three men did not seem to need to follow, they knew their destination based on the signal she had given. Without acknowledging each other's presence they headed along Mihailovskaya Street and up Nevsky Prospekt. Zmyeevich followed at a distance. On Nevsky Prospekt he saw the last of the men turning back on to the embankment of the Yekaterininsky Canal. He continued to follow. When he got to the canal he saw that the woman had crossed over to the far bank, while her three lieutenants remained on this side. Evidently she planned no direct part in the attack for herself.

Zmyeevich stuck with the three men. Once past the end of Inzhenernaya Street they began to lose momentum, loitering rather than walking with any purpose, as if waiting for something – which indeed they were. After leaving the Mihailovskiy Palace the tsar's coach would travel along Inzhenernaya Street and then turn on to the embankment. They were in the perfect place to trap him. It would be a delight to behold.

Zmyeevich loitered too – or rather sat, taking advantage of a bench which His Majesty had kindly provided for the benefit of the citizens of his capital. For once the appearance of age which the sun inflicted upon him would prove to be an advantage. He was a little way down from where the bombers stood in readiness, but that would be fine. He would wander over once Aleksandr arrived, and see what they had in store for him.

Mihail ran forward and darted into the cellar where he had earlier been waiting so calmly for Iuda. Everything that might protect his life was in there – he had not planned to encounter Iuda out in the passageway.

Inside stood Dusya. Mihail put his finger to his lips to silence her and then signalled she should step back from the door. She complied. Mihail was quickly across the room and snatched up the *arbalyet* from where he had left it. He turned and trained it on the doorway. Moments later, Iuda appeared. Mihail felt the urge to pull the trigger and release the bolt, but the weapon had proved ineffectual so far. Anyway, he did not want Iuda to die without knowing the reason.

'We meet at last,' said Iuda.

'We've met before,' replied Mihail. 'In Geok Tepe. I thought you might remember, but I suppose you had other things on your mind; just like you did at Saint Isaac's.'

'Oh, I remember – I remember both occasions – but on neither were we properly introduced. My name is . . .' He frowned. 'But I have so many – which would you prefer?'

'Iuda will do.'

'Ah! My favourite.'

Mihail glanced at Dusya and tried to signal with his eyes that she should move away from Iuda, and get safely behind him. She began to move cautiously, her back against the wall. Iuda turned and saw her. She froze.

'No, you carry on, my dear,' he said. 'I won't stop you.'

She took him at his word and marched across the room to stand at Mihail's side. The vampire could easily have reached out and grabbed her, but he did nothing.

'You, I take it,' Iuda continued, 'are Mihail Konstantinovich Lukin.'

Mihail offered no reply. He was happy to let Iuda go on thinking that for now.

'It's the Konstantinovich in all that which makes it interesting, of course – your eminent father.'

'What of it?'

'It's illustrious blood that runs in your veins.'

'You have no idea,' replied Mihail.

If Iuda was fazed by the remark, he showed it only momentarily. 'In fact it was your father – and more importantly your uncle – who so keenly wanted us to have this little chat. You have something that's rather troubling to them; and they've asked me to relieve you of it.'

'What do you mean?' It was Dusya's voice from behind him.

'I mean his life,' explained Iuda.

'This is nothing to do with her,' said Mihail. 'Let her go.'

'But I'm doing nothing to detain her,' protested Iuda. He stepped away from the door and offered an open palm to show her out. 'She is free to leave whenever she pleases.'

Mihail raised the crossbow higher, making it obvious that he was aiming at Iuda's heart. 'Get a little further back first.'

Iuda retreated until his shoulders touched the wall behind him.

'Further,' said Mihail, nodding with his head.

Iuda edged along the wall, the foresight of Mihail's crossbow tracking him as he moved. Now he was about as far from the doorway as he could be.

'Dusya,' said Mihail. 'Get going. Quickly. Don't worry about me. I'll come and find you.'

She did not move. Iuda's face broke into a broad smile. Mihail glanced over his shoulder, not wanting to take his eyes from Iuda for more than a second. He could see her standing – there was nothing to hinder her departure.

'I said go,' he hissed.

'I'd rather stay.'

'Trust me, Dusya, please. I know I've deceived you, but this is real. I have things under control. I know how dangerous he can be – but you have no idea, so please, do as I say.'

'No.'

Iuda laughed broadly. 'Oh, you've found yourself the perfect partner there, Romanov. You've got her twisted round your finger. I wonder what inspires her to be so disobedient.'

Mihail ignored him. 'Dusya—'

Iuda interrupted him. 'Dusya, my dear, why don't you just do what the poor fellow asks and leave the two of us alone?'

'Because,' she explained, 'I wouldn't be able to do this.'

'Do what?' Mihail asked.

He heard the cocking of a revolver, and felt the cold steel of its barrel pressing against his neck.

CHAPTER XXVI

IT WAS A STIR IN THE CROWD THAT ZMYEEVICH NOTICED EVEN before he heard the trotting of the horses' hooves, muffled in the compressed snow. He stood and walked along the canal, just far enough to look down Inzhenernaya Street. The cortège had set off from the Mihailovskiy Palace and was approaching at a gentle pace, first the Cossacks, then Aleksandr's carriage. The sleighs behind were obscured from view. Zmyeevich tried to picture it not as the majestic parade of an emperor returning to his palace, but as the sombre procession that took his lifeless body to its grave. It would not be long before such a vision became reality.

Zmyeevich imagined the horses transformed from the bay and chestnut of those ridden by the Cossacks to a sleek coal black, with black feathers sprouting from their harnesses. He pictured the tsar's coach elongated, so that His Majesty's motionless body could recline in its bier. The crowds, lining the route in mourning dress, looked on and wept instead of raising their arms to cheer in celebration. The destination was not the tsar's warm, comfortable home, but that place where ultimately every leader of Russia was destined to rot: the Peter and Paul Cathedral, just across the Neva. The tsar's namesake, Aleksandr I, was not buried there. He had cheated death – or at least postponed it. The possibility was there for the current Aleksandr too, if he would only accept Zmyeevich.

It was all as clear in Zmyeevich's mind as if the procession truly had been a funeral cortège, but it was no idle daydream on his part. Aleksandr could see his mind. If Zmyeevich looked upon the prophetic vision of the tsar's funeral, so Aleksandr himself would

412

see it, and understand his fate, and how he might be saved. The black, plumed horses reached the corner and swung away from Zmyeevich to continue alongside the canal, then the imperial hearse slowed and turned. As it did so, Aleksandr's recumbent corpse began to rise, sitting up, his head twisting to look into Zmyeevich's eyes.

The vision evaporated, but Aleksandr's eyes remained fixed on Zmyeevich's as the coach in which he sat turned the corner. He knew. He had seen what Zmyeevich wanted him to see. How he would react to it only time would tell, and the tsar had little enough of that.

Across the canal, the woman with the large forehead leaned against the railing, her face eager. On this side, two of the men with paper packages exchanged glances. The third, a thickset young man with a flat nose, stepped out into the road, behind the Cossacks and in front of the tsar's coach. He raised his arm, as if about to hurl a snowball.

The wooden bolt smashed into the brick wall, shattering on impact, its iron core clattering to the ground. Iuda pulled back the lever on the *arbalyet* to reset the bow then released the trigger with no bolt loaded. The twang of the vibrating string filled the air.

'An interesting weapon,' he commented. 'Is it actually effective? On a vampire, I mean.'

'I was hoping to find out,' said Mihail.

'So I gathered. But I have to ask, why? You're not working with Zmyeevich, but you seem to be entirely intent on my undoing.'

'I have my reasons.'

'But you refuse to explain them to me.'

Mihail said nothing.

'Dusya,' said Iuda, 'do you have any idea?'

She had moved to stand beside him, the revolver still in her hand. 'He's not mentioned you at all,' she replied, 'except when he asked me to watch the hotel. He knew Luka.'

'Ah, yes,' said Iuda. 'But then you'd have overheard us talking about him in Geok Tepe. And you wouldn't have had time since then to perfect a weapon like this.' He waved the crossbow from side to side.

Still Mihail remained silent, thinking. His plan still had a chance, but it did not account for the presence of Dusya, let alone for the fact that she was working alongside Iuda. All Mihail's work had been with the goal of trapping and killing a vampire. A human would be quite unaffected – otherwise how was Mihail himself supposed to survive? But with Dusya free to act for him, Iuda would easily escape. That assumed that she was human. Mihail had seen her in daylight, but not for a while; the change could have been recent. Did the scarf she had taken to wearing, that she wore even now, hide the marks of Iuda's teeth?

'Anyway, it doesn't matter,' Iuda continued. 'Once he's dead, he'll talk.'

'What?' Dusya almost giggled.

'Didn't you wonder why I called him "Romanov"? He is an illegitimate branch of that illustrious tree, and therefore the blood that runs in his veins is blood that was drunk by the great vampire Zmyeevich. Only days ago he in turn drank Zmyeevich's blood. He has exchanged blood with a vampire – to become one he now needs only to die.'

Dusya's eyes widened as he spoke, her hand went to her throat, caressing it through her scarf. 'So one only has to exchange blood,' she said. Evidently she was as yet no vampire.

'And die,' added Mihail.

'But it would not be death,' she insisted. 'It would be a new life.'

'No kind of life,' said Mihail. 'Worse than being simply a *voordalak* – I'd be a *voordalak* who shared his mind with Zmyeevich.'

'You share minds?' she said. 'How blissful.'

Iuda seemed as uninterested in her romanticism as Mihail was.

'It won't be blissful for either of them,' he said. 'Lukin will be my prisoner – my slave. Through him I will be able to inflict pain upon Zmyeevich wherever in the world he may be. You remember that chair to which I was bound in Geok Tepe? I have something like that in mind for you – with a few improvements.'

'Wouldn't you be afraid that Zmyeevich would find us?' asked Mihail. 'He'd know where I was. I'd be rescued – and you would die.'

Iuda smiled. 'I'll sort something out, don't you worry. The

important thing is for you to die. Dusya, go get me one of those.'
He pointed to the pile of wooden bolts that Mihail had laid out in
anticipation of his arrival. She went and fetched one.

'You're just going to kill him?' she asked. 'We still don't know
why he came after you.'

'As I say, that really isn't an issue.' Iuda pulled back the string
of the *arbalyet* once again as he spoke, slipping the bolt into
place. 'There'll be plenty of time to talk to him after he's dead.'
He raised the crossbow, aiming it at Mihail.

'In that case,' said Dusya, 'allow me.'

She placed the revolver on the floor beside her and held out
both hands towards Iuda. He thought for a moment and then
smiled, handing her the weapon.

'What do I do?' she asked.

He stood behind her, his arms around her, his hands over hers.
'Just like a gun,' he explained. 'Aim at the heart, and then squeeze
the trigger.'

She cocked her head to one side, examining Mihail dispas-
sionately. Then she grinned and her finger began to squeeze.

Mihail moved fast. He dived to the side, grabbing one of the
acid cells that Kibalchich had stored in the room and hurling it
towards them. The crossbow launched its bolt across the room,
but at a space Mihail no longer occupied. The lid came off the
battery in mid-flight and the liquid inside spilled through the air.
Most of it fell on their hands, and a little on the side of Dusya's
face. There was a hiss of burning flesh and smoke began to rise
into the air. Dusya squealed and dropped the crossbow. Even Iuda
reacted, pulling his hands away and wiping them on his jacket.

Mihail had changed direction the instant he threw the jar,
hurling himself across the room in its wake. He caught the crossbow as it fell from Dusya's hands, before it even reached the
ground. In the same movement he kicked at the revolver beside
her, sending it skidding across the flagstones and through the
door, out into the passageway. As it hit the wall it fired, the sound
of the blast echoing through all the chambers and tunnels around
them.

Mihail backed quickly away, rearming the crossbow as he did
so, but at the same time keeping his eyes on the two of them. Both

415

had managed to wipe away the splashes of acid. On Iuda's hands there was no sign of it – he had already healed – but his jacket had holes in it from which smoke still rose. Dusya bore further proof that she was not a vampire. Her clothes too showed the marks of where she had wiped her hands against them, but her hands themselves were scarred – the right merely raw and red, but the left blistered. The wound to her face was only a minor disfigurement; a single line of red where a drop of the acid had trickled, like a tear cutting through face powder. As Mihail watched, a genuine tear fell from her eyelid and ran down her cheek along a similar path. She winced as its salt water touched her wound. Mihail searched his heart to see if it held any sympathy for her, but he found none. Her alliance with Iuda was unexpected, but he had been too long planning his revenge to be distracted by it. He had been raised from boyhood to know that any friend of Iuda's was an enemy of his. That it was Dusya did not complicate the matter.

Iuda regained his presence of mind more quickly than Dusya and was already striding across the room towards Mihail. Mihail groped behind him until his fingers found the pile of bolts. He grasped one and a moment later the crossbow was loaded and aimed.

'Get back!' he shouted.

Iuda obeyed. Soon he was against the wall, standing alongside the weeping Dusya.

'I think we've been here before,' said Iuda.

'Except that Dusya is in no position to save you this time,' Mihail added. He raised the *arbalyet* and aimed. It was not what he had planned, but it would have to do. 'There's one thing I must tell you before I die, Iuda. And that is my name.'

Iuda laughed, though his voice revealed his fear. 'And what's that? Rumpelstilzchen?'

Mihail smiled. He could only admire Iuda's projection of calm. 'No,' he said. 'My name is . . .'

'Who gives a shit what your name is?' Dusya sprang suddenly to life, awakened from her shock at the acid burns. She took a few steps across the room and stood boldly in front of Iuda, her hands by her sides, clenched into tight fists, her chest stuck out defiantly, her blouse clinging tight against her breasts. 'If you want to kill him, you'll have to kill me first.'

Mihail thought about it, but not for very long. He pulled the trigger.

The bomb hit the ground between the legs of the horse pulling the tsar's coach and exploded in an instant. The noise filled the Saint Petersburg air, causing snow to cascade in miniature avalanches from the roofs of the buildings that looked on to the canal. It was met by a spray of earth, snow and fragments of horseflesh blown upwards by the blast. These heavier remnants of the explosion soon settled back down to the ground, but a bluish smoke remained hanging in the air.

After the initial shock the crowd began to close in around the tsar's broken carriage, Zmyeevich among them. Other than the shattered rear axle the coach didn't appear too badly damaged. That was no surprise; it was built to be bomb-proof – a gift from Napoleon III. Some of the material at the sides was torn and the glass of the windows was smashed – like the windows of every adjacent building – but from Zmyeevich's position it was impossible to see inside.

Those unlucky enough to have been around the carriage at the moment of the explosion had not escaped.

One of the Cossacks lay unmoving in the snow beside his horse. The creature raised its head and tried to get to its feet, little understanding that two of its legs were now no more than shredded skin and horsehair. The sound of its agonized screams filled the embankment. Nearby was a young lad – a butcher's boy, judging by his clothes and the joint of meat that lay beside him, half out of its wrapping paper, its blood mingling with that of the boy himself. His body twitched, and then lay still. Others stood dazed – soldiers, gendarmes and civilians – many with cuts to their faces and hands.

Within seconds order began to be restored. The colonel who had been riding in the sleigh behind Aleksandr's coach barked orders and his men obeyed, pushing the crowd away to keep the blasted area clear. Beyond, Zmyeevich could see that the man who had thrown the bomb was unharmed, but had been apprehended. Two soldiers had him pinned back against the canal railings.

The colonel marched over to the coach and opened the door to look inside. The tsar's bloodstained hand dropped down and hung loosely in the cold air.

That single shot revealed what an ineffective weapon a crossbow could be against a vampire, while still being entirely efficacious against a human. The boy had a good aim, but even so the bolt had missed Dusya's heart, piercing her torso instead just a little lower, around her solar plexus. At such close range and with no ribs to hinder it, the bolt buried itself deep in her body. Iuda had felt its tip thump against his own midriff, but it had lost the momentum to do any damage. For Dusya the wound would be fatal, though neither quick nor painless. Iuda could not deny that he was surprised at what had happened, and took a moment to admire Lukin's ruthlessness.

Dusya let out an unnatural, grating moan and her knees buckled. Iuda caught her under the arms and she twisted deliberately to face him. He stepped forward on to one knee so that he could support her. She looked up into his eyes.

'I saved you, Vasya,' she said. 'I saved you once, did you doubt that I would again?'

He said nothing. His eyes looked at her, but barely registered the image of her face. Instead he was gazing back a century into his past, into the face of Susanna. He pictured her the last time he had seen her, or believed he had seen her – he had never been sure. Her face had been pale then, just as Dusya's was now, and the reasons for both were not so very dissimilar.

He felt Dusya's hand reaching up to touch his cheek, smearing the blood from her wound across it.

'And I've never doubted you either,' she continued. 'And now you can save me.'

Iuda withdrew from his reminiscences and tried to make sense of what she meant. He frowned. What did she expect him to do?

She smiled and continued to stroke his face. 'My blood is in you, Vasya. You drank it to make you strong. Now give me just a little of yours, and then let me die, so that I will live.'

Iuda almost laughed. Perhaps she would have made a good companion as a *voordalak*, but he'd never taken a moment to consider it. Now was not the time to make such decisions. She had done enough to help him, but even if he chose to transform her into a vampire, it took weeks for the dead to become undead. The problems that Iuda faced were immediate.

He looked up. Lukin seemed stunned by what he had done to Dusya, but as soon as he locked eyes with Iuda he sprang into action, pulling back on the lever of the *arbalyet* to rearm it.

'Please, Vasya,' Dusya whimpered, blood now in her mouth and on her lips. 'Out of your love for me.'

Iuda launched himself across the room. He did not even bother to throw Dusya's limp body aside; she merely slumped to the ground as he stood, emitting an agonized gasp. Before Iuda was halfway Lukin had another bolt in his hand. He placed it into the groove at the same moment that Iuda's foot connected with the forestock, knocking it out of Lukin's hand and across the cellar. Both men dived for it, but Iuda was faster. He grabbed it, the string in one hand and the limb in the other, pulling hard until with the sharp precision of a gunshot the string snapped. He hurled the useless weapon to the floor.

Dusya emitted a noise that was impossible to categorize. Iuda and Lukin both turned to look at her. She was lying on her front, pushing her head and shoulders up with one hand pressed against the floor while the other reached out towards Iuda. She had managed to drag herself several feet – a fat trail of blood marking her path as though she were some great slug.

'Richard!' she gasped. Iuda felt suddenly weak – disoriented. Then he realized she had merely said, 'Vasya!' His mind had been toying with him. Again he recalled the final time he had seen – or believed he had seen – Susanna's face.

It had been on the very night when Iuda's father had died, when he had gone down beneath Saint George's to release his vampire captive in exchange for the death of Thomas Cain. Just as he had bid his farewell to Honoré, somewhere in the darkness beyond, he had seen her – Susanna – not the whole of her, just her pallid face peering out of the gloom as though she were lurking in the darkness there with Honoré, waiting like him for a chance of freedom. It was thirteen months since Richard had left her down there; thirteen months since her death. At the time Richard had put it down to his guilty conscience. Only later did he understand that that could not be; he had no conscience. Looking back he couldn't even be sure who it was had actually killed his father.

Dusya grunted and slumped forward, her arm no longer able to take her weight. Her forehead hit the stone with a thud and she lay still, her head to one side and her eyes open. Her last breath left her noisily and as her body slackened it collapsed on to the wooden bolt that had penetrated her stomach, forcing the bloody tip out a little further through her back.

Lukin walked over to her and checked her pulse, but it was obvious she was dead. He reached down and closed her eyelids with his fingertips. It was a sentimental act from the man who had killed her, but it didn't occupy him for long. He went over to his broken crossbow and examined it briefly, then threw it disconsolately into a corner of the room.

'Looks like you're going to have to kill me the old-fashioned way,' he said.

'Any mechanism will do,' said Iuda. 'I'm not sure I want to sully my lips with Romanov blood. I may simply strangle you, or rip your head off. Or use this.' He reached into his pocket and caressed his double-bladed knife, his weapon of choice for so many years.

'One question,' said Lukin.

Iuda shrugged.

'How did you get down here? You came through that gateway, I know – but where does it lead?'

Iuda smiled. He was happy to explain – at least to explain some of it. He would have to be careful. Once Lukin was dead, Zmyeevich would know his mind. Iuda would need to be circumspect as to exactly what was housed in that mind.

'We're standing in a very auspicious location, you and I,' he said. 'I take it you know the story of what took place between Zmyeevich and Pyotr I – your great-great-great-great-grandfather, I suppose.'

'Of course.'

'Well, there's a few details of the story that Pyotr didn't pass down to his descendants – or if he did they pretty soon got lost along the way. And Zmyeevich doesn't like to talk of it either.'

'The fate of Ascalon,' said Lukin.

Iuda nodded, impressed. 'A fragment of the lance with which George slayed his dragon. Zmyeevich used to wear it on a cord around his neck. He thought it gave him his power. How much of it's true I don't know. There may have been mountebanks all over Wallachia selling these things like popes selling splinters of the true cross. What matters is that Zmyeevich believes it.'

'And Pyotr stole it.'

'Exactly. Grabbed it from around Zmyeevich's neck just before he ordered Colonel Brodsky to kill him. Just before Zmyeevich escaped.'

'So what did he do with it?'

Iuda shrugged. 'What could he do with it? There was a story that if it was destroyed then Zmyeevich too would be destroyed; another that if the thing were not properly disposed of it could lead to Zmyeevich gaining the most enormous powers. All Pyotr knew was that Zmyeevich wanted it. The best thing to do was to hide it safely. But he didn't want to do it himself – the knowledge would be too dangerous.'

'So what did he do?' asked Lukin.

'At the time there were dozens of groups and sects trying to make a home in Petersburg, eager to ingratiate themselves with the tsar. Any might have helped him to conceal the thing, but in the end he chose the Armenians. Why them? Who knows? Perhaps they're the group which least venerates Saint George. I mean, you wouldn't entrust it to the English, would you?' He laughed, partly at the general absurdity of the concept, partly in the knowledge of where Ascalon now lay. 'The Armenians wanted to build a church. Pyotr tried to help, but he didn't want to appear to favour them. They made several attempts; in 1714, 1725, 1740. They finally got their church built in 1780. It's above us, almost – Saint Yekaterina's – on Nevsky Prospekt between—'

'I know. I've seen it.'

'I'm sure you have. Anyway, they were free to dig deep cellars and tunnel under the city and bury Ascalon in a nice safe shrine.'

'Near here?' asked Lukin.

'You're in it.'

Iuda walked over to the arched alcove in the wall opposite the door. It was empty now, but hadn't always been. Someone – Lukin or one of his comrades – had hung an electric light bulb just above it; a pathetic thing – so feeble that Iuda could gaze straight at it. He pointed to the carved letters.

Ասկադոն

'There it is, you see: "Ascalon", though I think it's more like "Ascaghon" here, a bit like that horrible sound the Dutch make – Armenian isn't my strongest language.'

Lukin gazed at the lettering, a look of awe spreading across his face. He reached out his hand as if to touch the relic where it had once stood. 'And here it remained, for all those years.'

Iuda turned away to show his disgust. 'Don't be like that. You know it's horseshit as well as I do. And "all those years" wasn't so very long. I bribed the *dyachok*, or whatever they call them here, back in '67 to let me down into the labyrinth below the church. It only took me three months to find it.'

'And where is it now?'

'Oh, somewhere safe, don't you worry.' Iuda turned back to face Lukin, who had moved away from the alcove and from Dusya's body towards the pile of junk in the corner. Iuda fingered the knife in his pocket.

'And Dmitry? – or should I say Shklovskiy? – or Otrepyev?'

'I don't know how he and Zmyeevich got on to this place; probably followed the same trail I did. They couldn't work out how to get in through the church, so Dmitry steered the Executive Committee into digging around here. Of course by the time they broke through, Ascalon was long gone.'

'They must have been disappointed.'

'Enough to chase all the way to Turkmenistan to find me. Which is where you came in.' He took the knife from his pocket. 'And here is where you're going to leave.' He saw the fear on Lukin's face. 'Don't worry, we'll have plenty more long conversations like this once you've arisen. I'm sure you'll become quite sick of me.'

He took a pace forward, the knife out in front of him, deciding how to use it. A cut to the throat was what it had been designed for, but that would be too swift. Iuda felt no need for revenge over Dusya, but he knew his Bible: 'life shall go for life, eye for eye, tooth for tooth, hand for hand, foot for foot'. Iuda's blade would enter Lukin just where the bolt had entered Dusya. After that he'd see how the mood took him, but his eye would not pity.

Lukin backed away until the wall prevented him from going any further. His hands pressed against it, as if clawing for some means of escape.

'Oh, before you go, though,' said Iuda, remembering their earlier conversation, 'you were going to tell me something; something about your real name.'

Lukin suddenly seemed to grow. He was no longer against the wall, merely beside it, though his right hand remained outstretched, touching the brickwork. Close to it Iuda noticed a small switch, presumably part of the dim electric lighting system they had down here, or even something to do with the bomb. Lukin's eyes flared and he breathed deeply before speaking.

'My name is Mihail Konstantinovich Danilov, son of Tamara Alekseevna Danilova, daughter of Aleksei Ivanovich Danilov. And you are about to die.'

He flicked the switch.

Aleksandr stepped down from his carriage on to the snowy embankment. He looked dazed and there was blood on his hands and arms, but he was very much alive. A few members of the crowd cheered at the sight of him, but it was a muted celebration – the carnage all around did not merit more.

'Please, Your Majesty, get back on board.' The coachman, unharmed in the explosion, was shouting down from his perch, his voice scarcely audible over the desperate whinnying of the dying Cossack horse.

'It's too badly damaged,' the colonel shouted back. 'It's not safe.'

'It's not safe to stay here. There may be more.'

'I don't need you to tell me that.' The colonel turned to his emperor. 'Sir, we should take my sleigh.'

Aleksandr looked bewildered – concussed even. He paused

for a moment before speaking, but then gradually began to gain resolve. 'Yes, yes, of course. But I want to see the fellow who did this first. I take it you've got him?'

The colonel exchanged a glance with one of his officers, but both clearly knew that the tsar's instructions could not be questioned. 'This way, sir,' he said.

He walked briskly, keen to be away as soon as possible. His head flicked from one side to the other, on the lookout for further trouble. Ordinarily the tsar's long legs would have allowed him easily to keep pace, but today he walked more slowly, like an old man, weakened in much the same way that Zmyeevich was by the sunlight.

A shot rang out. Some ducked, others turned their heads in the direction of the sound. Quietness followed and was a blessing for most. One of the gendarmes had fired his pistol into the head of the crippled horse, silencing it once and for all and in the process splattering its blood and brains over his uniform. The tsar merely stood, taking a moment to realize that the bullet had not been intended for him, and then continued walking towards his assailant.

The bomber was still pinioned against the railings by two of the tsar's escort. Aleksandr stood to face him. He raised his hand, his forefinger extended, as if to wag it as he berated his attacker, but instead he kept it still, shaking minutely, a jagged red cut showing at the base of his thumb. He asked just one question.

'What's your name?' His voice was rich with disgust.

'Glazov,' the man replied calmly. 'Makar Yegorovich.'

It was almost certainly a lie. Aleksandr could find no more words to utter. He turned away.

'The sled now, please, sir,' insisted the colonel.

Aleksandr looked across the scene of devastation and to the crowd beyond, straight into Zmyeevich's eyes. He seemed to form a sudden resolve.

'I want to see where it happened,' he said. He marched back along the embankment towards the funnel-shaped crater left by the bomb, but his eyes remained on Zmyeevich. He had confronted the bomb thrower and shown his defiance to him, now it seemed he wanted to demonstrate that same defiance to a far greater enemy. Zmyeevich smiled, coaxing him forward, knowing that there were two more assassins still out there, and at the same time trying to hide that knowledge from Aleksandr.

The tsar stopped at the side of the pit, the white of snow beneath his feet suddenly giving way to the brown, frozen soil of its steep sides. It was a wonder the canal hadn't broken through.

'Poor devils,' he muttered, looking down at the mutilated bodies of the Cossack and the butcher's boy. Then he looked back up at Zmyeevich. His eyes glared for a moment and he turned away.

'Let's go,' he said to the colonel.

The relief on the soldier's face was palpable. 'This way, Your Majesty,' he said, using his hand to indicate the path towards his sleigh. They set out back along the road, the heads of onlookers turning to follow them. But one of the crowd did not watch. His back was to the tsar as he leaned against the canal railing, gazing thoughtfully into the icy water, a newspaper parcel clutched to his chest.

The tsar passed him at a distance of scarcely three paces. At the moment Aleksandr was at his closest the young man swiftly turned, raised the package above his head and flung it down at the tsar's feet.

The current began to flow. The thin strand of fuse wire stretched between the two carbon blocks began to heat up. In less than a second its temperature was higher than the melting point of the zinc from which it was made. It became liquid and fell away, but the path that it had provided for the current remained, arcing through air itself between the carbon electrodes, producing a brilliant white light that in moments was at its full intensity. And it was more than simply white; it stretched into parts of the spectrum that were imperceptible to the human eye. Much like the light of the sun.

Mihail knew that all of this was happening without having to watch it. He had experimented many times and understood the physics perfectly. Today his only desire was to witness its effects.

It was not the same devastation that would have been meted out to Iuda if he'd truly been exposed to the sun's rays, but Mihail had known that. This was the second time he would be blessed with the opportunity to witness the effects of this great modern invention on a vampire. This time, though, it would be a far more enjoyable show. This time it was Iuda.

The *voordalak* stopped in his tracks. He narrowed his eyes and raised his arm to shade them. Even a human would have done much the same; Mihail's own eyelids were squeezed to thin slits. It was a bright light in a small room, and they were only feet away from its source. But then further effects became evident. A short violent spasm rippled through Iuda's body. His knife fell from his hand and clattered on the floor.

'What . . . what is that?' he asked. He did not sound afraid, but that was because he didn't understand. His mood was simply one of annoyance, as if he were hearing some high-pitched squeal that was inaudible to anyone else. For a moment the most unexpected sensation fluttered through Mihail's heart: a feeling of pity. He almost laughed, but the expression that briefly crossed Iuda's face was one that least became him – a look of puzzlement. Mihail pushed the emotion from his mind – with a little help from his dead mother. This was how it was supposed to be.

'That,' he explained, 'is the gift of one of Russia's greatest inventors, Pavel Nikolayevich Yablochkov. You'll have heard of him.'

Iuda made a movement that could have been a nod of agreement, or equally an involuntary twitch.

'It's called a Yablochkov Candle. It's a type of arc light. You may have seen them about town, outside the Aleksandrinsky Theatre and on Liteiny Bridge.'

'I have,' said Iuda, his voice low and level. Wisps of smoke or steam were beginning to rise from his face and hands, as though he had stepped from a hot bath into a cold room. His eyes were glazed and his arms hung limply at his side.

Suddenly he made a dash for the door, but Mihail had expected it and was quicker. He pulled the iron gate shut, locking it with a padlock he had brought for the purpose. Iuda grabbed the bars and rattled them, but to no avail. Even a healthy vampire would have found it hard to break through, and Iuda was already weak. Now there was nothing that he could do to save himself, though he still tried.

He approached the lamp itself. The wires protruding from it were flimsy and would be easy to rip out, if only Iuda could get close. He moved like a man walking against the wind, but with each step he took the light got brighter. It was an inescapable law of physics; halving the distance quadrupled the brilliance – and the pain. Mihail could see flakes of skin beginning to fall from Iuda's cheeks. Soon he gave up and obeyed the logic of his circumstances, backing away to the far corner of the room where the light was dimmest – but not too dim. He slumped against the wall, close to Dusya's body. It would be a slow death. It was better that way – it gave Mihail a chance to gloat.

'We captured one – a *voordalak*, I mean – Mama and I. You remember Mama, don't you? Tamara? Tamara Alekseevna?'

'Of course,' croaked Iuda.

'She remembered you. You were the one thing on her mind, every day of her life. She remembered what you did to her father, and her mother. And she remembered what you did to their friends. You remember the names?'

'Who cares?'

'I care! We care!' Mihail allowed his anger to flow through him and enjoyed the sensation. 'Do you remember Maks, or Vadim, or Dmitry Fetyukovich, or Margarita, or Irina? And let's not forget what you did to Dmitry Alekseevich.'

'I . . . I didn't.' Iuda was pathetic now. He spoke almost as if he believed in his own innocence.

'Not you yourself, no, but you caused it. You caused all their deaths. So Mama and I planned, planned for a long time. Eventually we captured one – locked him in a barn. We took a leaf out of your book – did things scientifically. Found out what hurt him, wrote it down. Found out what healed him, wrote it down.'

'How did you feed him?' asked Iuda.

Mihail stopped short. The question seemed like an irrelevance, a non sequitur, but even in death Iuda still possessed the cunning to inflict pain. Mihail simply did not know the answer. He hadn't asked. Tamara had dealt with that; she had not told him how and he, quite deliberately, had not asked. He would not let it distract him now.

'We could only kill him once though, that was the sad thing,' he continued. 'But we had to verify that this would work. And it did. We used a Gramme generator then. Mama wound the handle so that I could watch and take notes. I'm using batteries today – much more reliable.'

There had been nothing unreliable about Tamara as she frantically wound the handle to generate the current needed, a look of joy and hatred on her face. She was – she had confessed to him later – imagining that it was Iuda chained there in the barn. Mihail had even had to make her slow down – it was important to learn the minimum level of light needed for the process still to work.

'Of course,' Mihail continued, 'it's still weak compared with the sun. Not strong enough to penetrate cotton or linen.'

He walked across the room and picked up Iuda's knife where it had fallen, then he continued over to Iuda. He grabbed him by the lapels and heaved him upright, leaning him against the wall, then took a step back. He slashed the double-bladed knife harshly down the middle of Iuda's torso. His intent was to cut cloth, but he was happy for the blades to slice through flesh as well. He opened up Iuda's tattered jacket and shirt, exposing his chest and belly to the lamplight. Perhaps it was a mercy, hastening Iuda's end, but Mihail enjoyed taking advantage of his helplessness.

'*Pryestupleniye ee Nakazaniye,*' he said, referring to the late, great Dostoyevsky's finest work. 'You have committed the crime and now you face the punishment.'

'Who sentenced me?' asked Iuda. He was barely recognizable now. His skin had drawn tight across his chest and splits had begun to appear like tears in fabric. From them oozed blood and pus which quickly began to smoulder in the light. The smell was repellent, but Mihail could only feel joy at it.

'We did,' he replied. He and his mother had tried Iuda *in absentia* when Mihail was just eight years old. The verdict had never been in doubt. It had been a long wait to carry out the sentence.

'Then this isn't punishment,' said Iuda. He lurched forward as he spoke, but took a step and regained his balance. 'This is vengeance.'

'What's the difference?' asked Mihail. It was the same question he had discussed with Zhelyabov and the others, but for the life of him he could not see one, nor care if one existed.

Iuda produced something akin to a smile, in the process causing his top lip to split in the middle and rip open right up to his nose. Beneath it his teeth were revealed, still white, sharp and strong.

'I too can be avenged,' he said.

With that he flung himself forward at a speed of which Mihail had guessed him no longer capable. His momentum knocked Mihail backwards on to the floor, but Iuda remained with him, his hands grasping the back of Mihail's head, his fingers entwined in his hair. In the moment of death he had found a hideous new strength. For an instant Mihail saw a flash of his white teeth, brilliant in the arc light, and then his face descended on to Mihail's throat.

Mihail felt the sharp points press against his flesh, followed by searing pain as suddenly his skin yielded and Iuda's teeth sank into him. The sound of blood being sucked out of him filled his ears.

The blue smoke began once more to clear. This second bomb, though of the same size, had caused immeasurably greater devastation. The white snow was littered with debris – fragments of paper, splinters of wood, shards of cloth and shoe leather. A dozen or more bystanders lay wounded or dead. The bomber himself was on the ground, unmoving, as was the colonel whose duty it had been to protect the life of his tsar.

In that duty he had failed.

On the shattered paving stones in a pool of mostly his own blood lay Aleksandr. His hat had been knocked from his head. His clothes were in tatters. Below the knee both of his legs were shattered; there was nothing to see of them but shreds of his trousers. From somewhere within the mess, blood still pumped out on to the snow. He was not dead, but would not live.

Through the silence a single word penetrated. 'Yes!'

Zmyeevich turned to look. It was Glazov, the first bomber – the failed assassin. One of the soldiers beside him, still holding him against the railing, belted him across the face. He said no more.

Zmyeevich approached the dying tsar. He was conscious. His head turned from side to side, trying to take in what was going on around him. Then his eyes fixed upon Zmyeevich one final time. Zmyeevich concentrated, making this final offer in his mind, knowing that Aleksandr would hear.

'My blood. Take my blood and you shall live for ever.'

He raised one arm and pulled up his sleeve, then drew a knife and motioned as if to cut himself. He would have to shelter the blood from the sun, but it could be achieved. Aleksandr watched transfixed. All eyes were on him and his were on Zmyeevich. Then he coughed. He gave the slightest shake of his head and then turned away, breaking eye contact with Zmyeevich. The offer had been rejected. Aleksandr had chosen death. Unlike his namesake, he had not found so elegant a way to break the curse on his blood.

Zmyeevich stepped back into the crowd. The colonel was on his feet now, apparently uninjured. He began to organize the carrying of Aleksandr up on to the sleigh. With each jerk and jolt more blood spurted from his ravaged limbs, but no one seemed to have any understanding of medicine. The sole intent was to get him away from there.

At last they had him in the sled. Onlookers and soldiers helped to prop him up against cushions. Zmyeevich almost laughed; of all people, one of those who helped was the third bomb carrier – the newspaper package still tucked under his arm. Once he had done his duty by his emperor he turned and walked calmly away along the canal, unmolested by any of the tsar's men.

In the opposite direction, the sleigh pulled away, heading as fast as its horses could pull to the Winter Palace. Beside it ran Aleksandr's retinue. Those Cossacks who still had mounts rode ahead.

Behind it the sleigh left a bloody trail in the snow.

The agony did not come from Iuda's teeth, but from his mind. Mihail had expected it. As Iuda drew blood from him their minds were briefly as one – and one concept predominated in Iuda's mind; burning, torturing pain. It was a wonder that he could contain it; Mihail certainly could not. His screams filled the small bright cellar moments after Iuda bit into him, even though he knew it was not his own pain and could do him no physical harm.

What could harm him was Iuda's bite, draining blood from him and in doing so providing Iuda with sufficient sustenance to fight off the effects of the Yablochkov Candle for just a little longer, even though it would only prolong his torment. Iuda had spoken of vengeance, but this seemed self-defeating, causing him further pain to no beneficial end. And through the tortured thrashings of his mind Mihail could sense no emotion of revenge, only the cold, hard logic he would have expected from Iuda, though logic that followed a path that Mihail could not fathom; all paths ended only in Iuda's death. And even in the midst of all that there was more: a message; words forming in Iuda's mind that he was desperate for Mihail to hear.

It did not last long. From the moment that Iuda had launched his attack, Mihail had been pushing him away. The vampire's sudden strength had been a dying pulse; within seconds Mihail was able to overcome him, throwing his now insubstantial body across the cellar and closer to the candle that would do it so much harm. Mihail got to his feet.

Iuda lay still, but not yet quite dead. His eyes gazed up at Mihail and his mouth formed a lipless smile, Mihail's smeared blood forming an edge to the decaying flesh. Then with a jolt of energy he moved both head and eyes to gaze directly into the glow of the arc light. His eyeballs erupted into a blue flame which raged only a few seconds before guttering to nothing, leaving black gaping holes that looked in on his absent soul. Then only the holes themselves remained as the skin and fat and bone that surrounded them crumbled away and fell to the ground.

Mihail raced for his knapsack and brought from it his wooden dagger, along with a mallet with which to drive it into Iuda's heart, but by the time he returned to the body there was no heart to pierce. Iuda's head and trunk were dust. In the arms of his jacket and the legs of his trousers there was still some bulk. Mihail took Iuda's knife again and cut them open, exposing the flesh beneath to the light. It was paranoia, but it was a wise paranoia. He went over to the Yablochkov Candle and picked it up from where he had fastened it to the wall, using a cloth to protect him from the

431

heat. The wires were long enough to reach Iuda's remains. He held it up in the air, scanning it up and down across the man-shaped patch of dust on the floor as if to assist in looking at it closely, but in fact to make sure that all was destroyed. Occasionally some little lump of formerly protected flesh would catch the light and suddenly wither, or even produce a puff of flame, but soon there were no more of them. Mihail held the candle for another minute, then knew his work was done.

He returned the light to the wall and stood up, breathing deeply. His grandfather Aleksei had tried it before him. He had tried to drown him in the freezing Berezina, but somehow Iuda had survived. He had shot him on the ice of the Neva, and that time had killed him, but Iuda had cheated death and become undead. Tamara had never even come close. She had imprisoned Iuda, with Dmitry's help, but no more than that.

Now he, Mihail Konstantinovich Danilov, had avenged them all, and many more besides. He had done what none of them could and he felt proud of it. Richard Llywelyn Cain, born some time towards the end of the eighteenth century, a man who had thrown in his lot with *voordalaki* and then chosen to become one himself, who had conducted experiments on his own kind, who had plagued Russia for almost seventy years, was dead.

Iuda was no more.

CHAPTER XXVII

IT WAS A FAMILIAR MOMENT. IT WAS TWENTY TO FOUR IN THE afternoon of 1 March. Zmyeevich was not the only one gazing at the Winter Palace and at the flag bearing the double-headed eagle of the Romanov crest on the pole above it as it was lowered to half-mast. He had watched much the same thing from a boat moored off the town of Taganrog in 1825. Then it had been a ruse – Aleksandr I had not died. Today there could be no doubt. Zmyeevich had seen the wounds that Aleksandr II had suffered – death would not be cheated.

It was a hollow victory. Aleksandr had not cheated death because he had not wanted to – quite the contrary, he had sought it, knowing that in death he would defeat Zmyeevich, at least for a while. It was too small to see at this distance, but on the flag, on the double-headed eagle's chest, was a shield that bore the emblem of Saint George slaying the dragon – Ascalon held in both hands as he thrust it into the beast's heart. Even in death the Romanovs gloated and flew the emblem of their victory above the city.

Many of the crowd began to turn away, singly and in pairs – even families with children. There were tears on the faces of all the women and some of the men. One man – a naval captain – fell to his knees and sobbed loudly. Zmyeevich could only despise them, but he felt envious too. Even when a man, he had never been loved by his people like Aleksandr was. Perhaps that was why Zmyeevich craved to have power over Russia – so that he might be loved by the Russian people. It was preposterous, but the very idea of it frightened him.

Now Aleksandr III would take his father's place and take his people's love. Zmyeevich could wield no power over him, much as Aleksandr had seemed willing to give it. Danilov had seen to that; a new Danilov this time, but as troublesome as the first. Zmyeevich cursed the day he had met Aleksei Ivanovich, in that tavern in Moscow, so many years before.

But as to power in Russia, Zmyeevich would have to wait another generation. The new tsar had been at his father's side when death came and so, Zmyeevich guessed, had been the new tsarevich, Nikolai Aleksandrovich, a boy of just twelve. One day his father too would die, and he would become Tsar Nikolai II. But even of that, Zmyeevich could not be sure – that was always the problem. Zmyeevich could not act until Nikolai was tsar. He might die and leave the throne to a brother or son. Worse could happen. Perhaps the dreams of the People's Will would be fulfilled and the masses would take this opportunity to rise up and cast off their shackles.

Zmyeevich laughed. A few of those around him scowled, but he did not care. The idea was ridiculous. Who could imagine these tsar-loving peasants ever rising up to overthrow their masters? Zmyeevich did not need to worry. When he returned the Russian empire would still be there, still ruled by a Romanov – whoever it might be – and therefore still ripe for the plucking.

But what of the meantime? For over a hundred and sixty years Zmyeevich had seen in Russia two prizes combined: the Romanov throne and the return of Ascalon. Now those were separate. Dmitry might have chosen his own path, but not before Zmyeevich had read his mind and learned everything that Iuda had told him. Ascalon was no longer in Petersburg. It was in the country of Iuda's birth. Iuda had even given more precise clues, but it could well be bluff. It did not matter – Zmyeevich would go there and somehow he would reclaim Ascalon.

He smiled to himself. Iuda had quoted Shakespeare, and so would he. He spoke the words out loud.

'"To England will I steal, and there I'll steal."'

He walked on down the snowy street.

*

The boat rocked from side to side; waves splashed against its hull. Outside it was still daylight – outside the coffin, outside the hold, above the deck. Dmitry knew that it was a time for sleep, but he did not feel like it. He was not yet far enough from Zmyeevich to trust his dreams – not that vampires had dreams. He still wasn't far from Petersburg – somewhere out in the Baltic. He could sense Zmyeevich back there in the city. He still craved his blood. Dmitry squeezed his eyes shut and tried to dispel the idea. It was repellent – and he had done so much in his life that seemed to him repellent. Was it so strange that he should be the same in death?

At least now he was free. The ship might travel slowly with only the wind to propel it, but it would travel far. There would be stops along the way – Stockholm and London for sure – but Dmitry's coffin, disguised as a simple crate, would remain undisturbed. He had paid well to ensure that. After London there was only open sea to cover, the Atlantic, and then finally a great new city. Dmitry was going to a new life in a new world.

He was going to America.

It was a familiar moment. It was twenty to four in the afternoon of 1 March. Mihail was not the only one gazing at the Winter Palace and at the flag bearing the double-headed eagle of the Romanov crest on the pole above it as it was lowered to half-mast.

In fact, Mihail was not gazing at the Winter Palace at all. He was on the other side of the city. He knew that it was Zmyeevich's eyes through which he saw, but he pushed the vampire's presence from his mind.

Tamara had told him of the death of Aleksandr I, just as she had heard it from Aleksei. It had not been a true death, that had come later. It had been Aleksandr II, Mihail's uncle, who had told him precisely when. Tamara had told him too of Tsar Nikolai's death, how she had been with her family when they heard of it and how even she had been affected. That was the better death, since Zmyeevich had played no part in it. Nikolai had been protected by his brother, just as Aleksandr III was now protected by his cousin, Mihail.

Mihail did not know how long it would take for Zmyeevich's blood to fully leave him. Iuda's journals suggested weeks. If Mihail were to die in that time then he would save the whole Romanov dynasty, but he had done enough for them already. Aleksandr had repaid the favour by making sure that Iuda would be down in that cellar, whatever his motivation had been for it. Their debts had been cancelled, even though Aleksandr was now dead.

Iuda was dead too.

That was certain. It should have been clear enough from what had happened to him in the light of the Yablochkov Candle, but there was better proof still. Once back in the tunnel that led from the cheese shop, in the dim lamplight that could do it no harm, Mihail had again opened up the handkerchief and examined Iuda's severed ear. The folds of silk contained nothing but dust. It had not been directly exposed to the miraculous rays of the arc light, but when Iuda's body had died, so every part of it had died, the ear included. The same would have happened if the two had been separated by a thousand versts, but even so close, the fact of Iuda's death was irrefutable. Mihail had also taken another look at the hairs in his locket, but they survived, a remnant not of Iuda as a vampire but of his human self. He had thought to lay them with the dusty remains of Iuda's body, but it would have implied some hint of respect where none existed. Mihail used a little of Kibalchich's dynamite to cave in those old passageways, built by Armenian priests a century before, burying the evidence of what had happened. Iuda had left no obvious earthly remains, but it would be better if no one uncovered Dusya's corpse, at least not for a little while.

He'd found the key in her pocket and so been able to make an easy exit from the shop. He also searched Iuda's clothes, limp and empty, but spewing dust whenever he lifted them. There he found only one item of interest: a ring in the form of a dragon, with a body of gold, emerald eyes and red, forked tongue. Mihail had not noticed it when he had been in Zmyeevich's presence, but Aleksei had remembered it vividly and told Tamara. How it had got into Iuda's possession Mihail could only guess, but now it was his.

Mihail should have felt joy, but he did not. To destroy Iuda had been his life's one aim. Now there was nothing. He could chase off in pursuit of Zmyeevich, but that wasn't his quarrel

– let the Romanovs deal with their own foe for once, and leave the Danilovs in peace. That was why he didn't go to his father and ask for some nice country estate and a sinecure in one of the ministries. They would always see him as on hand, just in case Zmyeevich returned. He wouldn't have enjoyed the life anyway.

It was something he'd talked about with his mother on idle evenings when instead of planning how they would deal with Iuda, they imagined a world without him. He'd always said he'd return to Saratov to be with her, and she'd told him not to be silly, but he'd known she hoped he would. Now that was not an option. Wherever she was now, be it heaven or hell, then surely in a just universe she would be allowed the luxury of knowing that Iuda was dead, and that her son had lived. Without that, had any of it been worthwhile?

Tamara had told him how once when younger she had been in a similar position. For half her life she had been obsessed by a single goal – to find her real parents. It was a nobler goal than the one she had bequeathed to Mihail. She had wondered what she would do when she found them, what would drive her then. She had never needed to answer the question. She had been reunited with her parents and within hours they were both dead. She blamed Iuda, and the rest of her life gained a purpose: his death. Mihail had inherited that purpose too.

But now the task was complete; begun by the mother and completed by the son. Iuda was gone and Mihail's future was a blank page, still to be written. And yet he could not even fill out the first line; the first word. He had no family, no friends, no home and no desires. Worst of all, he had no dreams. All that remained was the same question that had so plagued his mother years in the past and to which he, like her, had no answer. What was he for?

And yet for all that the question troubled him, there was a greater puzzle on his mind. From the moment he left the shop and began to walk through the streets of Petersburg, Mihail had felt uneasy – even before he heard the news of Aleksandr's death. He had shared his mind, however briefly, with Iuda. He had done the same with Zmyeevich, but this had been far more unnerving. Iuda's icy calm, even in death, had been terrifying, but worse had been his apparent determination to get one piece of information across to Mihail. He had failed as his mind had collapsed along with his body and his thoughts had been cut off, mid-sentence, as Mihail pushed him away. Mihail had heard only the beginning, and it made no sense to him. Yet it was clearly worth more than death to Iuda. Just a few simple words which Iuda would never have the chance to explain, but which would haunt Mihail for ever:

'Tell Lyosha. It was . . .'

ENDNOTE

Of the members of the People's Will featured in this story, all are genuine historical characters with the obvious exceptions of Luka and Dusya. On 3 April 1881 five members of the organization were hanged in Semyonovskiy Square for the murder of Tsar Aleksandr II, the same number as had been executed as ringleaders of the failed Decembrist Uprising fifty-five years earlier. They were Nikolai Ivanovich Kibalchich, Timofei Mihailovich Mihailov, Sofia Lvovna Perovskaya, Andrei Ivanovich Zhelyabov and Nikolai Ivanovich Rysakov.

As with the Decembrists, the executions did not go smoothly. On the first attempt Mihailov's rope broke; on the second the noose itself unravelled. The crowd shouted that this was a sign from God that Mihailov should be pardoned, but their cries went unheeded. On the third attempt the rope held, but the knot was not tight enough and Mihailov thrashed in the air for several minutes. Eventually the hangman, Frolov, put a second noose around his neck without removing the first. Drawings of the execution show his body hanging strangely from two diagonal ropes instead of a single vertical.

Rysakov, who had betrayed his comrades under questioning, lost his nerve when his turn came, and clung to the scaffold, wrapping his legs around its wooden beam. Soldiers had to prise him loose before he could have the rope placed around his neck.

Kibalchich, the first to die, went calmly, having shown little interest in presenting a defence to the court. While in prison he spent most of his time developing his ideas for rocket-powered travel. He insisted that his lawyer present the work to the authorities in the hope that his invention could be used for the public good, but the papers were filed away and not seen again until 1918. While he had not devised a viable flying machine, many of his ideas foreshadowed those later used in rocket design.

A crater on the moon is named in his honour.

CHARACTERS OF THE
DANILOV QUINTET

Aleksei Ivanovich Danilov	Russian soldier and spy who defeated the Oprichniki in 1812 and saved Tsar Aleksandr I from Zmyeevich in 1825 by helping to fake his death. Sent into exile after the Decembrist Uprising
Dmitry Alekseevich Danilov	Only son of Aleksei Ivanovich Danilov. Became a vampire in 1856
Marfa Mihailovna Danilova	Wife of Aleksei and mother of Dmitry
Domnikiia Semyonovna Beketova	Aleksei's mistress, who accompanied him into exile in Siberia in 1826
Tamara Alekseevna Danilova also known as *Tamara Valentinovna Komarova*	Illegitimate daughter of Aleksei and Domnikiia
Iuda also known as *Vasiliy Denisovich Makarov, Vasiliy Innokyentievich Yudin, Vasiliy Grigoryevich Chernetskiy* and *Richard Llywelyn Cain*	The only human among the twelve Oprichniki who came to Russia in 1812. Under the name of Cain experimented on vampires. Became a vampire himself in 1825

Zmyeevich	The arch vampire who brought the Oprichniki to Russia in 1812 and who seeks revenge for the trickery played upon him by Tsar Pyotr the Great in 1712
Svetlana Nikitichna Danilova	Dmitry's wife
Vadim Fyodorovich Savin	Aleksei's commander, who died during the campaign of 1812
Maksim Sergeivich Lukin	Comrade of Aleksei, who died during the campaign of 1812
Dmitry Fetyukovich Petrenko	Comrade of Aleksei, who died during the campaign of 1812
The Oprichniki	The nickname for a band of vampires defeated by Aleksei in 1812. Individually they took the names of the twelve apostles
Prince Pyetr Mihailovich Volkonsky	Adjutant general to Tsar Aleksandr I, who conspired with Aleksei to fake the tsar's death
Raisa Styepanovna Tokoryeva	Vampire who helped Iuda to escape Chufut Kalye in 1825 and who turned Dmitry into a vampire
Vitaliy Igorevich Komarov	Tamara's husband
Luka Miroslavich Novikov	Tamara's son by Vitaliy

ABOUT THE AUTHOR

Jasper Kent was born in Worcestershire in 1968, studied Natural Sciences at Trinity Hall, Cambridge, and now lives in Brighton. As well as writing The Danilov Quintet (his Russian-set internationally acclaimed sequence of historical horror novels) Jasper works as a freelance software consultant. He has also written several musicals. To find out more, visit www.jasperkent.com